Also by Tony Flower

That Bloody Book

The Girl Downstairs

www.tonyflower.co.uk

The Resurrection of Skinny Ted and the Brothel Creepers

By Tony Flower

 New Generation Publishing

To Clare and Sean

Introduction

This book can be read with or without knowledge of, or indeed interest in, music. There is a riveting mystery to unravel, plenty of corny jokes and anecdotes, along with a healthy smattering of romance and pathos. However, for those of a musical bent, there are references scattered throughout, designed to drive you crazy or to reinforce what you already knew – that you are a walking, talking musical encyclopaedia. The corresponding notes at the end of the chapters are there to be absorbed or ignored as you wish and, hopefully, they don't detract from the story.

For those referenced, I have this message: thank you for the music and please don't sue me. For the most part the allusions are complimentary, written from a fan's perspective and with genuine respect. The characters are all fictional with warts and all; figuratively speaking that is, can't see any visible warts from here. Any resemblances to persons living or dead are purely coincidental. Likewise, locations are fictitious unless stated otherwise, although certain settings may bear a striking resemblance to my hometown of Aylesbury.

I hope you enjoy what follows as much as I have enjoyed its creation. It has been a long, loving and sometimes infuriating gestation; now it's time for my fledgling to fly the nest. Soar far and wide; and face the music.

Tony.

The Prologue

Is there a place in our hearts or a second chance for those on the periphery of fame; for those who burned in a blaze of short-lived glory, then fizzled out like a fart on the breeze; and whose work is eternally destined for the shelves of charity shops throughout the land?

They played anywhere back then and often for nothing. Pubs, clubs, village halls, youth clubs, parties; the unfortunate patrons of all were exposed to the fumbling formation of a legend. Wet behind the ears and rough around the edges, their manager argued that the only way they'd become more proficient would be to play, play and play some more. Perhaps the word 'manager' was a little flattering; Freddie was really just a geezer with the gift of the gab, who knew a few people. Any meagre recompense received from those willing to pay for the privilege, invariably ended up in his pocket under the guise of expenses.

Countless dives and bars frequented in the quest to perfect their craft; memorable and disastrous gigs aplenty and many a tale to tell. That village fete was the best one, though. The brass band had cancelled due to a tummy bug that had infected the entire ensemble; prompting the Mayor, who happened to be Freddie's uncle, to call in desperation. Freddie's suggestion that they upturn one of the trombones to use as an emergency backstage bog was met with a 'yuck' and a 'that's not funny', before Freddie agreed to provide the entertainment.

Nothing could have prepared the conservative villagers for the cacophony that was to follow on that infamous summer's day. Old ladies of a delicate disposition fled to the sanctuary of the nearby church, and gardeners participating in the largest vegetable challenge gathered up their marrows and ran, whilst contestants in the best-dressed dog competition howled in protest.

A fete worse than death, the local paper had called it!

Youthful and recalcitrant, the band all concurred that the natives had over-reacted when they pulled the plug; and that they'd rather be dead than reach old age and boredom. (1)

There once was a band that emerged from humble origins to almost compete with the best; then disappeared without trace or fanfare. I sometimes wonder; whatever happened to Skinny Ted and the Brothel Creepers?

3

1. Pete Townshend of the Who expressed similar sentiments when he wrote the incendiary *My Generation* back in '65.

'A pint of Gnarly Old Scrote please, Landlord.'

'Coming right up, Bill; and how are you today?'

'Can't complain Jack; wouldn't do me any bloody good if I did.'

'Had your mate Ken in the other day and that's all he does is complain. Emptied the pub he did - you could feel the ambience change; then all the punters left, one by one. Thinking of barring him if he darkens my door again; comes in here with a face like Manchester - he could turn the beer sour.'

'Hey, give him a break Jack; he's had a few problems with his love-life lately.'

'You surprise me. He's lucky he's got a love-life with a permanent expression like that. And if he does have problems there's no need to share them with the rest of us; people come in here to have a good time and a bit of banter.'

'And to escape; people come here to escape too.'

A trifle shy of two yards high, with skinny legs and a gaunt expression; a quiff of unkempt greasy black hair with flecks of grey, Bill scratched his three day-old stubble and stroked his impressive angular sideburns. Dressed in distressed denim jeans and a battered leather jacket, he bore a vague resemblance to an irreversibly faded Fonz. Bill looked thoughtful as he took in the familiar surroundings. A little warmth reached him from the flickering flames of the inglenook fireplace, a welcome respite from the bitter January cold of the elements outside. He felt cosy beneath the low, uneven beams and relaxed among the clichéd black and white pictures of his hometown.

He placed his rucksack on the floor beside him; it contained a couple of books from the library that he'd been looking forward to reading. Bill loved to read; he had a quest for knowledge, a longing for his mind to travel beyond his immediate sphere of awareness, to explore other ways of being; at least from the comfort of his armchair.

Jack, a seemingly reluctant host with weathered features and a large forehead, was the latest in a long line of landlords whom Bill had seen come and go; each with their own ambitions for this

4

ancient inn that dated back to the 16th century. For a while there was the guy who'd seen it as the town's premier music venue and the place was heaving each weekend, as bands of varying quality shook the rafters and rattled the windows; until the pushers and junkies moved in and the license was revoked. Then there was that smooth, smarmy git who tried to turn it into an upmarket eatery; and the regulars were squeezed out when the bar area was all but obliterated to make way for more diners. Now it was almost back to the way it was – a simple old comfortable pub, serving simple old comfort pub-grub and fine ale. Escape? Bill had been coming here to escape for longer than he cared to remember.

'Yeah, and that's exactly what all my customers did - escape,' continued Jack. 'Look, here's Tom, he was here. We were just talking about Ken and what a miserable bastard he was the other night.'

'He was that, but I've heard that Stella's left him again.'

'That was always going to be a difficult relationship,' said Bill; 'she's a popular lady and poor old Ken's hardly catch of the day, is he? The usual, Tom?'

'Yeah, go on then. Shall we sit over here?'

Tom, although similar in age and physique to Bill, had undeniably worn better. With an engaging smile and easy manner, he had laughter lines where others had wrinkles and his face told of a relatively contented life. He made himself at home at a corner table, while Bill ordered a pint of lager, a little of which spilled on his hand as he negotiated the irregular flagstones. Bill plonked the lager on the table, wiped his hand on his jeans and removed his jacket to reveal a faded tattoo on his forearm - a red heart jaggedly broken in two by a dagger, with the words "Stood Up, Again" etched in black on the blade that dripped with crimson blood. He pulled out a chair, sat down and wedged his gut against the table.

'Don't know how you drink this gnat's piss,' he said, 'it's just a glass full of bubbles, 'bout time you tried real ale.'

Bill held his pint up to the light and studied its clear, deep ruby hue, as if it were a thing of beauty and that he were a connoisseur. Apparently, Gnarly Old Scrote, an award winning ale and pinnacle of the brewers' art, was so named after a comment made to the master-brewer by a disrespectful young apprentice. Bill savoured its nutty flavour and licked his lips.

'So, what's happening, Tom?'

'Oh, you know, same shit, different day; I'm getting sick and tired of the regular old routine. Remember the time when we still had hope, when we were going to be the next big thing?'

'Yeah, and we nearly made it; had a pretty good following for a while, till it all fell apart. I often wonder how big we could have been.'

'Well, how do you fancy having another crack at it? Been talking to Clive; we're thinking of putting the band back together.' Tom ran his fingers through his hair and looked Bill in the eye. 'What do you reckon; think we've still got it?'

Bill coughed and spluttered his beer in shock - 'Ha, you can't be serious; aren't we getting a bit old for the rock'n'roll lifestyle?'

'Maybe, but we were good, man. All the bands from our era are back out on the road and cashing in; and most of them couldn't touch us live.'

Bill caught his reflection in a nearby mirror and sighed, 'You know, there's nothing sadder than a bunch of old crocks trying to relive their youth.'

'Yeah, but what else you got to do, except stagnate? I'd rather burn out than fade away.' (1)

'But we were toxic towards the end; ready to kill each other, friendships pushed to the limit.'

'And we're still here, aren't we?' reasoned Tom, his arms outstretched, 'a little older, but wiser. Look, I'll leave you to think about it while I get another round.'

As Tom made his way to the bar he stopped to allow two slightly-pissed young ladies in their mid-twenties to pass. He was rewarded with radiant smiles and giggles as, on heels ill designed for walking, they made their unsteady way to the door. Bill felt that familiar sadness, engendered by the passing of time. Long gone were the days when he and Tom would have clumsily attempted to engage them in conversation, before being unceremoniously rejected.

Bill took another swig of beer and considered the logic behind Tom's entreaty; a flicker of life dawned, the hint of a smile, a twinkle in the eye. Then reality rudely reappeared and he frowned. Nothing could have been further from his mind before Tom's bombshell and he'd resigned himself to the fact that it was all over a long time ago.

He still played his instrument from time to time, but in the privacy of his room; it had been years since he'd subjected an audience to it, and it wasn't particularly portable. The band had attempted to persuade him to trade it in for an electric one many times, but Bill always favoured authenticity; he loved that natural, simple sound that could never be recreated and he felt an affinity with his influences when he played. He remembered the time that they'd threatened to trade *him* in for a more contemporary musician if he didn't move with the times, but he'd stood his ground and prevailed.

Tom returned with two beers, a smile, and eyebrows raised in anticipation.

'Well?' he asked.

Bill shook his head. 'I think it's a fucking ridiculous idea; I mean, look at the state of us.'

'You speak for yourself,' protested Tom, as he preened his quiff and pouted his lips. 'This cat still has a few lives left.'

'And besides,' argued Bill, 'who did you have in mind for drums? He'd have to be bloody good to replace Stan, God rest his soul.'

'No-one could replace Stan, God rest his soul; short-arsed nutter; five-foot-four of whirling-dervish, but he never missed a beat. Wasn't it you that christened him the metro-gnome?' (2)

'Yeah, and he nearly took my eye out with that stick; still got the scar, look.'

Bill's finger traced the ancient indent above his left eye and he furrowed his brow as he recalled some of Stan's antics. His belief that he could fly when he was high and the time they had to persuade him that jumping out of that hotel window wasn't such a good idea. Then they'd tied him to the bed with Clive's guitar strap to stop him trying again. And the episode before a gig in Oxford when they'd been crossing a bridge and Stan decided he fancied a dip in the river. The stupid bastard couldn't swim and Tom had to jump in and pull him out.

Then there was Stan's contrary demeanour to deal with. To say that a small pot boils quickly was an understatement. When angry, his speech could be politely described as inarticulate, although it was invariably from the heart. He was an interesting character, but you wouldn't invite him to your house; not unless you'd had your tetanus. (3)

Bill recalled Stan's sensitivity about his lack of height. He had a theory that there is a phobia or an ism for everything; homophobia, racism, sexism etc., but that no-one ever talks about heightism. Bill remembered him saying that you often see tall geezers with short

7

girls, but rarely the other way around; unless, of course, said geezer is flush with cash. Stan maintained that this prejudice, reinforced by endless fairy-tales featuring tall, dark, handsome strangers, was enough to force vertically challenged individuals such as he to pursue DIY. But then he reckoned he had to deal with the prejudice of newsagents, who insisted on placing the magazines that specialised in DIY on the top shelf, where he couldn't reach them.

Add to that the fact that poor old Stan wasn't blessed with the best of looks, and he was always convinced that the odds were stacked against him when it came to partaking in the sport of rumpy-pumpy. Maybe that's why he was always so irate; not getting enough love. These days Bill could empathise.

'And he left us with the legacy of that bloody name,' continued Bill; 'can't imagine how we all agreed to that millstone.'

'Seemed like a good idea at the time,' Tom laughed, 'but it did somewhat inhibit our chances of mass appeal.'

'So, where do you start looking for musicians in our genre these days?'

'Bumped into Ray Arnold the other week' said Tom, 'you know, used to play with the Rockets; he doesn't have a gig at the moment.'

'Yeah, I remember Ray; drove a baby-shit brown Allegro, with diarrhoea-coloured upholstery and a square steering wheel. Decent drummer, though, as I recall.'

'He had to be, playing with that rabble; he was the only thing that held it all together, they were so pissed most of the time.'

'Ray did his fair share of the drinking too,' said Bill.

Andy Moon and the Rockets! Never was a man more aptly named than their singer; every time Bill looked at his face it reminded him of a pair of veiny buttocks pressed against a coach window. (4)

Jack sauntered over to collect their empty glasses. 'You two look pretty animated,' he said. 'What the hell are you arguing about?'

'We used to be in a band, would you believe,' said Bill. 'Tom thinks we should get back together.'

'Really!! And why not? I hear there's quite a demand for music in old folks' homes these days.'

'Hey, there's no need for that,' protested Tom, 'we could take our custom elsewhere you know.'

Jack made his way back to the bar, empty glasses clinking

together as his shoulders shook with mirth. Bill bristled at Jack's dismissal. He'd hit a nerve and nothing motivated Bill more than being ridiculed.

'OK, Tom, a hypothetical question. If we did reform, where would we play? There can't be much call for a little known punkabilly band these days.'

'You'd be surprised, there's a big nostalgia market. Things are starting to move around here; some of the pubs are putting bands on again and there's a thriving underground music scene if you dig deep enough. Finally, there's an alternative to the endless stream of tribute shows at the big theatre.'

'So, you think we'd get some gigs then?'

'Absolutely; we had a reputation on the circuit and they'd jump at the chance to book the band that once supported the Cats.' (5)

Bill shivered as he thought about that final tour. If it wasn't the crowd throwing glasses full of gob and God knows what else, it was the after gig parties. Then there was Clive; he wasn't the safest driver at the best of times, but after a night on the piss and no sleep he was positively lethal. It was a relief when they'd started earning and were able to delegate driving duties to Richard the Roadie.

'And that tour nearly killed us,' he reminded Tom.

'You always did look at the negatives in everything. Come on Bill, there were some great times too, weren't there? And we've all grown up since then; we'll be much more sensible this time around, as will the audience.'

'And what does Karen think about this? Can't imagine she'd be too keen on the idea. She saw it all, remember, the rise and fall; and she was there to pick up the pieces.'

'Haven't told her yet; I was waiting till I'd spoken to you first. She'll come round. The kids are older now and I'm just an embarrassment these days. They don't even notice when I'm not there.'

'Ha, don't they know that their dad used to be cool?'

Tom sighed - 'They wouldn't know cool if it bit them on the arse. I despair at what they watch and listen to; they don't even get off their backsides for their entertainment. All the pop stars these days have it on a plate. They just have to demean themselves in front of that vacuous panel on TV and it's - "sign here and we'll have you selling out the O2 in no time." None of them have paid their dues like we had to.' (6)

'Yeah, we paid our dues alright. Rattling around the country in that beat up Transit, stinking to high heaven in rat-infested dingy squats, getting ripped-off by promoters and record companies; and all for what - a number 27 hit and a footnote in the annals of rock?'

'It was character building; didn't do us any harm.'

'Character building? It nearly destroyed us, Tom. My God, you have a short memory. And you really want to go out and do it all again?'

'Not to go back on the road, no. We'll be selective, the odd gig here and there, festivals if we can get them. What do you say? Let's at least meet up for old time's sake, bring our instruments and have a jam; see if the spark's still there.'

1. I'd rather burn out than fade away paraphrases Neil Young's homage to rock'n'roll, *Hey Hey, My My (Into the Black),* or its acoustic counterpart, *My My, Hey Hey (Out of the Blue).*
2. A bad pun borrowed from David Bowie's *The Laughing Gnome.*
3. Van (the Man) Morrison's brilliant album, *Inarticulate Speech of the Heart.*
4. Never heard of Andy Moon and the Rockets? No, nor have I; they are a fictional band, made up for the purposes of this story.
5. The Cats? Could this be the legendary Stray Cats?
6. A not very thinly veiled swipe at the X-Factor; or is it Britain's Got Talent? I'll say no more.

Bill was deep in thought as he strolled home, taking care to avoid the icy side of the path where the winter sun's feeble rays hadn't reached all day. He felt the frozen extremities of his ears and wished he'd worn his hat. He knew the way without thinking; his feet on autopilot, he'd trod this route so many times. Over the footbridge, up the street with the timeworn terraced houses, past his old school (Jesus, that seemed like a long time ago), and past the school fields for the final stretch. Bill recalled the time that he and his friends had been forced to circuit those fields for a whole afternoon, after their PE teacher had caught them taking a shortcut in cross-country. He steeled his resolve and quickened his pace to bring closer the warmth of home. The streets were so deserted due to the bitter cold that he felt like the only soul in town.

Tom's words had set his mind racing and, in a nostalgic haze aided by a few pints of Gnarly Old Scrote, he wondered if it was possible. Could they really relight that burned out candle; be a force for good again? Many things had changed since their heyday; now the kids had other distractions to tempt them away from the holy grail of music - no-one took it seriously anymore. Back in the day that new record by your favourite band was an important event; life changing even. Every nuance and every word hung upon and shared with your peers; the record sleeve studied from top to bottom and back to front, lyrics learnt and repeated to reinforce your credibility. You would argue for hours about the respective merits of this band or that, thoroughly convinced you had it sussed, your finger on the pulse. Your taste was impeccable and you wore it well as you proudly strutted your stuff; in the misguided belief that you were the epitome of cool. Well, maybe it wasn't really like that for everyone, but it was for Bill and his cronies. (1)

He was a fan first, before that brief glimpse of stardom, aficionado turned celebrity; at least in his own hemisphere. It felt like an outdated attitude, from long ago. Before downloads and iTunes reduced the attention span to a soundbite; and before the alien technological age of the iPhone and gaming, with the whole world and beyond channelled through that tiny screen.

Bill felt sorry for young, aspiring musicians. How could they craft something new and original when every melodious variation had been explored before? Their predecessors had probably said the same about he and his band-mates; they too had been influenced by their forerunners, who would, no doubt, have berated them for their lack of originality. He indulged in a sardonic smile as he considered all they'd been through - 'Now, when those old enough to remember speak of those times, how many will recall our music?' he asked himself. 'Ha, that bloody name, maybe; but the music? Even among the cognisant we were a flame that burned fiercely, but fleetingly.'

All the way home he argued with his inner-self, weighed up the pros and cons and decided that logically, there were far more obstacles than opportunities. On the other hand Bill had always regretted that it was over too soon, their potential unfulfilled. Perhaps it *was* time to roll that rock again and see how far it would go.

1. Did you spot the reference to Rod Stewart's *You Wear It Well* hidden in this chapter?

11

By the time he'd reached his front door he'd almost convinced himself that it was a possibility. After all; what the hell did any of it have to do with rational thought? He struggled to turn the key in the lock due to his frozen fingers but eventually succeeded; to be met with the familiar greeting.

'Who is it? Who's there?'

'It's only me Mum, I'm home.'

'And where the fuck have you been?'

'Just for a drink with Tom; remember, I told you earlier and I phoned when I got to the pub to make sure you were OK. And please don't swear, Mum, it's not nice; you always taught us not to use bad language.'

'What do you think you're doing, coming back at this time of night; you'll wake up your father and he has to get up for work in the morning.'

'But it's only 10:30, Mum.'

There was no doubt it was getting worse and Bill was being subjected to this ritual more and more frequently on his arrival home. His father, Arthur, had passed away peacefully, nearly five years ago now. It was a blessing in many ways; he wouldn't have been able to cope with this. Never would you find a more devoted couple, inseparable since their immortal song, *True Love Ways*, had brought them together at the weekly dance at the Palais. He'd heard the story so many times that it was a fundamental part of him, the romantic precursor to his very existence. (1)

'What day is it?'

'It's Thursday, Mum.'

It wasn't really Thursday, but there were no longer any Fridays in this house. Friday was dance day; the day of the week that they would look forward to with eager anticipation. Dad was the Chairman, Mum was the Treasurer and, together, they were champions. No-one could conjure a more jubilant jive, a perfectly synchronised blur as they left their rivals quaking in their wake.

Surprisingly agile for one of such bulk, Dad had still been a capable dancer until a year or so before his untimely demise. He'd stand solid, slowly build momentum, then spin like the fulcrum of a fairground ride, as he threw Mum this way and that, until only fingertips held them together; before reeling her violently back in and holding her briefly close. Then the ride would begin another cycle and Mum would scream with fear and pleasure, like a teenage girl on the Whip. The centre of the ballroom was theirs and the other dancers kept a respectful distance for fear of humiliation or injury.

Bill knew where she'd be, the last time it was a Friday. He'd found her on Union Street, dressed in her best pink polka swing-dress, a little unstable on shiny stilettos but, from behind, she looked as she always had; immaculate, slender and ready to dance. The hall had long since been demolished to make way for a superstore, where robotic punters attempted to manoeuvre reluctant trolleys around the floor to a bland soundtrack of piped muzak. She'd sobbed a little as he put an arm round her shoulder; lost and confused, she'd offered no resistance as he led her home.

It broke his heart to think that Mum would never dance again. He'd tried taking her to some ballroom night at the community centre in a futile attempt to resurrect some interest, but Mum had only ever had one partner. He did his best but, whereas his father had the stature of a man-mountain, Bill was more of an average-sized hillock; his inheritance his mother's wiry frame and his father's predilection for all things alcoholic and dairy.

'Are you sure it's Thursday?'

'Yeah, it's Thursday. Have you had anything to eat?'

'I think so, there was some cold beef left over from Sunday.'

Bill shook his head. He knew that he'd used the last of the beef for his sandwiches during the week and that he'd left Mum an egg salad in the fridge. He went to the kitchen to take a look; still there and untouched.

'Come and sit down, Mum. You've got to eat, keep your strength up.'

Bill made her a cup of tea and watched as she half-heartedly picked at the withered lettuce leaves and dried-out tomatoes. She smothered it in salad-cream in an effort to make it edible. It was getting late, but time didn't matter anymore.

He sighed as he took a resigned look around. He tried to keep it tidy, but there was no denying that the old place could do with a lick of paint. It was like walking into a sepia museum dedicated to the memory of his old man; everything in its place, just has he'd left it before his heart stopped beating on that summer afternoon.

Mum had thought nothing of it, he often had a nap after lunch; it wasn't until she'd tried to wake him for their routine cup of tea that she realised he was gone. He looked at peace, she'd said, but then he always did. Nothing ever got his gander and he had a philosophical, laid back attitude to life - 'You can do nothing about most of the shit that happens in the world,' he opined often. 'What's the point in getting het up about it?'

It had taken four of them to lift him into the coffin – too much time spent in his second home; the White Swan, along with an ill-advised excess of cholesterol on his plate. He was a big man, but Bill wasn't sure what had done for him in the end; the apathy or the diet of real ale and cheese.

Now the house resembled a shrine; except Mum thought he was coming back. Every time Bill suggested that he redecorate he was advised to consult his dad when he got home - 'Your dad's in charge of things like that, he likes it just so.'

Just so was in danger of becoming retro – the place hadn't been revamped for so long that it was coming back into fashion.

It had seemed like the most practical solution after his divorce, to move back in with his mother; but Bill was starting to question the wisdom. Of course he loved her and felt responsible for her welfare, but he could see a desperate future panning out before him. Despite the onset of early Dementia, Mum was a physically fit lady; Bill envisaged at least another twenty years of gradual decline as she would, inevitably, turn into a stranger. He shivered and the walls seemed to close in around him.

The split from Elaine had been long and acrimonious. The maintenance payments were severe and he needed somewhere to live; it was either the luxury of a cardboard box in the subway or a return to the family home. What choice did he have?

Any recompense for his intermittent toil as a freelance Graphic Designer served only to keep Elaine and his kids in the luxury they thought they deserved. Despite the fact that it was she that had been unfaithful, broken the bond of trust that Bill took for granted, the Child Support Agency had insisted that he pay the price. He was permanently broke, with little or no prospect of the situation changing until the fruits of their long-dead love were capable of supporting themselves. That could be a while yet, he thought, taking into account that Lauren was entrenched in Psychology at uni, Rosie had flunked her A Levels due to family problems, Nathan was drowning in indifference, and Grace was only eight.

No matter that Elaine's new partner was an affluent entrepreneur, who had somehow emerged from the recession smelling of roses; the CSA were concerned only with the letter of the law and cared little about justice and the fact that Bill was a broken man. He wasn't a materialistic person - as long as he had his music collection and change for a few pints then he was contented. He didn't begrudge the money going to his kids; they could have everything as far as he was concerned, but it left a bad taste that its distribution was being managed by Elaine and that slimy bastard, with his flash car and holidays in the sun.

Recently, Bill had even been relatively solvent; a lucrative three month contract to resuscitate a tired but well-known high street brand, complete with web design. But the job was coming to an end, he could drag it out no further and, as yet, he had no work lined up to replace it. Maybe the resurrection of Skinny Ted and the Brothel Creepers could earn him a few quid and supplement his intermittent income. It was as good a plan as any; but how could he leave Mum for any length of time? Perhaps it was time that his brother, John, shared some of the burden; God knows it was long overdue.

As he climbed the stairs and entered his musty room, the fetid smell of yesterday's socks caught the back of his throat. Decorated with peeling dark green and taupe wallpaper, his sanctuary summed up his mood, tired and depressed. A large, ghostly white vision stood static in the corner, its expressionless face staring back at him. Bill smirked as he returned the gaze. His only companion would have terrified anyone else waking in the middle of the night, but Bill always found comfort in her presence.

As was his habit, he approached the inscrutable figure and ran his hands tenderly over her shoulders, then slowly down to a slender waist. He felt the curve of her hips and gently touched the G-string beneath her flimsy garment. Then he snatched the sheet from her body and spun her around, naked, until he could caress her from behind. As his fingers ran expertly up and down her neck, she shuddered to life once more in his grip and they moved in harmony to a sensual, rhythmic pulse; their bodies up close and intimate.

Rudely, an angry and insistent knock on the wall shattered the moment, and his irate neighbour bellowed - 'Do you have to play that fucking thing at this time of night?'

A wry grin as he softly placed the sheet back over her shoulders and leaned her back against the wall; he would resume her seduction in the morning. It was an indulgence of his, some might say a perverse one; but why shouldn't Bill imagine that his double-bass was a certain lady?

He flopped down on the bed, lay on his back, studied the ceiling and considered all the wonderful places he'd visited through that ever-expanding, shape-shifting damp-stain. In its infancy it had resembled the Maldives, a few specks and lines in a sea of nothingness; then he thought he'd try Sicily, the misshapen football on the toe of Italy's boot. Now boot and ball had merged and stretched to form Australia, his next exotic location; and all from the safety and comfort of his own crib. He'd travelled further in his mind than his body would ever carry him.

As a child he'd spend countless carefree hours digging his allotted plot of earth in the garden. When asked what he was doing, he'd reply - 'I'm going to Australia.' - as if it would merely be a matter of days before he'd burrow through the Earth's core. After exchanging pleasantries halfway through his journey with a man sporting long blonde hair and a flowing white robe, he would emerge on the other side of the world to be greeted by an upside-down kangaroo. Bill mourned the passing of the simple certainties of childhood, irreversibly tainted by the unwelcome knowledge of adulthood. Now, upon arrival down-under, there would stand the silhouette in the sunrise of a bespectacled, bearded old man, accompanied by the desolate drone of a didgeridoo. (2 – 3)

Like every night, his restless mind flitted from one scenario to another and, eventually, he drifted off to a fitful slumber. He'd be wide awake in the early hours again, of course.

1. *True Love Ways* was written by Buddy Holly for his wife Maria Elana as a wedding gift. It was created at his final recording session, before his tragic death in February 1959, aged just 22.
2. Could the mystery man at the Earth's core be Rick Wakeman, whose bombastic 1974 concept album *Journey to the Centre of the Earth* was based on Jules Verne's novel of the same name? Apart from the fact that Bill might have been a little old to dig holes to Australia at this time, it is plausible that he may have met Rick on his childhood journey!!
3. *Sun Arise*, among others by Rolf Harris, was part of the soundtrack to our childhood. Hence the reference to our memories being tainted by the unwelcome knowledge of adulthood.

Bill's weekend of access began, as usual, with him waiting impatiently outside his former home. Those trees could do with cutting back, he thought; that ivy's growing wild and the drive needs re-laying. It was with a mixture of relief and sadness that he remembered that these tasks were no longer his responsibility. With a sigh of resignation, he turned up the volume, closed his eyes, laid back and tapped the steering wheel as those familiar, soaring harmonies left him in wonder once more. Is there anything sadder than the tears of a clown? He'd felt much better since he'd resumed the self-medication of music. Now, whenever he questioned his existence, pondered as to why he was here, then that song alone was reason enough to be alive. (1)

He could picture what was going on inside the house. Inevitably, Rosie wasn't ready; she'd still be applying her make-up and attending to her immaculate image. Nathan would be stretched out on the sofa, with headphones on and iPad in his face, oblivious to time and anything else that happened to be going on around him as the bodies piled up in whatever dubious game he was playing. Only Grace would be jumping up and down excitedly, looking forward to seeing her dad and spending the weekend.

Like he'd done a hundred times, Bill involuntarily replayed the moment that he'd discovered his wife's affair. In retrospect he should have guessed long before he'd heard it through the grapevine. (2)

'But why?' he'd asked, utterly devastated.

'Well, you've been in another relationship for the last thirty years; I thought it was my turn.'

'Jesus, not that old chestnut; you can't use that as an excuse for your infidelity.'

'I'm sick of living in the same house as your fantasy, ideal woman. You have her memory tattooed on your arm for God's sake; and then there's that bloody song.'

Elaine proceeded to sing the words so cruelly; the words that had once meant so much to him, injected with such malice and venom, until he begged her to stop.

'But the tattoo is in homage to the song; a song that I'm very proud of. And I don't recall you ever turning down the royalties.'

'Whether she was real or not is irrelevant; she was your ultimate dream girl.'

'But that's all in the past; you're the one that I've chosen to spend my life with. We've raised a family together; doesn't that mean anything to you?'

'A womb to carry your children; that's all I ever was. You

never wrote a song for me.'

'You know the band was all over by then. I haven't written a song since long before we met.'

'And why's that? Lack of inspiration, that's why.' Elaine started to sing his song, *Stood Up, Again*, once more; only this time with her own name inserted. 'See, doesn't fit, does it? It doesn't rhyme, the words don't belong together and neither do we.'

'Utter nonsense; you had relationships before we met and they were more tangible than the one that you're so jealous of.'

'But I never had them indelibly inked into my skin, or immortalised in song. How can I compete with that?'

'I never asked you to compete. Ours is a completely different kind of relationship.'

'Exactly; it's easier to love someone when you've only known them in a song; it gets much harder with the passing of time.'

Bill considered her words. They'd had this argument before of course, but Elaine had never previously acted on her discontent. This time she'd really gone out and found another, apparently to punish him for daring to write a lyric for someone else three decades ago.

His mind drifted back to that night, when he'd spied a vision in the crowd; a lone dancer in a yellow mini-skirt and black Dr Martens, shining among a sea of gloomy, uniform and intimidating punters. It was her smile that drew him in. The spotlights aimed at the stage were dazzling enough, but that smile radiated more light than all of them put together. He'd played the rest of the gig just for her, as if they were the only two people in the hall; and he was over the moon when she'd waited for him backstage.

During the subsequent few months he'd returned to the venue whenever he could (regardless of what god-awful band was playing), in the hope of seeing her again. Cruelly, she'd taken him halfway to paradise and left him there, with no way back to reality. Maybe he'd dreamt the whole thing. (3)

Did Elaine have a point? Could anyone ever contest that ephemeral youthful infatuation, that one girl who makes your heart ache and your loins tingle; and thoughts of whom fill every waking hour and expectant dream? In your mind she's perfect as you project all you ever wanted onto the beautiful blank canvass of your illusions. A tattoo and a song was the least she deserved, wasn't it?

Real long-term relationships take a lot more effort and, once the

18

first flush of ardour is over, you gradually discover each other's attributes, idiosyncrasies and irritating habits. You learn how to compromise, to live together and respect each other's space. You celebrate the good times, endure the bad times, and offer mutual support during the tragic times. You share your children's evolution, from the sleepless nights of crying babies, their first days at school, their achievements and disappointments; through to the joys of adolescence and first boyfriends or girlfriends; and you wait up, worried sick, until they return in the early hours without so much as a sorry for putting you through hell.

Surely such momentous experiences should forge an unbreakable bond that transcends a fleeting fascination from the past. Or maybe you simply grow bored, nothing new to discover or say, until temptation and the greener grass break the invisible chains that hold you together. If you're lucky the cycle will begin again, but Bill didn't feel much like an eligible bachelor. Who would be interested in a middle aged divorcee with no career prospects? He'd reached that time of life where he felt too long in the tooth to start anew, but too young to throw in the towel.

Ah well, things are as they are, he sighed, as he looked at his watch; the weekend would be over if he sat out here much longer.

Eventually, they all tumbled out of the front door, Rosie and Nathan exchanging less than affectionate insults as they approached. Bill climbed out of the car as Grace ran to give him one of her special hugs that he'd missed so much. He wistfully recalled the days when all his kids used to greet him in such a way; a spontaneous outpouring of unconditional love. His youngest daughter was a beautiful accident; unplanned and much younger than her siblings, for a while she'd been a ray of sunshine in the tempestuous sky of their failing marriage. Bill ruffled Grace's hair, gave Nathan a manly punch on the shoulder and stuck out his tongue as he traded a customary glare with Rosie.

'Have them back by three tomorrow,' ordered Elaine, 'Nathan and Grace have homework and school on Monday.'

'Yes, Boss,' replied Bill. He couldn't be bothered to argue; and besides, he knew that he and Rosie at least, would run out of things to talk about long before then. He looked Elaine in the eye - 'So, how are you?' he asked.

'Don't pretend you care. I'll see you tomorrow.'

'Cool,' was all he could think to say. How had it come to this? How could two people who had shared so much, find so few words for each other?

'So, where are you taking them?' asked Elaine.

'Don't know; thought we'd play it by ear.'

'As organised as ever; and don't forget - three o'clock tomorrow.' She turned and strode back into the house.

Bill resisted the temptation to kick the brand new Range Rover in the drive and made his way to his somewhat worse-for-wear Renault Laguna. The electronics were temperamental, the aerial was broken and the passenger door creaked excruciatingly when opened, but the engine would probably last forever. Rosie won the tussle to sit in the front and, in the absence of an auxiliary socket and without asking, proceeded to play her music through her phone. Within seconds they were all listening to Justin Beaver; whether they liked it or not. Bill cringed, turned the key in the ignition and pulled away, ignoring the twitching curtains of Mrs May next door. (4)

Bill caught Nathan's eye in the rear-view mirror. 'So, how was the school trip to France?'

'Great; wasn't too keen on the food though, had live on burgers and pomme frites.'

'So, you didn't eat anything healthy.'

'I did have a couple of apples.'

'Well, that's something I suppose.'

'Yeah, but they were on a stick and covered in toffee.'

'So, what shall we do this weekend then, folks?' asked Bill, with enthusiasm. He took care not to use the word kids, for fear of appearing condescending toward his older offspring.

'Dunno,' said Rosie.

'Don't care,' said Nathan.

'Can we go to the park?' squealed Grace.

'How about a walk along the canal and a spot of lunch at the Grand Junction Arms,' Bill suggested. 'It's a beautiful day; look, barely a cloud in the sky.'

'No, I don't like walking, it's boring,' replied Rosie, as she Snapchatted her best friend.

'But you used to like the outdoors and the countryside,' recalled Bill.

'Well, not anymore.'

'But there are so many things to see; flowers growing, rivers flowing, boats to row, bikes to ride, trees to climb, air to breathe, sun to feel on your face. There's a whole world to discover out there and you're missing it.'

'Boring; it's all boring.'

For a moment he was angry at her apathy, but then he just felt sad; sad for the loss of her childlike wonder at new things, new experiences; sad that she'd grown into this seemingly indifferent individual that he no longer knew. Now her whole world seemed contained in the banality of that tablet, the flickering screen reflected in her blank face.

'And it's bloody freezing out there,' observed Nathan.

'So, we'll wrap up warm,' reasoned Bill, 'get some fresh air into your lungs. It'll do you good.'

'But we're not kids anymore, Dad; we don't like all that stuff now,' insisted Rosie.

'I'm still a kid,' said Grace, 'I'll come and climb a tree with you.'

'That's the spirit,' enthused Bill. 'Come on guys, you'll love it once we get out there.'

'Well, I guess there's nothing else to do,' conceded Nathan. 'Do they do pizza at this pub then?'

'Don't know, not been for a while; but I'm sure they'll have something you like on the menu.'

Rosie sighed - 'What about vegetarian? I'm not eating dead animals.'

'How long have you been a vegetarian?'

'About two weeks,' Nathan answered on her behalf, 'it's her latest crusade. Mum is always getting wound up because she has to cook something different for Rosie.'

'Well good for you,' said Bill, 'you should stand up for what you believe in.'

It was indeed a beautiful day, bright, crisp and fresh as a new dawn; albeit bloody freezing, as Nathan had pointed out. Bill held Grace's hand as she skipped beside him along the towpath, Rosie and Nathan trailing reluctantly behind. Bill loved this walk and had been coming here since he was a kid. Nothing much had changed, except the path was better maintained these days and you no longer had to negotiate your way through nettles and brambles. They stopped at the lock gates as a colourful barge named *The Drifter II* came near; a three-legged brindle Greyhound jumped excitedly from the boat and approached them with a friendly bark and a floppy tongue. Bill bent to stroke its bony head and asked the owner, a thinning, rotund man in his fifties, - 'Need a hand with the lock?'

'Yeah, thanks; could always use a bit of extra muscle.'

Rosie groaned and leaned against a nearby fence, as Bill, Nathan and Grace put their backs into the lock beam and pushed; their combined weight making the task easy. The barge was expertly manoeuvred into the lock by a lady in paint splattered dungarees, as the man wound the windlass to close the gates. Rosie breathed impatiently as they watched the lock fill with water and the boat rise to the next level. Bill noticed an old guitar propped against the cabin door and nodded in recognition of a fellow musician. The man whistled and yelled - 'Elvis' - and the dog jumped back in; the couple smiled and thanked them as they made their way out of the lock and meandered leisurely away. This was a way of life where the journey meant everything and the destination mattered little.

'Why do they call their dog Elvis?' asked Grace, as she cheerfully waved them on their way.

'Cos it ain't nothing but a hound dog?' suggested Bill. (5)

Grace looked confused.

'OK, let's find a good climbing tree,' enthused Bill.

'How about that one,' proposed Nathan, 'come on little Grace; let's see how high you can climb.'

'Don't call me little,' shouted Grace, as she chased Nathan towards an abundantly branched Cypress. Nathan helped her onto the first limb then, from below, advised the next steps.

'So, are you ready for your A Level retakes then?' Bill asked Rosie.

'It's none of your business; nothing to do with you.'

'Hey, no need for that; I'm only taking an interest. What subjects do you have to do again?'

'Business Studies, English and Maths.'

'Is there anything I can do to help?'

'Like what, Dad? What do you know about it?'

Bill knew she was right, of course; what did he know about it? Once his offspring had mastered the basics, he'd always felt hopeless and inadequate when it came to helping with the homework. His business acumen was sketchy to say the least and Veritable Visuals, his graphic design empire of one, was barely afloat. His English credentials amounted to co-writing credits on a couple of albums full of three minute rock/pop ditties; and his mathematical skills were practically non-existent. Given his own rather embarrassing academic achievements, he knew he couldn't lecture his kids about theirs. He felt like a laggard; and Rosie wasn't inclined to make him feel any better.

'Well, my English is pretty good,' he ventured, 'I speak it like a native.'

'A native of where, exactly?'

Their futile conversation was rudely interrupted by frantic cries of – 'DADDY, DADDY; HELP!!'

They turned to see Grace suspended from a branch by the seat of her jeans and waving hysterically. Nathan was about half-way up, but couldn't reach her.

'Jesus, Nathan; why did you let her climb so high?' Bill remonstrated, as he ran to the base of the tree and looked up. 'It's OK Grace, I'll come and get you; just keep still please and don't panic.'

After much scraping of knees and banging of head, Bill managed to reach his increasingly anxious daughter and negotiate a safe route down for them both; as well as for Nathan, who wasn't about to admit that he was stuck too. Bill was reassured to find that at least, after all these years he hadn't lost his tree-climbing skills. They reached terra-firma without further incident and there was relief at a happy outcome for one and all. Bill hadn't seen Rosie laugh so much in years.

1. Smokey Robinson and the Miracles' *Tears of a Clown*. It doesn't get any better than this!!
2. More Motown magic; Marvin Gaye's *I Heard it Through the Grapevine*.
3. Written by the prolific Carole King and Gerry Goffin, *Halfway to Paradise* was a massive hit for Billy Fury in 1961.
4. Justin Beaver? I'm sure this analogy has been used before!!
5. *Hound Dog* was written by the legendary Jerry Leiber and Mile Stoller. Originally recorded by Big Mamma Thornton in 1953, Elvis's version hit the charts in 1956.

The Reunion - Meet the Band:

Tom Milston (lead vocals/rhythm guitar/harmonica): Founder member and predominantly responsible for the musical element of the song-writing, Tom started the band with school-friend Bill

Harris in 1978. An enthusiastic but perfunctory guitarist, he was perfectly positioned for the 'anyone can do it' ethos of the day. Credited with the creation of their on-edge energy, Tom is a charismatic front-man and singer with a powerful, rasping range.

Tom studied Accountancy and set up his own firm in the immediate aftermath of the demise of the group. He married his childhood sweetheart, Karen Humphries, and they have two offspring; Richard, 25; who lives at home due to student debt and a lack of means to enter the housing market; and Siobhan, 22, a trainee shop-manager, who lives in a dingy rented flat with her boyfriend.

Tom has the appearance of a man ten years his junior and still sports an impressive blonde quiff, similar to that worn by the top Cat himself. He likes to dress simply, in black skinny jeans, leather jacket and well-polished winklepickers (black of course). (1)

Bill Harris (double-bass/backing vocals): Founder member and lyricist, Bill's words were initially panned by the critics for their clichéd subject matter - primarily cars and girls; but two songs raised his profile and enhanced his bourgeoning reputation as a post-punk poet. *Shafted* evoked the pride and solidarity of the miners' strike and the inspirational people they'd met after a benefit gig for Red Wedge. Bill was aware that the song would alienate some of their more disagreeable right wing fans, but that was exactly what he wanted to achieve. A fortunate by-product was acclaim in the radical music press of the day, who hailed the song as subversive, due to its incisive, cutting-edge lyrics wed to a traditional rockabilly rhythm. The uncharacteristic ballad B-Side, *Stood Up, Again*, an aching lament for lost love, was later covered successfully by Shaky and the Sunsets, among others, and for a while, Tom and Bill were able to live comfortably from the royalties. (2 - 4)

Bill is recently divorced from Elaine, with whom he had four children; Lauren, 21; Rosie, 18; Nathan, 16; and Grace, 8. Although the same age as Tom, Bill looks like an ageing negative of his song-writing partner and favours a jet-black quiff with matching attire.

Clive Hunt (lead guitar/keyboards/backing vocals): A brilliant, well respected musician and Blues aficionado, it was often said that Clive was wasted as a Brothel Creeper. However, he showed great loyalty to Bill and Tom, who had discovered him busking in the bowels of Baker Street and invited him to join the band. Clive was the only member who'd continued in the industry after the split, and he's carved out a lucrative career as a session musician. He has also been known to play the pub circuit under the pseudonym, Carsick Kevin. (5)

Clive is a bit of a loner and finds it difficult to nurture long-term relationships; a wet weekend in Weymouth with Wendy Williams his most erotic encounter to date. He still harbours hopes of happiness and looks for love in all the likely places, the anonymity of internet dating promising perfectly-matched partners. His on-line personal profile testifies to tons of talent and an annoying aptitude for alliteration. As bald as a bowling ball, he is happy for others to take the spotlight.

Ray Arnold (drums): New recruit and veteran rhythm-meister, Ray made his name with Andy Moon and the Rockets; the Brothel Creepers' nearest rivals in their heyday. As a recovering alcoholic, life back on the road with this bunch of former reprobates is probably not the wisest career choice. An accomplished drummer, but somewhat lacking in flamboyance and stage presence, Ray will do well to emerge from the formidable shadow of Stan, God rest his soul.

Ray has buggered-up just about every relationship he's ever been in, mainly due to his predilection for booze. He has an estranged twenty year old son named Keith, who has hinted at a chance of reconciliation should his dad stay on the waggon for a year. Ray hasn't touched a drop for over a month and is making reluctant but determined progress. A defiant expression shines through bushy beard and watery eyes, his bulbous rubicund nose like a beacon of hope for the dispossessed. (6)

'1-2-3-4,' shouted Ray with some gusto. As the keeper of the beat, he felt it was his responsibility to count in the intro. They'd decided upon *Shakin' All Over*, a rousing staple of their past live set, to kick-off the reunion rehearsal. They hadn't got beyond the first bar, before the whole thing fell haphazardly apart and the once accomplished ensemble stuttered to an uncoordinated halt.

'What the fuck was that?' exclaimed Clive, a screech of feedback accentuating his point.

'I think it was Tom,' said Ray; 'he came in too late.'

'And how am I supposed to know when to come in,' pleaded Tom, 'when you sound like a blind man with a wooden leg falling down the stairs? My gran could play better than that and she suffers from arthritis.'

'Whoa, come on guys,' said Bill, 'we're all bound to be a little rusty; it has been a while you know. Let's keep it simple and take it one step at a time.'

Upstairs at the Oddfellows Arms; a decidedly underwhelming location for an occasion so significant, but Tom knew the landlord, who'd agreed to let them use the room in return for a free gig once they were ready. Small mouse-bait boxes hugged the skirting boards and the place reeked of rising-damp and the hoppy aroma of the spent beer-barrels stacked in the corner. Ultimately they would be converted into uncomfortable chairs for any punter too old, too tired or too drunk to lean on the bar.

Splintered and cracked old oak beams brushed their heads, as they got back to basics and re-dug the foundations of the rhythm. The floorboards vibrated to the boom of Bill's bass and the forty watt light bulb flickered in protest at the theft of its current. Their second attempt was little better, but Bill perceived some progress and sensed the tiniest hint of the old feeling return. Until Tom broke a guitar-string and it went to pieces again.

Whilst Tom fitted a new string, Bill and Clive retreated to the sparsely populated bar below to order refreshments. A few heads swivelled to appraise the source of the recent racket from above then returned with indifference to their conversations or newspapers.

It had been a long, long time since Bill had seen Clive and there was an awkward reticence between them, a residue of the rancour that split the band the first time around. Clive's main gripe was that Bill and Tom had earned more, due to their song-writing royalties, than he and Stan, God rest his soul. Each time Clive had made a suggestion Bill and Tom had either been dismissive, or they'd commandeered and adapted it until it was unrecognisable. There were a number of songs where Clive had argued that he should have a co-writing credit and it evidently still rankled.

They stood silently, side-by-side at the bar before, eventually, Clive asked Bill what he was drinking. In the absence of any Gnarly Old Scrote, Bill chose an American IPA, the most expensive beer on offer. Clive bristled and ordered the round.

'So you think this is gonna work, then?' he asked.

'Not based on what I've heard so far, no,' replied Bill, 'but I guess it is early days. You and Tom must have thought it worth a try or we wouldn't be here.'

'But Tom told me it was all your idea!'

'Interesting,' said Bill, 'so he's got us both here under false pretences, the devious bastard. Come on, let's sort this out.'

Bill and Clive returned with stern expressions, three pints, and a Coke for Ray; they glared at Tom with their arms folded.

'I think you have some explaining to do,' demanded Bill.

'Did you think we wouldn't talk to each other?' asked Clive.

'What's up?' enquired Ray.

'It appears that Tom here has spun us all a different yarn,' said Bill, 'in order to get us together against our better judgement.'

'Well let's face it,' protested Tom, 'you all thought it was a joke. None of you would have turned up if I hadn't told a few white lies.'

'And it is a joke,' said Clive. 'Look at this place, look at us; and you only have to listen to what we've just played. We're no better than our first rehearsal all those years ago; and we haven't even got youthful energy to make up for it this time.'

And with that he knocked back his pint, unplugged his guitar and began to pack away.

'Wait,' pleaded Tom. 'You're by far the best musician in the band and I admit that we may not have treated you right in the past. What do you say we're all equal footing this time and you can be the musical director? We'll split everything four ways.'

'Great,' laughed Clive; 'a quarter of bugger-all is still bugger-all, you know.'

'I have to agree with Clive,' said Bill. 'Let's face reality, Tom. There's nothing left, man.'

'OK; go back to your miserable existences, if that's what you want. Your marriage has collapsed, Bill; you're living with your mum. Clive, you earn your crust playing what others pay you to play; doing as you're told. Ray, what were your prospects before I asked you along for the ride? And me, I'm utterly sick of the rat-race. Tell me, what else have you all got to live for? Alternatively we can take one last shot at it. I believed in this band back then and I still do. We were one of the best and there's no reason why we can't be again.'

Clive hesitated, halfway to the door; whilst Ray provided a rim-shot to emphasise the crescendo of Tom's tirade. Bill looked at his watch and sighed.

'Well, as I've already cancelled my date with Clare Grogan to be here tonight, I suppose we may as well carry on. If we're still shit at the end of the evening then we can knock it on the head.' (7)

Clive shook his head, exhaled loudly, removed his jacket and threw it on the floor. 'OK, but it's a complete waste of time.'

'What about you, Ray?' asked Bill.

'Yeah, I've got nothing better to do.'

Clive strapped his guitar back over his shoulder, plugged it in and let loose a deafening chord. He clearly didn't want to be there, but gradually, his instinctive professionalism took over. In that moment, he became the band's musical director and wherever things were going wrong he recommended ways to put them right. Bill and Tom bowed to his superior musical knowledge and went along with whatever he said; partly to keep the fragile peace, and partly because Clive knew what he was doing. Ray did what Ray did best and delivered a rock-solid and steady beat.

And so it was that little by little, row by row, the bricks of bop were laid until they were almost as one again - Ba-ba-dum-dum-dum-dum-dum-dum-dum. Blammm!! 'Shakin' All Over!!' - Maybe not quite as buccaneering as the original Pirates, but more than enough to set Jolly Roger's foot a-tapping in the bar downstairs. (8)

Three parts original and one part reconditioned, the rickety old motor was systematically and meticulously restored to a decent facsimile of its former glory. Sure, it looked old and knackered; but by God could it go.

Apart from the fact that they weren't sure which metaphor to use, things were starting to go well. Rough and almost ready, a provisional set list was lovingly formulated as the evening flew by and they rediscovered their mojo. They were all pretty good musicians with an instinctive feel for what sounded right and, after the shaky and acrimonious start, it was simply a matter of time before they were rocking again. Bill would have happily stayed there all night, had the bell not tolled and the landlord not called – 'LAST-ORDERS; AND THAT GOES FOR YOU NOISY BASTARDS UP THERE TOO!!'

Tom looked at Bill and they beamed simultaneously - 'What do you say; think we've still got it?'

Bill turned to see Clive and Ray smiling too - 'Was there ever any doubt,' he said, 'when's the first gig?'

1. Of course frontman, Tom, would resemble the iconic Brian Setzer of Stray Cats' fame.
2. *Cars and Girls* by Prefab Sprout was a respectful swipe at Bruce Springsteen and what singer/writer Paddy McAloon perceived as the limited subject-matter of his songs.
3. Red Wedge – a musician's collective formed by Billy Bragg, Paul Weller and Jimmy Sommerville that promoted support for the Labour Party in the run up to the 1987 general election. Some of the major acts of the day joined tours organised by Red Wedge, including Elvis Costello, Madness and the Smiths.
4. You haven't lived till you've heard Shakin' Stevens' version of the fictional classic, *Stood Up, Again*.
5. Carsick Kevin; a landlocked tribute to Seasick Steve. Born Steve Wold, the American blues musician spent much of his early life as a hobo, hopping freight-trains in search of work. His career really took off after an appearance on Jools Holland's Hootenanny in 2006. Since then he has enjoyed great success with songs inspired by his formative years on the road, played on his trademark homemade guitars.
6. Ray named his son in memory of legendary Who drummer, Keith Moon. Famed for his flamboyant and debauched lifestyle, Moon the Loon finally went too far and died of an overdose in September 1978.
7. Best known as singer with the 80s New-Wave band Altered Images and the subject of many a young man's dreams, Clare Grogan is also a successful actress famed for roles in *Gregory's Girl* and *Red Dwarf.*
8. *Shakin' All Over* by Johnny Kidd and the Pirates. A classic slice of English rock'n'roll from 1960. An influence on the Who and Dr Feelgood, among others.

Bill invariably felt small and inferior on his rare forays on the mock-Tudor mansion, in which older brother John resided when not gallivanting around the world on business. He checked himself out in the massive antique hall-mirror, which didn't lie, and wished he'd taken the trouble to shave prior to his visit.

John's immaculately dressed wife, Jessica, led him towards the living room where a large oil-painting hung above the fireplace; the branches of a majestic oak in the foreground, surrounded by a carpet of bluebells. An erratic path drew you into the misty distance, where a barely visible hint of the archetypal family (husband, wife, little boy and younger sister, plus the obligatory dog), gambolled along the forest path towards a gap in the trees. Bill had always admired the painting, but it made him feel sad. It evoked distant memories of his own childhood; innocent days full of love and hope and, at the same time, reminded him what he missed about fatherhood and being with his kids.

John barely looked up from the financial pages of his *Telegraph*, as Jessica announced, with a barely disguised hint of distaste in her voice - 'John dear, it's Bill.'

John Deere; that was Bill's nickname for his vexatious brother, ever since that visit when no-one was in. He'd passed the time of day with John's neighbour who happened to be out washing his car.

'I wouldn't want to be the gardener in there,' the neighbour had opined, 'all you ever hear is "John Deere do this, John Deere do that".

Jessica, a horsey lady in her late forties, whiled away her hours on coffee mornings, gentle gym workouts, or on criticising the work of their longsuffering cleaner, whilst testing everything that didn't move for dust with her index finger. She'd never forgiven Bill for his use of bad language in conversation with her father on the occasion of her and John's wedding.

'It's amazing how many doors the old school tie can open,' Jessica's father had stated.

'My old school never had a fucking tie, mate,' was Bill's inebriated response.

Bill wondered if he might be invited to stay for lunch, but Jessica only offered the option of tea or coffee. He would have preferred a beer, but simply replied - 'Black coffee please, no sugar.'

Jessica exited the room, nose first.

'Are you serious?' asked John, when informed of the intent to resuscitate the long-dead corpse of the Brothel Creepers. The newspaper was still on his lap, implying that his Sunday morning routine was sacrosanct and not to be interrupted.

'I'm deadly serious,' replied Bill. 'And why shouldn't I be?'

'Well, it's a bit sad isn't it; at your age? Isn't it about time you got a proper job? Haven't you got maintenance payments to keep up; and what about Mum - who's going to be there when you're out trying to relive your misspent youth?'

'I *have* a proper job; I run my own business, remember? Any income from the band will simply supplement what I earn. As for Mum, I thought it was about time that you did your share. When's the last time you even paid her a visit?'

'What's the point? She didn't know who the hell I was the last time I came round.'

'Yeah, and I had to think twice,' said Bill, 'not seen you for so long.'

'Hey, that's not fair; you know how much responsibility I have. The bank is in trouble again due to some newly-discovered mis-selling in the 90s and it's my job to sort out the unholy mess they left behind. I have to go to New York next week and then to Dubai in May. You simply have more time than me; I hardly get the chance to see my *own* family.'

'Mum *is* your own family, in case you've forgotten. You always thought that your career was somehow more important than mine, didn't you. Well, just because you wear a suit, live in a big house and drive a BMW, it doesn't give you the right to look down your nose at me. I'm proud of my music and creativity and I intend to realise my potential again before it's too late. All I'm asking is that we come to an arrangement about Mum's care when I'm on the road. If you can't be arsed to do it yourself then perhaps you can pay a carer to come in.'

'And how much will that cost?'

'No idea; but let me know when you find out 'cos you've been getting your share for free so far. If you were to invest the time, it would cost you nothing.'

'But time is money for me; you know that.'

'And money is God, right?'

John groaned - 'We're not going to have that argument again, are we; the one about Capitalism versus Socialism? Anyway, you were happy to visit the bank of John, when you needed bailing out.'

'Desperate, not happy; and you'll never let me forget it. I would have paid you back; it was you that wrote off the loan.'

'At the rate that you were making the payments, you'd have still been in debt on your death bed. No, I've made twenty times that in investments, so it's forgotten.'

'And I was grateful. You know we were just about to break in the U.S.A. when Stan, God rest his soul, decided to quit.'

Bill still bristled when thinking about it. The tour had been lined up, a contract signed with a big advance; then they had to let everyone down, pay back the promoter and record company. No-one would touch them after that fiasco.

'It'll be different this time,' he promised, 'lessons have been learned and we're more mature.'

'So, when and where is this great cultural happening taking place?' asked John, with his customary disdainful expression.

'Not sure; we're in the process of calling promoters and venues, testing the water.'

'So, you don't have any gigs lined up; a UK tour or a record deal perhaps?'

'Not yet, no; I'm just giving you prior warning for when things do take off.'

John shook his head - 'Are you sure the world's ready for this cutting-edge, revolutionary movement; or are you just going to reprise the same old tunes?'

'Don't worry about that,' blagged Bill, 'Tom and I have plenty of new material; enough for a double album in fact. We're checking out our old contacts at the record labels; it's simply a matter of time before someone picks us up.'

'Hmm, if you say so; I'd have thought all your contacts would be retired or dead by now. By the way; did you ever get that hip replacement?'

'Hip replacement? What hip replacement?'

'Well you're going to need one, because you're certainly not hip anymore.' John chuckled and looked pretty proud of his joke.

'Hilarious,' scoffed Bill. He was becoming more irritated with each sentence uttered by his sceptical sibling, his face turning a deeper shade of red with every snide put-down.

'Look, if all you can do is criticise,' he fumed, 'then don't say anything at all. This is going to happen, with or without your support.'

John held up his hands - 'OK Little Brother; it's your life, you can waste it as you choose. But don't come crawling back to me when it all goes tits-up again.'

Bill hated being referred to as "Little Brother" and John knew it - 'It won't go tits-up; rehearsals are going well and we sound better than ever; the new songs are great too. I haven't felt this optimistic in years.'

'Very well,' conceded John, 'you're obviously determined to make a fool of yourself. You come to me with some dates and I'll make some arrangements for Mum.'

'Tom, I want to write some new songs,' announced Bill; 'make another album.'

'Don't you think we should walk before we try to run,' answered Tom, 'it was only a few weeks ago that you were the cynical one; said there was nothing sadder than a bunch of old crocks trying to relive their youth.'

'That was before I remembered how good we were; and before we started playing again. I have a hunch that things will go well this time. I can feel it, Tom; it's as if we have a guardian angel watching over us.'

Bill had another incentive now: the pressing matter of proving his brother wrong. He already had a poem, written in the style of Attila, just waiting to be put to music.

'And do you have any lyrics for me to work with?' asked Tom.

'Yeah, I have a couple; the first one's called *Sun Soaked Murdoch Marionette*, and there's another called *Never Had a Dirty Mind (Till I Laid Eyes on You)*.' (1)

'Well those both have hit written all over them,' laughed Tom. 'Do you think we'll be able to handle all the fame and adulation that's bound to come our way?'

'I agree that they may be album tracks, but I've just got started. Leave it with me and I'll come up with something more commercial too.'

Tom sighed - 'OK, email them over and I'll see what I can do.'

A couple of hours later and Tom phoned back.

'Well, what do you think?' asked Bill.

'I like the *Dirty Mind* one and I think I've got a pretty good riff for it; but I'm having a little trouble getting that *Murdoch* rant to fit. The words don't pan particularly well; and besides, it's too political.'

'Well, you know me Tom; I've never shied away from difficult subjects and these things have to be said.'

'Yeah, but nobody writes in-your-face protest songs anymore; even the Bard of Barking's last album was more reflective and less confrontational. He still has the same outlook, but with a little more subtlety. Anyway; aren't you supposed to mellow as you get older, become more tolerant?' (2)

'No; the more I see of those bastards, the angrier I get. Someone has to stand up to them and tell it like it is.'

'I don't disagree with the sentiments,' said Tom, 'but you won't get any decent press with lyrics like that; you know how powerful they are and they'll come up with an angle to shoot us down.

That's if they even bother to acknowledge our existence.'

'So, you're asking me to compromise my lyrics to pander to the media. It's not gonna happen Tom.'

'Okay, okay; you can climb down from your pulpit. Next thing we know you'll be wearing ragged trousers too. Let me sleep on it and I'll have another go tomorrow.'

'Thanks,' said Bill, 'you're the one who'll have to sing this shit, so you have to mean it too.'

'Yeah; we mean it maaaan,' sang Tom; perhaps a step too far for his out-of-shape vocal chords. (3)

Bill held the phone away from his ear and laughed - 'See; you can still do it.'

Tom's coughing fit reverberated down the line. Eventually he caught his breath - 'Not sure I can carry off the angry young man stuff anymore,' he rasped.

'Then write it how you can sing it; I really don't mind, providing the words aren't watered down and it's not Country and Western.'

And Bill did mean it maaaan; more than ever. He considered himself an activist and often spent his weekends at anti-capitalist demos and the like. There he rubbed shoulders with a microcosm of society's disenfranchised; old and young, black and white, male and female, gay and straight: all with one aim, to protest at the insidious erosion of the basic rights that had been hard-won by our forefathers. Bill never felt more empowered than on a march through the city, standing up for what he believed in.

His political conscience had been awoken a lifetime ago by an inspirational man he would later call a good friend. He recalled the day he'd met Kev; before a gig in Rotherham at the height of Miners' dispute. It was the middle of summer and Kev certainly made an impression when he entered the bar. A larger-than-life character, he was dressed in incredibly baggy shorts that predated the Madchester scene by some years. (4)

Bill had been invited back to meet Kev's family and was overwhelmed by their hospitality and generosity, bearing in mind that they'd been on strike for some time and were being starved back to work by a callous government, intent on the vicious destruction of whole communities. The experience had inspired the song *Shafted*, and a series of benefit gigs would follow, along with a long affinity. Bill had graced his appearance on Top of the Pops with a National Union of Miners t-shirt and one of his most prized possessions is a letter of thanks from the N.U.M., for his help in publicising their plight; it hangs upon his wall to this day. Henceforth, Bill made it his business to fight injustice and inequality, both through his lyrics and affiliation to a number of worthy causes.

The marches were social gatherings too and he enjoyed mixing with kindred spirits and meeting new people. You never knew who you would end up talking to and connecting with; the fascinating stories that you would overhear.

He recalled a recent conversation that he'd earwigged; between a young lad and a seasoned cop. In some ways it was progress that they were even talking to each other. In Bill's day the Special Patrol Group would have waded in without question; puppets of the state with batons flailing and scant regard for the rights and wrongs of the argument. One positive to come from the intrusion of the Surveillance Society and instant recording; the authorities are under scrutiny too and any injustice can be captured and shared on social media within minutes.

The kid was about 18 and sported a leather jacket with 'Anarchy in the UK' emblazoned across the back in metal studs. Not even a stirring in his father's loins when the Gender Weapons were challenging the status-quo, he nonetheless knew his stuff. Despite the vivid red Mohican, the stubble and the torn denim jeans, he looked pretty clean-cut, like he was well educated, from a well-off family and this was just his rebellious phase; after all, we all have one, don't we? Bill just hadn't grown out of his yet and hoped that he never would. (5)

As there was a lull in proceedings the cop thought he'd try a bit of community relations, engage the kid in conversation and try to work out what made him tick.

'Anarchy,' he scoffed. 'What do you think would happen if we had real anarchy in the UK; if there were no laws to stop all those evil bastards out there, no reprisals for their wickedness? I've seen what men do to women, what adults do to kids, what drunks and junkies do to each other. Civilisation is a thin veneer; it wouldn't take much for us all to descend into chaos and cruelty. Trust me, we need rules, we need control; otherwise society would fall apart. Is that what you really want?'

Bill listened intently as the kid fired back: 'But what if the guys that make the rules, the establishment, the judges, the police, are more dishonest than your fellow citizens; those who you think you have to control to avert chaos?'

'Then you vote them out; that's what democracy is all about.'

'How do you vote them out when, ultimately, they all end up the same; corrupted by power, money and the influence of big business?'

The kid had a point, thought Bill; it was a universal truth. How many times had a MP been elected on a wave of good intentions, only to be derailed at every parliamentary point of order? The power-brokers had it all sewn up, regardless of who was the latest figurehead. On the other hand, real anarchy relied upon individuals taking total responsibility for their actions, helping their fellow human beings. In reality it could never work because it doesn't take into account the inherent selfishness of human nature.

Bill considered the perpetually insurmountable impasse between society's opposites, personified by the kid and the cop, and wondered if there was a song or two in it. He cracked open a beer, sat back and began to write; relishing the surprise resurgence of his creativity. Nobody writes in-your-face protest songs anymore, Tom had said. Well, perhaps it was about time they did.

1. Attila the Stockbroker describes himself as a "social surrealist poet and songwriter". His brilliant autobiography, *Arguments Yard*, is a cutting-edge social history, as well as a touching personal memoir. Attila's poems resonate with truth and a razor-sharp wit. *Sun Soaked Murdoch Marionette* is a title I've made up, but I challenge Mr Stockbroker to make it real.

2. Billy Bragg of course. The bard of Barking remains true to his roots and is still barking on about socialism to this day; and long may he continue. While there are people like Billy in the world, we still have hope.

3. A proclamation from the Sex Pistols' *God Save the Queen*. John Lydon sneered his way to prominence in '76 and continues to challenge with Public Image Limited. With well-directed rage, the Pistols blew everything away; and their like will never be seen again.

4. The Madchester scene is a cultural movement that emanated from the Manchester area in the early '90s. Its finest and best known exponents were the *Happy Mondays* and the *Stone Roses*.

5. The Gender Weapons could be a great name for a female tribute act to the aforementioned Sex Pistols; *Anarchy in the UK* their inflammatory, anarchic calling-card.

Bill's dream was rudely interrupted by his radio alarm clock. He rolled over, looked at the time through bleary eyes, groaned and hit the snooze button. Six minutes later and he awoke again to the immaculate sound of the Aylesbury Brewery Company singing about solitude, followed by an unnaturally cheery DJ, wishing him a happy Valentine's Day. (1)

'Yeah, you too, mate,' he replied, as he rolled out of his lonely bed and began his daily routine.

Over a bowl of Cornflakes, a slice of toast and a glass of orange juice, he finished off an article he'd been reading from Saturday's Guardian concerning remedies for insomnia. He had a meeting in town that morning, with a potential new client and had decided to travel by bus. It would be less stressful than driving through the school traffic and would also circumvent the town's exorbitant parking fees.

Upon leaving the house, he bumped into the postman who, with a jovial grin, pronounced - 'Looks like it's your lucky day, Pal,' as he handed Bill a pale blue envelope containing a card.

'But my birthday's not till June,' said Bill, his brow furrowed with confusion.

'Don't you know what day it is?' asked the postman.

'Yeah, but I've not been sent a Valentine's card since I was a teenager. Are you sure you've got the right address?'

'Well, take a look. That's your name on there, isn't it?'

Bill studied the perfectly formed calligraphy and had to admit that it looked as if he was, indeed, the intended recipient. He shook his head, wished the postman good day and walked briskly towards the bus stop. As usual he was running late. Once on the bus he held the envelope before him and contemplated its possible source. Probably just a joke by one of the band, he concluded; but deep down he knew that none of them were renowned for such elaborate handwriting.

'Aren't you going to open it, then?' asked the familiar old lady in the seat opposite. 'It could be from someone special.'

Bill had helped the friendly octogenarian with her shopping the previous week, after he'd seen her struggle under the weight of what appeared to be a bag-full of spuds. With a weak nod, he carefully removed the card, as if fearing that an arrow from Cupid's bow could shoot out at any moment and pierce his beating heart. With shaking hands he held the mysterious missive before him; an unostentatious plea to "Be My Valentine" beneath a simple red heart. The card design was from another era, no barcode, brand or pretentious flourishes on the back. A look inside revealed an almost menacing message - "Old flames can still burn; I'll be in touch", embellished with four kisses; all lovingly crafted in elegant script.

'So, who's it from?' asked the curious old lady.

'I have absolutely no idea,' answered an incredulous Bill.

'But that's the fun part; finding out,' said the voice of age and wisdom.

1. The long defunct Aylesbury Brewery Company, otherwise known as ABC; not to be confused with the Martin Fry fronted band of the same name, whose song *Valentine's Day* was a highlight of their classic *Lexicon of Love* album from 1982. ABC Bitter was a watery accompaniment to a misspent youth, but it hadn't actually been brewed in Aylesbury since 1937. The beer was manufactured by Ind Coope and distributed to most of the pubs in the area; it tasted horrible but, apart from Double Diamond from the same brewery, there was little choice in those days. In contrast, the brilliant Trevor Horn produced *Lexicon of Love* still resonates.

A shiver overcame Bill as the four of them stood in silence, surveying the venue that they'd last played over thirty years ago. Surprisingly, not all of their old contacts were retired or dead as John had suggested; and Tom had managed to cobble together a mini-tour, taking in half-a-dozen dates around the South of the country. Clive had been sceptical, arguing that they were hardly massive in their previous life. Who would bother to come out and see them now?

Tom smiled as the Winter Gardens' manager approached, looked them up and down, and asked the inevitable question that they'd heard a hundred times before - 'So, which one's Skinny Ted, then?'

Viewed in profile they looked like four pears balanced on cocktail sticks and people never tired of alluding to the incongruity of their name. As Tom was the lead singer, it was usually assumed that Skinny Ted and he were one and the same; a misnomer that he always endured with resigned good grace.

Fortunately, the manager wasn't the same fella as on their previous visit; otherwise they'd have been run out of town. At the time it had enhanced their brief flirtation with fame; or was it notoriety? As usual, it was Stan's fault, but it sure as hell got them some headlines and sales; along with a reputation they could have done without.

They'd been strolling along the promenade on the afternoon prior to the gig when Stan, prompted by a few too many lunchtime beers, had staggered into the road, causing a passing motorcyclist to swerve. The biker, a large and threatening-looking man, adorned from head to toe in black leather with matching headgear, stopped to enquire of Stan whether or not he would be so kind as to watch where he was going. To which Stan, in his inimitable style, had retorted: 'Hey dickhead, are you sure that helmet's the right colour; shouldn't it be purple?' (1)

He knew no fear did Stan, God rest his soul; but Bill had seen the words in pewter studs on the back of the jacket – "OUTLAW ANGELS".

'Might be a good idea to make ourselves scarce', he suggested, 'think that guy might have a few unsavoury friends.'

They'd dragged a reluctant Stan into an alleyway as the Angel returned with about twenty (or fifty, as Stan told it) identically dressed members of his Chapter. Their engines roared like thunder and the quaking Brothel Creepers cowered among the bins, until the gang had given up their search and rumbled away along the prom.

'You bunch of cowards,' Stan had shouted, after they were long out of sight and earshot, 'send us your four best men and we'll take them on.'

'Nice one Stan' said Tom, as he picked the remnants of a discarded takeaway off his jeans. Keeping their eyes peeled, they'd made their way back to their homely B & B to lie low and prepare for that night's gig.

"BROTHEL CREEPERS' ANGEL FANS TRASH VENUE" the headline had run in the following week's music press. Despite protestations that these degenerates were nothing to do with them, Skinny Ted and the Brothel Creepers were told in no uncertain terms, never to darken this door again.

Now, three decades on and the sound-check was going well. As Bill instinctively picked out the bass line to their cover of *I Fought the Law*, he closed his eyes, stepped back in time to '84 and recalled the scene. (2)

They were at the pinnacle of their live brilliance; the place was heaving and the band was rocking like they'd never rocked before. It felt as if they were at one with their fans, whose palpable energy fuelled their virtuosity to unprecedented heights. Then, as the Angels descended, utter chaos ensued. Whilst pandemonium reigned, they'd dragged as much of their gear as they could carry through the stage door, while half-a-dozen brave bouncers temporarily held off their adversaries. Stan had stood defiantly before his drum-kit, shouting obscenities whilst it was being frantically dismantled behind him. Tom staggered with blood pouring from a large wound on his temple, the result of a well-aimed bottle.

Richard the Roadie had the engine revved but, as they were about to make a hasty exit, the police appeared in numbers, offering both protection and a night in the cells. Deciding that it would probably be unwise to emulate the song and fight the law, they'd gone quietly. Any attempts to sleep had been somewhat disturbed, as Stan and the lead angel exchanged vociferous insults throughout their nocturnal incarceration.

Their growing ignominy was cemented the following month; at the legendry and infamous Holloway show - 'It'll be good for our image,' Stan had insisted, 'those prison gigs never did the man in black any harm. We should record if for prosperity too.'

At the conclusion of the second encore (a frenzied rendition of *Folsom Prison Blues*), a formidable lady who had taken an unlikely shine to the pocket-sized percussionist, yelled – 'What are you doing Saturday night, Stan?' (3)

To which he inadvisably retorted, 'I'm going out; what are you doing?'

"THERE'S A RIOT GOIN' ON" was the inevitable headline. (4)

Back in the present, Bill turned and nodded at Stan's replacement; after just a few rehearsals they'd built up a rapport and were turning into a pretty tight rhythm-section. Although Ray could never hope to replicate Stan's manic presence, it was reassuring to know that they would probably get out of the place alive.

Sound-check over, they watched curiously from the back of the stage, hidden in darkness, as the punters began to arrive. They had no idea how the announcement of the first gig of their second incarnation would be received; how many people would actually show up. Yes, they used to be a renowned live act and could attract

40

a reasonable crowd, but that was a long time ago. How many people would bother to rise from their armchairs to watch this bunch of old rockers attempt to rekindle a flame that had been long extinguished?

The doors had opened at 6:30 and by 7:00 the crowd had barely reached double figures. Clive and Ray looked dejected and, not for the first time, Bill questioned the wisdom of reforming; anxiety was etched across his face.

'Don't worry,' said Tom. 'Have you seen the price of a pint in here? They're probably loading up in that pub across the street first. It'll be buzzing with fans before you know it.'

'Ever the optimist,' replied Bill, less than convinced.

By 7:30 Bill was feeling desolate and pronounced that he might have to take off his shoes and socks to count how many were in the audience. Tom didn't comment, but looked equally disconsolate. Clive wore a told-you-so expression and Ray picked his nose. There was nowhere to hide and, even if this was to be the full extent of their following, they'd still have to play and suffer the humiliation.

At 7:45, Clive was ready to walk out, declaring that the whole thing was a farce and bellyaching about how the hell he'd been talked into it to start with. Then gradually, the place began to fill up; a few more people at first, but definitely more promising.

Bill was pleasantly surprised that, as well as the anticipated ancient aficionados, there were a number of youngish dudes filing through the doors too. Maybe the parents had brought their kids, he thought, with some jealousy; his own bored brood wouldn't be seen dead at a gig with their dad. Besides, they were probably permanently scarred from the last time he'd taken them out. He thought they were going to see a sock-puppet manipulated by ventriloquist Shari Lewis, but ended up watching a melancholic alternative country band. (5)

Bill cast an eye over the crowd. Those of the older generation that still boasted hair, sported an array of magnificent quiffs and sideburns that put his and Tom's to shame; their attire impressively completing the bygone Teddy Boy look that identified them as dyed-in-the-wool Brothel Creepers' fans. In time honoured tradition, most of them headed straight for the bar, until they were about five deep and staring impatiently, straight into the eyes of the insufficient bar-staff.

There was a growing buzz about the place; an almost physical intensity that could be felt in the wings, as a nervous perspiration began to spring from Bill's brow. Anticipant punters were shouting to make themselves heard above the fifties rockabilly compilation that Tom had lovingly put together to set the scene for what was to come.

They exchanged handshakes with their old friends and support act for the evening, who had agreed to play for nothing to help launch the second coming of the Brothel Creepers.

'What, really free?' Bill had asked, astounded by their generosity.

'Yeah, really, really, really free,' answered Tom.

These veteran cults were the real deal and had been playing the circuit to a loyal fan-base, off and on for the past forty-plus years. It would be an honour to share a stage with them for old times' sake. Bill and Tom stayed hidden, stage left, as the eccentric duo prowled the boards with their renowned comic telepathy. (6)

In front of the stage, an over-zealous security man harangued a lady who had the audacity to smoke an e-cigarette. How times had changed, thought Bill; the last time we were here it was difficult to breathe through an all-encompassing mushroom-cloud of ganja. Having said that, the support band were renowned for their fondness of the international herb. (7)

It was Tom who saw them first and nudged Bill.

'Don't want to worry you mate, but take a look over there.' He pointed to the right of the bar where, foreboding and more than menacing, they stood; a group of about half-a-dozen Angels.

Bill froze and replied, 'It's them alright; I'd recognise that big, ugly bastard at the front anywhere.'

Still sporting the same styled studded leathers, albeit a few sizes bigger, they were undoubtedly the very chaps with whom they'd briefly shared Her Majesty's pleasure all those years ago.

'So, what do we do?' asked Tom.

'Come on,' said Bill, 'let's go and introduce ourselves.'

He strode resolutely towards the eye of the potential storm, as Tom followed apprehensively; whilst in the background, the singer caterwauled something manifestly tragic about Cheryl going home. The Angels huddled ominously, as the visibly quaking Bill and Tom approached. (8)

With a shudder, Bill stared up at the colossus that filled his eyes and shut out the light; he looked even bigger than he remembered.

'Look, we don't want any trouble,' squeaked Bill. 'We're just here for the music; all that violence belongs in the past.'

The lead seraphim stood static and glared back at Bill, his eyes piercing and bloodshot, a look of apparent contempt for the quaking Teds before him. The other Angels gathered round to form an intimidating presence as their leader slowly reached into the inside pocket of his leather jacket. Bill and Tom took a few steps back as the light flashed off something metallic; was it the blade of a knife? They were too young to die.

Bill grabbed Tom's arm in readiness to run back to the relative safety of the dressing-room, or even to sacrifice their comeback gig to preserve their good looks. Then a hint of a smile invaded the dark demeanour of their ex-adversary, as he stepped forward and held out his hand.

'Gabriel's the name, Messenger's the game.'

He opened the small silver box that he'd removed from his jacket and presented them each with an elaborately designed business card. The inscription read: *Gabriel Cherubim; Marketing Consultant*

Bill was a little thrown by this unexpected greeting and wondered if he'd got the wrong man - 'Hey, aren't you the guys that wrecked this place and tried to maim us the last time we were here?'

'The very same; and it sure got you some publicity, didn't it? You'd still be wallowing in obscurity if not for us. It was after that night that I realised my calling; found out that I had a talent for P.R. I've been running a very successful consultancy since then and have some pretty high-profile clients.'

Bill glanced at Tom, who looked equally flummoxed, then turned his attention back to the imposing figure of Gabriel.

'Marketing Consultant! Are you serious?'

'Absolutely; if you're looking for an agent to represent your rise from the ashes, then I'm your man. We specialise in the entertainment business. Do you still have Tiny Temper on drums? I could sell him anywhere.' (9)

'No,' answered Bill, 'Stan, God rest his soul, is no longer with us.'

'That's a shame,' said Gabriel, 'plucky little character; I admired his spirit.'

'So, you're not here to cause trouble then,' said Tom.

'Not unless you want some more headlines, no. We're here for the music too. You were a decent band at your zenith; we've just come to see if you've still got it.'

They exchanged handshakes again and Bill and Tom withdrew backstage to prepare for the gig. Bill studied the card again and shook his head.

'Gabriel Cherubim, Marketing Consultant; wasn't expecting that. Do you think that's his real name?'

'I doubt it; but a man has to make a living and I guess we've all matured a bit since then,' said Tom.

Bill smiled - 'Speak for yourself; come on, let's set this place on fire.'

And hot they were. The drums kicked in with a crisp staccato on the snare and the rest of the band made a perfectly timed entrance; they were soaring again as if they'd never been away. From the moment that Ray hit the first beat, the flame was lit and he remained rock-solid, thunderous and sharp throughout. Clive had become even more accomplished in the intervening years and his guitar wept gently one minute, then exploded with joy the next. He posed stage-left; self-conscious in his brand-new trilby with the blue feather on the side. Unfortunately his newly-shaven dome caused the hat to slide around each time he moved his head. He felt like a boiled egg in a non-stick saucepan, and he spent the entire gig trying to avoid sudden movement for fear of humiliation. (10)

Tom had been training his voice and all that gargling in the bathroom, whilst he practised his scales, had payed-off. He sounded better than ever. Bill wore a permanent grin, (apart from during Tom's aching rendition of *Stood Up, Again*), and he span his bass on its axis like a man who'd rediscovered fun. It felt so good, as his fingers walked easily across the strings; as natural as putting one foot in front of the other.

The audience felt it too and a surge of electric excitement spread like wildfire through the crowd. Bill scanned the horde and located Gabriel and his cronies, bopping like teenagers as a large space opened up around them. Gabriel nodded his approval and smiled.

As their set reached its climax, Ray's sticks were a blur and even Clive tapped his foot to the unrelenting beat. Tom jumped and twisted like a man possessed, a frenzied expression accentuating every syllable. Bill finished the gig on his back, his double bass atop him like a passionate lover, in ecstasy as he shook all over.

All over, encores and band exhausted, they returned to the dressing-room and collapsed in a euphoric heap. An undeniably triumphant return; how could they follow that?

1. The Purple Helmets were a tastefully named band put together by JJ Burnel and Dave Greenfield of the Stranglers, to enable them to gig between Stranglers projects. They released one album; *Ride Again*, in 1988.

2. Written by Sonny Curtis when he joined the Crickets after Buddy Holly's death, the superb *I Fought the Law* was a hit for the Bobby Fuller Four in 1966. It was later recorded by the Clash in 1979.

3. Johnny Cash, otherwise known as the man in black, was well-known for playing gigs for the incarcerated. *Folsom Prison Blues* was originally released in 1955, but a live version, recorded where else but Folsom Prison, reached number one on the Country charts in 1968. Cash also famously played San Quentin prison in 1969; the resulting live album was nominated for a number of Grammy awards.

4. *There's a Riot Gion' On* is a magnificent slab of psychedelic funk from 1971 by Sly and the Family Stone. Their fifth album, it spawned the hit singles *Family Affair* and *Runnin' Away*. The title track, bizarrely, is 0.04 seconds of silence.

5. OK, this is probably another bad pun. Who could possibly mistake ventriloquist and children's entertainer Shari Lewis's puppet Lamb Chop, for the beautifully melodic and plaintive band from Nashville, Lambchop?

6. John Otway and Wild Willy Barrett's *Cor Baby, That's Really Free* reached number 27 in the UK charts in 1977, followed by a series of valiant but failed attempts at stardom. Otway finally achieved his longed-for second hit with *Bunsen Burner*, a mere 25 years later in 2002. Still recording and playing live to a loyal fan-base; check out the review of *Otway, The Movie (Rock and Roll's Greatest Failure)* on my website for a more in-depth analysis of Otway's cultural contribution. www.tonyflower.co.uk

7. Could the support have been the magnificent reggae stalwarts, Culture? *International Herb* is a song that eulogises the benefits of marijuana. Culture are best known for their 1977 album *Two Sevens Clash*, based on a prediction by Pan-Africanism leader Marcus Garvey that chaos would ensue when the two sevens met on 7 July 1977. Turned out to be just another day.

8. Otway's emotional version of American folkie Bob Lind's *Cheryl's Goin' Home*. In 1991 Otway collaborated with Attila the Stockbroker to produce *Cheryl, A Rock Opera*, based on the song.

9. I've borrowed this ideal nom de plume for Stan from rapper and mixer, Tinie Tempah. A little research has revealed that Tinie grew up on the Aylesbury Estate in East London.

10. Clive's guitar wept gently; a gentle reference to the George Harrison penned Beatles' tune *While My Guitar Gently Weeps*.

Vanessa stared at her PC and waited for the inspiration to come. She was supposed to be writing an urgent report for the Headmistress, about how she included differentiation in her teaching methods to accommodate the requirements of all her pupils. It was only because bloody OFSTED were due in next week; differentiation came instinctively and she seldom gave it any thought. It was obvious that she couldn't use the same vocabulary when speaking to Johnny as she could in conversation with Sinead, that their capacities for understanding the subtleties of the English language were poles apart; but how to put something that came as second-nature into words? Perhaps she should just write a couple of case studies, using her two most disparate pupils as examples of how to simultaneously teach the same staid syllabus to the behavioural equivalents of Denis the Menace and Sister Bernadette.

Ah, Johnny - it was hard not to think of the stereotypical inhabitant of every old joke about the class-clown. But Johnny was a talented artist and musician - why shouldn't he be allowed to nurture his creativity in a supportive environment, instead of being penalised for not fitting into their pre-conceived version of education? This wasn't what she'd signed up for and Vanessa was beginning to hate what teaching had become; taking a chisel to the rough edges of the square pegs, until they could be rammed into the round holes of conformity. And what about poor Sinead – the inevitable subject of cruel taunts, bullied by her peers for being teacher's pet, simply for her desire to learn and show of genuine interest.

It was a tumultuous time for all of her pupils; a time when every fibre is battered by the onslaught of hormonal fluctuations, when the body is racked with growing pains and unwelcome new hairs sprout daily. It is, of course, at this very moment that the powers-that-be choose to heap undue pressure upon these dazed and confused individuals, by asking them to pass the essential exams that will determine their future. Ah well, it was good preparation for the bullshit that was to come if they were fortunate enough to gain employment.

Vanessa recalled her own traumatic teenage turmoil, when she'd been cruelly parted from her first love, the week before her exams. It had taken all of her inner-strength and fortitude to get through and emerge with some half-decent results. It was an act of defiance, as much as determination; she was the only-child of a single-parent and was used to facing up to things alone. She'd be damned if she'd let these circumstances destroy her. These were just some of the experiences that shaped what she'd become, the scars that hardened to form a thicker skin.

She'd left many a besotted fella in her wake as she ploughed a lonely furrow through her own space, in search of new frontiers to conquer and abandon. Those deep blue eyes below a jet-black fringe, and lithe figure beneath her customary jet-black t-shirt and jeans were enough to keep them coming back; but she eschewed commitment for the illusion of freedom. It wasn't that she didn't want to settle down; she was just embittered by experience and scared of getting hurt again. Besides, it was probably too late now.

With a sigh, Vanessa attempted to blot out any distractions and refocus her mind on the task in hand. She'd recently returned to work after being signed-off due to stress and the pressures hadn't gone away; the work had simply piled-up higher in her absence. It didn't help with the creation of her insightful report that her mind was very much elsewhere; and she couldn't concentrate since she'd seen the headline in the local rag: "Brighton's Premier Rock Venue Welcomes Back Skinny Ted and the Brothel Creepers".

'Who the hell are they?' her colleague, Jill, had asked when Vanessa excitedly showed her the tiny piece, tucked away in the corner of a back page. The accompanying picture presented the band captured in their prime, eternally youthful and smiling.

'Only one of Britain's finest exponents of the art of rock'n'roll, that's all,' answered Vanessa. Her tone implied that it was a stupid question and that everybody should know of this iconic ensemble.

'Never heard of them,' said Jill.

'Well, I guess you wouldn't have; they split years ago. I had no idea they'd got back together till I saw this.'

'Isn't rock'n'roll a bit before your time?'

'Yeah, but good music never dies; doesn't matter how old you are,' argued Vanessa. She'd always looked younger than her years, a blessing that she'd hated in adolescence when she ached to appear older, but that had its advantages in adulthood.

'You should hear them,' she continued, 'they're really good. What do you say; fancy coming along?'

'When is it?' asked Jill, with a less than enthusiastic expression.

'This Saturday; trust me it'll be a great night.'

'Well, I guess I've got nothing better to do,' Jill sighed. 'Been a bit quiet since I kicked Bobby out; might do me some good to hit the town. Won't we look a bit out of place, though; it'll be full of old rockers, won't it?'

'We're out of place wherever we go these days,' argued Vanessa; 'the clubs are full of teenagers, and the last time I went to the Concorde half of my class were there. Bloody embarrassing it was, and they've not let me forget it; every Friday it's, "See you in town, Miss", or "Can I have the first dance, Miss?"' (1)

'Ha, ha, yeah, I remember,' said Jill, her shoulders shaking with amusement. 'It was all round the playground; and Joey Wilson was boasting that he got to first base.'

'It's not funny. There should be a place especially for teachers to socialise, without the risk of bumping into students or parents. There's nowhere you can go to relax.'

Jill picked up the newspaper again and re-read the headline - 'Well, I doubt that 11D will be interested in Skinny Ted and the Brothel Creepers, although we may bump into their grandparents. OK, I'll come, but the minute some fifty-something lothario tries to chat me up, I'm out of there.'

'Yeah, it winds me up when guys assume that any single woman of advancing years has got to be desperate and on the pull, but you never know; you could meet your dream man.'

'Well, I might make an exception for Daniel Craig if he's on the guest-list,' said Jill, ever the optimist, with her cheery smile and peroxide blonde curls. She was great company was Jill, and Vanessa often called upon her when she needed cheering-up.

'Funny you should say that; they do a pretty good version of the James Bond Theme. I'll lend you some of their music,' offered Vanessa, 'so you can get in the mood.' (2)

'I can't wait,' said Jill.

A smile slowly crept across Vanessa's face; at least she had something to look forward to.

1. The Concorde is billed as Brighton's No. 1 Music Venue. Never been, but a peek at the website reveals some pretty impressive gigs.
2. The iconic *James Bond Theme* is credited to Monty Norman as writer, but its authorship was disputed by John Barry who claimed that he wrote it. Whoever its creator; John Barry's arrangement forms part of an iconic soundtrack for a very British hero.

Bill listened to the rhythm of the rain as it cascaded down the window. He had no reason to get up early and, for once, he'd had a peaceful, uninterrupted slumber through to the relatively civilised hour of 8:30 a.m. They had three days off prior to the next gig and intended to chill out and indulge in a little male bonding; some rest and recreation by the seaside, pub lunches, maybe take in one or two local bands. Bill yawned and stretched serenely; characterless and uniform they may be, he thought, but the one thing you can say about Premier Inns is that their beds are comfortable. Since waking he'd been contentedly lying back as he relived the previous night's glorious performance and considered his mixed feelings about the coming Saturday's return to Brighton. (1)

He loved its vibrant, cosmopolitan atmosphere and appreciated its pulsating and varied music scene; but it was also a place that had had a profound effect on his life. For there it was that he'd met his dream girl; the fleeting happenstance that had momentarily made him feel so alive, and subsequently, so bereft and empty. For God's sake grow up, he berated himself. It's about time you forgot about her and moved on. He studied the indelible tattoo on his arm and wished, not for the first time, that soap and water could wash it away. He couldn't even recall getting it done on his return to the city some months later, the anaesthetic attributes of alcohol numbing the pain and the memory.

'For God's sake, why didn't you stop me,' he'd asked Tom the next day.

'I tried, but you wouldn't listen; kept insisting that you wanted to immortalise your best song.'

In an attempt to put a more positive slant on the forthcoming trip down Memory Lane, Bill recalled the unconventional pre-gig junket to Brighton Racecourse on their last visit. He smiled as he remembered how Stan, God rest his soul, had blagged them into the VIP lounge by pretending that he was a jockey; and how he'd got away with it due to his diminutive stature. In fact, he was so convincing that a desperate trainer wanted him to ride in the 3:30, as the proper rider had fallen badly in an earlier race and was injured. They'd even gone so far as to get the reluctant Stan kitted up and ready. Bill had never seen him so terrified.

'What am I gonna do?' he'd cried. 'I've never ridden a fuckin' horse in me life.'

Fortunately they'd sussed him out when he couldn't mount the colossal stallion; otherwise he'd have probably broken his neck. Of course they'd all been kicked out, whilst Stan complained vociferously that he didn't even have time to collect his winnings. Bill chuckled to himself; hopefully their impending Brighton come-back would be less eventful.

A glance at the clock confirmed that it was time to roll out of bed and join the others for breakfast. After a refreshing shower and a shave he felt more awake and ready to meet the coming day; at least he thought he was ready until the familiar *Batman Theme* ring-tone on his phone rudely interrupted his ablutions. Bill frowned as he saw his brother's name on the screen and an immediate pessimism entered his mind. John never called. It must be something important. Something must have happened to Mum. (2)

His fears were soon realised as John recounted how Mum had locked the carer out of the house and refused John entry, claiming that they were both burglars, intent on stealing the family silver.

'Can you come home and talk to her?' pleaded John. 'I'm getting nowhere.'

And so it was that, after promising the guys that he'd meet them in Brighton on Saturday, Bill found himself back on the road and back down to Earth. Large droplets of rain bounced off his windscreen, as he negotiated the creeping crawl that was the M25 and the rolling grey clouds echoed his mood; dark and ominous.

A long, lonely trudge through the gloom, a deep sense of foreboding prevailed as he drove in silence. It was rare that he travelled without music, but he simply wasn't in the mood. Eventually, he turned the corner into his mother's road, his heart heavy with what he might find. As arranged, John was waiting outside in his BMW and he jumped out upon Bill's arrival and shook his hand.

'Thanks for coming back, and I'm sorry to drag you away, but Mum was asking for you; said she wouldn't talk to anyone else.'

'So, how long has she been in there by herself?'

'Since first thing this morning; the carer left her keys on the hall table while she went to get some cleaning stuff from her car and Mum locked her out. She won't let me in either; says she only has one son and he's left home. I'm sorry, Bill; I didn't realise she'd got this bad. How do you cope?'

Bill was surprised at his brother's apparent empathy and felt himself welling up.

'Not sure if I have been coping, to be honest. I have to work from home most of the time and keep Mum to some kind of a routine. Don't have a life of my own anymore; and I guess that's partly what the band is about – my chance to reclaim something for myself. I have to confess that I thought something like this might happen.'

'Then why didn't you tell me?' asked John, his hands outstretched.

'I have tried to, but you were always too busy; away on business or counting your money.'

John chose to ignore Bill's cheap shot - 'Look, we have to get Mum some professional help; find her somewhere safe where she is looked after properly.'

'Put her in a home, you mean?'

'If that's the best solution for her and you, then yes; or do you have any better ideas?'

Bill took a look at the house and sighed; all of the windows closed and the curtains shut. That wasn't Mum; she always liked fresh air and daylight.

'I'd best go in and make sure she's OK,' he said.

As he walked up the familiar garden path he saw the curtains move slightly and he motioned for John to stay back. He turned the key in the lock and shouted his familiar greeting - 'It's only me Mum, I'm home.' No answer. He looked in the kitchen, dining room, living room and bathroom; and finally found her cowered behind her bed.

'Who are those people trying to break in?' she asked, her voice shaking with fear.

Bill sat on the edge of the bed and spoke quietly - 'It's only John, Mum. You know, your eldest son. The lady is called Sandra. You remember, you met her the other day and we said she could come in and help out while I'm away for a few days.' Bill held out his hand. 'Come on, Mum; you can stop hiding. There's nothing to worry about.'

As she emerged reluctantly, Bill could tell she hadn't eaten. She looked so frail and tiny, still dressed in exactly the same clothes as when he'd left; her once immaculate hair knotted and unkempt. At this moment he realised that John was right; Mum needed proper care in a safe environment and he wasn't the one who could provide it 24/7 anymore. It was almost a relief that it was out in the open, that John acknowledged what he'd been going through; and that he could admit that he was on the verge of a breakdown. An accumulation of events had conspired to bring him to this point; the break-up of his marriage, his estrangement from his kids, the struggle to keep up the maintenance payments and the daily responsibility for his mother's welfare. Bill put his head in his hands and sobbed uncontrollably, while Mum looked on impassively; she didn't even have the capacity to comfort her son in distress.

Composure partly regained, Bill guided Mum downstairs to the kitchen table, where sat John; oldest son and head of the family. Bill wrinkled his nose as a strong smell emanated from the kitchen bin. Carefully, he opened it up and immediately closed it again; as maggots writhed around a piece of uncooked chicken.

Characteristically, John took charge and, in a business-like manner, spoke only of the practicalities. It emerged that, whist waiting for Bill, John had busied himself on Google, looking up possible places that could accommodate Mum. Once he'd made up his mind about the logical solution he hadn't hung around; he'd phoned a few residential homes and had made appointments for the following morning.

'But don't we have to go through Social Services?' asked Bill. 'Aren't there procedures to follow; funding to sort out?'

'No, these are private residential care homes; only the best for Mum. I'll cover the costs.'

'It's funny how the posh ones are called residential,' observed Bill, 'but the ones for ordinary people are nursing homes. So, the parents of those that can afford it get to vegetate in luxury, while the masses have to sell their homes to pay for basic care.'

'It's the way of the world Bill; always has been, always will be.'

Mum sat silently, emotionless, as these two strangers argued about her future as if she weren't there.

The next morning they took their confused mother to these strange pristine places, full of strange pristine people in pristine white coats; where empty shells who used to be somebodies could while away their days in relative comfort. They chose a nice home that overlooked a lake, where swans, ducks and geese swam serenely before a picture-postcard landscape. Bill had to admit that he couldn't imagine anywhere better.

And there they left the amazing lady that had brought them both into the world, nurtured them through childhood and adolescence, and shared all of their joys and sorrows. Familiar artefacts, pictures and ornaments that Mum had accumulated were left too, to aid the transition from the old to the new, from the young to the old and back to the dependency of childhood.

It's the way of the world; always has been, always will be.

1. A tender lament for lost love, The Cascades' *Rhythm of the Rain* referenced at the beginning of this chapter, was released in 1962. It still brings a shiver to the spine of this sentimental old sod.
2. As familiar as James Bond, the *Batman Theme* has been covered by, among others, The Who, the Kinks, Link Wray and the Jam. Which version do you think Bill might have on his phone?

Upon Bill's return to the fray he met up with the others in a local pub and was surprised to see Gabriel and another man in attendance. He gave Tom a quizzical look, as if to ask, 'What the fuck are they doing here?'

Tom pre-empted the question - 'Gabriel has a proposition for us, Bill. He has brought a copy of his portfolio and there are some pretty impressive names on here. Subject to us proving that we're serious, he might like to become our manager, handle all of our promotion. They even supply gig security, so all we'll have to do is play.'

Gabriel introduced his partner, a slight young man with blonde hair, high cheekbones and piercing blue eyes, resplendent in tight black leather trousers.

'Bill, I'd like you to meet Victor, head of the Security arm of our business. We are very lucky to have him, you know. He was going to be a professional dancer and they were speaking of him as a modern-day Nijinsky; until he injured his poor knee and had to retire.'

'Wow, that's illustrious company,' said Tom; 'he must have been good.'

'Not really; it was because he danced like a horse.' (1)

Bill took another disbelieving look at this unlikely couple and asked Gabriel - 'Are you sure you have this the right way around? Given our previous encounter, I'd say you were more suited to Security; and Victor, here, looks a more likely Marketing Consultant.'

'Oh, don't judge by appearances,' replied Gabriel, 'Victor is a very capable manager of people. He certainly keeps me in my place.'

Bill shook his head - 'Look, can you handle this, Tom? I'll go along with whatever you think is best; I'm really not in a fit state to make decisions at the moment.'

'Yeah, sure, sorry man; how's your mum?'

'Not so good, Tom; we've had to put her in a home.'

Bill didn't want to elaborate. He felt like a failure for his inability to support his ailing mother in her hour of need; and inadequate, now that big brother John had, once again, solved the problem instantly with one swipe of his credit card.

Tom took Bill to the bar and ordered him a pint of the local brew - 'Look, we can cancel the rest of the tour, you know, if you're not up to it at the moment; reschedule for later in the year.'

Bill took a deep swig of his ale - 'I did consider throwing in the towel; but it was John, of all people, who persuaded me to carry on. He said that Mum and Dad loved rock'n'roll, that they were so proud when we were on Top of the Pops; never stopped telling anyone who would listen that their son was a pop star. John said he was pretty envious for a while. No, the show must go on and you have keep on rockin' while you still can. What's the alternative?'

1. Vaslav Nijinsky was a Russian male ballet dancer who rose to prominence in the early 20th century and reaped acclaim as the greatest of his era. Fast forward sixty years and Nijinsky the racehorse, named after the aforesaid dancer, left all competition in its wake. I think this is the best joke in the book; which doesn't augur well for the rest of it.

To begin with, Brighton felt like something of an anti-climax after their triumphant come-back. For a start the place was only about a third-full - they were in competition with a multitude of entertainment options in this thriving musical metropolis - and, to add to the somewhat subdued atmosphere, Bill was hardly in the right frame of mind. Uncharacteristic bum-notes littered the set and his fingers felt like sausages as he fumbled amateurishly with his instrument. Aided by pointed glares from his colleagues however, he gradually overcame his self-pity and commenced to groove. He fuelled his stuttering performance with the emotions of the past few days and channelled his feelings into the music. They tried out some of the new songs and received a reasonable response, considering that no-one had heard them before.

Bill turned and smiled at Ray, a man who found it difficult to function on a day-to-day basis; often a gibbering wreck among civilised human-beings in social situations, but completely combobulated when on stage. Clive appeared to be, as usual, in a world of his own and perfectly happy to be there; eyes closed and undoubtedly in a place preferable to reality. Tom was growing in stature with each song, as he drilled into the inspiration that had lit his fire all those years ago. It was still there and he nodded in appreciation of their distinctive sound. In that moment, Bill felt an overwhelming sense of affection and loyalty for his fellow musicians. As individuals they were, at best, average (with the notable exception of Clive), but together they were explosive; the sum of their parts combined to create something truly special.

So, why did Bill suddenly stop playing mid-tune? A statue with a shocked and glazed expression, he stood motionless and stared into the audience with mouth agape, as if a ghost had entered the room. Were his eyes playing tricks on him? For an instant she was there; in exactly the same spot and wearing the same yellow skirt, as if the sun had opened up a hole in the clouds and sucked him into a time-warp. Back in time he went; to the very second that his eyes had first rested on the girl of his dreams. It all came flooding back, the shiver down his spine, the increase in his heart rate, the wobble in his knees. He blinked and shook his head vigorously; and when he opened his eyes once more she was gone. He scanned the audience for any flash of yellow, but saw only uniform black, a sea of dour hostility staring back at him. Then, through the haze of his memories, he became vaguely aware of some urgency going on around him and he abruptly returned to reality. Tom shouted something obscene and he tried to pick up the rhythm again, but the crowd had latched on to his hesitancy and began to boo. A few disgruntled punters yelled something about wanting their money back and Bill wished the stage would swallow him up.

Try as they might, the vibe had gone and recovery proved elusive, as the set ground to a faltering halt. A minority of hard-core fans stayed to demand an encore, Gabriel and Victor included, and they dutifully returned for a final song, before retiring dejected to the dressing room.

'Look, I'm really sorry guys,' said Bill, his head down to avoid eye-contact. 'Thought I was in a fit state to play, but I've let you and the fans down tonight.'

Clive was in no mood to let him off the hook - 'That's our reputation out there, you know. You seem to forget that I make my living from music; unlike you bunch of part-timers. It only takes a few bad reviews and I start losing work.'

Ray said nothing, but seemed equally pissed off; but then, he always looked like that.

'Hey, give him a break, lads,' pleaded Tom, 'Bill's had a bad few days and we all have an off-night now and again.'

'An off-night I can forgive,' argued Clive, 'but to simply give up half way through a song is just unprofessional. What were you thinking of?'

Bill didn't answer. He felt foolish enough already, without confessing that he'd just seen a vision of the past in the crowd. In not so many words, they'd probably send him away, with the suggestion that he seek psychiatric assistance.

'Let's go for a beer,' suggested Tom, 'it won't seem so bad after a few pints.'

'Go for a beer,' scoffed Clive, 'that's your answer to everything.'

'Well, I've never come across a better way.'

Again, Ray said nothing. He'd been drinking lemonade since they'd got back together; on doctor's orders he said, as he was on tablets that couldn't be mixed with alcohol.

For the first time, Bill became aware of a single pressed red rose in front of the mirror by his side; it looked ancient, the petals withered and faded. An elaborately scripted card addressed to him had been tied to its stem. "A thing of beauty, but beware the thorns when you try to pick it up."

'What does it say?' asked Tom.

Bill passed him the card.

'Who's it from?' said Tom.

'I don't know; it's not signed.'

'Well, either you have an admirer or someone's trying to scare you.'

Bill shivered as he considered the message, then linked it to the vision he'd seen in the crowd.

'Both options are pretty intimidating,' he said. 'Come on, let's get out of here.'

He left the solitary rose on the dressing-table.

As nobody could come up with a more civilised venue to discuss whether or not they dare show their faces in public again, they retired to the Prince Albert for an honest exchange of views; Clive still seething silently. Once Tom had explained in more detail how Bill had spent the last few days however, Clive and Ray seemed a little more acquiescent.

'So, why didn't you tell us?' asked Clive. 'We could have postponed the gig until you were in a better frame of mind. We're not that insensitive, you know.'

'Yes, I know. I can only apologise again.'

Just then, Gabriel and Victor entered the pub and made a beeline for the contrite combo. Tom looked up and asked: 'Well, do you still want to manage us, after that debacle?'

'I'd like to manage the band that I saw in Margate, yes,' answered Gabriel, 'not the shower of shit that I've just witnessed. What the hell happened?'

Bill explained his lack of focus once more, leaving out the bit about the yellow attired vision that was still playing on his mind.

'It won't happen again,' he promised.

Then, over Gabriel's shoulder, Bill thought he saw yet another face from the past, standing at the bar. Yes, he'd aged a bit, a few grey hairs on a receding hairline, but that familiar contemptuous expression remained. Bill blinked again, but this time when he opened his eyes, unfortunately, the vision was still there.

'Hey, isn't that the bastard from the NME that used to give us all those bad reviews? We used to call him Anti, remember; bearing in mind that he was anti everything we did. God, I hope he wasn't at the gig.'

Bill's worst fears were realised, when Anti sauntered over and smirked - 'See you haven't improved with age, then. Are you sure it's such a good idea to subject us to your plagiaristic nonsense all over again? Haven't we suffered enough?'

Bill was ready for an argument, but Tom stayed cool.

'Hi Anti, long time no see. No doubt we can expect yet another of your well-considered hatchet-jobs. Tell me, what did we ever do to you to deserve such vindictive vitriol?'

'I was just doing my job. The general public are not savvy enough to tell the difference between good and bad taste; they need a little help to make the right decisions when choosing the

57

soundtrack to their lives. At the time I thought that your music was derivative and Ted culture was pretty unpleasant in those days; remember that Punks and Teds didn't mix particularly well. It wasn't until you wrote *Shafted* that you nailed it. Shame you split up soon after that; it deserved a follow-up. Anyway, you've nothing to worry about; I'm only here out of curiosity and for old times' sake. Make my living writing novels these days.'

'Yeah, I'd heard,' said Tom, 'pretty successful, too.'

'I get by; and it gives one more scope to be creative. You know all those times when you look back on a conversation or an argument and think - I wish I'd said that? Well, when you write a novel you have the time for consideration before you open your mouth and insert your size tens. In real-life the topic of discussion generally moves on and leaves you mourning the waste of that priceless quip that you thought of too late, or regretting an opportunity missed forever. Of course, that doesn't stop you reviewing your work post-publication and thinking - I wish I'd said that.'

'And what about some of the vicious stuff that you used to write?' asked Bill. 'You had the power to make or break careers; do you ever look back and think - I wish I *hadn't* said that?'

'No, not really, because I was usually right. And I saw little tonight to make me change my mind.'

'As arrogant as ever,' observed Bill. 'Look, if you've got nothing nice to say then piss off; this is a private conversation.'

'Very well, but just a word of advice before I go - stop peddling that left-wing crap; it's old hat in music and an outdated ideology. I changed my allegiance years ago.'

'You surprise me,' sneered Bill. 'It's been an absolute pleasure catching up with you; let's meet up again in another thirty years.'

Anti had to have the last word as he walked away - 'Maybe you'll have learnt how to play by then.' (1 - 2)

'Well, that's just the cherry on top of the perfect day,' seethed Bill, 'that's all I needed was to bump into that prick. What else can go wrong?'

'The important thing is to look forward,' advised Gabriel. 'You must forget about tonight, move on and think about your future. In the meantime Victor and I have some serious thinking to do about whether we want to invest our time and money in this band. We will come to the next gig and make our decision then.'

1. The NME was once an influential publication and considered itself the guardian of musical taste; with the power to decide, hit or miss. After 66 years of publication, the NME ceased printing the magazine in 2018 and moved to an on-line only format.
2. There were numerous reports of violence between Punks and Teddy Boys in the mid-1970s. Boy George has told of the time he was beaten up for wearing paint-splattered brothel creepers at the height of the punk era. Apparently some Teds objected to the Punks stealing their fashion, ripping it up and repairing it with safety pins.

Vanessa knew what was coming as she stood at the coffee machine on Monday morning and, on reflection, thought it was probably justified. Jill approached with an expression that said it all – the next time you have any suggestions as to how we spend our Saturday evenings then keep them to yourself. They'd parted somewhat acrimoniously, Vanessa insistent that she just wanted to go home; and Jill equally adamant that she wished to go somewhere else so that it wasn't a completely wasted evening. By the time they'd finished arguing the point and Jill had flounced away in a huff, Skinny Ted had left the building and his Brothel Creepers had crept away behind him, with tails between their legs. Jill had moved on to meet some other friends for a nightcap, whilst Vanessa, in disappointment, hailed a cab and retreated to the sanctuary of her flat. (1)

Vanessa held up her hands in a submissive gesture - 'OK, you don't have to say a word. I know the evening didn't meet expectations, but you have to admit there were some redeeming features; a few moments of genius.'

'I didn't have any expectations, to be honest,' said Jill; 'before you started extoling their virtues. I'd never heard of then, remember, until you explained that they were; what was it? - "the missing link between Little Dick and the Beatific Newcomers, combining the romance of rock'n'roll with a punk attitude", whatever the hell that means. What more could a girl ask for? I should have listened to my instincts and stayed away.' (2 - 3)

'So, you don't want to come and see them again in Hastings on Wednesday, then.'

'Are you serious? What is it about a bunch of smelly old rockers that's so appealing? This is turning into an obsession and, quite frankly, it's pretty unhealthy.'

Vanessa looked down at her feet and muttered beneath her breath - 'It's personal, OK. If you won't come with me then I'll go by myself.'

'What was that?'

'I said if you won't come with me then I'll go by myself.'

'What, all the way to Hastings on a Wednesday night? You're crazy.'

'Crazy, yeah, that's me; but I'd rather be crazy than sit in that flat and fester every night. What's so special about this job that you have to commit every waking hour to it? I'm still marking last week's past papers and there's another lot tomorrow. Well, I've had enough and I will spend my leisure time as I choose.'

'And the marking will still be there tomorrow. It's the kids that suffer, you know; when we're so overworked that we can barely function in the classroom. A night on the piss midweek isn't the answer; it'll just add to the workload and the stress.'

'Who said anything about stress? I've been liberated since I decided that I don't give a shit anymore.'

'I don't believe you,' said Jill. 'You're one of the most dedicated teachers in the school and you care about your students. Something's changed since that dodgy band hit town. What's going on, Vanessa?'

'Nothing; I've just discovered that there is a life beyond this place and I intend to live it.'

'Oh, I give up,' sighed Jill. 'Let me know when you decide to return to reality.'

And with that she stomped away and left Vanessa contemplating her coffee.

1. An indirect reference to the famous announcement – "Elvis has left the building".
2. Veteran rock'n'roller, Little Richard, of *Tutti Frutti* and *Good Golly Miss Molly* fame. A charismatic and flamboyant performer, Little Richard is credited with helping to break down barriers between black and white audiences, during a time of strict segregation in the U.S.A. I have no knowledge of, or indeed interest in, the size of Mr Penniman's pecker, but thought that Little Dick was an amusing pseudonym.
3. The Beatific Newcomers – The Angelic Upstarts are an anti-fascist, socialist punk band from South Shields, whose early gigs were marred with violence when National Front sympathisers infiltrated their audience. Singer, Mensi, has explained that their reputation for trouble

was unjustified, as the band often had to defend themselves and physically eject these unsavoury individuals from their shows.

Bill took a deep breath of fishy sea air, as the band strolled among the fishermen's huts on the Hastings sea-front. He'd always loved the seaside, ever since those carefree holidays with Mum and Dad; along with big brother John before he forgot how to have fun. There was only three years between them, but John had always seemed much older and more responsible.

A glorious early-summer's day and a beautiful blue sky; a gentle sea breeze masked the power of the sun's rays and wafted the odour of Seabass and Gurnard among wandering tourists. Bill recalled the last time he was here; on a family long-weekend with Elaine and the kids. Lauren wanted to be elsewhere as her parents were embarrassing, but at least Rosie and Nathan were still young enough to enjoy the playground. Grace had escaped from her pushchair to join them and Bill had reached her just in time to prevent her running in front of the swings.

They'd spent the afternoon on a packed beach, with sun-worshipers stretched out for as far as the eye could see. The pastel shades of blue, orange and yellow windbreaks sheltered bathers in various stages of tanning.

'Why haven't we got a windbreak, Mum?' Rosie had asked.

'We don't need one, Dear; your father is the best there is at breaking wind,' was Elaine's witty riposte.

Bill had loved watching his kids grow up and achingly missed those days that could never be recreated.

He jumped as a young seagull landed with a clang on a nearby sloping tin roof and attempted to climb to the top. The hungover group laughed hysterically, as the gangly gull tried the manoeuvre numerous times, before repeatedly sliding to the bottom. Its clumsy efforts caused a loud metallic clattering din and its frantic cries shattered the tranquillity, before the hapless bird, eventually, fell off the roof and flew away.

'Crashes about like one of your drum solos, Ray,' observed Tom.

'Yeah, and it sings like you, Tom,' said Clive. 'We could sign it up and replace the two of you in one fell-swoop. What do you think, Bill?'

61

'Sounds like a good idea; it dances a bit like Tom too, same kind of co-ordination as when he does the Hippy-Hippy-Shake.'

'For goodness' sake,' cried Tom, 'I haven't tried that for years.' (1)

The good-natured banter could only be born of a collection of geezers who had known each other a long time and they were feeling a little more optimistic after the Brighton fiasco. Bill had consigned his yellow-clad apparition to the past and had put it down to the strain of recent events playing tricks on his mind. The next hurdle would be the rapidly-approaching Hastings gig and the attempt to restore their fragile reputation.

'You OK, mate?' Tom asked Bill, as they passed the Shipwreck Museum.

'Feel like I qualify to be in there. A nervous wreck and old enough to be a museum exhibit; but at least I have something to live for now. Listen, thanks Tom; thanks for persuading me that putting the band back together was a good idea. Dread to think how I would have dealt with things, without the hope that you guys have given me. Probably misguided, but at least we're having a go.'

'Don't mention it. Think you can get through tonight's gig without any mishaps, then?'

'Yeah, I'll be totally focused this time,' promised Bill, 'my mind will be wiped clean of all but the music.'

1. A feature of the Beatles' early live shows, *Hippy Hippy Shake* was a hit for The Swinging Blue Jeans in 1964.

It was hardly appropriate for the forthcoming event, but the venue had insisted upon employing their resident DJ to warm up the anticipant audience. It wasn't that they were against other forms of music, but Tom's devotedly crafted, sympathetic compilation of classics of the rockabilly genre was usually guaranteed to get people in the mood for their set. Not this time, however.

He cringed as the speakers blasted out some macho misogynist named Cold Tea, who rapped aggressively about his fantasy sexual conquests whilst surfing an unrelenting pneumatic beat.

"Schoolgirls, Call girls, Tall girls,
Titch girls, Bitch girls, Rich girls,
Poor girls, Four girls, More girls,

The one girl, Fun girls, Sun girls,
Cool girls, Cruel girls, Drool girls,
Hippy girls, Mississippi girls, Lippy girls,
Leggy girls, Vegie girls, Smeggy girls,
Clean girls, Lean girls, Teen girls,
Old girls, Bold girls, Bald girls..."

There was probably more of the same, but it seemed he'd run out of rhymes and made his point. The crowd appeared to be unimpressed too and stood around chatting and swigging beer. (1)

Eventually our heroes took to the stage and squinted into the dazzling spotlights; so bright that they could barely see who or how many were there. Finally, their eyes became accustomed to the glare and Tom shouted the time-honoured greeting – 'GOOD EVENING HASTINGS, LET'S ROCK.'

Four clicks of Ray's sticks and they were away, recreating the energy and precision for which they were renowned. Bill nodded at the now familiar figures of Gabriel and Victor, who danced like seasoned coryphées and attracted their own curious crowd.

Audience suitably warmed-up, Tom decided to introduce one of the new songs – 'We had the pleasure of playing this in front of the President of the United Dairies; he didn't like it either.'

As Bill added basic harmonies to his pasquinade, *Sun Soaked Murdoch Marionette*, he tried to gauge how their new masterpiece was going down with the fans. He was encouraged to see numerous feet a-tapping and smiles all around, along with one inebriated consumer who staggered from one side of the floor to the other with little sense of rhythm. They followed with *'billy Dub*, a double-bass-heavy instrumental fusion of Bill's two musical loves - rockabilly and reggae – resplendent in reverb and space.

'Thank you very much,' said Tom, as an appreciative roar of approval filled the hall. He gestured towards Gabriel and Victor. 'I'd like to thank our fan club for turning up again tonight; I saw their tandem parked outside.'

Sweat dripped from their brows, soaked their clothes and lubricated the beat. Tom played the crowd like an old pro and decided to ease the tempo. Warm applause rippled through the auditorium as the familiar intro to *Stood Up, Again* evoked echoes of a bygone era.

This time Bill didn't miss a stroke when he saw her standing there. It was as if she had appeared from nowhere, just at the moment that Tom crooned the immortal lines – *A vision in yellow, she lit up the night, then just like the sunset, vanished from sight. I waited for a sunrise that never came, Oh, oh, stood up, again.* (2)

Tom had seen her too, and glanced at Bill for confirmation that she wasn't a figment of his imagination. And when they both looked back to that spot on the dancefloor, she was gone.

Successful encores completed, they retreated backstage, where an incredulous Tom asked Bill - 'Was that who I think it was out there?'

'Well you saw her too; what do you think?'

'We only have your word that she ever existed,' said Tom, 'the rest of us never met her, remember; all we have is your fawning description to go on. But surely not; not after all this time.'

'She was a long way away, but there's an uncanny resemblance. That's why things went tits-up in Brighton on Saturday; she was there too and I just froze.'

'You never did get over her, did you?'

'No, I guess not.'

'What was so different from all the others? She was just another girl you picked up after a gig; happened all the time in those days.'

Bill considered Tom's cold words. Back then the world was a different, confusing place, generally viewed through the single voracious eye of a permanent erection. He recalled that fading feeling with a mixture of relief and sadness. It was like being unshackled from a lunatic and, these days, he wasn't quite so bound by the chains of libido; but he missed the illusion of hope, hope that the discovery of that one soulmate would put everything right. (3)

In the cruelly brief time they'd spent together, Bill instinctively knew that she was the one. That's why he'd gone back so many times, in the futile hope that she'd be there again, awaiting his return. He'd spent the subsequent years following his dick around in a fruitless attempt to find a substitute; a substitute for the real thing.

For a while there'd been groupies, a series of often pretty girls, willing to do almost anything for the chance to sleep with a rock star. It was their appearance on Top of the Pops that did it; that somehow, overnight, miraculously transformed him from a greasy, unattractive, backstreet rocker into something more desirable. He wondered how the hell that had happened.

'No, she was special, Tom. It was much more than just another one-night stand.'

'Well, it obviously wasn't for her; otherwise she'd have shown up the next day.'

Bill looked hurt - 'No, something must have happened to stop her from coming. She'd have been there if she could.'

Tom sighed - 'Well, if it makes you feel better to believe that. At least you got a decent song out of the experience and lived off the proceeds for a few years. So, if not her, then who is the mystery lady in yellow that is seemingly following us from town to town?'

'Who knows? Could be a ghost for all we know.'

1. A comment on the rap genre's often misogynistic content. To imagine what Cold Tea might sound like, think of a polite English version of Ice T.
2. Did you spot the reference to the Beatles' classic *I Saw Her Standing There* in this chapter? The opening-track on their 1963 debut album, *Please Please Me.*
3. "The male libido is like being chained to a madman" has been variously attributed to Socrates, Sophocles and Plato. The late jazz singer George Melly paraphrased by describing his loss of libido in later life as "like being unchained from a lunatic."

'God, Vanessa, you look like shit,' observed Jill with candour. 'Good night, was it?'

Vanessa had barely slept since her arrival home at 1 a.m. Her face had taken on a ghostly pallor, apart from the darkness of the bags beneath her eyes that some hastily applied make-up had failed to disguise. With reluctance she'd dragged her sorry carcass into work, despite the mirror confirming her resemblance to a panda, though not quite as cute. She was hardly in the mood for Jill's honest and disapproving appraisal of the situation.

'Yeah, it was a great night as it happens. The band were superb; all that I expected and more. Guess they just had a bad night on Saturday. I'm sorry you missed it.'

'I'll survive,' said Jill. 'So, where to next then; will you be following them on their dodgy-dives world tour? New York, London, Paris, Rasnov, perhaps?' (1)

'Very funny; where the hell is Rasnov anyway?'

'Romania; it's where one of the girls in my class comes from. Apparently they have a thriving rock scene and a dinosaur park. I'm sure your lot would fit into one or the other.' (2)

'Humph, I'll bear it in mind when I'm booking my holidays. Actually, the next date on the tour is in London and I intend to be there.'

Jill shook her head - 'Look, Vanessa, I know I take the piss, but some of us are worried about you. You're like another girl on another planet these days; is there anything I can do?' (3)

'Yeah; you can leave me alone. There's nothing wrong, apart from a bunch of judgemental do-gooders interfering in my life.'

'Suit yourself,' answered Jill, as she turned away, 'only trying to help. Oh, and by the way; the Head wants to see you in her office at break-time.'

1. The original lyric from the 1979 hit *Pop Muzic* by M. Writer Robin Scott changed it slightly after realising that Rasnov doesn't rhyme with muzic.
2. Rasnov in Romania hosts an annual Extreme Metal festival, which has featured bands such as Napalm Death, Decapitated and Primordial, among others of a similar ilk.
3. *Another Girl, Another Planet* was a 1978 single by The Only Ones, and a John Peel favourite.

It was hardly the front page of the Melody Maker of yore, but at least the Hastings and St Leonards Spectator wanted to speak to them. They'd convened at a small coffee bar on the seafront for the interview at the ungodly hour of 10 a.m. With a certain amount of trepidation, they nursed their assorted fancy methods of expensive bean infusion as they awaited their first interview since reforming. The place was deserted, as if the whole world were ignorant that there were authentic rock stars in town. Young reporter Rachel obviously wasn't even born when they'd last played here, but she oozed enthusiasm and had clearly done her research.

'So, *Shafted* was the song that first brought you to the attention of the mass-public. Can you tell me what inspired the song?'

'Yeah, it was my mate, Kev,' answered Bill. 'For some reason he took offence to the government of the day systematically destroying his livelihood and his community. We felt it was our duty to expose the scoundrels who perpetrated these acts of industrial vandalism. It's still happening now by the way, but it's more insidious and not as barefaced.'

'Tom, do you think that current bands have lost the sense of rebellion that epitomised the music scene in those days?'

'The scene in general was much more politicised back then. We often shared the bill with dreads, punks, goths and pub-rockers, any genre you can think of really; and what brought us all together was a common enemy. We probably don't have our fingers sufficiently on the pulse of modern music to comment, but I would hope there's still someone out there to rage against the machine. We all sang *Free Nelson Mandela*, when Thatcher was referring to him as a terrorist; we were all *Glad to be Gay*, whether we were gay or not; we implored Margaret to stand down at the top of our voices; and we all knew that Babylon was burning. Not that any of it made any fucking difference, but music was our voice, our way of standing up to the many injustices in our society.' (1 - 5)

'We're just wandering minstrels,' added Bill. 'Long before there were newspapers and people doing your job; musicians, storytellers and poets used to travel the country to tell the populace what was happening in the world. We're simply offering a public service; and we did write the odd love song too.'

'So, who was she; the girl that inspired *Stood Up, Again*?' asked Rachel.

'I'd rather not say,' replied Bill. 'It was a long time ago and you've got to allow us a little mystery.'

'Does the lady in question know that she had a song written for her?'

'How do you know that she wasn't a fictitious character, a figment of my imagination?'

'A woman's instinct. I was hoping that I could use the headline – "Stood Up, But Still Searching", or something like that.'

'Who says we're searching?'

'Aren't you even a little curious, to know what happened to her?'

'You're wasted here, you know. You should be working for the tabloids.'

'I'm only looking for the story behind your best track. The public would be very interested.'

'There is no story,' insisted Bill, 'that chapter closed years ago.'

Ray attempted to lighten the mood and dig Bill out of his hole - 'Hey, don't you want to talk to the new drummer too? I could tell you a few stories about lost love.'

'No, the interview is over,' Bill decided. 'Come on, let's get out of here.'

'Well, that went well,' said Clive, as they left the Coffee Bean Café, 'just what we needed - more negative publicity.'

'We've had plenty of that in our time,' pointed out Bill, 'and we're still here, aren't we? The papers will print what they want anyway.'

'You always were over-sensitive about that song,' said Clive. 'Surely you can put it in perspective, after all these years.'

'I wish I'd never written it and, if it were down to me, we'd never play it again. But I know that song is the reason that half of the punters show-up to see us; it's certainly not for the new stuff, is it?'

'Give it time,' said Tom, '*Never Had a Dirty Mind (Till I Laid Eyes on You)* is a sleeping classic. They'll still be coming back for that in thirty years.'

'Ha, not the way you sing it,' laughed Bill, 'it's quite inappropriate for a man of your age.'

'And how the hell else am I supposed to sing a lyric like that? It's the words that are inappropriate, not my performance.'

'It's supposed to be tongue-in-cheek,' argued Bill.

'It's a bloody rock'n'roll tune, for God's sake; nobody's going to pick up the subtle nuances of your intentions, no matter how it's sung.'

'Well, I like it,' said Ray; 'it has that feel-good factor. Just what the doctor ordered.' (6)

Disastrous interview forgotten, they all chortled as they strolled back along the seafront. It wasn't such a bad life, this.

1. Rage Against The Machine were a highly politicised rock band from Los Angeles, who once tried to storm the New York Stock Exchange. In 2009 a campaign was launched to end the Christmas number one dominance of X-Factor winners and, as a result, *Killing in the Name* became that year's U.K. festive tree-topper.
2. *Free Nelson Mandela* was a rousing Jerry Dammers penned anti-apartheid anthem performed by the Special A.K.A. Released in 1984 it was a protest against the continued imprisonment of Nelson Mandela by the South African government.
3. *Glad to be Gay* is a gay pride song by the Tom Robinson Band, which lampooned British attitudes towards the gay community. Released in 1978, it was the follow up to their first single, *2-4-6-8 Motorway*.
4. *Stand Down Margaret*, combined with their version of Prince Buster's *Whine & Grine*, was a track from the Beat's brilliant first album *I Just Can't Stop It*. I recall singing this at the top of my voice when the Beat played Friars Aylesbury in 1980, and feeling temporarily empowered.

5. *Babylon's Burning* was a hit for the Ruts in 1979. A reggae-influenced punk band, they performed many benefits for Rock Against Racism and supported members of Misty in Roots, when some of their People Unite collective were beaten by the Special Patrol Group, during a protest against a National Front march in Southall. The Ruts lead singer, Malcolm Owen, tragically died of a heroin overdose at the age of 26.

6. Dr Feelgood were formed in Canvey Island in 1971 by Wilko Johnson, Lee Brilleaux and John B Sparks; they were soon joined by drummer John Martin (a.k.a. the Big Figure). The high energy of their pared down R & B was cited as a major influence on the punk scene, whose protagonists would have witnessed the Feelgoods on the pub rock circuit in the 70s. They were never the same after songwriter and guitarist, Wilko Johnson, was ousted from the band. A version of Dr Feelgood is still touring but, like Trigger's broom, there are no original components left.

Vanessa stood apprehensively before the Headmistress's door, like a wayward child awaiting her punishment. She knew that the impending meeting was not likely to be about her long-overdue promotion and she felt her blood-pressure rising, as she attempted to make her knock sound confident.

'Come in,' came the predictable response. 'Ah, Vanessa, please sit down.'

Vanessa blinked as the sun shone through the venetian blinds and made a striped pattern on her white blouse; whilst Mrs Mohair, a self-assured lady in black in her mid-fifties, sat importantly behind her fake mahogany desk, with head tilted to one side in apparent concern.

'So, Vanessa, how are things going?'

'Fine; why, is anything wrong?'

'That's what we're here to find out. In my job it pays to have your ear to the ground and I've heard that some of your recent behaviour could be described as a little eccentric.'

'Described by whom, exactly?'

'Oh, this has come from various sources. Look, we all know that you've had time off with stress lately. Some of your colleagues are simply concerned for your welfare, that's all; as am I.'

'And I appreciate your concern, but I'm OK. There's nothing to worry about.'

'But that's not reflected in your performance this term; you are

constantly behind on your marking, your lessons lack preparation and your students' work is somewhat below the required standard.'

'Wow, you have been busy with your ear to the ground. How long have I been under such scrutiny?'

'I'm simply doing my job. My responsibility is to make sure that this school meets the highest possible standards, and my primary focus has to be on ensuring that our pupils reach their full potential. If any of my teachers are underperforming then I have a duty to find out why and act accordingly.'

'So, is this a disciplinary meeting, then?' asked Vanessa, her voice shaking.

Mrs Mohair hesitated, as if in consideration of a decision she'd already made - 'I have to act in the best interests of the school and our students. The formal procedure is to issue a verbal warning in the first instance, followed by a written warning if performance doesn't improve. Ultimately the process can lead to dismissal, but I'd prefer to find a way to support you through this difficult time. I know from your previous results that you are a good teacher; but you have to start by telling me what is wrong, to enable me to help you to achieve again.'

Vanessa felt the words like a knife to the heart, as she thought about all the years of dedication she'd given to the school. But, deep down, she knew that Mrs Mohair was right; her current performance wasn't up to scratch. The tears began to well and she sobbed as she heard herself speak, as if it were another person making the decision for her.

'How about I save you the trouble,' she said. 'I quit! How much notice do I have to give?'

For a moment Mrs Mohair looked shocked, before it dawned that Vanessa was offering a far more convenient way out, which would involve a lot less paperwork.

'For someone with your length of service, it would normally be three months; but given your apparent state of mind, I would like to offer gardening leave whilst HR sort out the details. I'm truly sorry that you feel this way, Vanessa, and I'd like to thank you for the service you have given to the school.'

So, that's it then, thought Vanessa. What did you expect; that they'd beg you to stay? That all those years of commitment and loyalty would actually mean something? She was overcome by a cocktail of dudgeon and relief; there was no turning back, but at least it was over. There'd be a different kind of pressure now; that of finding another way to pay the rent and put food on the table. At least she had a bit of breathing space; a recent inheritance that would tide her over for the next year if necessary. She took a deep breath and tried to sound nonchalant through her mixed emotions.

'Can I say goodbye to my class?' she asked.

'I think it would be less traumatic for us all if you didn't. I'll accompany you while you collect your personal things and escort you from the premises. That's the correct procedure in circumstance such as these, as laid down in the staff handbook.'

'So, you checked out the staff handbook before our meeting then? I can't imagine that you've ever had to deal with anything like this before.'

'I had to be prepared for every eventuality.'

Oh my God, what have you done thought Vanessa, as she packed her meagre personal effects into the boot of her Mini Cooper. They didn't amount to much; a coffee-stained 'Best Teacher in the World' mug, emotionally presented by one of her classes at the end of their time at the school; the battered dictionary and thesaurus that she used to read out definitions of the student-chosen word of the day; and a box of thank-you cards from pupils who had appreciated her modest efforts to help them along their way in life.

Mrs Mohair stood over her as she closed the boot, handed over her drawer and locker keys, sat in the driver's seat and turned the key in the ignition. Vanessa said nothing; she knew that tears would flow if she tried to express her feelings. It was a sad end to years of teaching; it had always meant more than just a career and she knew no other life. She drove sadly out of the school gates for the final time and into the void that stretched out before her.

So, where do you go from here, Vanessa Jones?

In the scheme of things it wasn't a disaster, thought Bill; Gabriel's blowing it all out of proportion. Their prospective manager sat before them with a frown on his face and his laptop open on the table. The meeting to discuss their potential professional relationship had been arranged at a half-way-house; a typically homogenous motorway services off the M25. They all nursed their typically homogenous coffees in silence, as typically homogenous travelling-businessmen and women went about their business about

71

them. A small child wandered near, followed by a harassed mother, eager to steer him away from the scary-looking men. Nonetheless, Bill smiled at the boisterous toddler and awaited Gabriel's appraisal of their situation.

'Are you determined to sabotage your comeback before it's even started?' he fumed. 'Look what it says here – "The band were opinionated, surly and obstinate; particularly bassist, Bill Harris, who appears to have a chip on his shoulder about one of his ancient compositions."'

'We weren't that bad,' said Tom, 'the article has been somewhat exaggerated.'

'Regardless of the fact that this is a provincial newspaper with a limited readership, you must consider how it goes down if you speak to a young journalist in this way. You must show respect to everyone, or gain a reputation for contempt. Social Media can spread this shit faster than you can say goodbye to your career, you know. Hopefully, on this occasion, the damage is minimal. If, and I repeat, if, I am to become your manager, then I will require your agreement that all future publicity is managed by me; that way we can avoid further debacles like this.'

'Fine by me,' said Bill, 'I always hated talking to the press. As far as I'm concerned the music can do the talking.'

'And one would hope that it can be more eloquent than you,' huffed Gabriel. 'I have been pondering as to whether or not you are a viable business proposition and have come to the conclusion that, with a little polish, you could be.'

'Hey, no-one polishes us,' insisted Tom, 'we like the rough edges just the way they are.'

'Musically, that's fine,' said Gabriel. 'I have no interest in influencing your artistic direction; I am merely suggesting that you take a more professional approach if you're serious about this. I've had the pleasure of observing all three of your recent gigs, two of which were very good indeed. If we can harness that energy and creativity then I think you have potential.'

'Gee, thanks,' said Bill. 'We have done this before, you know. We're not wet-behind-the-ears beginners.'

'Not in the modern marketplace you haven't. Believe me, things have changed; a lot. I have taken the liberty of preparing this contract. Should you approve then, essentially, I will be like a fifth member and have a twenty per-cent interest in the band. Given my expertise in the industry it is a good deal and I suggest that you give it serious consideration.'

'A fifth member,' repeated Bill; 'and what can you play?'

'The game,' boasted Gabriel, 'I can play the game. All you have to do is make music and leave me to deal with the rest of the bullshit. You'll have peace of mind that everything else is will be taken care of in an efficient and professional manner.'

There was that word 'professional' again; somehow it conjured up the antithesis of fun. The band had been discussing their situation on the way to the meeting. All had agreed that they needed someone to manage the business side of things; preferably someone with their finger on the pulse and with useful contacts. They'd studied Gabriel's portfolio and were suitably impressed with his roster. Clive had asked around and established that he had a good reputation; he looked after his acts and maximised their opportunities. All in all, they considered that Gabriel might be the very man.

'What do you think, Clive?' asked Tom. 'You have more experience in the industry than us.'

'Twenty per-cent isn't unusual for an up-and-coming band; which I guess, in effect, is where we are, back on the bottom rung.'

'You should listen to Clive,' Gabriel addressed them all. 'He is very astute. You are starting anew and I would like to join you on your journey.'

'Subject to the provisos in the small-print, no doubt,' said Bill.

'All contracts have small-print, but a relationship is built on trust and, as the snake said in *Jungle Book*, "you can trussst in me".'

Bill stared into Gabriel's eyes and, although still wary, was reassured that he wasn't immediately hypnotised by swirly bits. Gabriel went outside to make a few calls and to allow the band to peruse the contract and make their decision. He returned half-an-hour later to a serious-looking combo and coughed to announce his presence.

'OK, where do we sign?' said Tom.

It had been a while since Bill had attended a decent protest but, fortuitously, there happened to be a worthy one in London on the afternoon prior to the next gig. It was heaving too, and he relished the positive party atmosphere as the mantras grew louder. Austerity was a political choice, not a necessity; and he'd not witnessed a single government minister tighten their belt in empathy with the victims of their cruel cuts. Despite their platitudes about the country living within its means, the rich continued to bleed us all dry with their dodgy deals and tax evasion. As always, their targets were society's most vulnerable, those that could least afford to lose and those that barely had anything more to give.

As the crowd swelled to frightening proportions Bill observed an enormous man at the fulcrum of the melee. He stood at least a foot above the average protester and Bill wondered if he was the very chap that used to show up wherever Stan, God rest his soul, went. "It's the same fella," Stan would insist; "every time I go to the cinema, or to a football match or a gig, that bastard is sat in front of me. Six-foot-five, built like a brick shithouse and with a head you need a periscope to see over. I swear I'm going to report him for harassment if he keeps following me."

For that very reason, Stan had grown adept at the pogo; it was the only dance he was any good at and at least he got to see half of the show. No matter what the act, Stan could be seen jumping up and down in a frenzy of frustration. Bill recalled the time they'd been thrown out of a Constabulary gig after their humourless front-man took exception to Stan's over-exuberance. Bill laughed inwardly at the memory. (1)

Suddenly, the gathering ground to a halt, as a counter-protest hove into view. In stark contrast to the genial bonhomie of those around him, these guys looked evil and menacing; predominantly dressed in black, with Nazi sun-wheel symbols on leather jackets and t-shirts, their knuckles dragged along the ground as they chanted slogans of bigotry and intolerance. They'd commandeered their country's flag as evidence of their patriotism and obviously failed to see the irony in accompanying it with a Nazi salute. Their argument appeared to centre around immigration being the cause of all evil and that austerity wouldn't be necessary if there were fewer mouths to feed, jobs to find, immigrants to house etc. This was all wrapped up in catchy chants like "terrorist scum off our streets" and "Britain for the British."

Bill watched in admiration as the colossus on his side of the argument lifted a frail but defiant old lady out of the throng and to safety; then re-join the horde to continue his peaceful remonstrations. The plucky old lady was having none of it, though, and fought her way back in to add her not inconsiderable voice to the cause. It would take more than a few fascists to stop her.

Being a bit of a coward, Bill kept to the periphery and away from the potential flashpoints. He was full of respect for those prepared to shed blood for their principles, but Bill aspired to pacifism; at least that's what he told himself anyway. Until, that is, he was shocked into action.

For a moment he couldn't believe his eyes, but it was definitely her. Lauren, his eldest daughter, was there at the very front and on collision course with a particularly nasty-looking specimen of hatred. What the hell was she doing here? Immediately, the protective fatherly instincts kicked-in and, with some difficulty, Bill fought his way through the ruckus. As he got nearer he could see the malice in the thug's eyes; and all Lauren did was stand and smile at him, her expression one of non-confrontational mockery that appeared to have, at least temporarily, stopped him in his tracks.

His accomplices weren't so restrained however and Bill was shocked to suddenly feel the full force of a size eleven steel toe-cap. With a well-aimed punch at the nearest Neanderthal nose, he swept Lauren up and, in one movement, bundled her away from trouble, just as the police stepped in to keep the warring factions apart.

Looks of shock, indignation and admiration battled for supremacy on Lauren's face; quickly turning to anger as she demanded - 'Why are you following me? This is the most embarrassing thing you've ever done. What are my friends going to think?'

Bill hopped in agony, wondered if his shin-bone was broken and stared back at his ungrateful offspring.

'I'm not following you,' he frowned, 'I've been supporting events such as this since long before you were born. We're on the same side, would you believe.'

Lauren glared back at him - 'I don't believe you. Are you trying to tell me that this is coincidence?'

'Completely; I had no idea you'd developed a political conscience. Oh, and I'm fine by the way; thank you for your concern.' Bill hopped around some more in pain. 'Does your mother know you're here?'

'Of course not; and it's got nothing to do with either of you. I'm old enough to make my own decisions.'

Bill held up his hands in submission - 'Absolutely; I'm proud that you're involved in such a worthy cause, but do you have to put yourself right in the firing-line? You poke those vicious dogs with sticks and they tend to bite back, you know.'

'I had everything under control, and there was no violence until you showed up. That's part of the problem, when we sink to their level and fight back physically. There are better ways, you know.'

Just then, a tall, gangly youth with thick black glasses arrived on the scene. A wispy beard thinly disguised the pock-marks left by the recent eruptions of adolescence, his lank blond hair was dishevelled and his striped red and green jacket ripped at the shoulder.

'Hey, Lauren, what happened? Are you OK? Who's this dude, then?'

'Jacob, this is my dad; Dad, this is Jacob.' Lauren's face reddened in discomfort.

'Hey, Dude,' said Jacob, as he confidently shook Bill's hand, 'I'm not one to advocate violence, but that was some punch you threw back there. Pretty sure that guy's nose is broken.'

Bill winced at Jacob's firm handshake. He hadn't realised how hard he'd hit that thug, and it was dawning that his string-plucking fingers were throbbing with pain.

'Pleased to meet you, Jacob,' he grimaced. 'So, tell me what you think you're doing, leading my daughter astray?'

'Hey, Lauren doesn't need any leader; it's more the other way around, Dude. It was her idea that we come here today.'

Although he was somewhat irritated by Jacob's insistence on calling him Dude, Bill took an instant liking to the fervent young man before him. They struggled to make themselves heard, as the chants and slogans grew louder on each side; and the police, with riot shields to the fore, fought against the throng. Again, Bill saw the gentle giant in the middle of the crowd, his only thought to protect the more defenceless protesters around him from injury.

'Look, this could turn pretty ugly,' observed Bill, 'how about we get out of here and I buy you guys a coffee?'

Lauren looked appalled by the idea, but Jacob replied: 'Sounds cool, Dude; there's an excellent independent Fairtrade place around the corner. Lauren and I don't use the corporate Costa Fortunes or Starfucks.'

'Fine by me,' said Bill, 'lead the way.'

Simply furnished with rustic coffee crates and decorated with used coffee sacks from around the world, the cosy Daily Grind was crammed with trendy customers, all conscious that they were in the place to be. The inviting aroma drew them in and they found a cramped table in the corner. Lauren looked decidedly uncomfortable and not only due to the confined space.

'So, how come none of us knew that you were a seasoned protester, then?' she asked. 'You've never mentioned it before.'

'All down to your mother; she always disapproved of my involvement, as she did with most of the things I did. She argued that you should all be allowed to reach your own conclusions with regard to politics. I may have sneaked in the odd comment to entice you along the righteous path, but it was rarely a topic of conversation around the dinner table, was it? So, how did you two get involved?'

'We met at the Students' Union, Dude,' said Jacob; 'started by campaigning against the astronomical tuition fees and it snowballed from there. The more we delved into the issues, the more we found that was unjust and corrupt. We figured that if our generation simply sat back and did nothing then things weren't going to get any better.'

Bill smiled at Lauren - 'That's my girl. You always did like a good argument; just glad that you've come out on the right side.'

From her expression it didn't seem that Lauren relished her father's pride. Her parents' break-up had hit her hard, coming as it did in the middle of her exams, and she appeared more concerned with matters closer to home, than of national import.

'Talking of arguments, are you and Mum talking to each other these days?'

'Depends what you mean by talking. We discuss what we need to discuss in a relatively civilised manner, but it's never going to be happy families again, is it? One thing that we do agree on is that we don't want you kids taking sides; we're your mum and dad and we both love you very much, regardless of our own problems.'

'And have you found anyone else?'

'No; been inundated with offers, somebody even sent me a Valentine's card, but thought I'd spend some time on my own. I've been a bit preoccupied, what with your Gran's illness and all.'

Lauren's eyes moistened - 'Yeah, we went to see her last week and she didn't even know me. It must have been awful to watch her change like that.'

Jacob fidgeted uneasily on his chair, as if he were eavesdropping on a private conversation. He attempted to lighten the mood a little - 'Hey Dude, Lauren told me that you used to be in a band.'

'Not used to be; still am,' said Bill. 'We've reformed and hit the road again.'

Lauren groaned - 'Yes, Mum said you were out making an exhibition of yourself again; well, that's how she put it anyway. Aren't you a bit old for all that, Dad?'

'Why don't you come and see for yourself? That's why we're in London; we have a gig tonight. What do you say; shall I put you both on the guest list?'

Jacob didn't wait for Lauren's response - 'Hey, that'll be cool, Dude. I play a bit of guitar and write the odd melody myself; it'd be great to pick up some tips from the experts.'

He turned to Lauren and asked - 'We're not doing anything tonight, are we my little revolutionary?'

'I guess not,' sighed Lauren, 'as long as you don't tell anyone. It'll be ancient music, played and watched by ancient people and, trust me, it won't be cool.'

Bill winked at Jacob with a conspiratorial smile - 'We'll see about that; you'd better get that jacket stitched up, son, cos it'll be cooler than you can handle.'

1. Could this have been the Police? It's a little harsh maybe, but check out Richard Thompson's song *Here Comes Geordie*, for a hilarious swipe at Sting's mock Jamaican accent.

Gabriel frowned as he held Bill's bruised and swollen fingers gently in his hand.

'What on Earth were you thinking of? These delicate digits are the tools of your trade and you should treat them with respect. You can barely lift a pint, let alone play a guitar.'

'I'll manage; and it wouldn't be the first time. You remember, Tom; the time that Stan, God rest his soul, tried to break my fingers when I suggested that he was playing too loud?'

'How could I forget? You were like a pair of kids; I lost count of the number of times I had to prise the two of you apart.'

Gabriel addressed the imminent prospect of that evening's gig - 'It's got to be good tonight boys. I've called in some favours and I have enticed various luminaries of the music press and a few A &

R men from the top record labels. This could be your big chance to get back in the limelight. Please, don't let me down; I have my reputation to consider and, already, the word on the street is that old Gabriel's lost his marbles, hitching up with those decrepit old has-beens.'

'Charmed, I'm sure,' said Bill. 'Don't worry; my eldest daughter and her new beau will be there too. I'll be playing my heart out to impress and to prove that I'm not an embarrassment.'

'Lauren's coming?' said Tom. 'You never told me.'

'Only bumped in to her today; she didn't even know we were in town.'

'Well, it'll be great to catch up with my beautiful Goddaughter. I consider it my duty to vet the suitability of her boyfriends and I'll send him packing with a flea in his ear if he doesn't come up to scratch.'

'Seems like a nice guy, as it happens,' said Bill, 'providing you don't mind being referred to as Dude.'

'Trust me, there are worse things you can be called,' declared Gabriel.

'Yeah, I can imagine you've had it tough,' said Bill, 'there can't be many gay Hell's Angels out there. Couldn't you have found a more sympathetic environment?'

'It was my rite of passage, I guess. My father spent all his life in the forces and I spent my childhood moving from one place to another. Each time I'd settled somewhere and made some friends, it was time to move on. The Angels were somewhere to belong. They were my rebel yell and, at the same time, an attempt to impress the old man; to prove I was a tough guy that he could be proud of.' (1)

Victor lifted Gabriel's left arm, squeezed his bicep and pointed at his flexed muscle - 'Still in pretty good shape don't you think?'

'What? Yes, absolutely,' agreed Bill.

'The Angels were my army, the leathers my uniform,' continued Gabriel, in full flow and seemingly oblivious to the flattery. 'It took years for me to admit the truth, to acknowledge who I really was. And, you know what Pater said, when I came out? - "I'm not surprised; always thought you were a bit of a fairy. Well good luck to you son, if that's your bailiwick and it's what makes you happy." - Would have saved a lot of heartache if he'd told me that earlier.'

Gabriel pulled a tatty old photo from his wallet, of an imposing man in uniform, and placed it on the table in front of Bill and Tom.

'That's the ugly old bastard, look.'

'Yes, I can see the resemblance,' said Bill. 'Not that you're ugly of course,' he added hastily.

'No, you're right,' sighed Gabriel. 'I have the same intimidating look that scares people away. I don't mean to.'

'It was more the unfettered violence that terrified us back then,' said Tom, 'that and the scary fancy dress.'

'Yeah, I guess it's the only things left from those days,' smiled Gabriel, as he felt the luxury of his jacket; 'that and a few friends from the Chapter, who stuck by me. Guess I'm still wearing the uniform to impress someone.'

Victor put his arm through Gabriel's and smiled - 'Well, you sure impressed me,' he gushed.

'Yes, but you're just a tramp,' teased Gabriel, 'you'll go for anything in leather.'

Bill and Tom made their excuses and left the happy couple to it. They had a little time to kill before joining Clive and Ray to prepare for the evening. The remnants of that afternoon's protest were drifting through the streets; the earlier mood of celebration and hope engendered by the union of kindred spirits, replaced by one of resignation and futility. Nothing had changed.

The heat of the day turned to the cool of early evening; the cool of early evening would later turn to the heat of the night.

1. *Rebel Yell* was a song by ex-Generation X frontman, Billy Idol, first released in 1983. The song has resonated more down the years than its original chart position of 62 would suggest, although it did reach no. 6 when re-released two years later.

Vanessa had been back to the doctor, who'd prescribed some different drugs to control her anxiety. There was no doubt that the medication was working, but they simply rendered her numb, her emotions supressed until she felt nothing. All her history and associated fears and worries were still there, the root-cause of the problem unaddressed. She took the tablets every day as the doctor ordered, but it felt useless; like putting make-up on skin cancer. This wasn't a life, it was an existence.

She remembered the time when she saw the world as a place of endless possibilities, a daily adventure as she casually cast aside any fella who didn't live up to her ideals; in search of the perfect man, the perfect relationship. And there were a few back in the day, when she had more of the glow of youth about her and a spring in the step. For a while she thought she'd found him but, ultimately, he couldn't live up to her expectations. That lothario on her arm, who induced envious glances from her peers, was just a shallow bully who treated her like a possession. These days she was more wary and a shield of apparent indifference kept potential suitors at arm's length.

Her reflection hid a multitude of insecurities as she brushed her hair and applied mascara, in preparation for the evening ahead. Not only had she managed to persuade Kelly, her old university room-mate, to put her up for the night, but she'd also cajoled her into attending the gig, by use of the same arguments that had coaxed the reluctant Jill along, barely two weeks ago. Kelly was also a little sceptical.

'Who the hell are they?'

'Only one of Britain's finest exponents of the art of rock'n'roll, that's all,' answered Vanessa. Once again, her tone implied that it was a stupid question and that everybody should know of this iconic ensemble.

'Never heard of them,' said Kelly.

'Trust me; it'll be a great night,' reassured Vanessa for the tenth time, as they headed for the underground.

Vanessa disliked tube travel, but had to concede that it was the most efficient way of getting from A to B in London. Cosmopolitan commuters wore blank expressions, each in their own little world of mystery and intrigue. She scowled at the City 'gent' opposite, who was none too subtle in his attempts to look up her skirt. Eventually he got the message and returned his attentions to his Evening Standard.

Their carriage to the ball was one of London Transport's older trains that rattled and whined towards its destination. Beneath the worn and stained fabric of its aged upholstery, Vanessa could feel the springs pressing into her thighs and the stifling heat added to her discomfort. Beside her, Kelly studied something intently on her phone and there was an awkward silence between them. Once they'd caught up on each other's news and the novelty of their reunion had worn off, they found they had taken different paths into adulthood and had little in common.

Kelly had majored in politics and now worked as a Researcher; apparently for any hue of politician with a will to stump up the cash. *Understandably, given her line of work, she had become more cynical than the idealistic youth of Vanessa's memory - 'You just tell them what they want to hear and back it up with a few statistics,' was how she portrayed her chosen profession.*

It was obvious that Kelly was already regretting the decision to accompany Vanessa and, with hair barely threatened with a brush and still in the sweatshirt and jeans that she wore around the flat, had made little effort to get into the spirit of things. Nowadays this was alien territory for Kelly and she was more likely to be found hobnobbing with local dignitaries, than hitting the town with the hoi-polloi.

The minute they entered the heaving venue, Vanessa could tell from the expression on Kelly's face that she wanted to be somewhere else. By the unpretentious standards of rock it wasn't such a bad place – your feet didn't stick to the floor too much, the walls weren't dripping with sweat, and somebody had at least attempted to clean the piss-stained toilets.

Posters of past and future performers adorned every available space, from triumphant heydays to desperate reunions, with varying degrees of authenticity and line-up changes. Vanessa was disappointed to see that the Bezcocks had appeared the previous night – a trippy, poppy, punky Manic Mondays, the poster boasted. Had she known, she would have timed her visit a day earlier and made a weekender of it. She ordered a bottle of Mexican lager for herself and a dry white for her reluctant companion and baulked at London club prices. (1)

'Cheers,' said Vanessa, 'here's to old friends.'

'Yeah, cheers,' replied Kelly, doing little to conceal her lack of enthusiasm.

Vanessa determined to enjoy the evening nonetheless.

1. The Bezcocks - a made-up hybrid of Mancunian punks the Buzzcocks and the Happy Mondays, featuring their dancer/percussionist, Bez; if you can imagine such a thing. The Happy Mondays have also been renamed the Manic Mondays in homage to the classic Prince penned hit for the Bangles. Yes, I'm confused too!

Backstage, the boys ravenously demolished a pre-gig takeaway curry, which emitted an inescapable odour that pervaded every corner of the poky dressing room. At the height of their infamy they'd ridden on the back of a rider commanded by the headline act that catered to each of their varied and exotic tastes. Bill had been the least pretentious and contented himself with pie and chips, whilst Tom favoured moules-marinière. Clive was partial to anything Italian, whether pizza, pasta or ice cream; and then there was Stan, God rest his soul, who insisted upon the finest Istrian truffles on bruschetta, accompanied by salami and olives, all washed down with copious quantities of expensive champagne.

How times had changed, and Bill mopped his brow and swilled beer after inadvertently biting into a particularly red-hot chilli pepper. Inevitably, the curry did what curries do and the show was punctuated by a series of pungent farts. Fortunately no-one lit a match, or the performance would have been enhanced by unintentional pyrotechnics. Those in the mosh-pit wrinkled their noses in distaste and wondered if they'd happened upon a modern-day enactment of Le Petomane. (1 - 2)

Musically, things were going well and Clive's guitar chimed with all the clarity of a clarion call, the rhythm-section responding to thunderous effect, as Tom sang like a bit of a lark. Strong painkillers had numbed the ache in Bill's fingers, but they'd also made him a little drowsy and a hazy feeling replaced his usual exuberance. He'd reached the stage where his eyes unconsciously scanned the audience each night, as they searched in expectation for that flash of yellow. Sure enough, she was there and Bill reeled in shock at the realisation that she was dancing enthusiastically next to Lauren and Jacob.

The next song required all their concentration. The muse had certainly returned and, that afternoon, Bill and Tom had cobbled together a promising new nonsense number called *Jacob's Ladder*; inspired by Bill's brief encounter with Lauren's new boyfriend. They'd run through it with Clive and Ray during the sound-check and all were sufficiently impressed to include it on the set-list. As they reached the catchy chorus – *"He's tall and thin, ain't no-one badder, all the young dudes climb Jacob's Ladder"* – a smile of recognition spread across Lauren's face and she prodded her oblivious partner to listen to the words. Jacob soon caught on too and gave Bill an appreciative thumbs-up. (3 - 4)

By their side, the lady in yellow applauded rapturously; maybe with a little more vigour than the tune warranted. Then she leaned over and shouted something in Lauren's ear. Somehow, Bill resisted the temptation to leap off the stage, grab her by the shoulders and yell - 'Who the hell are you? Why are you following us?' Instead, he played on professionally to the end of the set, his eyes fixed on that spot. He was damned if he'd let her escape this time without discovering her identity.

With Ray's cymbals still vibrating from the closing crash, Bill climbed down from the stage and made his way through the surprised and still cheering crowd. Most people stood aside to let him pass, but some wanted to clap him on the shoulder and congratulate him on his performance, thereby hindering his progress.

Eventually he reached the startled Lauren and Jacob. Too late; she was gone. Bill span around, his breath heavy. He looked among the crowd and towards the exits, but to no avail. He turned to Lauren - 'Where did she go? Who is she? How do you know her?'

'What; who?' asked Lauren.

'That woman in yellow who was standing here; she was talking to you.'

'Never seen her before in my life,' said Lauren. 'She just shouted something about the band being brilliant and that she would kill to get closer. I resisted the temptation to bristle with pride and say, yeah, that's my dad up there. After that she disappeared and I assumed she went to get nearer to the stage. Why, what's the problem?'

Bill shook his head, a little embarrassed by his display of emotion - 'It's nothing; don't worry. I just thought I recognised her, that's all.'

1. The Red Hot Chilli Peppers are hidden in this paragraph. Formed in Los Angeles in 1983, they have sold over 80 million records worldwide and won six Grammy Awards. Apparently the band in its original form was named Tony Flow and the Miraculously Majestic Masters of Mayhem!

2. Le Petomane was the stage name of Joseph Pujol, the French flatulist (professional farter). One of the highlights of his show involved playing *O Sole Mio* and *La Marsseillaise* on an ocarina connected to a tube in his anus. The character has been immortalised numerous times in film, most notably in *Le Petomane*, written by Galton and Simpson of *Steptoe and Son* fame, and starring Leonard Rossiter. And if you think that any part of this book is unbelievable then consider that Joseph Pujol was for real!!

3. *All the Young Dudes* was written by David Bowie and gifted to the iconic Mott the Hoople in 1972. It effectively saved their career as they were about to split before they recorded the song. Mott went on to score further hits with *Honaloochie Boogie, All The Way from Memphis* and *Roll Away The Stone,* among other works of genius predominantly penned by Ian Hunter. Hunter went on to work with former Bowie guitarist Mick Ronson, before enjoying a prolonged and prolific solo career.
4. Bill and Tom's new composition has nothing to do with the African American slave spiritual *We Are Climbing Jacob's Ladder,* which has been recorded by Paul Robeson, Pete Seeger and Bruce Springsteen, among others.

Morning had come way too soon for Bill. He'd hardly slept due to a combination of throbbing shin and fingers. Add to that the fact that the fire-alarm had woken them at 2 a.m. and they'd been obliged to evacuate the building, then Bill and Tom were hardly bright-eyed and bushy-tailed.

'Do they know what caused it?' asked Tom over breakfast.

'Apparently it was someone spraying deodorant,' said Bill. 'I spoke to the security guard and he said that some aerosol had set the alarm off.'

Bill had been unable to return to the land of nod after that, and had spent the rest of the night in speculation as to the identity of the enigmatic lady. His insomnia showed on his haggard face, as he sat opposite his writing partner in the hotel lobby.

'You're paranoid,' insisted Tom, 'she's probably just a fan who's listened to the words of the song and decided to dress like its protagonist.'

'You know that fan is short for fanatic, don't you?' Bill pointed out. 'And why was she standing next to my daughter and speaking to her? That's not the behaviour of your average fan; I'd say it verges on stalking and invasion of privacy. I'm thinking of going to the police.'

'The police; isn't that a bit over the top? Do you think it's really her?'

'I don't know; I've not got close enough to be absolutely certain either way. And if she is just a fan, as you say, then why can't she simply come and say hello and get an autograph like any normal person.'

'Hmm, I see your point,' said Tom, 'but she's hardly committed any crime or displayed any threatening behaviour, has she? What have you got to go to the police with? Attendance of a gig without an explanation; dressing like your fantasy woman; over-enthusiastic dancing? Think a little more evidence might be required before they drop their latest murder case and open an investigation.'

'I guess you're right, but I don't like it. There's something strange going on and I intend to find out what she's up to.'

The small hotel was busy with people finishing their breakfast, checking out and going about their daily business. It wasn't the height of luxury, but comfortable enough, clean and tidy, with helpful and friendly staff. On the back of last night's show and their new manager's connections, a meeting had been arranged for later that morning, with an executive from a well-known record company, and Bill and Tom were awaiting Gabriel's arrival. They didn't have to linger long before he entered with his usual flourish, accompanied by an unnaturally bright, for the time of morning, Victor. Both were garbed in their customary black leather, the tightness of which left little to the imagination; a look that sat with more sartorial elegance on Victor than on his noticeably bulging companion. Unfortunately Victor had also decided to top-off his image with a large white beret, reminiscent of those worn by the Pubettes in their prime; a cap-it-all offence against fashion, if ever Bill had seen one, it balanced on his head like a futon on a bottle of Beaujolais. (1 - 2)

'Morning campers,' said Gabriel, as he looked Bill and Tom up and down with a critical eye. 'This is an important meeting that I've managed to swing, you know; thought you could at least have made some kind of effort.'

Bill looked offended - 'This is us, man; this is the image that has stood us in good stead for all these years and it's too late to change now. How did you expect us to dress; like A Flock of Shitehawks?' (3)

'Well, I guess you'll have to do,' sighed Gabriel. 'Where are your fellow Brothel Creepers, then? Still creeping out of a brothel, I'll wager.'

'Clive said he'd meet us there,' replied Tom, 'and Ray's still in bed; said he'd go along with anything we decide.'

'Very well,' said Gabriel, 'it's a pleasant morning for a stroll. Thought we could take in the local culture as we walk; we have plenty of time and it's only twenty minutes away.'

Victor had other business to attend to, so they wished him good day and made their way outside. As they walked, Gabriel excitedly told them of a show that he and Victor were intending to catch that evening, featuring a pair of drag queens named Burly Chassis and Rusty Springboard. His dream, he said, was to present a variety show, similar to the old Sunday Night at the London Palladium, but with a cross-section of gay, straight, black, white, male, female acts. (4 - 5)

'It will be a celebration of individuality and acceptance,' he declared, 'and it will be called *Neither Gay nor Gloria*. I'm going to ask Mylie Kinogue to headline. How would you guys like to be involved?' (6 - 7)

'Sounds very ambitious,' said Bill. 'Let us know if it ever gets off the ground and we'll talk about it.'

The Saturday morning London streets buzzed with multi-cultural businesses and punters, and the clamour of conversation and commerce assaulted their senses. Bill loved the life-affirming racket of the place and the different smells and music emanating from every shop or stall they passed. The spicy aroma of samosas blended with the sultry smell of jerk-chicken, and the sounds segued from bhangra to reggae as they emerged from beneath a graffiti festooned railway bridge.

Bill stopped in his tracks; he was familiar with the iconic bass-heavy dub of Tubby King that boomed from impressive speakers, but he'd never heard the like of the dreadlocked greengrocer who improvised ingenious rhymes as he tended the display outside his shop. Bill held the others back and put his finger to his lips as he paused to listen; before the man sensed their presence, fell silent and turned. He was about to meet the rockers uptown. (8)

'Wh'appen, brethren? Yah here fe a free show or you wan buy vegetable?'

'We were just admiring your talent,' answered Bill, 'you should be on the stage.'

'Yeah, me know, man; the first stage outa town.'

Bill smiled and offered his hand - 'You're good; where did you learn to toast like that?'

The man hesitated, as if weighing up the strangers before him; a look of suspicion on his face. His eyes lingered on Gabriel for a few moments then he stared at Tom, before turning his attention back to Bill. Apparently satisfied that they weren't cops or tax

87

inspectors, he firmly shook Bill's hand.

'Ras Putin, at your service. It come natural, man. Back a yard I and I play in a band; nah roots, but one o' dem Babylon system cabaret act that play hotel for tourist. Nah good for me image, but it pay well. Soon come this Russian oligarch name Romin Arounabit; he on vacation and he wan tek we home with him. It too cold for me man, even colder than here. Then he try to mek we sing that bloodclaat Bony tune, so me come to Englan' fe to set up me shop. Rest of the band still there; and now he send them on tour fe try sell Russian reggae to the world. Even ship them back to Jamaica, as if we nah remember who they are. Russian reggae! Pah! You ever hear such a ting?'

'Ras Putin; it's a great stage name,' said Bill.

'The label jus' stuck, man; and me have the name long before that crazy baldhead tief it an become president.'

'And are you happy in your shop?' asked Bill. 'Don't you miss the music?'

'Me like the community, man. They some good people round here, despite them pickney tief me cabbage fe use as football. Then there's the rassclaat who come pon me shop every week an' break the stalk from the broccoli fe to mek it weigh less; me surprise him nah peel the sweet potato too.'

In the background Gabriel was becoming a little impatient. He prodded Bill and tapped his watch. Ras Putin glared at him over Bill's shoulder.

'Hey, you have somewhere to go, man? Me entertain you with me life story, leas' you can do is buy a likkle someting before yah go. This the finest mango outside Jamaica; sweeter than yah first girlfriend, and it nah bring you so much trouble.'

Bill wondered what this Rasta street-poet knew about his first girlfriend, but then assumed he was just generalising.

'I'll take two,' said Bill.

Gabriel, feeling a little intimidated, grabbed the nearest thing to hand; a rather large cucumber. Ras Putin took his money, looked him up and down and declared - 'Thanks batty man; Jah only know a wah you gwan do with it.'

'I intend to put in my sandwiches and, if I'm feeling particularly extravagant, I may add it to a salad with a splash of vinaigrette.'

'Hey, you buy it, man, you do whatever you want.'

Ras Putin thanked them for their custom and they made their

way briskly along the street, conscious that the little interlude had made them late for their appointment.

'Do you think he concocted that whole Russian reggae story to justify his name?' asked Tom.

'It's possible,' said Bill, 'but you heard him, Tom; he was brilliant and I'd like him on the album.'

'Over my dead body,' asserted Gabriel. 'Besides, we haven't got the deal yet. I spoke to all of my contacts that attended last night and, despite my gushing enthusiasm, Jeff is the only one that's agreed to meet us. Let's face it you're not exactly the next big thing, are you.' (9 - 11)

'Yeah, but you knew what you were getting when you signed us,' argued Tom.

'It's not me you have to convince,' said Gabriel, almost running now, in his haste to make up for lost time. 'We're already late because you stopped to talk to that awful man. It doesn't look very professional if you can't even be bothered to turn up on time. I hate being late for appointments.'

'It'll be fine,' said Bill, panting in his effort to keep up. 'With our talent and your charm, what could possibly go wrong?'

1. The Pubettes, I think, is a better name than The Rubettes, who emerged during the glam-rock era of the 70s with the falsetto fuelled *Sugar Baby Love*. Their trademark white stage suits were topped with white berets, similar to the one that Victor is wearing here. Worth checking out is *Your Baby Ain't Your Baby Anymore*, the solo single by Paul Da Vinci, who provided the distinctive vocals on *Sugar Baby Love*.
2. "It balanced on his head like a futon on a bottle of Beaujolais" paraphrases a line from Bob Dylan's *Leopard Skin Pillbox Hat*. The song featured on Dylan's 1966 *Blonde on Blonde* album. Now, has anyone ever referenced the Rubettes and Bob Dylan in the same sentence before?
3. A Flock of Seagulls, the 1980s synth pop band from Liverpool. Their fashion sense and hairstyles have been lampooned by many and would have represented the antithesis of Skinny Ted and the Brothel Creepers. *Wishing (If I Had a Photograph of You)* was a decent song, though.
4. Burly Chassis is a play on the name of Welsh diva, Dame Shirley Bassey, who I hope will forgive the pun. Shirley is, of course, a British institution famed for recording no less than three James Bond theme songs – *Goldfinger, Diamonds Are Forever* and *Moonraker*. A Google search however, reveals that Burly Chassis are both a rock

band from the North West UK and, (spelt Burley Chassis), a drag queen from Sydney, Australia.

5. And Rusty Springboard is the brilliant English soul singer and gay icon Dusty Springfield. As well as soothing our souls with that effortless, husky voice, Dusty was responsible for hosting many of the top Motown acts on her TV show and bringing them to the attention of a UK audience. Who can top the perfection of hits such as *You Don't Have to Say You Love Me* or *Son of a Preacher Man*? Neither Burly Chassis nor Rusty Springboard are original non de plumes, and I recall my father using both of these spoonerisms way back in the 70s.

6. Neither Gay nor Gloria is a reference to Gloria Gaynor, whose 1978 disco favourite, *I Will Survive* (a declaration of strength and defiance after the break-up of a relationship), has been adopted as a gay anthem.

7. Mylie Kinogue – yet another spoonerism, Kylie Minogue is the Australian actress and singer who rose to fame in the TV soap, Neighbours. A vivacious and glamorous performer, Kylie boasts a large gay audience.

8. King Tubby was a Jamaican sound engineer who worked with the top reggae producers, such as Lee Scratch Perry and Bunny Lee. His best known work is the excellent dub album, *King Tubby Meets the Rockers Uptown*, recorded with melodica maestro, Augustus Pablo, in 1976. King Tubby was shot dead outside his home in Kingston in 1989 after returning from his studio.

9. So, where does one begin to justify this bizarre episode? My woeful attempts at Jamaican patois were inspired by the Booker Prize winning epic novel *A Brief History of Seven Killings* by Marcus James. The story is based around the attempted assassination of Bob Marley in 1976. Being black, gay and Jamaican, Marcus has more authority (and the skill to pull it off), than an old white geezer from Buckinghamshire, U.K., to write about the homophobic and sexist culture propagated by some reggae artists. Yes, I know; after writing this I have no right to take the piss out of Sting's bogus Jamaican twang.

10. The reference to "that bloodclaat Bony tune" is, of course, Bony M's euro-disco ode to Russia's greatest love machine, *Rasputin*; a big hit and irritating earworm from 1978.

11. Also hidden in this strange chapter are two of Bob Marley's finest songs, *Babylon System*, from the 1979 *Survival* album; and *Crazy Baldhead*, from my favourite Wailers album, *Rastaman Vibration*, released in 1976.

Barely a short bus-ride away, Vanessa packed her modest overnight bag and thanked Kelly for her hospitality. She knew she'd never see her again and that the same applied to Jill and all her other ex-colleagues; her circumstances determined that she was alone in the world and she felt both liberated and abandoned. Beholden to no-one, she once again negotiated one of the busiest but loneliest places on the planet, the London Underground; before boarding the 11:15 to nowhere.

Across the aisle, a doting mother entertained her young daughter with nursery rhymes and colouring books. Vanessa smiled as she retrieved a pink crayon from beneath her seat and handed it back to the beaming little girl, whose face was the very picture of innocence. Enjoy it while it lasts, thought Vanessa, you have no idea what this world can do to you.

Now that she was a lady of leisure, the small matter of how to fill the days engrossed her thoughts and, with all this time on her hands, there was no end to the potential mischief she could get up to. A number of jobs had been applied for, most with the customary polite but negative responses; but she had secured one interview, scheduled for two weeks hence, for the role of Care Assistant. The position offered flexible hours and promised regular work, a competitive salary and benefits; although said salary and benefits were unspecified.

With the next Brothel Creepers' gig some weeks away, would there be a hiatus in her preoccupation, or could she dare to get closer? As the countryside sped by outside, Vanessa leant her head against the window, fixed her eyes on the green blur of motion and allowed the train's vibrations to clear her mind.

It was only fifteen minutes, but Jeff was obviously unimpressed by their tardiness. He stared askance at them from behind his desk, as Bill tried to conceal the fact that he was carrying two large mangoes. Gabriel was less successful with his cucumber, which protruded conspicuously from his trouser pocket and, when invited to take a seat, was unable to do so until he'd removed the offending gourd and placed it on the desk before him.

'It's for my sandwiches,' explained Gabriel, in response to Jeff's quizzical expression. 'I must apologise for our lateness, but we suffered a small distraction on our journey.'

'No matter,' said Jeff, 'Clive here, at least, was on time and has kept me entertained with stories of the impressive roster of acts he has played with. I take it that no-one else in the band has such a remarkable CV?'

'I toured with Mark Walnut for a while, after we split up,' ventured Bill, 'but it was a fleeting gig. The moment I said hello, he waved goodbye.' (1)

'I can testify for their musicianship,' said Clive. 'Besides, you were there last night; you must have seen something worth talking about, or we wouldn't be here.'

'Hmm, Gabriel can be very persuasive when he has a passion for something,' said Jeff, 'and it seems that you are his latest project. However, I can't deny that it was a good show, with a positive response from a mixed-age audience. Add to that the fact that you are writing new material, rather than simply regurgitating old glories, then I am prepared to listen to your demos.'

'What demos?' asked Tom. 'We haven't done any demos. Surely you can check out our old albums.'

'I am familiar with your previous work, but that was a long time ago. I want to know what you have to offer now.'

'No problem,' said Gabriel, 'I'll book a studio and we'll let you have a couple of new tracks.'

Bill looked around the spacious office and studied the inspirational images that covered every wall. He would have no qualms about describing some of the inhabitants of these action shots as his heroes and he could be proud to share a label with them. There was no doubt that they would be keeping illustrious company if they signed for Coarse Craft and he felt that thrill again; the same sensation as the first time around, when they'd signed on the dotted line for one of the big labels as teenagers. But then he recalled the small-print that determined that they would never reap the just rewards for their endeavour. (2)

'OK, let's assume that you're happy with the demos once we've laid them down,' he said. 'What kind of deal would you offer?'

'We'd start with one album, preferably containing a few songs we can issue as singles,' replied Jeff. 'It's the standard arrangement that we have with all of our acts and you won't find a better one. We're not in the business of ripping people off and Gabriel will back me up on that point.'

'It's true; this is a reputable label and Jeff is one of the good guys.' Gabriel turned back to their possible benefactor - 'We'll come back with the demos next week. I'm sure you'll understand that we have a couple of other labels to speak with in the meantime.'

'That's not what I heard,' smiled Jeff, 'we do talk to each other, you know. All the other execs who were there last night think I'm mad to even consider signing you guys.'

'But imagine their faces when we prove them wrong,' said Gabriel.

'Hmm, I'll try,' said Jeff. 'Just one thing before you go; about your choice of drummer. Is this guy more mature and responsible than the wanker from your previous incarnation? As I recall he upset a lot of people and made quite a few enemies with his, shall we say, eccentric behaviour.'

'Yeah, Ray's sound,' promised Tom. 'Stan, God rest his soul, was fortunately a one-off. Besides, we're all too long in the tooth to put up with all that crap these days.'

1. Mark Walnut is a less glamorous version of Marc Almond who, alongside David Ball, formed Soft Cell. *Say Hello, Wave Goodbye* was a no. 3 hit for the duo in 1982. Bill may have played with Marc's mid-80s band, the Willing Sinners, though no record exists of his involvement.
2. Coarse Craft; a fictional equivalent to Rough Trade, the independent record label formed in 1978 by Geoff Travis and named after his Ladbroke Grove record store of the same name. The label helped to launch the careers of such illustrious acts as The Smiths and Stiff Little Fingers.

It was a long time since the band had been in a studio, but Clive was fortunately a master at the craft of recording demos. They decided upon *Sun Soaked Murdoch Marionette and 'billy Dub* as representative of their new material, due to the fact that they constituted two thirds of their new material. Once happy with the performance and sound, the recordings were submitted to Jeff, who promised to come back to them once he'd discussed matters with his colleagues.

They used the lengthy break between gigs to hone the new songs and to compose a few more. Both Bill and Tom were surprised at how naturally it came to them and, somehow, song-writing seemed less arduous than it was in their troubled youth.

They'd each accrued a wealth of life experience on which to draw for inspiration and their new compositions had a maturity about them (with the notable exception of *Never Had a Dirty Mind (Till I laid Eyes On You)*), whilst still retaining the energy for which they were renowned. Clive had also weighed in with a pair of bluesy numbers that showcased his virtuosity and gave him the opportunity to exercise his somewhat melancholic vocal-chords. He was a little put out when Tom likened his vocal style to Murky Waters with constipation. (1)

It took more than a fortnight for Jeff to return with his verdict and they'd almost given up hope, but eventually and with unbridled enthusiasm, he offered to put his reputation on the line and take a chance. With a recording and publishing deal signed, the next step would be to record the songs properly. Bill nearly fainted however, when Jeff announced that he'd enlisted the services of two top producers. Dennis Roy, who'd worked with some legendary reggae acts, had been recruited due to Bill's insistence that he wanted to experiment with a dub sound; whilst Richie Stevens had been enticed from the States to compliment the band's more traditional, pared-down vibe. (2 - 3)

'How on Earth did you get those two?' asked an incredulous Clive.

'Well Dennis is always up for a challenge; and would you believe that Richie is a fan? Just happened to be chatting with him in New York last week and I mentioned you guys; to be honest that's what made my decision easy. If Richie wants to work with you then you definitely have kudos.'

An unexpected live engagement was to dissect their recording process and Gabriel had been very excited about the prospect when he'd swung the deal some months ago.

'I've got some good news,' he'd announced. 'I've managed to get you on the bill at the *Blaze On Weekender* at Bunter's Holiday Camp in Pithead. There will be thousands of punters there and it will be worth ten regular gigs.' (4)

'Won't we look a bit out of place?' said Bill. 'It'll be all jangly guitars, floppy hats and Northern accents; and we'll be about ten years older than the other bands.'

Bill had studied the provisional line-up and it featured the likes of Reverb and the Rabbitmen and The Marvel Stuff; both bands for whom he had a lot of respect, but of a very different genre and fan-base than their own. (5 - 6)

'Yes, but there's no such thing as bad publicity,' Gabriel retorted; 'and it'll put you back on the circuit.'

'So, how did you persuade them that we'd be a good fit?' asked a sceptical Bill.

'Apparently you were an early influence on the Magic Carpets and I'm also told that, if you listen carefully, one of your bass-lines is hidden in the mix on the Stoned Flowers' first album. Hey, what have you got to lose? It'll be a great weekend by the seaside; you can even take your buckets and spades if you want.' (7 - 8)

'You make Pithead in November sound positively attractive,' said Tom. 'I'm up for it if the others are. Will we be staying on-site?'

'Yes,' affirmed Gabriel, 'forgive me for saying so, but you're anonymous enough to blend in with the crowd. The accommodation is cheap too.'

All in all, a busy few months lay ahead. They would begin recording with Richie Stevens, followed by their seaside sojourn, before returning to complete the album with Dennis Roy. They were all thrilled that everything appeared to be coming together. It was as if they'd never been away.

In the meantime, though, they still had to live. Things hadn't changed that much with regard to the imbalance between income and expenditure for a working band on the road, and no-one was too surprised that the balance-sheet was in the red. Unanimous in the view that they were way too old to sleep in the van or in the squats of yore, they'd grown accustomed to a little comfort in their dotage and favoured a hotel or B & B. Although ticket sales had been encouraging, they barely covered the hire of the venues, let alone accommodation. Reluctantly, they all agreed to a partial return to their previous employments to revive the coffers.

Tom had no problem whatsoever. His accountancy business was stable and he had a number of regular small-business customers, who'd been with him for many years. Work had been coming in regularly throughout the tour and Tom had suffered the reproaches of his fellow musicians on the frequent occasions that he'd had to interrupt rehearsals to deal with a business call.

Clive, as usual, was in demand in the studio and was the subject of some mockery due to his involvement in a jingle for a toilet-roll commercial. His admonishers however, were silenced when told how much he was earning from the project.

Ray put on a brave front, but was barely keeping it together.

Unbeknown to the rest of the band, he hadn't worked for the past four years due to ill-health and was reliant on Employment and Support Allowance. He'd missed a recent appointment at the Job Centre to discuss why his benefits had been stopped, as he'd been on tour. Ray didn't know where his next meal was going to come from.

Through recommendation from a previous client, Bill had secured a substantial graphic and web-design project that would, hopefully, tide him over for the foreseeable and bring in some much-needed revenue. All things considered, he felt optimistic about the coming months, despite his constant concerns about the health and happiness of his ailing mother. His brother's timeworn excuse that he'd been too busy would have been convenient, but it didn't feel right. He'd prevaricated long enough, he thought; it was about time he paid her another visit.

This time it was John's turn to reproach him about his lack of consideration, and adherence to his duty as a loving son.

'But I hate these places,' protested Bill, 'they're a portent of what we've all got to look forward to; old age, the loss of our faculties and independence. Wiping your drool as you wait for your gruel; next stop the graveyard.'

They'd met in the car park and were attempting to enter the home, the security system designed equally to keep the residents in and intruders out. Once inside they sought a responsible looking person, for an update on their mother's condition. Matron, a smart and efficient, business-like lady in her late-thirties who bore scant resemblance to the starchy Hattie Jacques stereotype, proceeded to give them an honest appraisal.

'She's settled in quite well, but she has a tendency to upset some of our other residents with her industrial language and inappropriate sense of humour. To be honest, she's had the nurses in hysterics on occasion and I'm sure she doesn't mean any offence, but we often have to take her back to her room for the sake of keeping the peace.'

'Well, good for her,' said Bill, 'we should all have the right to spend our twilight years kicking and screaming into oblivion and saying whatever the hell we like.'

'That's all very well, but she won't let anyone watch TV without demanding, rather loudly, that we switch over to Top of the Pops; says her son is a pop star and he's in a band that have a hit record.'

John groaned - 'Not again. But surely that's all part of her illness, living in the past and all that.'

'Absolutely,' said Matron, 'and we obviously understand that her intermittent outbursts are out of character. So, which one of you is the pop star then?'

'That'll be my little brother here,' answered John.

'I prefer rock star,' said Bill, 'but Mum always referred to us as pop stars.'

'I'm sorry, but I don't recognise you. What band were you in?'

'Skinny Ted and the Brothel Creepers.'

'I've never heard of them,' said Matron. 'Were you very famous?'

'Not really,' said Bill, 'but you may know one of our numbers.'

At which point he proceeded to sing an acapella middle-eight of *Stood Up, Again*, whilst John cringed by his side.

'*You said you'd meet me by the pier, In stockings delicate and sheer, So I dressed up in my best gear, The strides that won rear of the year, But look around there's no-one here, So I'll just have another beer, And this clown will shed another tear, For a broken heart so hard to bear...*' (9)

Matron joined in the next line, '*...You left me crying in the rain, Oh, oh, stood up, again,*' before exclaiming - 'Wow, did you write that? I love that song; it's so poignant.' (10)

'That's just one of our masterpieces,' boasted Bill, 'there's plenty more where that came from.'

'Well, I'm impressed,' said Matron, her manner suddenly a little flirtatious, 'and I've never met a pop star, sorry, rock star, before. I'd better let you two boys visit your mother now, but please pop in and say hello next time you're here.'

Bill made sure he read Matron's name-badge as he shook her hand and thanked her for her time. He might indeed pop in and say hello to Wilma on his next visit.

'Jesus, that was embarrassing,' said John, as they walked along the corridor, 'you'll let me know if I'm cramping your style, won't you.'

When they entered her room, their mother was sitting quietly by the window, gazing into the distance over the lake and to the trees beyond. Bill put his finger to his lips in a gesture to John to stay silent; and they watched for a few minutes, a dignified lady at peace with the world. Eventually John cleared his throat to announce their presence and their mother turned; a confused expression, a flicker of recognition, followed by blank indifference.

'Hello; are you here to take me home?'

'No, Mum,' answered Bill, 'this is your home now. It's nice here isn't it?'

'It's a good hotel and the staff are very friendly, but I'm ready to go home now. Arthur will be waiting for his tea.'

Despite their attempts to make small talk and share their news, both Bill and John found that there was little to say that could penetrate her lack of curiosity. Embarrassed silence ensued, until Bill pulled up a chair, sat beside his mother and took in the vista. He held her hand and spoke softly - 'You won't get a view like this at home, you know Mum. Take a look at that; it's so peaceful, and you know how much you've always enjoyed bird-watching. You feed them all the time and there must be all kinds of birds out there.'

'Yes, I saw some Goldfinches today, just outside the window. They're my favourites, so colourful and quick; blink and you'll miss them.'

'Then stay for a bit longer,' pleaded Bill; 'next time I'll bring a book with all the different birds in and you can tick off the ones you see.'

John lounged silently on the bed and fidgeted uncomfortably. He looked like an intruder at his own family gathering.

'Look Mum, I've brought you a little present,' continued Bill, as he handed her an iPod, upon which he'd painstakingly downloaded all her favourite songs. She looked confused at this shiny tiny box, as he gently placed the headphones over her ears, pressed play and watched his mother's eyes light up in recognition of a song that had once meant so much. She smiled to herself and sat back in the chair, the picture of contentment; while it lasted. Bill nodded towards the door and he and John left quietly.

Back outside and they each took in a breath of late-summer air; the sky was deep blue and this really was an idyllic setting but, despite the blazing sunshine and well-intended attempts to make it feel like home, the whole place seemed so cold and clinical.

'Well, at least we're not her only visitors,' said John.

'Yeah, Lauren said she'd been recently; and I think Elaine's brought the kids a few times. Much as we don't get on these days, I have to give her credit for that.'

'There was another lady here too, last time I came; left in a bit of a hurry when I showed up. Said she was an old friend, but I didn't recognise her.'

'What did she look like?' asked Bill.

'Very attractive, dark hair, blue eyes, yellow mini-skirt, Dr Martens; didn't get the chance to ask her name or how she knew Mum. Hey, are you OK? You've gone white as a sheet; look like you've seen a ghost.'

Bill made it to a nearby bench and John followed with an expression of brotherly concern - 'So, who is she?'

'I wish I knew. She's been at every gig since we reformed; always dressed the same and the spitting-image of the girl that inspired *Stood Up, Again.*'

'Ah, yes, the lovely lady of legend and song; I remember you moping around like a lovelorn teenager back then. You wouldn't eat a thing and you couldn't sleep; jumping down everyone's throat whenever we tried to make you see sense. And now she's returned to haunt us, has she? Oh, whoopy-doo!'

'I *was* a lovelorn teenager; just turned nineteen I think. And it's not funny, John. It's one thing stalking me, but why would she come to visit Mum? Anyway, she can't be the same lady; from a distance she looks pretty much the same as she did all those years ago. It's as if I've stepped back in time.'

'Are you sure? You can do a lot with make-up these days; and then there's the wonder of cosmetic surgery where you too can look like Barry Manifold, a taut plastic parody of your former-self and indistinguishable from your waxwork dummy. And what is it that the over-fifties are saying now: fifty is the new forty? There's an element of truth in it too - people do seem to be looking younger; or is that just from the perspective of someone who's nearly sixty?' (11)

Bill shook his head - 'I don't know, John; I'm confused and, whoever she is, she gives me the creeps. Maybe it wasn't such a good idea to reform the band, to rake up the past and to play that bloody song again. You know the wounds still feel raw, even after all this time.'

'You always were the sensitive one. Thought you'd grow out of it one day, but I guess that's the curse of the creative gene. Look, why don't we go back in and speak with your new friend the Matron and ask if they have any CCTV footage? I remember reading somewhere that they have to show the images if requested by the service user or their family. Perhaps we can get a closer look at our anonymous lady.'

Contrary to the warmth of the day, Bill shivered and nodded - 'OK, guess it's worth a try.'

Fifteen minutes later and they were huddled round a small screen in Matron's office while she scanned the footage for the day in question.

'I don't like all these cameras around the place,' said Matron. 'They were put in after all the abuse scandals, you know; but there's a fine line between consideration for the safety of our residents and invasion of privacy.'

'Wait, there she is,' exclaimed Bill, 'can you go back a bit please.'

The grainy picture grew more animated as a blur of yellow sped backwards through the entrance, then in slow-motion they viewed the mysterious apparition as she walked furtively, oblivious to the camera above her head. Pausing to sign the visitor's book, she looked around the lobby to get her bearings and asked a nurse for directions, before disappearing along a corridor. Bill strained his eyes in an attempt to recognise the star of the show, but could only confirm that it was the very same lady who'd been at their gigs. The camera angles and picture quality negated any further identification.

'Is that all you have?' asked Bill.

'I'm afraid so. We've stopped short of placing cameras in the rooms, although families are welcome to install their own if they have any concerns. No, the welfare and dignity of our guests is our priority and we are not here to spy on our staff and visitors.'

'Can we look at the book in reception?' asked John. 'We can get her name from there.'

'Be my guest,' said Matron, 'and please let me know if there's anything we have to worry about. I can get Security to stop her if she shows up again.'

Bill thanked Matron for her time and was rewarded with a coquettish smile - 'Please, call me Wilma,' she said, as she shook his hand for a little longer than etiquette required.

'Will you behave yourself,' said John, as they walked back to the reception area, 'it's not appropriate for you to chat-up the staff.'

'I didn't do anything,' protested Bill; 'it's not my fault if I'm irresistible.'

John flicked through the pages of the book until he came to the correct date - 'Here's my name at 2 p.m., so she must have been here in the hour or so prior to that.'

'Look, there's Lauren's name,' said Bill, 'visiting Peggy Harris. I know for a fact that Lauren was in London that day; it was the day after our gig and I phoned her that morning.'

'So our mystery lady has signed-in with a false name then; must mean she has something to hide.'

'This isn't right, John. How does she know Lauren's name? Do you think we should report it to the police?'

'Not sure that they'll be able to do anything, but I guess it won't do any harm to make them aware of your fears.'

'I'll go on my way home,' offered Bill, 'I'm sure you have better things to do.'

'Yeah, I do have a lot of work to catch up on. You'll let me know how you get on, won't you.'

'Sure.'

'And don't worry; I'm sure there's a perfectly innocent explanation.'

1. They don't come much more influential than McKinley Morganfield (better known as Muddy Waters). He inspired both the U.S. rock'n'roll musicians of the 50s and the U.K. rhythm & blues bands of the 60s, as well as giving the Rolling Stones their name. Muddy Waters enjoyed a resurgence in the late 70s with the brilliant *Hard Again* album. The father of Chicago blues left us in 1983.
2. Dennis Roy is a fictional character whose name is a hybrid of well-respected producer, Dennis Bovell, and the legendary reggae DJs, U Roy and I Roy.
3. Richie Stevens – another fictional character who may bear a passing resemblance to someone else.
4. This is a reference to a fantastic live music event, held at a well-known holiday camp in the west of England that a friend and I attended in 2016. The weekend featured a number of predominantly Alternative bands that were popular in the 1990s; but more of that later!!
5. Reverb and the Rabbitmen pay homage to Liverpool's finest, Echo and the Bunnymen. Formed in 1978, the original line-up consisted of Ian McCulloch, Will Sergeant, Les Pattinson, and a drum machine that was subsequently replaced by the late Pete de Freitas. Their album, *Ocean Rain*, is the "greatest album ever made", according to the ever-modest McCulloch. To be fair, it is pretty good.
6. The Marvel Stuff might be a superhero version of Black Country Alternative Rockers, The Wonder Stuff. An exuberant live band, their

biggest hits were *Size of a Cow*, and a version of Tommy Roe's *Dizzy* (in collaboration with comedian, Vic Reeves); both in 1991.

7. Would you rather have Magic Carpets or Inspiral Carpets? Part of the Madchester scene in the late 80s, the Inspiral variety once employed Noel Gallagher as a roadie and technician. The band courted controversy when an Oxford University student was prosecuted for obscenity after wearing one of their 'Cool as Fuck' T-shirts.

8. The Stone Roses' eponymous 1989 debut was heralded by critics as one of the greatest albums of all time. Ian Brown, John Squire, Mani and Reni constitute the original and most recent line-up.

9. Another nod to Smoky Robinson and the Miracles' Motown masterpiece, *Tears of a Clown*.

10. Not to be confused with the Everly Brothers' *Crying in the Rain*. One of the most beautiful sounds in music, the Everlys seemed almost telepathic in the way their voices complimented each other. The height of their career straddled the late 50s/early 60s and Don and Phil's harmonies graced some great songs, such as *Cathy's Clown, Walk Right Back* and *When Will I Be Loved? Crying in the Rain* was released in 1962. Their relationship was blighted in the latter years by their diametrically opposed political views. Phil Everly passed away in 2014.

11. Barry Manilow would probably prefer to be famed for being one of the world's best-selling artists, rather than for his proclivity for plastic-surgery. Best known for 70s middle of the road ballads *Mandy* and *I Write the Songs,* along with the up-tempo Latin movie theme *Copacabana*, Mr Manilow has an enormous worldwide following.

The bored-looking old-school Desk Sergeant peered over his glasses, straightened his tie and appraised Bill with an expression of suspicion. Perhaps he looked at all of his visitors that way, but it made Bill feel like the suspect in a heinous crime before he'd even uttered a word.

'Good afternoon, sir. How may I help you?'

'Am I supposed to call you Jake?' asked Bill.

The sergeant fingered his name-badge with some discomfort - 'Oh, these are an initiative by the new Super; they are supposed to make us more accessible to the general public; community-policing and all that. I prefer Sergeant Watson.'

'Well, Sergeant Watson; I'm not sure if you can help, but I'd like to report some suspicious behaviour.'

The cynical policeman listened impassively, whilst jotting down the odd note and asking the occasional question for the sake of clarification.

'And what band did you say you were in?'

'Skinny Ted and the Brothel Creepers.'

'I'm sorry, but I've never heard of them.'

'No, not many people have,' said Bill, growing increasingly irritated by the general populace's lack of musical nous, 'but that's not the point. I think I am being stalked and want to know if you can do anything about it.'

'So, this young lady that you met - back in the 80s wasn't it; and how old would she have been?'

'I have no idea. I didn't ask, but she looked about the same age as me or thereabouts. Hey, hang on; what are you implying?'

'Nothing at all, sir; I'm simply trying to establish the facts.'

Bill went red and questioned, not for the first time, the wisdom of reporting his fears to the police. How dare this desk-bound detective sully their brief but beautiful relationship with his sordid suppositions?

'Look, are you able to help or not? If you won't take my case seriously, then we should stop wasting each other's time.'

'I will put your concerns on record, sir; but at this stage the lady hasn't committed any crime that I can think of. Presumably she has paid for her tickets to your shows and there has been no threatening behaviour. I understand that it happens from time to time, that a lady becomes enamoured with a particular popular entertainer and behaves in a way that may seem irrational to us mere mortals. In fact I had a Welsh guy named Thomas the Tank-top in the other day, complaining that women kept throwing their underwear at him. I'm sorry, sir, but unless you can give me more to go on, then there is little we can do.' (1)

'But this woman is not only following me, but she has also visited my mother. I pay my taxes and I demand that you investigate.'

'My poor old mother is in a nursing home too, sir, albeit somewhat downmarket from the one where yours resides. She is always complaining that she never gets any visitors. Perhaps you should consider it a blessing that this lady is prepared to give up her time to offer companionship to a lonely old woman.'

'So, you won't do anything about it, then,' said Bill.

'Police resources are stretched to the bone, sir, and in this age of austerity I'm afraid that we have to prioritise. We now have your details and if you feel that there is imminent danger to yourself or anyone else, then please contact us again. In the meantime I wish you luck in your resurgent career; I will follow it with interest.'

Bill felt foolish as he left the police station. He'd escaped a warning for wasting police time, but nevertheless, Sergeant Jake Watson had made it abundantly clear that Bill's anxieties were not top of his list when it came to the never-ending battle against crime. He sat in his car for a short time and stared up at the blue police sign on the white wall, whilst trying to clear his head. Maybe the sergeant was right and he was overreacting; after all, no-one had been hurt and the only person making a big deal out all this was him. Was it really all in his mind; a paranoia brought about by a series of stressful events? Bill resolved to put his youthful crush, or her creepy imitator, out of his mind and to focus on the good things in his life; the band, his kids, his friends and a promising future.

Simultaneously he turned the key in the ignition and hit the windscreen-wiper stick to clear the few drops of rain that had settled during his embarrassing brush with the law. It had been a glorious day, but dark rain-clouds were rolling in from the West and a strong breeze was building up. As he joined the early evening traffic a flash of yellow caught his peripheral vision and, in panic, his eyes darted to the other side of the street. Bill shook his head and smiled as a lady in a plastic mac struggled to control a lemon umbrella. Yeah, he was getting paranoid.

It should have only taken ten minutes, but roadworks on the ring-road meant a slow crawl back home. Eventually familiar streets emerged from the gloom. Each time he approached his road, Bill dreaded the emptiness of that house; a lonely shack for a lonesome guy. Spoilt by the recent anonymity and relative luxury of hotels and B & B's the old family home felt even more run down and barren than before. With Mum no longer in residence, Bill knew that he should start redecorating, but he found it hard to muster the enthusiasm. Whenever he did contemplate a new colour scheme or rearrange the furniture, he could feel the presence of his old man offering the sage advice: 'You don't want to do it like that, son.'

I'll oil that gate tomorrow, he thought, as the rusty hinges played the timeworn theme to Coronation Street. Bill glanced up at the cracked glass that caused a draft in his bedroom; the result of a particularly exuberant bass spin that had volleyed an unsuspecting vase towards the window.

He stopped abruptly on the garden path and squinted through the dusk. It appeared that somebody had dumped a load of old rags on his front doorstep. He moved a little closer then hesitated as the rags slowly began to move; then, through a slit in the fabric, a pair of eyes blinked at him. Finally a bushy beard beneath a red nose emerged and greeted him by name.

'You took your bloody time, Bill; been out on the town have we?'

'Ray?'

'Look, I'm sorry to intrude, mate, but I'm after a favour; I need a place to crash for a few days. Only a week or two behind on the rent, but the bastards still evicted me, didn't they? I've been on the streets for the past few nights, but looks like it's gonna piss it down tonight.'

'On the streets; you mean sleeping rough? Haven't you got anywhere to go?'

'No, I don't like to be a burden; and it's not the first time I've used the stars for a roof.'

'For God's sake man, why didn't you tell us? You're part of the band; of course I'll help.'

'I don't always feel like part of the band. You're always talking about Stan, God rest his soul.'

'Stan's long gone, man. All that reminiscing is just a symptom of old age; we all talk about the glory days, don't we? Now shift your festering carcass and let me open the door.' (2)

Bill retched a little, as he realised that festering carcass wasn't too far from the truth and that Ray didn't smell too good.

'Thanks mate,' said Ray, as he hauled himself up from the floor and stood aside, 'I'll make it up to you, I promise.'

Bill took a deep breath and showed Ray in - 'First things first; let's get you a shower and a change of clothes then I'll rustle up something to eat. Dump all that stuff by the washing machine and we'll see if any of it is salvageable. My God man, how has it come to this?'

Once washed and clothed in some of Bill's more casual, lounging around the house gear, Ray brought Bill up to speed with recent events.

'I've been on Employment and Support Allowance because, for one reason or another, I was unfit for work. At my last Work Capability Assessment however, the bastards disagreed with my

GP's prognosis and stopped my benefits. Since then I've had to declare my meagre income from the band and, after taking away my rent and costs while we were on the road, there's nothing left. The only thing I have is my drum-kit and I'm gonna have to sell that to eat. I don't know what to do, Bill.'

'And where's your drum-kit now, if you've been thrown out of your home?'

'In my sister's garage; she took it in reluctantly, but her hospitality didn't run to her big brother. Can't blame her I suppose; I'm not the best role-model for her kids, am I?'

Bill took a long look at Ray and, for the first time, saw a desperate human-being instead of the steady beat-keeper that he thought he was. He felt guilty that he'd been so preoccupied with his own problems that he'd failed to notice a fellow band-member and friend in trouble.

'Well you can stay here for as long as you need; providing you pull your weight and treat the place with respect. I could do with the company to be honest.'

With the faintest hint of a smile and a sigh of relief, Ray sank back into the sofa and took in his surroundings.

'Hope you don't mind me saying so, mate, but it looks like the old place could do with sprucing up a bit. I've done a bit of decorating in my time; how about I pay my way by splashing a lick of paint here and there?'

'Bloody cheek,' said Bill, 'I offer you my hospitality and all you can do is diss the décor. I have some old cardboard boxes in the shed that you can sleep on if you'd prefer.'

Ray held up his hands - 'Sorry, mate, no disrespect intended.'

'No, you're quite right,' conceded Bill, 'the place is a fuckin' tip, but this ole house is all I have left of Mum and Dad and it has their imprint all over it. Been meaning to get round to it, but I haven't had time to oil those hinges, nor to replace the window pane.' (3)

'So, let me do it then; all you have to do is choose the colours and buy the paint and you won't recognise it when I'm done.'

'Yeah, that's what I'm afraid of.'

Ray twisted the extremities of his newly shampooed beard between thumb and forefinger and furrowed his brow in thought.

'Tell you what we'll do,' he said at last; 'you pick a feature or two from each room, whether it be a painting of sentimental value or a bit of faded wallpaper, and I'll incorporate them into the design in a tasteful manner. That way you'll have your memories intact and a habitable house in one package. What do you say?'

'OK, why not?' sighed Bill. 'I'll think about what shade of magnolia I want tomorrow. Don't forget that we're due in the studio next week, though; and there's no way you're selling that drum-kit.'

'Thanks mate, you're a lifesaver.'

'Well, us background boys in the rhythm-section should stick together. It's always the guitarists and singers that get all the limelight.'

'Yeah, that's true,' laughed Ray. 'Let's face it, you don't become a drummer if you want to get the girls, do you. The pulling-power of the percussionist pales into insignificance when compared to the seductive overtures of your average guitarist.'

'That's settled then,' said Bill, 'you can stay here for a bit and we can depress each other with tales of our lonely lives.'

1. Thomas the Tank Top could be the voice of the valleys, Tom Jones. Not sure if it still happens but, at the height of his career, it wasn't unusual for him to dodge underwear thrown by some female members of the audience. Tank top jumpers were a dodgy, sleeveless fashion accessory, prevalent for a while in the 1970s. As an indicator of how cool I was; I had one that was knitted by my mum!!
2. A track from Bruce Springsteen's 1984 *Born in the USA* album, *Glory Days* spoke of the tendency for men of advancing years to reminisce about and exaggerate past glories.
3. A few people have lived in *This Ole House*, but the best known are Rosemary Clooney in 1954 and, who could forget, Shakin' Stevens in 1981.

Wow, thought Vanessa, as she drove into the grounds of the venue for her interview. Flanked by immaculate lawns and newly planted saplings, the gravel road concluded with an ornate fountain, behind which stood an impressive Tudor edifice.

Feeling small, she parked her modest yellow Mini alongside a brazenly beautiful Mercedes Convertible, smoothed down her best black trouser-suit and approached the front door. Once inside she looked around the lavish reception area and wondered if she should have used the tradesmen's entrance. Despite her almost overwhelming inferiority complex she attempted to sound confident as she announced her arrival.

'Good morning, my name is Vanessa Jones and I have an appointment with Ms Stephenson.'

The very picture of organised efficiency, the middle-aged receptionist swung round on her chair and looked Vanessa up and down. Vanessa got the impression that not many applicants would actually reach the interview stage without this lady's approval.

'Welcome, Ms Jones; if you'd care to sign in and take a seat over there, I'll let Ms Stephenson know you are here.'

Apparently she'd overcome the first hurdle. Vanessa tried to focus on the forthcoming interrogation and to make herself comfortable on the plush, generously upholstered red sofa; only for the cushions to sink beneath her as if it were attempting to swallow her whole. She admired the tasteful décor and the picture of the ex-Mayoress, resplendent in her chains of office as she cut the ribbon that had declared the home open ten years ago. Vanessa considered the possible history of the house prior to refurbishment for its current use. Who had lived here and how many servants had waited upon their every whim? What secrets could these walls tell?

Surprised that she'd even survived the selection for interview process, Vanessa pondered how she could explain the abrupt termination of her previous employment. She decided that honesty was the best policy; or at least a selective, abridged version of honesty. After all, she thought, we all have some secrets that even our closest family and best friends are not privy to.

Alone with her rambling thoughts, she jumped as a self-assured lady offered her hand. By this time she'd sunk so far into the sofa's softness that she feared she would need a crane to extract her, but she managed to stand without too much loss of dignity.

'Ah, Ms Jones, forgive me for keeping you waiting; please come through to my office. Can I get you any refreshments; tea, coffee?'

'Could I have a glass of water please,' squeaked Vanessa. 'I thank you for the opportunity to apply for this position. I'm sure you have many well qualified candidates.'

'Oh, yes; there have been dozens of applicants to sift through,' Ms Stephenson sighed, as she handed Vanessa a plastic beaker of water from the dispenser outside her office, 'all with qualifications coming out of their ears. No, to tell you the truth I'm not spoilt for choice. The money's pretty crap; then there's the unsociable hours and, let's face it, who wants to clear up somebody else's shit?'

Vanessa assumed this was a rhetorical question and said

nothing.

'On the plus side,' continued Ms Stephenson, 'it's a nice place to work and most of the residents are pleasant enough. That's not the job description that they put in the advert, but it's an honest assessment of what's involved. From that I deduce that anyone who wants to work here is either dedicated or desperate. Now, tell me, which of those categories do you fit in to?'

Vanessa sat in the chair indicated by Ms Stephenson's outstretched arm and her disarmingly candid interviewer occupied the seat behind her desk and looked Vanessa in the eye. She was a little thrown by this unorthodox interview technique and was unsure of how to pitch her response.

'I am looking for a change in career and want a job that's rewarding and enables me to help others.'

'And do you have any experience in looking after the elderly?'

'A little, yes. I have recently contributed to the care of a close relative who was terminally ill.'

'I'm sorry to hear that; it is hard enough to remain detached once you get to know the people here, but it must be doubly difficult with someone that you care about.'

'Yes, it was hard,' said Vanessa, taking a sip of water; she didn't want to elaborate.

'I understand from your application that you were previously a teacher. This is a step or two down career wise, isn't it?'

'I don't see it that way. It is merely a question of assisting people in the latter stages of their life, rather than in their formative years.'

Next, came the inevitable question that Vanessa had been waiting for; the one that she felt could potentially scupper her chances.

'So, why did you leave your previous job?'

'I had become somewhat disillusioned with the way the profession was going and, at the same time, had a few issues in my personal life. We parted company by mutual consent.'

'And these personal issues; are they resolved or will they affect your work here?'

'I am in a better place, but I would rather have a job that I can leave at the door. Teaching doesn't allow you to do that. I am a hard-working and conscientious person and will do a good job, but I'd rather not take it home with me.'

Ms Stephenson flicked through the papers before her; the

109

prepared questions, Vanessa's application and CV, and the job description. She tapped her pen on the table and stroked her chin in thought; keeping Vanessa in suspense and milking the moment. Vanessa wondered if she had been too frank in her answers, but her interrogator had set the tone in that respect. Eventually Ms Stephenson looked up and smiled.

'Very well, Vanessa; I am inclined to offer you the position on a trial basis and subject to references. How about we start with one month's probation and, if everything is satisfactory, we'll look at making it permanent? When would you be able to start?'

Vanessa breathed a sigh of relief that she hoped wasn't too obvious. Confidence wasn't something that she had in abundance and her expectations upon leaving home that morning had been low. She couldn't believe that she'd successfully negotiated her first interview for many years. With a smile and surge of self-belief she held out her hand.

'Thank you Ms Stephenson, I can start as soon as you wish.'

'Please, call me Wilma. We'll make it three weeks Monday then; give us time to process the paperwork and to let HR do their bit. I'm very much looking forward to working with you.'

A large, impressively bearded man surrounded by an impenetrable aura, Richie Stevens sat cross-legged with eyes closed in the centre of the studio floor. Dressed in a simple white t-shirt with black knee-length shorts and multi-colour striped espadrilles, he looked the picture of relaxation, his long grey hair cascading over his shoulders. Consisting of an elaborate mixing-board, a compact recording space and two small isolation booths, there wasn't a great deal of room in this state of the art studio and it seemed that everyone was there for this historical event. Nobody spoke, either out of deference or for fear of disturbing the guru's meditation.

Richie rarely ventured outside of the U.S.A., so it was some scoop to get him to produce part of the album; apparently he'd been a fan since acquiring the Brothel Creepers' first album many years ago from a New York back-street record store. Known for his sparse, pared-back production, he'd guided an eclectic array of artists to achieve their best work and was a perfect fit for the sound the band were looking for.

Eventually he sensed their presence, opened his eyes and stood in one graceful movement. His eyes slowly surveyed the room as if in appraisal of each occupant, before focusing on Bill. He stepped forward, took Bill's hand in a firm shake and broke into a genial smile.

'Hey, man; it's a pleasure to meet you. It's Bill, isn't it? Bass guitar, I think. Now, don't tell me; all of you guys have aged a little since that record sleeve. This is Tom, right? Lead vocals and rhythm. And you must be Clive; a great guitarist, man. What about Stan, though? Don't see him around.'

'No, Stan, God rest his soul, is no longer with us,' said Bill.

'Hey, that's a shame. He was an exceptional drummer; bit of a head-case from what I've heard, but every band should have at least one of those.'

'Yeah, things are a bit quieter these days,' said Tom. 'Allow me to introduce Ray, Stan's replacement.'

'That's cool; I like a man with a beard,' beamed Richie, as he clapped Ray on the arm. 'Now, that's the important people dealt with; who the hell are all these hangers-on?'

He swept his arm in the general direction of Gabriel and Victor, along with Jeff, who had also brought a small entourage from the record company. Gabriel looked particularly put-out by being described as a hanger-on and stepped forward to introduce himself.

'Gabriel Cherubim, at your service. I am the band's manager and this is my partner, Victor.'

'Gabriel Cherubim, huh; is that for real? What about all these guys over here?'

'Well, you know Jeff from the record company of course,' said Gabriel; 'he's just brought a few of his associates.'

Richie nodded sagely, as if he'd seen it all before - 'Look, I'm sure all of you guys serve a useful purpose, but I'm here to work with the band and I don't like a busy studio. Too many distractions detract from the music and that's what we're all her for, right? I have some rules, whoever I'm working with - no managers, record company execs, girlfriends, boyfriends, mothers, fathers, groupies, pets or children, unless they happen to be singing on the record. What say you give us some space, guys?'

'Absolutely,' conceded Gabriel, 'we're only here to ensure that everything's in place. We'll leave you to it then. Good luck fellas and call me if you need anything.'

And with that the studio emptied of all but Richie, the band and the engineer. Gabriel glared as he exited, whilst Victor attempted to smooth the waters of his indignation - 'Have you ever heard such rudeness?' Gabriel was heard to say, as the door slammed behind him.

'Hey, that's better,' said Richie, as he cracked open a can of beer and held it up. 'Cheers; here's to a successful relationship. Help yourselves to a libation or two. Now, how about you guys play me some of your new materiel?'

In the scheme of things it was a pretty seamless move. Vanessa had given her old landlord the required notice and she found herself in a strange town; a fresh beginning, nearer to her new job. Alone in her new flat, a modest and basic dwelling above a row of shops and takeaways, Vanessa took another sip of white wine and opened the box of memorabilia once again. She doubted if there was another archive in existence so lovingly and comprehensively assembled, on the subject matter of Skinny Ted and the Brothel Creepers. Everything was there; from vinyl to CDs; from music paper interviews to features; and from gig, single and album reviews to t-shirts; along with detailed journals that mapped their short, but tempestuous journey. (1)

In an attempt to get inside the head of the band, she sat back in her armchair and perused a music paper interview from the latter stages of their first incarnation. If judged by the politically-correct values of today, some of the comments were pretty distasteful and unsavoury; but most of these were attributed to the drummer, Stan, whose reputation for putting his foot in it was legendary. The answers given by the rest of the band were positively intellectual by comparison and Bill seemed particularly articulate when the subject matter veered towards their musical inspirations. He was often asked about the contradiction of his left-leaning lyrics and their traditional teddy-boy accompaniment, but Bill answered that they were simply reclaiming rockabilly from the rednecks.

It was a feature of the era that a lot of music was politicised, to the extent that bands were invariably probed about their opinions on any number of the hot topics of the day. Evidently Bill and Tom had required little encouragement to share their worldview.

On the Falklands war: "It's just a publicity stunt for Thatcher – her popularity is on the wane and there's nothing like a war to get the masses to rally round the flag."

On fox hunting: "I'd rather have a fox in my garden than a bunch of Tories on horseback - they're the real vermin."

On apartheid: "An abomination – how can it still exist in this day and age?"

Clive had been a little more circumspect: "I'm just a guitarist; who gives a shit what I think?"

Another rummage in the box revealed its most valuable artefact. Vanessa carefully removed the eponymous debut album from its sleeve and placed it on her newly acquired record deck. The Brothel Creepers had straddled the period of transition from vinyl to CD, but somehow the traditional format held more romance, and some argued that it sounded better. The speakers amplified every scratch and crackle as the opening bass-line was joined by an incendiary rattle of drums and a searing guitar. (2)

That inaugural track heralded their appearance on the scene to dramatic effect, a statement of intent that would be difficult to follow. But follow it they did, with each song as urgent and brazen as the last. Made before the politics and pain had too much of a stranglehold, the subject matter explored the domain of your average young man, whilst the sound empathised, with short, sharp and hurried ejaculations of noise.

Vanessa held the empty sleeve and studied its design, a picture of four sullen youths, with hints of a rugged handsomeness breaking out of a troubled adolescence. The name emblazoned across the top in blood-red ink indicated, wrongly, that the contents would lack subtlety and finesse – what a treat lay inside for those who ventured further. She flipped over the twelve-inch-square cardboard relic of a bygone era and read the track-listing once more.

Side 1
Spread the Word
Grain of Sand
Beat Up Buick
Candy's Gone
Love's Young Dream
You Got a Stranglehold On Me

Side 2

Scandal
You Scratch My Itch
Red Mist
A Song For Peggy
I'll Be Your Action Man
Slave Wages

An occasional sweet sentiment peeped through the juvenile macho posturing, and the relentless beat paused for breath now and again to make way for the odd romantic undertone, but the overall impression was one of urgency and vigour.

Vanessa's foot tapped involuntarily as she poured another glass of wine. The yellow mini-skirt hung on the airer by her side, awaiting the warmth of the iron, and the Dr Martens boots stood proud and polished on the rack by the front door. The next time she intended to wear her favourite outfit would be this coming weekend at Bunter's, by which time the band would have been entrenched in the studio for nearly a week, recording their latest masterpiece. Vanessa was excited about a potential album of fresh materiel and, from what she'd heard live, the new songs were well up to scratch.

Blaze On at Bunter's would be her last weekend of freedom, before the start of her new job. Twelve hour shifts had been agreed, three days on, two days off. It would feel strange at first, to be employed in what were essentially other people's homes; a stark contrast to the hustle and bustle battleground of her previous labours. She would miss the companionship of her ex-colleagues and the backs-against-the-wall togetherness engendered by the daily onslaught. A lonelier path lay ahead; a less predictable future and she wondered again if she'd been a little hasty in burning her bridges.

It was a time of transformation for Vanessa; a time of reflection, a time to take stock and a time to plan. Everything had changed in the last year; all that she once held true turned upside-down, all that had seemed so real denied, all that once mattered rendered trivial by cataclysmic revelations.

She turned up the volume and the music resonated and reverberated as she ran her finger over Bill's face on the record sleeve.

1. One of my favourite Jam songs, *Strange Town* was released in 1979 amidst a run of incendiary Paul Weller penned singles. The lyric deals with the loneliness of London, but can equally be applied to any move to a town full of strangers. Reportedly, Weller rates it as one of the best songs he has written.
2. Skinny Ted and the Brothel Creepers would have been around at the dawn of the CD, the first commercial ones produced in 1982. They were hailed as a digital revolution and the end of the old scratched record format. To this day though, I can listen to an old song on the radio and expect to hear that scratch in exactly the same place as on my old 45s. There has been a decline in CD sales in recent years, due to the emergence of digital downloads and the resurgence of vinyl.

Bill and Tom were less than enamoured with their accommodation. They'd registered their arrival, hauled their bags and stage gear from the car park and perused row upon row of uniform huts, before stumbling upon their billet in Block C.

'Jesus, these have to be the original chalets, modelled on Stalag 13', complained Bill, 'and those beds must have seen a few holidaymakers. Not exactly the height of luxury, is it?'

'Yeah, it's pretty basic,' agreed Tom, as he plonked his bag on the bed; 'it's a good job we're only here for a few nights. What room do you want; the double or the twin?'

'You can have the double,' said Bill, 'you've got more chance of pulling than me.'

'I'll have you know I'm a happily married man,' protested Tom. 'Besides, from what I've seen so far the place is full of blokes.'

The white walled square room contained a double bed, a rickety wardrobe and a chest of drawers. Apart from a small TV that occupied the other corner, that was essentially it. Through a dented door they entered the twin room; two tiny single beds with metal legs crammed into a space intended for children. An even smaller wardrobe and a bedside cabinet that barely separated the sleeping arrangements were the only other accoutrements, not even a picture or two to deflect from the depressing banality. Bill looked in despair at the place where he would be expected to slumber. Another door led to a rudimentary bathroom; no shower, just a bath, sink and toilet.

'God, what a desperate place,' said Bill, 'and every time you need a piss in the middle of the night you'll have to stagger through my room and wake me up.'

A knock on the door sent them back outside.

'Is your place as bad as ours?' asked Clive. Ray stood behind him, looking even more dejected than usual.

'I'm assuming they're all the same,' said Tom, as he glared at Gabriel, who appeared a little sheepish. 'Is this the best you could do?'

'We have to do this on a budget,' reasoned Gabriel, 'the band is running at a loss at the moment. Once you've made it again, then you can stay in the Ritz; in the meantime this will have to do. For God's sake cheer up; we're in a holiday camp by the seaside. It'll be like going back to our childhood.'

Bill was unconvinced - 'And where are you and Victor staying?'

'Our chalet is just around the corner. We won't be far away should you need us.'

A huge seagull landed on the strip of threadbare grass that separated the rows of huts and appraised this improbable mob for any chance of food. It walked towards them with all the swagger of a Cockney nightclub bouncer, its thick neck moving back and forth as if to say – 'come and have a go if you think you're hard enough.' They'd only been there for half-an-hour, but Bill had already noticed that the gulls were enormous. He wondered if, in bird-world, there was a researcher reporting on an obesity crisis in Pithead, owing to their preference for discarded junk-food. Eventually the funny tern waddled away to try its luck with another group of nascent holidaymakers.

They decided to freshen up, as best they could within the limitations of the facilities, then head for the Horizon where the headline bands would be playing. It was Friday afternoon and the Brothel Creepers weren't due on until Sunday, so there would be plenty of time to savour the entertainment. Besides, Gabriel was right, they were in a holiday camp by the seaside; it wouldn't hurt to rough it for a bit.

The guitarist and drummer emerged first, due to the fact that Clive had no hair to wash (he didn't so much wash and go, as buff and bugger off), and that Ray spent somewhat less time on his look than the more image-conscious bassist and singer. Tom was waxing his quiff when they rapped on the door and Bill was deciding which shirt to wear.

116

'Where do you two think you're going, then?' enquired Ray, as Tom allowed them access. 'I didn't know it was fancy dress.'

'Nothing wrong with taking a bit of pride in your appearance,' said Tom. 'I'm thinking of setting up as a fashion advisor to the over-fifties. Just because you get old it doesn't mean you have to dress like your dad.'

'Are you implying that I have no dress-sense?' asked Ray.

'Not in so many words, but let's just say that I'm glad you can hide behind that drum-kit.'

'At least I don't throw a hissy-fit every time we play somewhere without a mirror in the dressing-room.'

Ray ducked as Tom's hairbrush flew towards him.

The Horizon was a cavernous marquee-like structure, with the stage at one end and the bars, merchandise and amusements at the back. It was already filling up fast when our heroes sauntered in, waiting for someone to recognise them and ask for autographs. A few heads turned and clocked Bill and Tom's atypical attire, then promptly resumed the business in hand – supping ale and tapping their feet to the agreeable jangle of the Railway Set. Clive and Ray were able to blend in with the predominantly nondescript mass; only the odd paint-splattered floppy hat to punctuate the uniformity of jeans and baggy t-shirts. (1 – 2)

Bill nudged Tom and Clive and raised an imaginary glass to his lips. They both nodded in agreement and followed Bill towards one of the many makeshift bars, as Ray slunk along behind. It was every man or woman for themselves, as Bill buffeted against the thirsty throng in a determined effort to reach the front.

'Three pints of Butcombe Gold and a Diet Coke please,' shouted Bill, struggling to make himself heard over an impressive cacophony of guitars. 'At last,' he sighed. He must have been stood there for at least fifteen minutes while the beleaguered bar staff struggled to cope with the hordes. Each time he thought he was about to be served, he'd been overlooked in favour of a guy who'd just joined the pack. He was beginning to think he was invisible before an amenable Scotsman had uttered the words he'd been waiting to hear – 'Hey, my good man; this gentlemen was first.'

Bill expressed his thanks with a smile and a nod. Once served he parted with his cash and turned in search of his parched companions who were, of course, well out of earshot and reach. With a curse he carried two overflowing pints to Clive and Tom, before thanking them for their help and fighting his way back through the crowd to retrieve his beer and Ray's Coke. At least it wasn't his round next.

The Sportsbar at the back was showing the England v Scotland World Cup Qualifier match, but recent yawn-inducing performances by their national team had decided their priorities. Besides, they were here for the music and wanted to catch the House of Lust, whose wonderful songs deserved a larger and more appreciative audience. The party atmosphere ignited with the appearance of The Marvel Stuff and the hall filled with revellers and ravers, who danced ecstatically to the harlequin-skirted fiddler's tune. (3 - 4)

Bill surveyed the dancing, smiling crowd and wondered again at the power of music, its capacity to bring people together, to inspire and to move. He'd witnessed it many times and still felt the vibe; it was the very reason that he kept coming back for more, the reason he'd not grown old gracefully, if ever that were possible. Whether the general bonhomie was fuelled by good nature, alcohol or something stronger, Bill didn't know, but an atmosphere of peace and tolerance prevailed. The bulky security staff dotted around the hall looked like they'd worked-out how to handle themselves but, apart from one stoned punter who needed help standing up, their expertise wasn't required.

Everything ran like clockwork, the bands forced to stick religiously to their allotted time-slots, and the main-stage entertainment was terminated at 10 p.m. as scheduled. For those with staying-power, satellite bars and clubs provided further entertainment, but the Brothel Creepers' hell-raising days were long since passed and they decided to call it a night in order to pace themselves for the rest of the weekend.

Back at their billet Bill and Tom caught up with the football highlights and prepared for bed. The aim was to get some sleep before the piss and pot-heads returned shouting and hollering in the early hours. While Bill used the bathroom, Tom idly flicked through some sketches that he'd found on Bill's bed.

'Hey, what are these?' he asked on Bill's return.

'It's an idea for a card game that I've invented; it's called Bottom Trumps.'

'Bottom Trumps?'

'Yeah, it's like Top Trumps, but in my version the player with the lowest human standards wins the game. You get points for xenophobia, intolerance, sexism etc. In fact the more obnoxious you are the greater the chance you have to win. I'm thinking it could catch on in America.'

'Sadly, you could be right,' said Tom. 'Goodnight.'

1. The Railway Set - to start their weekend our heroes would have done a bit of trainspotting, as first, the Train Set took to the stage, followed by the Railway Children (see what I did there?). Formed in the 80s, the Train Set are an Indie band from Crewe who have toured with the Happy Mondays and James. Now back together, they are gigging and writing new material.
2. An agreeably jangly Alternative Rock foursome from Wigan, the Railway Children's biggest hit was *Every Beat of the Heart* in 1990. They have supported R.E.M. and the Sugarcubes and the original line-up reformed in 2016.
3. Perhaps the House of Lust could be a racier version of the House of Love. Their first two albums were both eponymous; the one with the butterfly on the cover is outstanding and contains their best known single, *Shine On*.
4. Another reference to the wonderful Wonder Stuff. The harlequin skirted fiddler is Erica Nockalls, a brilliant violinist who has also played with the Proclaimers.

The place is full of blokes, Vanessa thought as she toured the site at Bunter's in an attempt to get her bearings. She found the shop, a perfunctory Spar that had everything necessary to survive a weekend away from home. A magazine would help to while away the hours when there was no-one performing; and that jumbo packet of Wotsits looked tempting – ah, look; buy one, get one half-price. A conversation between the two older guys in the queue before her broached the subject of dental hygiene.

'I can't resist the smell of bacon, but you spend the rest of the day trying to get it out of your teeth. You didn't bring any dental-floss with you by any chance, did you?'

'Wasn't top of my list; it's as much as I can do to remember to bring a change of underpants.'

Vanessa decided to grab a coffee, attune herself to the ambience and flick through her magazine. She alternated between people watching and an article about the benefits of grape-seed polyphenols; apparently they are powerful antioxidants that fight free radicals, slow premature ageing and boost the skin's natural regeneration process. Although she had no argument with free radicals, she was all for slowing premature ageing. Wiping away her cappuccino moustache with a serviette, she listened to the eager anticipation of the dialogue around her, each group of friends looking forward to different elements of the entertainment to follow.

As she entered the Horizon, she had to admit that she felt a little vulnerable; a lone woman among a swarm of sweaty geezers but, at the same time, there was an atmosphere of affability that made her solitude more comfortable. It wasn't as if she was the only lady; some of the lads had obviously brought their wives or girlfriends and there were even a few families with teenage kids, but the male/female ratio had to be about ten to one. She clocked a hen-party that, in the absence of Teutonic towels, had commandeered a large proportion of the stripy deckchairs at the back of the hall; placed there to conjure a seaside vibe but also pretty handy if you could barely stand – and it was only three-o'clock in the afternoon. Someone was going to miss the headline acts, but no-one seemed to care.

Vanessa had dressed simply in order to blend in to the background; an unassuming dark-blue t-shirt, black jeans turned up at the bottom, black trainers and a faded denim jacket, but still she attracted admiring glances from many of the groups of men who passed her way. She couldn't make out what they were saying to each other, but the not too subtle nudges followed by uproarious laughter indicated the gist.

'Cor, I'd give her one.'

'You should be so lucky.'

Thankfully their attention was diverted when the bands began to play and Vanessa could enjoy the music unhindered. And the quality was generally very good; musicians who had been around long enough to master their instruments, but not so long that they'd lost their enthusiasm and passion.

The crowds at the bars were about eight-deep, but she was getting thirsty and could put it off no longer. It took her a while to get to the front, but one advantage of being a relatively small lady is that courteous men often allow you to go first. Then she saw him and recoiled in shock. Barely a few punters along, Bill was clearly increasingly frustrated at his failure to be served. The Brothel Creepers weren't on the bill until Sunday and Vanessa was surprised to see him here already. They'd obviously decided to make a weekend of it and enjoy the rest of the programme, as had *she.*

She raised her hand to the side of her face to conceal her identity, but needn't have worried; Bill was far too preoccupied with getting the attention of the bar staff. Finally, the amenable Scotsman next to her had helped him out with the words - 'Hey, my good man; this gentlemen was first.'

Bill looked left to acknowledge his intervention and Vanessa tried to turn her back and sink into the ground simultaneously. If she'd had on the yellow mini-skirt outfit then she may have been seen, but Bill was more concerned with his hard-earned pint than with those around him. Vanessa watched to see where the Brothel Creepers were standing and removed herself to a safe distance. That was close and she'd have to be on the lookout for the remainder of the weekend.

Vanessa watched with one eye on the stage and the other on Bill then slipped away before the culmination of events. Back at her chalet she prepared for bed and lay there with tears in her eyes; this was the closest she'd been to Bill Harris, the closest she'd been to the man she wanted so much to be close to.

Although Bill, Tom and Clive had all promised themselves that they'd go for the healthy continental option, a full-English is always hard to turn down when on offer and the waft of fried pig in various guises proved too much to resist. Only Ray tucked in without guilt and he was determined to take full advantage of the all-inclusive eat-as-much-as-you-like buffet.

'Just what we need to start the day,' said Tom, 'an overdose of cholesterol.'

'It's not as if we do it every day,' reasoned Bill. 'How about we take a stroll into town after breakfast; get some sea air and walk off some of these calories. Besides, I've hardly slept in that crappy bed and could do with waking up.'

Tom took a look out of the window to see grey skies and a fine drizzle, with just a hint of blue on the horizon - 'Could be a bit damp out there.'

'Got nothing else to do though,' said Clive, 'I'm up for it if you are.'

'Yeah, me too,' said Ray, 'blow the cobwebs out.'

As they emerged into the open air Bill held them all back with an outstretched arm - 'Wait, isn't that Gabriel and Victor over there?'

'Yeah, that's them alright,' said Tom, 'just coming out of the Yacht Club restaurant. Bet they've gone upmarket and had the smoked salmon and poached egg.'

'Let's follow them,' suggested Bill, 'be interesting to see where they're staying.'

At a discreet distance they trailed their manager and his companion, past two storey blocks that appeared more attractive than their own accommodation. Tom took a peek through the window of one and commented that it was decidedly posh in comparison to their place. They followed through the holiday camp's equivalent of leafy suburbs until Gabriel and Victor turned into their apartment; by Bunter's standards an exclusive residence with patio and private parking. They waited a few minutes then rapped upon the door. Gabriel answered, with an uncomfortable smile.

'Ah, good morning gentlemen; I trust you had a good evening and a hearty breakfast.'

Bill entered without being invited and was greeted by the sight of a shocked Victor in what appeared to be a silver silk thong. Victor screamed and retreated to the bedroom. The others joined Bill in the living room as Gabriel stood aside and said with undisguised acerbity - 'Please, come in.'

'Well, this is all very cosy,' observed Bill, as he took in the expansive room with comfortable sofa, armchair and table, 'I thought we had to do this on a budget; I don't see you two slumming it for the sake of austerity.'

'It's for your own good,' proclaimed Gabriel, 'it'll keep you sharp and edgy. Bands get bloated and lose their creativity when they get too comfy.'

'Yeah, I tend to be sharp and edgy when I've had no sleep,' said Bill, as he made himself at home on the sofa. 'All we want is a decent bed and a bloody shower. We know we're not superstars and we're not asking for our every whim to be tended to by beautiful maidens...'

'Though that'd be nice,' interjected Tom.

'...but some basic amenities would be good,' continued Bill.

'You should check out the Boss's autobiography,' suggested Gabriel, looking decidedly indignant as Ray too sat down. 'Read about some of the places he had to sleep when he was trying to make it.' (1)

'I have read it,' Bill retorted, 'and that all happened when he was a young man. We stayed in some dives the first time around too, even slept in the van a few times, but we're a bit long in the tooth for all that now, in case you hadn't noticed. I'm far too old to sleep under the boardwalk, especially in November. Besides, I don't even know if they have a boardwalk in Pithead.'

'I'll sleep under the boardwalk,' said Ray, 'probably be more comfortable than that chalet.' (2)

'Look, Victor and I have paid for the excess cost of this accommodation out of our own pockets. You are welcome to check the band accounts anytime you wish and I resent the fact that you are suggesting that we're somehow pulling a fast one.'

'Well it wouldn't be the first time,' said Tom, as he straightened the mirror and stood back to admire his reflection. 'History is littered with bands that have been ripped-off by their managers.'

'Well, not any more,' said Gabriel, 'this is a reputable profession and we're all above board.'

'It wasn't that long ago that the music-biz had links to organised crime,' continued Tom. 'Who was our first manager - the guy with the double-barrelled surname?'

'Yeah, I remember,' said Bill, 'Freddie Shotgun, wasn't it? He used to live the high-life too, while we scrabbled around in the gutter. Owned a vintage Mercedes, until the thing spontaneously combusted one night; he was giving me a lift home after a gig and it went WOOF, smoke everywhere.'

'I thought it was Rovers that went WOOF, not Mercedes,' said Tom.

Everyone looked at Tom and groaned.

'Very well,' conceded Gabriel with a sigh, as the tumbleweed rolled across the room in homage to Tom's pun, 'I will go to reception and ask if they have any upgrades available. Don't get your hopes too high though, as I think the place is pretty full.'

'Thank you,' said Bill, as he hauled himself to his feet, 'that's all we ask. We're going for a walk into town; we'll catch up on our return.'

Ray made a point of fluffing-up the cushions before they left. 'There, good as new,' he smiled, 'sorry to intrude.'

1. Otherwise known as the Boss, Bruce Springsteen's honest and compelling autobiography, *Born to Run*, tells of the hard work and

hard life of his formative years in rock'n'roll, as he and his bandmates gigged around the bars and clubs of New Jersey.

2. *Under the Boardwalk* is where Bruce may have slept and it's also the title of the Drifters' 1964 classic. You can almost feel the sun beating down and hear the waves crashing on the shore, as the lovers lay out their blanket and hit the shade, under the boardwalk, down by the sea...

An all-encompassing sea mist invaded Vanessa's eyes and nostrils as she stared across the bay from beneath her hood. A few dog-walkers and shell-seekers had braved the beach but, apart from these brave souls, the shore and promenade were deserted. It was too early or too grey for the majority of Bunter's clientele and the few that she passed appeared hungover and bleary-eyed.

She took a deep breath of salty air and resumed her walk; part of her daily constitutional she told herself but, in reality, a chance to clear her head of all but untainted thoughts. The golden sand was pristine, apart from a set of footprints accompanied by the tracks of frantic paws that disappeared beneath the surf and back again. Vanessa liked it here by the seaside, regardless of the weather. The sounds of crashing waves and plaintive seagulls had the power to cleanse the soul and to instil a sense of possibility; the possibility that things could change. A walk by the sea was better than any medication.

A window-seat at the Flotsam and Jetsam Café looked inviting and she ordered a coffee, accompanied by a pecan and maple syrup Danish. The hot coffee slipped down so well that she asked for a top-up and settled back to enjoy the view. The misty outline of a distant ship clung to the horizon, in danger of falling off the edge of the world; and a buoy bobbed in the bay, a warning to whoever was foolish enough to be out on the waves on a day like this.

Vanessa turned to appraise the few other customers; a smartly dressed older gentleman, engrossed in his newspaper; a young couple enjoying the simple delights of a fry-up and gazing into each other's eyes over a forkful of sausage; and, in the corner, a timeworn lady with eyes like coal, whose bags overflowed with all her earthly possessions. Vanessa sighed and sensed the heaviness of her eyelids; she'd had another bad night and sleep had eluded her once more. Only the caffeine kept her awake and she felt like driftwood, floating on a tide she couldn't control.

It was warm in here, despite the paucity of patrons. This modest café had a homely feel, as if the owners cared about the creation of a comfortable environment for lonely travellers like her, far from home and familiarity. She closed her eyes, took deep breaths and tried to relax; until a commotion outside disturbed her thoughts. Four men of middle years were arguing vociferously about something or other, apparently a matter of great importance; though Vanessa couldn't catch what.

It took a moment for her to recognise the quarrelsome quartet and she ducked back behind the window-frame, before anyone could look in. For a second she thought they might enter, but instead they continued their walk without a glance, gesticulating to emphasise their points of view as they went. Vanessa watched as they wended their way along the prom, until they reached their predictable destination; a distant inn across the harbour.

Safe in the assumption that they'd probably be in the pub for a while, Vanessa leisurely finished her coffee and settled the bill, as well as anonymously paying for the breakfast of the lady in the corner. She took a short stroll into town to kill some time and check out the retail-therapy options but, apart from the odd tattoo parlour and a shop specialising in mod gear and memorabilia, there was little to catch her attention. Eventually, she made her way back to Bunter's, where the security guard on the gate glanced at her wrist-band, leered and nodded to allow her access. Rays of sunlight punctured the clouds and a hint of optimism permeated her mood. Early afternoon and the entertainment would soon be underway.

There were a couple of pseudo pubs on camp, where up-and-coming bands of varying talent had the opportunity to ply their trade. It was good to see that the mini-gigs at the Tavern on the Green were heaving, loud and bouncing. Tribute acts paid tribute to their heroes; copycat cameos that complimented the crème-de-la-crème of Indie that filled the Horizon.

The Moon and Sun hosted a self-proclaimed raconteur whose claims to fame were that he once managed a couple of well-known bands and had shagged a very famous person (allegedly), whilst high on cocaine. His expletive-ridden rant was punctuated by the odd amusing anecdote and the punters, male and female alike, hung on his every word. Vanessa's hackles rose at his macho posturing and glorification of the drug-culture prevalent in his youth. How many lives had been wasted by being wasted? But then she wondered if some of this unique music could have been created without artificial stimuli. Drugs were certainly a major part of the equation; but she'd also seen what they'd done to some of her ex-pupils and it broke her heart. There was rarely a happy ending. (1)

Rock stars can afford the best high, the finest cut, the rehab. They venerate the mind-bending creative qualities of their drug of choice, but choose not to see the misery of the masses they influence; desperate for their next fix, dependent upon unscrupulous dealers who take their last penny without a thought and leave them to beg in frozen doorways. Of all the contemptible scum on this Earth, she despised the pushers the most; their ill-gotten profits gleaned from others' despair.

With a sigh, Vanessa finished her drink and removed herself from this poisonous place. She would spend the rest of the afternoon in her chalet, in relaxation and preparation for the evening ahead.

1.   OK, I'm not going to name this geezer, but he certainly relates a good story and has a few to tell. During his slot at Bunter's he regaled us with tales of his time as manager of a couple of the top bands of the era, during which he (allegedly) had a sexual encounter with someone famous. He had no qualms about naming the lady in question, but I will not repeat it here. His casual glorification of the drugs culture prevalent at the time would not have impressed Vanessa.

Bill had to admit that it was an improvement. Warm in the afterglow of a couple of lunchtime pints, he and Tom surveyed their new accommodation and agreed that they would be more comfortable here. Gabriel had arranged two upgrades, at surprisingly little extra cost and effort, and the band were sorted for the remaining two nights of their stay. Their rooms were separated by a short hallway that housed a relatively spacious bathroom containing the sought-after shower; and the beds at least had a hint of bounce in them. There were even pictures on the wall, albeit bland and uninspiring.

Bill laid back and considered the turmoil of his life of the past few years. He achingly missed his kids and the comfort of his old home; the family he'd helped to build and the house they'd struggled to attain; the constant background clamour of his offspring, as they fought for noisy dominance of their domain. It was all for them, all they'd scrimped and saved for and sacrificed; and he didn't begrudge them any of it. He just wished that he was still there to share it.

Regardless of proximity, parents inevitably lose that precious connection with their kids as they grow more independent but, banished from the security of the family home, Bill felt even more out of contact. Each access weekend accumulated to make him more of a stranger, the bonds forged by familiarity loosened by absence. On the flipside, he'd somehow become cooler. No longer responsible for routines such as homework and bedtime, he could remain detached; there for support when required, but relieved of the unpopular duty of day-to-day discipline.

Bill wistfully recalled the ritual when Nathan left for school each morning.

'Alligator,' Bill would say.

'Crocodile,' was Nathan's habitual response. (1)

He tossed and turned to lessen the discomfort of his thoughts and sensed a spring in the small of his back that threatened to pierce the fabric of the mattress. His mind drifted back to a conversation he'd once had with Rosie.

'Dad, I need a new mattress.'

'What's wrong with the one you have?'

'Well, it said on the telly that you're supposed to change it every eight years. I'm sure mine's older than that.'

'It's an advert by mattress manufacturers,' Bill had patiently explained, 'it's in their interests to sell you a new one every eight years. In fact, our mattress is over twenty years old and still going strong. You and your siblings were conceived on that mattress and, if it can survive your mother's thrashing around, it must have been built to last.'

'Dad, that's far too much information,' Rosie had complained, as she'd turned an embarrassed shade of red and left the room. Bill always knew how to win an argument when it came to spending money unnecessarily.

Jolted from his reminiscences by a knock on the door, he turned to see Tom in the doorway, a towel round his waist, a rogue soapsud on his torso and his quiff flattened by the weight of water.

'Shower's free when you want it,' said Tom, 'shall we head down at about 4'ish?'

'Sounds good; who are you looking forward to seeing tonight?'

'Well I like Boomtummy; not sure about Dubious; a bit

lightweight for me, but we can take a look.'

'They wrote a couple of decent pop tunes, though,' argued Bill.

'Yeah, they were a passing soundtrack to a summer's day.'

'Nothing wrong with that; it's more than most of us can aspire to.' (2 - 3)

'True,' said Tom, 'but I like to think that we helped a few angst-ridden adolescents through Thatcher's summers of discontent; even if they were only ourselves.'

'Yeah, I guess we did our bit. Better have that shower then; it's nearly time to put on our glad-rags and hit the town again.'

'All of my rags are glad,' said Tom, 'they're on me.'

And with that, he retired to his room to make love to the mirror.

1. Originally recorded by Bobby Charles in 1955, the best known version of *See You Later Alligator* was by Bill Haley and His Comets the following year. The catchy chorus consisted of the title, followed by the response – after a while crocodile. Still sounds good!!
2. Boomtummy? Who else but Echobelly. Led by the exuberant and beautiful Sonya Madan, they were one of the best bits of a high-quality weekend. In the interests of research I have just listened to their recent single *Hey Hey Hey* and it's wonderful.
3. The passing soundtrack to a summer's day refers to the 1994 hit by Dodgy – *Staying Out for the Summer*; a song which, quite simply, exudes sunshine.

The evening picked up where last night had left off, the entertainment generally of the highest quality. Boomtummy would prove to be one of the highlights of the weekend, the band's musical exuberance only exceeded by the sheer happy-to-be-here enthusiasm of their impish singer, a breath of fresh air amid a sea of serious geezers.

Punctuated by a rota of occasional trips to the bar, Bill, Tom, Clive and Ray stuck to the same spot. They'd marked out their territory adjacent to the mixing desks; always the location of the clearest sound in the auditorium, Clive had reasoned, due to the fact that the sound-engineers would adjust the mix until it was right for them. It was a little way back, but the obligatory screens either side of the stage allowed them to see all that was happening.

Bill was happily indulged in a spot of dad-dancing, safe in the knowledge that none of his offspring could see him, when a pair of hands covered his eyes and a female voice from behind shouted, 'Surprise.'

Bill turned quickly to see the beaming face of his first-born, Lauren, who stepped back and joined in with the dance, imitating Bill's best moves with comical accuracy. Behind her stood the ever-jovial Jacob; his glasses at a jaunty angle and that now familiar red and green striped jacket, still torn at the shoulder. Bill smiled through his shock and hugged his daughter.

'What the hell are you doing here?'

'Wasn't my idea,' replied Lauren, 'Jacob enjoyed the last show so much, he persuaded me that it would be a good idea to come down and surprise you.'

'Well it's great to see you both,' said Bill, as he shook Jacob vigorously by the hand.

'Hey Dude,' smiled Jacob.

Tom hugged his goddaughter as Bill introduced Jacob to the rest of the band.

'Hey Dude,' said Jacob, in response to each introduction.

Too loud for conversation, the next thirty minutes were spent with the odd shouted word passing for communication, until the latest band on the conveyor-belt finished their set with a wail of feedback and crashing cymbals. Bill, Lauren and Jacob made their way to a bar at the side of the hall to catch up on each other's news.

'So, how did you manage to get away from uni then?' asked Bill.

'It's the weekend, Dad. They do allow us out sometimes.'

'We'll be missing a lecture on Monday morning,' added Jacob, 'but I have a friend who will record it for us and we can catch up. So, how's the weekend been so far?'

'Brilliant,' said Bill, 'the perfect place for a bit of bonding and the music's been excellent. It's good to have a break from recording and tomorrow will be our chance to engage with a new audience. Don't know what they'll make of us though; we're not exactly compatible with the rest of the line-up.'

'Don't worry, Dude' said Jacob, 'you play like you did the other week and you can win over any crowd. Even the sceptical Lauren had to admit that you were pretty good.'

Bill beamed; the approval of his daughter meant a lot - 'So, you thought we were cool after all then?'

'I said you were pretty good; dads aren't meant to be cool.'

'Well, I guess pretty good will have to do for now,' smiled Bill.

'Any sign of our mystery lady?' asked Lauren.

'No, not yet; been trying to forget about her to be honest. Tom says I'm suffering from paranoia and that she's probably just a fan who's taken things a little too far. The police said pretty much the same thing too.'

'You've been to the police?'

'Yeah, but they didn't take it seriously. I've come to terms with her coming to the gigs dressed like a blast from the past, but when she visited your Gran, that kind of spooked me. There's something not quite right about that.'

'We'll keep our eyes peeled,' said Lauren. 'You can't do anything from the stage, but I can have a word if she shows up again.'

'When you say, "have a word", what do you mean exactly? I don't want any trouble.'

'Dad, do I look like a violent person? No, I'll just politely ask her to explain what the hell she thinks she's doing and, whatever it is, suggest that she stops doing it with immediate effect.'

'Perhaps I should put things in context,' said Bill. 'One of the countless things that your mother and I fell out about was a song that I composed many moons ago. *Stood Up, Again* was written for a girl that I met after a gig; long before your mother and I met, I hasten to add. The lady that keeps showing up bears an uncanny resemblance, and dresses identically too. Whoever she is, she must know something about my history.'

'Ah, yes,' said Lauren, 'Mum told me about your unhealthy obsession, *and* I've grown up with the evidence tattooed on your arm, remember.'

'I would argue that it is your mother that's obsessed. It's all in the past as far as I'm concerned.'

'Until she turned up again; there's something quite romantic about it, if it really is her.'

'Look, you've been closer to her than I have. From where I'm standing she looks too young. Do you think it's possible?'

Lauren looked pensive - 'I didn't really take much notice to be honest. I thought she was just another punter until you came down after the show, with that look of panic on your face.'

'Well, there's no point in worrying ourselves about it,' said Bill, 'if she wants to make contact, I'm sure she will, in her own time. Let's just enjoy the weekend.'

The remainder of the evening passed in pleasant revelry, Bill contented in his natural environment, with his bandmates, daughter and Jacob apparently relishing the vibe as much as he. In fact they were having such a good time that they decided to stay up late and continue the party in the Middle Point, a kind of gaudy on-site nightclub where the DJ was definitely on Bill's wavelength.

Practically every song a classic in its own right, the music veered between the Trojan, Stax and Motown labels, with a spattering of early rock'n'roll and the best punk and new wave thrown in for good measure. It was almost as if they'd asked Bill to suggest a soundtrack for the movie of his life and he spent the night with an inane grin on his face, in awe of the sheer brilliance of his musical idols. (1)

He could have listened to this stuff all night, but the DJ eventually gave way to the advertised live acts. The recently reformed and decimalised Thousand Metre Glare set the place aglow, with their energetic set and self-depreciating banter; followed by the amiable Candid and Walters, who entertained with pure pop melodies and Celtic charm. (2 - 3)

Eventually, our contented revellers spilled out into the cool November night, warmed by the glow of the perfect evening and quite a few late night whiskies; with the exception of Ray who, devoid of alcoholic stimuli seemed equally happy with his night's amusement.

As Bill's head hit the pillow, he focused on the positive elements of his existence and reflected upon how privileged he was to have been born in an era that produced so much exceptional music. He wouldn't have wanted to live in any other time.

1. No attempts at witty wordplay here, the Trojan, Motown and Stax labels have hosted some amazing music; a seemingly endless treasure-trove of talent.
2. Thousand Metre Glare - belying the adage that the best thing to come out of Slough is the A4, Thousand Yard Stare are an underrated band that emerged in the early-90s, but never achieved widespread acclaim. In May 2017 they released their first studio recordings for 24 years.
3. An alternative band from Cork in Ireland, the Frank and Walters specialise in a jaunty tune and wistful lyric. I defy anyone not to be charmed by their beguiling songs. Check out *Indie Love Song* for the essence of their sound and dive in from there.

Vanessa watched from a safe distance, unbearably jealous of the close camaraderie and familial bond. She would have loved to join in, but could hardly saunter over and say - 'Hi, let me introduce myself; I'm your past, come back to haunt you.' At least not yet; she simply wasn't ready and didn't know what reaction she would get. Her time would come; that much she knew.

Instead she contented herself with the performers before her; across the weekend a veritable who's who of popular culture for those of a certain age. In truth, she felt little different to the youthful lady who'd seen some of these acts before. Sure, she tired easier these days, and her ability and desire to stay up all night had waned somewhat, but that party animal was still inside. It just barely ventured out these days.

Perhaps she should have walked away when he spoke to her, but she was feeling lonely and cautiously welcomed his friendly smile and the first social interaction she'd had for a while. The final act on the main stage, had finished their set to rapturous applause, but Vanessa wasn't ready for bed. She was about to wander off to check-out the entertainment on offer elsewhere on-site, when a sound in her left ear stopped her short.

'So, what's a nice girl like you doing in a place like this?' asked a voice akin to gravel being poured into a dumper truck; coated in a treacly Californian drawl.

She turned abruptly, her view somewhat hindered by Joey. She knew it was Joey from the badge immediately before her eyes, pinned to an impressively broad chest flanked by bulging biceps; all wrapped-up in a security uniform. A glance up at the six-foot-plus source of this incredibly corny chat-up line revealed a friendly Bohemian face with piercing blue eyes beneath a shock of unruly brown hair. This would-be Adonis wasn't the type that she normally went for, but that didn't stop Vanessa replying - 'And how many times have you used that line?'

'Oh, all the time, Ma'am; doesn't usually get me anywhere. Seriously though; I couldn't help but notice that you are here on your own. Saw you last night too and wondered why a lady would come alone to an event such as this. Tell me to mind my own business if you wish.'

'Mind your own business,' said Vanessa. She kind of meant it too, but her demeanour left the door ajar.

Joey smiled again and raised his hands - 'OK, no more questions. Look, I have a thirty minute break before my next shift.

Can I buy you a drink?'

'Can I buy you a drink; isn't that a question?' reasoned Vanessa. 'Let me buy you *a drink; you're the one working to keep the peace here.'*

'Sounds cool to me,' said Joey, 'it's not often that I get such an offer from a beautiful lady.'

Vanessa looked him up and down - 'I don't believe you. They must be queuing up for the privilege.'

'Will you allow me one more question? May I ask your name?'

'Vanessa.'

'Vanessa,' repeated Joey; 'the name was invented by Jonathan Swift for his poem 'Cadenus and Vanessa' way back in the 1700s, I believe.'

'I didn't know that.'

'Oh, I'm a mine of random facts Ma'am; pick them up in junk-stores and from used-poetry salesmen, whenever I can.'

As they walked towards the bar, Vanessa wondered what the hell she was doing, but then she thought; why not? It wasn't every day that she was propositioned by a handsome, muscular man; or did he just think she looked desperate? A woman alone, as he'd already observed, she vowed to stay safe.

'Do you really like all this kind of music?' asked Joey, as he savoured his pint of diet-lemonade. He wasn't permitted to drink on duty, he'd told her, and rarely touched alcohol anyway; said it jeopardised his fitness regime.

'Why else would I be here? What about you, then? I guess you don't have a choice about which events you work.'

'Not really my scene. I'm more of a jazz aficionado, myself; can't be doing with all that navel-gazing. A good crowd, though; not been any trouble so far and everyone seems friendly enough. Are you here to see anyone in particular?'

'Skinny Ted and the Brothel Creepers; they're on tomorrow night.'

'Sorry, never heard of them.'

Vanessa was getting used to this inevitable response whenever she mentioned the name of her pursuit - 'Stick around,' she suggested, 'they'll be the best thing on this weekend.'

'I'll look forward to it,' said Joey.

Vanessa looked quizzical - 'From your accent I'd say that you're a long way from home.'

'Very observant Ma'am; I left L.A. five years ago after my

designs on a waitress went unreciprocated. Hightailed it here to escape and it suits me just fine. Turned to whisky for a while, but the doctor said if I carried on drinking I'd end up dead. Now I spend my nights providing security and my days pumping iron and body-building.'

'It's an impressive body,' observed Vanessa and immediately sensed her face reddening.

'Thank you, Ma'am', smiled Joey, 'it's the only one I have, so I try to look after it.'

Despite her better judgement, Vanessa felt herself surrendering to his husky tones and she couldn't help but picture that beefy body, perspiring to a rhythm forged from steel girders, pummelled into the ground by a steam-hammer. Whoa, steady on, she warned herself.

Joey took a peak at his Rolex and took her hand - 'Sorry, Lady Vanessa, have to get back to work, I'm afraid. How about we meet up again tomorrow, or am I being too presumptuous?'

Vanessa thought for a moment; this wasn't why she was here and Joey was a totally unexpected distraction, albeit a very tempting one. She glanced over to see Bill and his entourage disappearing into the Middle Point.

'Tomorrow's not too presumptuous,' she replied with a nervous smile; 'tonight would have been presumptuous. How about lunch somewhere?'

'It will be an honour Ma'am. Shall we meet outside reception at 11 a.m. and take a stroll into town?'

'OK, I'll be there.' Vanessa felt herself blush as Joey kissed her hand, turned and melted into the crowd. Did that really just happen?

It was the morning of the big gig and Bill opened his eyes gradually. Too much light at once could permanently damage his eyesight. He blinked, before burying his head beneath the covers once more. Slowly, he re-emerged and squinted at the shaft of sunlight that pierced the slit in the curtains. A sorrowful chorus of gulls aided the internal Sat-Nav that confirmed his location; and the incessant throb behind his temples was a painful reminder of the previous night's excesses. Bill glanced sideways at his travel alarm-clock and read its blurred digital message: 8:45 a.m. He groaned, laid his head back on the pillow and closed his eyes. He felt like shit.

With unerring accuracy, he reached down to his left and retrieved the bottle of water that he'd somehow had the forethought to leave by his bedside. Years of bad practice had at least taught him one thing; that when you awake after a night on the lash, you crave water to wash away the bad taste from a sandpaper mouth. It was a routine that he followed religiously, no matter how pissed he returned.

Gently, he sat up, rearranged the pillows to support his back and took a couple of glugs of H2O. His head felt as if it belonged to someone else; someone with little regard for their own wellbeing and for the importance of the day ahead. From the room next door he heard deep snoring, akin to a pig on vacation, and he had a hunch that Tom would feel just as bad when he finally awoke.

Steadily, Bill swung his legs over the side of the bed and tried to fix both of his eyes on a point in the picture in front of him; a pretty mundane piece depicting a solitary tree against a lurid orange sunset. Once focused, he considered his priorities and pondered his next move. There were things to do; breakfast to be had, stage clothes to iron, sound-check at 11:00 a.m. His body and mind told him that there was plenty of time, but his instincts said otherwise. It wasn't just the practicalities that had to be taken care of, they had to be in the right frame of mind too; at the top of their mettle. This audience was not their own and they'd have to be won over.

Cautiously he stood and staggered to the bathroom, the mirror doing little to offer reassurance. The first piss of the day seemed eternal and he wondered what the Guinness Book of Records had to say on the subject. Finally, the endless flow ceased and he took two steps to the right, turned on the cold tap, cupped his hands and splashed water on his haggard face; his senses temporarily revived.

As Tom's snoring was no longer audible, Bill concluded that he must be awake. A loud rap on his door confirmed as much.

'What?'

'Are you awake?'

'No; fuck off.'

'And top of the morning to you too,' replied Bill. 'Are you getting up for breakfast?'

'Maybe; are you buying?'

'Yeah, it's my turn.'

'Be with you in fifteen,' growled Tom.

Bill knew that Tom was aware that breakfast was included in their package, but at least his answer was relatively coherent for one who'd just surfaced. Perhaps he too felt the gravitas of the forthcoming day and was mindful that he had to get up and face the music.

Twenty minutes later and the bleary-eyed duo entered the restaurant. All of the eateries on site were decked-out in blue and white with a nautical theme and they stood before a large ship's wheel, while the hostess scanned their cards. Clive and Ray were there already, their plates devoid of all but a thin film of grease where their fry-ups used to be. Ray sipped at his fourth mug of black coffee and took in the sight of the band's two prominent members.

'Good of you to join us,' he said, 'hope you're going to look better than that tonight.'

'You're no oil painting yourself,' pointed out Tom.

'Yeah, but I can hide behind the drum-kit, as you've previously mentioned.'

'How come you're so chipper?' asked Tom. 'Oh, I forgot, you don't drink anymore.'

Ray scowled - 'Not allowed to, remember. Was up soon after dawn and I've already been for a walk along the beach; sleep is a rare luxury these days anyway, due to the nightmares. Most people count sheep, but I count Dracula.'

'An early morning walk along the beach, eh? Well, good for you,' scorned Tom, 'if only we could all be so clean-living and wholesome. Oh, and by the way; you've got egg in your beard.'

Tom looked as if he were about to chunder; his face pale and drawn, with sunken and bloodshot eyes. He stared at his breakfast for a few seconds, before taking a deep breath and tucking in hungrily. The others looked on in disbelief, until Tom sensed their eyes upon him and glanced up.

'What?'

Bill shook his head - 'You always did have the constitution of an ox.'

Bill too, made an effort to re-line his stomach, but with less enthusiasm and in dainty mouthfuls. Each swallow was an achievement and he was applauded by the others when he eventually emptied his plate.

'That's better,' he said. 'So, are we all ready for our forty-five minutes of fame, then?'

'I'll be happier once we've sound-checked,' said Clive, 'but we've been known to play in far worse condition than this back in the day.'

'Somehow it seemed much easier to recover back then,' mused Bill; 'takes me best part of a week these days.'

'Well, regardless of how we feel, we must remain professional,' insisted Clive. 'I probably enjoy about twenty per cent of the sessions that I play on, but I'm there to do a job and I just get on with it.'

'Hey, the Brothel Creepers were much more than just a job,' proclaimed Bill, 'and still are to me.'

'Yeah, me too,' said Clive, 'I'm simply suggesting a strategy to overcome the hangovers. Concentrate on playing the right notes at the right times and the rest will follow.'

And that's how they approached the sound-check, one note at a time, until the mojo gradually returned. An underestimated antidote to the blues, Bill wondered why music wasn't available on the NHS, as he exchanged satisfied smiles with Tom.

Lauren and Jacob watched from the side of the stage, arms around each other's waists and feet a-tapping, as the band reached the climax of *Jacob's Ladder*. Bill glanced at them and the seeds of an idea entered his head. He sauntered over and addressed Jacob.

'Hey, do you have your guitar with you?'

'Yeah, it's back in the chalet, Dude. Why?'

'Well, as you were the inspiration for the song, how do you fancy playing on it?'

Jacob looked sceptical - 'I've only ever played in front of a few friends before, never anything on this scale. Besides, shouldn't you ask the rest of the guys?'

Bill convened a short band meeting.

'OK by me,' said Clive, 'providing he can play and it sounds good. It's never a bad thing to break up the show with something a bit different; keeps the audience interested.'

Tom and Ray agreed too, and Jacob was dispatched to fetch his guitar. When he returned Clive went through the song's chord sequence; a simple classic three chord number with a middle-eight, and well within Jacob's capabilities. While their guest learnt his lines, Bill wandered backstage and passed the time of day with one of the technicians, a thickset young man with greasy black hair and geometric sideburns.

'You guys sound pretty good,' he complimented Bill. 'What are you called?'

'Skinny Ted and the Brothel Creepers.'

'Sorry, never heard of you.'

Bill was growing accustomed to this inevitable response, but wasn't bothered this time; for over the technician's shoulder something had caught his eye.

'Hey, can we borrow that?' he asked.

The technician turned in the direction that Bill was pointing - 'What the hell do you want that for?'

'A stage prop. Don't worry, we'll look after it and I'll put it back afterwards.'

'What the fuck are you doing with that?' asked Tom as Bill returned, struggling with the weight of a large stand-alone ladder under his arm.

'Don't just stand there, give me a hand,' pleaded Bill.

Tom shook his head and assisted Bill in unfolding the steps and erecting them centre stage. The rest of the band, along with Jacob and Lauren gathered round with quizzical expressions.

'Now, it's just an idea,' said Bill, 'and you can tell me it's a bloody stupid one if you wish, but I thought that maybe Jacob could play his part up there; bearing in mind the name of the song and all that...' Bill's words tailed off, as he began to feel unsure of his brilliant suggestion.

'Well I like it,' laughed Tom, 'sounds like the kind of plan that Stan, God rest his soul might have come up with. However the remainder of the show goes, people will remember that bit.'

Jacob looked up uneasily - 'But I don't like heights, Dude; and it doesn't look particularly steady.'

Bill grabbed both legs of the ladder and shook it vigorously - 'Solid as a rock; you'll be safe as houses up there.'

'Go on Jacob,' encouraged Tom, 'let's just rehearse it and see how it goes. If it doesn't work or you feel too uncomfortable, we'll knock it on the head.'

'Well, I guess it's the only way I'll reach the top as a guitarist,' sighed Jacob.

Guitar slung over his shoulder, Jacob reluctantly took one rung at a time, until he was perched precariously atop with a look of abject fear. Clive said nothing, but his expression said it all: I am a serious musician; how has it come to this? As Ray counted in the song, Jacob came in right on cue and strummed his chords proficiently, but with little enthusiasm. With both hands required to play his instrument, he was reliant on balance to prevent gravity taking its course and he didn't want to move around too much. Performance complete, he descended slowly to applause from his fellow musicians. Feet gratefully back on terra-firma, he fell into the arms of the waiting Lauren, who pecked him on the cheek and squeezed him tight.

Tom clapped him on the arm - 'Well done young man. Think you can pull that off again tonight?'

'Can but try, Dude; I'll be petrified in front of all those people anyway, so may as well have a good reason to be scared.'

'All in the name of showbiz,' said Bill, 'bet you're glad you came now.'

'It's an experience, Dude, and something to add to the C.V.'

Bill turned to the technician, who had been observing curiously in the wings - 'What do you think, man; can we use the ladder again tonight?'

'Nothing to do with me, Pal. Probably contravenes all the health and safety rules and I don't suppose you've completed a risk assessment, but if it's left lying around I haven't seen anything, right?'

'Goes without saying, my friend,' said Bill, 'and thank you.'

'No problem; good luck with the show.'

Sound-check concluded to everyone's satisfaction and hangovers forgotten, the band members retired to make their individual preparations.

A slight breeze ruffled the immaculate hair that Vanessa had spent the past hour perfecting in preparation for her date. The weather had turned unnaturally mild for the time of year and a powder-blue sky, peppered with fluffy cumulus clouds, aroused in her a rare optimistic mood. Despite the accumulated cynicism, shaped by years of disappointment, Vanessa couldn't help but feel a little excited at the prospect of lunch with this enigmatic Californian.

In fact it had been a while since she'd had the confidence or inclination to have lunch with anyone; convincing herself that her own company was preferable to the inevitable conflict of a relationship. When she talked to herself she was assured of a sensible answer, or at least one that she agreed with. More than enough problems of her own, she had no desire to share someone else's.

Trapped in a perpetual cycle of hope and despair, she always waited for utter loneliness to dictate that she emerge once more from self-imposed hibernation and dare to dream again. Until another glance at her watch determined that he was fifteen minutes late.

Vanessa felt foolish and angry; how many times had she been let down and still come back for more punishment. She was about to return bereft to the solitary confinement of her chalet, when an awkward-looking, sallow youth approached.

'Excuse me Ma'am; is your name Vanessa?'

'It might be. Who's asking?'

'Joey sends his apologies, but he's been asked to cover the lunchtime shift, as Frank has called in sick again, due to too many wild years. Said he's really sorry, but he had no choice and that he hopes to catch up with you this evening.' (1)

Down to earth with a thud, Vanessa stared at the unfortunate messenger, who stepped back from her seething eyes.

'I don't think so,' she snapped. 'You can tell Joey he's had his chance and there won't be another. You have a nice day now.'

And with that she walked away, head held high, but with the familiar tear of regret welling-up. No matter that his excuse may have been genuine and that he'd at least had the courtesy to send someone with a message; she'd be damned if she'd let yet another disillusionment destroy her weekend. Tonight would be awesome, despite Joey and despite everything and everyone.

1.   A reference to one of Tom Waits' many classics; *Frank's Wild Years*. A brilliant, innovative songwriter whose voice could be described as an acquired taste. Once acquired though, a veritable treasure trove awaits.

They weren't due on till six and Bill fancied some time on his own, a chance to clear his head and relax prior to the demands of the evening onslaught. Making his excuses, he grabbed his iPod and headphones and made his way to the seafront, where weathered fishermen perched on rocks and cast their lines to the swell. Bill had never fished (unlike his near namesake, who has fished all over the world), but could see the attraction and he admired the universal attitude of anglers. They cared little whether or not they caught anything, it was the sport and tranquillity that mattered, the escape from whatever wound them up at work or at home.

A cool sea breeze filled his lungs, caused his eyes to water and his nose to run, but the serenity made up for any discomfort. His chilled playlist provided the perfect background and he found an empty bench on the prom from where he could take in the entire vista of the bay. A group of children crowded round a rock-pool, excitedly searching for crabs and tempting them with bacon fat on a string. Their buckets were full of the unfortunate creatures, clambering over each other in a futile quest to escape. Hopefully, they would be returned to the pool when the kids had had their fun.

It could only be global-warming that encouraged people to wander so freely in the West of England on a November afternoon, a light jacket sufficient to maintain a comfortable temperature. Even the ice-cream van enjoyed a roaring trade, as Bunter's clientele meandered amiably among the locals. Some looked a little worse for wear; it was coming to the end of a long weekend, predominantly fuelled by adrenalin, alcohol and God knows what else. An air of submission to days of excess prevailed, as these old-enough-to-know-better ravers contemplated the prospect of going home.

Bill pondered on life's paradoxes; how he'd somehow come full circle and found himself back where he was thirty-five years ago, on the road with a bunch of misfits and malcontents. It felt right though; it was where he belonged and nothing could replace that buzz at the culmination of a successful gig. He was looking forward to getting back on stage again that evening.

The ice-cream man; it was always the ice-cream man when he was young. But times had changed, he thought, as he approached the colourful van with Miss Whippy emblazoned across the side. Despite his best efforts he couldn't help but envisage a dominatrix, dressed from head to toe in black leather, with whip at the ready.

'Er, a large sixty-nine please,' he stammered.

'I beg your pardon,' glared the imposing Italian lady at the counter.

'A large ninety-nine; I mean a large ninety-nine.' Bill's face grew redder with each word.

'That'll be two-pounds-fifty, sir.' She injected the word, sir, with venom and looked at him as if he were some kind of pervert.

Bill slunk away to enjoy his ice-cream. He checked his watch, decided there was sufficient time for a forty-five minute stroll and headed away from town along the coast road. On his iPod, Southside Jimmy and the Aylesbury Ducks were suffering from the *Fever* and Bill's footsteps kept pace with the beat, as the rhythm caressed his eardrums. His stride determined by whatever was playing at the time, he savoured the solitude and sounds as he wended his way. (1)

Cocooned in his own little world, he only gradually became aware of a commotion from somewhere behind him. At first it sounded like distant shouting but, when he turned off his music, it was evidently much closer. Bill removed his headphones in an effort to determine the source of the unwelcome interruption and was rewarded by a fast approaching shriek of what sounded like - 'GET OUT OF MY WAY, I'M A PSYCHOPATH; GET OUT OF MY WAY, I'M A PSYCHOPATH.'

In panic he turned towards the utterer of this fearsome declaration. Instinctively he cowered back against the wall and raised his hands to protect his face, just as a lady in luminous lemon Lycra sped by with a look of rage in her eyes - 'GET OUT OF MY WAY, YOU'RE ON THE CYCLE PATH; GET OUT OF MY WAY, YOU'RE ON THE CYCLE PATH.' This livid blur of yellow was soon followed by a group of similarly attired cyclists, all of whom glared angrily at him as they zipped past within inches of his feet and covered his black jeans in dust. Bill watched petrified, as an assemblage of athletic arses swayed away into the distance.

With his heart racing as fast as they had come and gone, he belatedly took the lady's advice and removed himself to the footpath, where a group of onlookers could barely conceal their amusement. Bill brushed himself down, regained his composure and attempted to stride away with some dignity intact. Still in shock, he decided to head back to base; it was a perilous business, this walking.

1. I believe Southside Jimmy are originally from Glasgow, but are now based in Milton Keynes. Not had the pleasure of seeing them live yet, but they have played the Shoot Pool venue in Aylesbury a few times, where a friend of mine quipped that maybe they should bill themselves as Southside Jimmy and the Aylesbury Ducks. This would, of course, be in homage to Springsteen contemporaries, Southside Johnny and the Asbury Jukes; whose Boss penned 1976 classic *The Fever* is referenced here.

Clive bit into his ham and cucumber sandwich with an expression of distaste. He turned over the packaging and shook his head.

'What's up?' asked Tom.

'Nothing; it just tastes a bit funny, that's all. It's in date, so it should be OK.'

'Give it a sniff,' suggested Tom. 'It's a philosophy that can be applied to any aspect of life: if something doesn't smell too good, then you're probably better off staying away from it.'

Clive did as advised, wrinkled his nose and put the sandwich to one side.

'Don't know how you can eat at a time like this, anyway,' said Bill. 'I know we've all done this hundreds of times before, but somehow I'm more nervous about this one.'

Bill took a peek through the backstage curtain and saw the hall slowly filling up. It was a good time to go on, as most people were out of their chalets by now and ready for their evening's entertainment. He studied the faces of those closest to the stage. Some looked as if they were on the final straight of a marathon, their endurance tested to the limit; with a steely resolve in their half-closed eyes and barely able to stand, they still exhibited a determination to continue to the end. We'll have to be good to raise this lot from the dead, thought Bill, as he turned to face the others.

'Are you ready for this?' he asked.

'As ready as I'll ever be,' answered Ray.

'Absolutely,' smiled Tom, as he jumped from one foot to the other.

'I'm always ready,' said Clive. 'Come on, let's go.'

And with a rush of enthusiasm, they bounced on stage and took their positions; to be met with a murmur of indifference.

'Good evening, we're Skinny Ted and the Brothel Creepers.' Tom's fervent announcement was rewarded by a ripple of polite applause.

'Never heard of you,' shouted the obligatory heckler.

'I've never heard of you either,' retorted Tom. 'Come on guys, let's rock.'

They'd decided to open with the classic *Panic in Detroit*, in tribute to its legendary composer, who'd recently passed away. As it wasn't one of their own there was a better chance that the crowd might recognise the song and get them off to a good start. Bill was encouraged to observe some movement in the mosh-pit, where a lad danced insanely, but further back there was little reaction. Despite it being one of its prolific author's finest songs with an iconic descending bassline, it was an album track and perhaps lesser known than his many hits; particularly among an audience who were barely born upon its original release. (1)

'Thank you,' said Tom, in reaction to a smattering of respectful clapping. 'This one was a hit for us, way back when you lot were babies; it's called *Shafted.*'

'Never heard of it,' yelled the inarticulate heckler.

Tom glared at the spot from whence the criticism came and uttered the words that got everyone on their side - 'Hey man, we're here to have a good time; I don't know about you.' He turned to the rest of the crowd with his arms outstretched - 'We all go home tomorrow guys; what do you say we make this the best night of the weekend?'

A loud roar indicated that the majority were in agreement and the heckler wasn't heard again. A couple of crowd-pleasing raw rockers (*You Scratch My Itch* and *Red Mist*) from the first album followed, along with a number of their tried and tested favourites, before Jacob was cordially invited to join the party.

'Ladies and Gentlemen,' announced Tom, 'please welcome Jacob to the stage, the inspiration for the next song.'

With his characteristic gangly gait, a nervous Jacob entered stage left. Apprehensively, he made his way to the ladder that Bill and Clive had already erected, took a deep breath and climbed carefully to the top. Predominantly confused expressions greeted him as he took his position and turned, terrified, to face the audience. A nod from Ray, four clicks and they had lift-off; the crowd catching on to the concept once they reached the catchy chorus. By this time, the spaced-out spectators were well and truly on-board and smiles and handclaps prevailed as Clive stepped forward for his solo.

Unfortunately, he failed to notice that his lead was wrapped around one of the ladder's legs and, as Clive instinctively manoeuvred his guitar, Jacob's only means of support wobbled dangerously. Lost in the music and oblivious to all around him, Clive suddenly lifted his instrument and let rip a screaming crescendo then fell to his knees at the front of the stage. Behind him, the rest of the band watched in helpless horror as, in apparent slow-motion, the ladder began to topple. A look of abject fear came over Jacob's face and he headed head-first towards the boards. Then, in one amazing, almost graceful movement, he performed a perfect head-over-heels and, still sporting his guitar, landed back on his feet and continued to play. Apparently thinking that it was all part of the act, the audience went wild and lifted the roof in appreciation. (2)

Clive grinned from ear to ear as the song came to a close; he had an inherent confidence in his own ability, but he'd never before received such a rapturous reaction to one of his solos. He took a well-earned bow then turned to see Bill and Tom holding Jacob's arms aloft in celebration. With a what-the-hell-just-happened expression, Clive joined his colleagues centre stage as they milked the applause.

Tom walked to the mic and gestured towards their guest - 'Ladies and gentlemen, please give it up one more time for Jacob.'

If the crowd weren't already standing it would have been a standing ovation, as Jacob waved back and staggered off stage relieved, to the safety of Lauren's arms.

'Wow, how do we follow that?' asked Tom of a now anticipant audience. 'Let's bring it down guys. Is there anyone out there who's been stood up tonight?'

Bill looked daggers at Tom then scanned the crowd for any response. A brief silence ensued, before a large, muscular, tattooed man raised his hand and hollered - 'Yeah, that's me; I've been stood up, again.'

A flurry of laughter filled the hall, as Tom shielded his eyes from the spotlights and gazed out towards the source of this surprise declaration. He smiled at the colossus who, bursting out of a tight denim jacket and white t-shirt, resembled a builder on his tea break.

'Well,' he announced, 'this one's for you.'

Bill shook his head as Tom proceeded to sing, whilst hamming it up and gazing lovingly at the builder. Blinding lights and vast distances, this wasn't the intimate kind of venue that they were used to and Bill struggled to pick out any individuals, as his eyes mechanically drifted from one side of the hall to the other. He played in a dream, before the song reached its final refrain; then his gaze rested on a flash of yellow to the right of the crowd. Bill squinted and blinked and then she was gone; again.

The schedule was designed to run like clockwork and each band had been briefed that, should their set exceed the allotted forty-five minutes then the plug would be pulled. Bill felt that they'd done enough to deserve an encore and their new-found fans certainly wanted more, but they had no choice but to thank everyone for their time and, still buzzing, leave the stage. In the wings, Jacob and Lauren were waiting with solemn faces.

Tom grinned at Jacob - 'That was brilliant, man. Do you fancy doing it again sometime?'

For some reason, Jacob's customary laid-back demeanour had temporarily deserted him - 'No chance, Dude. You're fucking mad, the lot of you. I could have broken my neck out there and my back is killing me. And you ask if I want to do it again?'

'I can recommend a good osteopath,' offered Tom; 'he was glad to see the back of me.'

'Hey, accidents happen,' said Ray, 'I wouldn't exist otherwise.'

Lauren sternly addressed her father - 'Jacob could have been seriously injured out there and you would have been to blame; it was your stupid idea. As it is, he may have damaged his back.'

'Yeah, I'm sorry,' Bill held up his hands, 'it seemed like a good idea at the time; and the audience loved it.'

Lauren punched Bill hard on the arm. 'You always were irresponsible,' she shouted, 'it's about time you grew up.'

'Ouch, that hurt,' said Bill.

'And next time you can employ a stunt-man, Dude,' suggested Jacob, 'because I quit!!'

And with that he hobbled away, with Lauren attempting to provide some support.

Bill looked crestfallen. He'd wanted to build some bridges with his daughter and he genuinely approved of her choice of boyfriend. Jacob was obviously a good bloke and he felt bad that he'd been the cause of his discomfort. Bill should have been celebrating the culmination of another successful gig on their road to resurrection, but instead he felt down.

Tom put an arm around his shoulder - 'Don't worry, man; he'll come round in the morning. The poor sod's probably suffering from shock at the moment.'

'What was all that about?' asked Clive, still totally unaware of what had occurred behind him.

'Your lead was tangled round the ladder,' explained Tom. 'When you went into overdrive the whole thing came tumbling down; Jacob too. Somehow he pulled off this amazing stunt and landed back on his feet. That's why the crowd were going crazy.'

'Jesus; and I thought they were cheering my solo. No wonder he's none too happy. I feel kind of responsible.'

'No, Lauren's right,' said Bill, 'it may have been you that nearly killed him, but it was my idea, so it's my responsibility. We'll go and see him to apologise in the morning. In the meantime, I think we've earned a beer.'

'Yeah, that was some show,' agreed Tom.

'Bravo, bravo,' came a shout from the side-lines. They all turned to see an inebriated Gabriel, sporting his customary leathers and a wide grin, alongside an equally pissed Victor. It was difficult to tell who was holding who up.

'Now that's what I call showmanship,' continued Gabriel. 'Where on Earth did you find that sweet young acrobat and when can we sign him up?'

Bill studied the two wobbling jellies before him; apparently invertebrate, it was as if somebody had poured molten leather into a swimming pool and left it to float, without any visible means of support.

'Well, you certainly look as if you've had a good time,' he said. 'Unfortunately, I think Jacob's appearance was a one-off and he's not keen to repeat the experience.'

'Just send him to see me,' slurred Gabriel, 'I'll persuade him that it's in his best interests.'

'We'll bear it in mind,' said Bill, distracted, for over Gabriel's shoulder he saw the lady in the yellow mini-skirt exiting the hall by a side door some distance away. Making his excuses he followed, determined to solve the mystery.

1.   *Panic In Detroit* is a stand-out track from David Bowie's ground-breaking *Aladdin Sane* album (a lad danced insanely; geddit?) from 1973. The Starman left us on 10 January 2016. A statue in his honour was unveiled in Aylesbury's Market Square (immortalised in his song *Five Years*) in March 2018, to mark the fact that Bowie debuted both the *Hunky Dory* and *Ziggy Stardust* albums live at Friars Club, Aylesbury. www.aylesburyfriars.co.uk

2.   A staple of his live show, John Otway has been known to perform this stunt with the ladder during his cover of *Cheryl's Going Home*; although, unlike Jacob, Otway used to do it on purpose! Somehow, he would invariably land back on his feet and continue to play, whether the guitar was still plugged in or not.

For some reason, Vanessa hadn't enjoyed tonight's performance as much as the previous gigs. Maybe it was due to the larger, less intimate venue which made the band seem distant and detached; or perhaps it was down to the new gimmix, the man on the ladder and his gymnastics; or was it that the audience weren't in on the secret of the magic that was Skinny Ted and the Brothel Creepers? Also, she hadn't been impressed with the finale; their special song treated as a joke by Tom, as he serenaded Bob the builder. Of course, it could have been that she simply wasn't in the mood, after the earlier disappointment of being stood-up by Joey. (1)

Whatever the cause, Vanessa decided she'd had enough and made her way to the exit. She would return to her chalet, try to sleep and make an early start tomorrow; get away before the rest of the punters hit the road. The cool evening air hit her hard, as she left the hustle and bustle of the hall behind and stepped outside. It was a clear, starlit night and she took a deep breath and shivered in her inadequate attire; at least it was only a short walk to her accommodation.

The still night made her starkly aware that she was on her own and she stepped quickly along the shortest, but dimly lit route. There weren't many people around, most of the chalets were in darkness and Vanessa wondered if she were the only one who'd decided on an early night. Then, as she turned a shady corner, she literally bumped into a couple who were taking their time to get to where they were going. Vanessa realised that the man was in some kind of pain, apologised and continued on her journey; she really didn't want to talk to anyone. Suddenly, she felt someone grab her arms and pin her to the wall.

'Hold it right there,' said the young lady who'd restrained her.

Vanessa was shocked, frightened and unsure how to react. The lady was about her height and build, and Vanessa knew who she was.

'OK, start talking,' growled her captor. 'Why are you following my dad?'

'Hey Lauren, take it easy,' said the young man in the background. Vanessa noticed that he was struggling to stand up straight and that his hand was held in the small of his back.

'I'm sorry; I don't know what you mean. What makes you think that I'm following your father?'

'He says you've been at every gig, always dressed the same, and that you look like someone he once knew. You've also been to

visit my Gran.'

From the shadows, Vanessa became aware of another man approaching and her heart skipped a beat as she realised his identity.

'Lauren, let her go please,' ordered Bill, 'there's no need for any unpleasantness.'

Vanessa felt Lauren's grip loosen and speculated whether or not she could run faster than her assailants. The young man was obviously in no fit state to pursue anyone and she thought she'd probably be quicker than Bill, but Lauren looked at least her equal in physique and was a fair bit younger.

'So, who are you?' asked Bill, his voice gentle and unthreatening.

'I'm no-one,' replied Vanessa, 'just a fan and I think you're brilliant. Can I have your autograph?'

Bill patted his pockets - 'Don't seem to have a pen on me at the moment, but if you want to come back inside and tell us what's going on then I'm sure we can find one. You can meet the rest of the band too.'

Oh shit, this could get ugly, thought Vanessa as she saw an imposing figure approaching from behind Bill; how many people are tailing me tonight?

'Hey, what's going on here; are you OK, Vanessa?' asked Joey.

Vanessa saw the look of confusion on Bill's face - 'It's all fine, Joey,' she said, 'we've finished our conversation and I'm going to bed.'

'Look, I'm really sorry about earlier. Can we catch up tomorrow, before you leave?'

'Maybe; I'll let you know.'

And, as they all looked on speechless, Vanessa walked swiftly away. She had a hunch that none of them would follow; Bill and Lauren too concerned about causing a scene; especially with that scary looking security man around; and Joey, she hoped, too much of a gentleman. All the same, she quickened her pace and, with a racing pulse, kept going until she was out of sight.

Back at her chalet, she gathered her thoughts, emptied the drawers and wardrobe and threw her things haphazardly into her suitcase. She made her way hastily to her car and, stopping only to check-out, left this weekend of folly behind her and sped off into the darkness. It would be a long, lonely drive home.

1. *Gimmix! (Play Loud)* was Mancunian punk-poet genius John Cooper Clarke's only hit single (so far); it reached the dizzy heights of no. 39 in 1978.

A contrite knock on the door and, eventually, Lauren answered. Bill's sleep had been fitful and he was knackered and on autopilot. He would have preferred to stay in bed for a little longer, but checkout time was 10 a.m., so he'd had little choice but to emerge to face another day. He came bearing a gift for Jacob by way of an apology; one of Clive's myriad guitars that Jacob had strummed and admired the previous day. It was a generous peace-offering and Bill hoped it would ease Jacob's pain somewhat and pave the way for congenial relations.

Obviously still in some discomfort, Jacob was nonetheless impressed with the gesture - 'Hey Dude, it's a Fender Mustang; I can't take this.' (1)

'Clive was insistent,' said Bill. 'Besides, he's got so many guitars, that he's hardly going to miss this one. It's the least we can do after what we put you through and we're all very sorry.'

'Apology accepted, Dude. This is amazing and I'm sure I'll survive.'

'And if you want to join us on stage again, you'll be very welcome; and no ladders next time, I promise.'

Lauren's dark demeanour lightened a little as she saw the look of pleasure in Jacob's eyes.

'So, are we any closer to finding out the identity of your sinister stalker?' she asked.

'A stalker,' said Bill; 'do you think that's what she is?'

'Well, I can't think of a better word to describe her behaviour.'

'It was too dark and you were both in the shadows. She looked somehow familiar, but it's all still a mystery to me. Why would anyone go to all that trouble?'

'At least now we know that her name is Vanessa.'

'And that makes it even more mysterious,' said Bill. 'Maybe we could have found out a bit more if that security guy hadn't turned up, but it looks like she wishes to remain anonymous at the moment. Not a lot we can do I guess.'

'Well, we're getting closer. I could have interrogated her to within an inch of her life, if you hadn't made me let her go.'

'Yeah, that's what I was afraid of.'

In the corner, Jacob began to improvise a slow blues on his new toy, the picture of contentment.

'Say thanks to Clive for us,' she smiled, 'and tell him that he's made Jacob's day.'

Bill hugged his daughter and it appeared that he was at least partially forgiven. He shook Jacob's hand and wished them both a safe trip home, before making his way to join the others. He wasn't looking forward to the return journey, cramped and uncomfortable in Clive's mid-life crisis; a Fiat 500 Abarth with a 1.4 litre turbocharged engine. It was a nice car in gun-metal grey with a black go-faster stripe on the side, but hardly the most practical vehicle for transporting four fairly bulky men. It had taken Bill an hour to straighten out after the trip here and he'd feared he'd be stuck with his knees to his nipples for the entire weekend.

It had been decided that Ray would drive back. He'd been pestering Clive to have a go and, furthermore, hadn't been drinking; whereas Clive was probably still over the limit after the weekend's overindulgences. Gabriel and Victor were hauling their gear in a hired van and had already left. Bill shook his head and took a deep breath, before wedging himself in next to Tom in the back seat.

'You know that if you keep the box, this'll be worth a lot of money one day,' he told Clive.

'Very funny,' replied Clive. 'You can always walk back if you'd prefer.'

'I'm all for a man driving his dream car,' continued Bill, 'but you've left it a bit late in life to be buying a fanny magnet, haven't you?'

'Ha; if that's what it's meant to be then I'm getting my money back,' laughed Clive, as he set his iPod to shuffle, 'cos it's not working.'

An eclectic soundtrack was to accompany them home and Clive boasted that he had over ten thousand songs in that little box; constantly surprised by the next track. There were a few comments about Clive's often melancholic taste, but among the obscurities shone a few gems that they recognised. All smiled as a familiar intro kicked in; Bill and Tom contributing hitherto unheard falsetto harmonies, akin to the din of packs of howling wolves on barren nights – 'ooh, ooh, ooh, ooh; baby love'... Unfortunately, the laughter triggered by their caterwauling caused Ray to swerve a little, just as he passed a police car that was partially hidden behind some bushes on a side street. Inevitably, the rear-view mirror was soon filled with a flashing blue light and Ray pulled over at the next layby. (2 - 3)

The obviously experienced, grey-bearded policeman peered through the window and appraised the car's inhabitants with some suspicion. Bill quaked in the back, terrified that they had been stopped in relation to health and safety breaches after their show's ladder incident; or that the security guard had reported him for harassment subsequent to his late night altercation with the lady in yellow. The hirsute bobby's eyes rested briefly on Bill before he returned his attention to the man behind the wheel.

'Good morning, officer,' said Ray. 'Is anything wrong?'

1. The Fender Mustang is a favourite among punk and grunge guitarists and one was famously played by the late Kurt Cobain of Nirvana.
2. Howlin' Wolf, the legendary Chicago blues singer, guitarist and harmonica maestro, who was recorded by Sam Phillips in the 1950s. Howlin' Wolf's *Little Red Rooster* was later covered by the Rolling Stones and he collaborated in the 60s with British rock musicians, Eric Clapton, Steve Winwood and Charlie Watts, among others.
3. *Baby Love* was, of course, a massive hit for the Supremes in 1964; but the version that Bill and Tom's car-journey caterwauling resembles, featured on the Barron Knights' *Pop Go The Workers* the following year. A humorous pop group, they supported both the Beatles and the Stones in their heyday. Special mention for original Barron Knight Butch Baker's little brother, Ralph, who has been my trusty companion on many a musical adventure.

Vanessa had arrived home at around 2:30 a.m., a straightforward journey as the roads were practically deserted in the early hours. She'd gone straight to bed, her mind in turmoil after the tribulations of the weekend, culminating in that late-night stand-off in the darkness.

Besides managing her anxiety, the tablets helped her sleep too; although they couldn't control her dreams and she often wondered if they contributed to her nightmares. She'd spent the night frantically running through a graffiti-adorned high-walled labyrinth, with seemingly no way out. Clowns leant grinning against the walls to her left, whilst jokers cackled and swung on lampposts to her right. Around each corner a different figure would stand, blocking her way and laughing in her face. (1)

First, there was her old work colleague, Jill, with a contemptuous look - 'Are you still following that dodgy band? How's the new career?'

Next, there stood the Headmistress, Mrs Mohair - 'The school's running just fine and all of the kids are doing well. In fact we're better off without you.'

Then Kelly, her old university buddy - 'Thanks for a great night out. Don't hurry back.'

Joey returned to taunt her some more - 'My name is Temptation. Did you really think you could be happy?'

Lauren looked angry - 'Leave my father alone, or you'll have me to answer to.'

Around the next corner and in the distance was Bill, looking fearfully over his shoulder as he ran away. Vanessa followed as fast as she could, but was blocked at every juncture by faces both familiar and vague. No matter how long her steps, the distance remained the same; tantalisingly in sight but heartbreakingly out of reach.

Her covers were everywhere as Vanessa awoke thrashing around in a cold sweat. She grabbed a handful of duvet and stuffed it in her mouth to stifle a scream. Would her torment ever cease?

1. Surrounded by clowns and jokers? Stealers Wheel knew the feeling back in '73 when they were *Stuck in the Middle With You.*

The policeman greeted Ray in a deep voice and broad west-country accent - 'Good morning, sir; had a good weekend have we?'

'Very good, thank you,' answered Ray.

The others remained silent and tried to look innocent as the officer's eyes gave them the once-over once again.

'Well this is a fine bunch of specimens. I'm sure we have some photo-fit pictures back at the station that feature you lot.'

'Whatever it was we have an alibi,' said Tom.

It was probably too late for Bill's attempt to appear inconspicuous, by gazing indifferently through the window. The policeman addressed Ray.

'Can you tell me when you last had a drink, sir?'

153

'That'll be December 31st last year, officer.'

'Then I assume you won't mind breathing into this.'

Much to the apparent disappointment of the sceptical cop, Ray passed the breathalyser with flying colours.

'So, if you're not pissed, sir, may I ask the reason for your somewhat erratic driving?'

'Just a temporary loss of concentration, officer; it won't happen again.'

'Please ensure that it doesn't; it only takes a second to cause an accident and I'd rather not be scraping you gentlemen off the windscreen. So, what was the highlight of the weekend?'

'We were,' retorted Ray, 'we're one of the bands.'

'You don't look much like rock stars,' observed the cop, as he took another look at this motley crew, packed into Clive's Fiat like sardines. 'What do you call yourselves?'

'Skinny Ted and the Brothel Creepers,' answered Ray.

'Never heard of you, I'm afraid. Drive safely now.'

They all thanked him and bade him good day. Bill breathed a sigh of relief. Ray took care to check his mirrors and indicate, before hitting the road once more.

'I'd appreciate if you kept your strangled cat impressions to yourselves for the remainder of the journey,' he pleaded. 'It's a good job one of us is sober.'

When she'd accepted the job, Vanessa wasn't sure if it would be compatible with her disposition, her experience and her capabilities; yet, surprisingly, she found it natural and rewarding. The residents were, for the most part, grateful for her assistance and she enjoyed engaging them in conversation and learning a little of their life-stories.

Ivy had been a midwife and told of the hundreds of babies she had helped to deliver; of the times when people didn't have immediate access to a phone and had to run or cycle to the nearest public callbox to summon assistance. Eloquent and captivating, she spoke of the amazing advances in medical science and mourned lost babies and mothers, who may have survived with the advantages of modern treatment. There couldn't be a more worthy profession, thought Vanessa; a more positive contribution to the wellbeing of the world.

In a previous life Duncan had been a Naval Officer and he regaled the other residents with tales of exotic locations and girls in every port. There was a suspicion that his anecdotes had been somewhat enhanced with each telling but, as he was such an entertaining raconteur, he was forgiven the exaggerations. Invariably smartly dressed and dignified, his nickname of 'The Captain' was as inevitable as it was fitting.

Grace was once an actress, her beautiful face still caked with makeup as she waited for her next audition. The smears of lipstick applied by shaking hands told of desperate endeavours to retain her boisterous youth; there were few parts for faded stars, she said. She told of endless B-movies and obscurity, long-gone days when the clipper-clapper would clap his clipper board and shout 'ACTION'; before her big Hollywood break was scuppered by a volatile six-month-long set-decorators' strike. On her return to the UK, she'd scratched a living from theatre productions and minor TV roles. Vanessa was fascinated by this graceful lady's scrap-book of sepia newspaper reviews and tattered theatre bills and tickets, of leading-men who led her on then moved on to their next conquest.

These were just a surface-scratch of the lives of those still articulate enough to convey their own stories. The sagas of others were lost forever in silence and blank expressions. For most, visitors were few and far between, families scattered to the four corners of the Earth, and friends either passed-on or too infirm to travel.

And then there was Peggy Harris, whose flame burned intermittently and distant; occasionally ignited by the past, but more often doused by the present. A ballroom dancer of obvious repute, her trophies filled a purpose-built display-cabinet, the centre of which was dominated by a picture of this elegant lady held by her handsome partner, both in their full ballroom regalia heyday.

Two schoolboys beamed from a frame on her dresser, one aged about ten, assured and serious; and the other a few years his junior, his tie askew and a mischievous glint in his eye that hinted of a rebellious nature. Vanessa smiled as she handed Peggy her cup of afternoon tea; strong and no sugar, just as she liked it. She picked up the picture and studied it hard.

'So, who are these handsome young men, then?' she asked.

'The oldest is John and the youngest is Bill,' answered Peggy, particularly assured and lucid today. 'He was christened William, but he hates the name. It's been Bill since he learned how to argue and that was at an early age. What time is it? They will be home from school soon.'

Vanessa pretended to check her watch - 'Plenty of time; they won't be back for ages yet. You must be very proud; tell me more about them.'

'Oh, yes; they are wonderful children, but completely different. John studies hard and always does his homework. He gets top marks every time and wants to go to the grammar school. He'll make it too; he's very determined. Bill is the opposite; as soon as he gets home he's out on his bike, or kicking a football around the park. Arthur is forever out looking for him when it's teatime and he always has some excuse; he had a puncture, or they had to get the ball down from a tree. I get worried sick, but Bill is a free spirit and I don't think we'll ever tame him. He's the more affectionate of the two. Don't get me wrong, I love John just as much, but I get more cuddles from Bill.'

'What do you think they'll grow up to be?' probed Vanessa. She was fascinated by Peggy's perspective from a bygone era.

'Oh, John will do something responsible; an accountant or something like that. Bill, I'm not so sure; he loves drawing and he's always listening to our music and watching us practice our dances. He'll be something creative if he can stick at it for long enough.'

Vanessa nodded. She had the benefit of current knowledge, whereas Peggy's suppositions were entrenched where her mind resided; way in the past. Was there a hint of awareness of what her sons had actually become, or were these predictions uncanny in their accuracy? Vanessa had only been there a few weeks but, on the days when the light still flickered, a natural affinity had developed between her and Peggy; a trust evolved from a willingness to spend some time in conversation. Vanessa did manipulate the dialogue on occasion, but mostly she allowed Peggy to talk and to live in her own antediluvian world.

With her shift coming to a close, Vanessa replaced the picture and took Peggy's empty teacup. She fluffed up her pillows and drew the right-hand curtain a little to inhibit the sun that was shining in Peggy's eyes. Once content that her ward was as comfortable as possible, Vanessa said her goodbyes and promised to come back tomorrow.

'Don't go,' pleaded Peggy, 'I don't like it here on my own.'

Vanessa held her hands - 'But I have to go and get my beauty sleep; that way I'll be wide awake when I see you again.'

The drive out of Lakeside was viewed through blurred eyes glazed with tears and, once through the gates, Vanessa pulled in and blinked until roadworthy vision returned. Gathering her senses, she resumed her journey, the early-evening rays dancing through trees and bushes, like the flickering imageries of an old movie reel. The low sun made her trip more hazardous and she could barely see the obscured curvatures of the road ahead. Too late, the brakes applied, but the resplendent pheasant was squashed beneath her wheels, its handsome plumage caked in blood and guts; an evening meal for the fortunate crows and magpies that hopped judiciously and expertly away from oncoming traffic, before resuming their feast.

Vanessa had an appointment before going home; to visit a local youth club, with a view to volunteering her services when she could. The lady on the phone had seemed keen to meet her and was impressed with her credentials - 'We can always use an extra pair of hands,' she'd said, 'we're constantly looking for people to run the café and to supervise activities.'

Located in a reasonably respectable area, this club wasn't like the ones in which she'd previously assisted, in her former pupils' neglected neighbourhoods. The place had windows for a start; and none of them were broken. As she approached the entrance, a group of clean-cut lads stepped aside to let her pass and one of them held the door for her. She thanked them and went inside; with a lewd sounding ooh, followed by lusty guffaws at her stern. With the hint of a smile, Vanessa made a bee-line for a substantial woman in distressed denim; her hair knotted and tangled like the mane of a tinker's mare, it was as if this well-attended club were her vocation and that she had little time to tend to her own wellbeing.

'Hi, you must be Paula; I'm Vanessa, we spoke on the phone.'

'Ah, yes, pleasure to meet you,' Paula smiled and shook Vanessa strongly by the hand; she exuded enthusiasm and dedication to the cause. 'Welcome to our humble little club; it's not much, but we try to make a difference and give these guys something to do. Let's grab a coffee and sit over here and you can tell my all about yourself.'

Games of pool and table-tennis went on around them, while

groups of teenage girls and boys huddled around their phones in corners and at tables. Cans of Coke and Fanta were the predominant tipples of Hobson's choice and the place was buzzing with laughter and banter. Grime and hip hop thuds made conversation difficult, but Vanessa went through an abridged version of her recent history, before declaring – 'I miss being around young people and having a positive impact and I'm looking for somewhere I can help out, without the constraints of a curriculum. Due to my shifts I can't commit to every week, but I'm happy to give my time if it's needed.'

'Absolutely,' enthused Paula, 'and you seem like our kind of person - willing to volunteer your services for a start. I'll give you some forms to complete and we'll need to check your DBS credentials. Once we've gone through the formalities you can come in for a trial run and see if it suits you. What do you say?'

'Perfect,' said Vanessa, 'I'll drop the forms in tomorrow, along with copies of my certificates and you can let me know when you want me to begin.'

Paula showed Vanessa round and introduced her to Dick, an intense, ponytailed man in his forties and a committed volunteer. She also met some of the club's clientele, who largely met her greetings with indifference; apart from the young man who'd held the door for her, whose face went red upon ribbing from his mates.

'They're good kids, mostly,' said Paula, as she accompanied Vanessa to the carpark. 'Some have their problems, but don't we all. The most important thing we can do is be non-judgemental, gain their trust and be there when they need us. We quite often hear things that they won't tell their parents; but hey, I'm teaching you to suck eggs – you'll know all this stuff if you used to be a teacher.'

Darkness had fallen and Vanessa was exhausted after a long day. A glass of white to complement another ready-meal awaited her return to an empty flat. She'd be asleep as soon as her head hit the pillow.

Their successful charming of the holiday-camp crowd two weeks' past, Bill and Ray headed towards London to record the next instalment of their new album. Bill was relieved to escape the overpowering pong of paint, as Ray had fulfilled his promise to redecorate the house and was making a pretty good fist of it so far.

They'd decided to take the train, as neither of them relished the prospect of driving in the city. They hadn't got far before they rattled to a halt at a stereotypical suburban station and a shabbily-garbed young woman staggered on-board. Although their carriage was sparsely populated, she took a look around and promptly plonked herself opposite Bill and Ray.

Despite the early hour, the vision before them appeared to be a little intoxicated; whether from breakfast or the night before they couldn't tell, but she was definitely unsteady on her feet and bleary eyed. Bill and Ray attempted to look out of the window to evade conversation, but this young lady had other ideas.

'So, what are your names then?' she asked.

'I'm Bill and this is my friend, Ray.'

'Are you gay?' she slurred.

'Err, no,' answered Bill, 'we're just good friends.'

'Where are you going?'

'We're in a band,' said Bill, 'we're off to London to record some tracks.'

'What are you called?' She looked momentarily impressed.

'Skinny Ted and the Brothel Creepers.'

'Never heard of you,' she said, turning to Ray. 'How old are you, then?'

'I'm 55. Why do you ask?'

'Wow, you don't look it. My mum's a bit of a slapper and she'd be all over you, given the chance.'

'Well, I guess that's some kind of compliment,' said Ray.

Bill tried to muffle a chuckle, as she offered Ray her hand. 'Hi, my name is Cressida.'

Ray shook it reluctantly then returned to staring out of the window.

'Cressida,' repeated Bill; 'as in Shakespeare?'

'Yes, that's who I was named after. Pretty apt really, because I've been a bit of a tragedy ever since.' She returned her flitting attention to Ray - 'Hey, why are you avoiding eye-contact?'

'I'm not avoiding eye-contact,' he protested, 'I'm just looking at the scenery.'

'Hmm, if you say so. I get off at the next stop and I need a hug from both of you before I go.'

Ray glanced uneasily at Bill as Cressida stood and stretched out her arms - 'You first,' she insisted. Ray stood reluctantly and returned an awkward hug, before she turned her attention to Bill, who too, hesitantly reciprocated. A powerful whiff of alcohol wafted under his nose as she gathered her rucksack and prepared to leave.

'Now, that wasn't so bad was it?' she said. 'The world would be a better place if strangers hugged more often. You boys take care, now.'

And with that, she made her wobbly way to the doors, just as the train reached her stop. They watched as she made unsteady progress along the platform, before stopping to wave.

'Maybe you should have got her mum's number,' laughed Bill, as he waved back.

'Why do they always sit near me?' asked Ray. 'I must have a strange magnetism that attracts the nutter on the train. There he is, they'll say; he'll talk to me. The carriage is practically empty for God's sake, and she has to sit here. All I wanted to do was look out of the window.'

'No, I reckon you were avoiding eye-contact,' sniggered Bill.

Ray punched him on the arm and continued to watch the world speed by.

Now, this really is something different, thought Bill, as they all sat and listened to the early takes of their recording session with Dennis Roy. Bill and Ray had been practicing at home in an attempt to master the rhythmic subtleties of reggae, and it sounded like their efforts had paid off. Ray had a natural, deft touch that suited the vibe and there was unanimous agreement that the resultant effects could never have been achieved with the more aggressive style of Stan, God rest his soul. Ray looked made up when told as much. It had taken their music to another dimension and, although a rockabilly/reggae fusion had surely been tried at some point in the past, nobody in attendance had heard anything like it before.

Dennis had a more relaxed approach in the studio than Richie, so Gabriel and Victor were present and relishing the creation of something truly innovative. In fact, Gabriel was so excited at the prospect of promoting this new sound that he danced around the overcrowded sound-booth and stood on a number of toes in the process. His enthusiasm was soon curtailed however, upon the appearance of a dreadlocked vision in the doorway.

'What the hell is he doing here?' he asked, with a face like thunder.

'Er, sorry, I invited him,' admitted Bill. 'Dennis, this is the guy I was telling you about; I'd like you to meet Ras Putin.'

'Weh yuh ah seh, Rasta,' greeted Dennis, 'welcome to me studio.'

'It's an honour, man; you a legend in these parts.'

They exchanged a convoluted street-handshake, the kind that looks excruciating when a white man tries to emulate it.

'Yes, all very cordial,' fumed Gabriel. He turned to Bill - 'I'm surprised at you for inviting him here; you know he is homophobic and I thought better of you than that.'

Bill felt embarrassed. He knew that Gabriel was right, but was equally convinced that Ras Putin could provide exactly the vocals he wanted over an extended version of '*billy Dub*. He tried a conciliatory tone.

'Unfortunately, there are a lot of homophobic people in the world; surely the only way to educate is to engage with them. Besides, it took me ages to persuade him to come here; had to buy half the bloody shop before he'd agree. I'm OK for my five-a-day for the rest of the year.'

'Hey, chill-out battyman,' Ras Putin addressed Gabriel, 'me here fe work, nah fight.'

'I'm not happy about this,' protested Gabriel, as he stood by Victor for support. He sulked, hands on hips, and stared for a moment at Ras Putin. Eventually he turned and addressed Bill - 'OK; I am willing to listen to what he has to offer, provided that his lyrics aren't as offensive as those of some of his contemporaries. And, if he calls me battyman one more time, I swear he'll come to a sticky end.'

'We ah nah wan know 'bout your sticky end,' teased Ras Putin.

'Don't be so uncouth,' said Gabriel. 'There are all kinds of discrimination, you know, and I'm sure you've experienced some of it. Think about it; we have far more in common than that which divides us. Now, let us find out if you are as good in the studio as you are in the street.'

And he was. Even Dennis, who'd worked with the best in the business, had to admit that Ras Putin was a cat that really was no longer here. Whether in deference to the sensibilities of Gabriel and Victor, or whether he wasn't such a bad guy after all, his ostensibly improvised rhymes were inventive and inoffensive, and concerned the musical adventures of a mixed-race cool runner named Billy Dub. Bill had briefed him on the concept of what they were trying to achieve and he was impressed that Ras Putin had prepared a plethora of lyrical couplets that fitted the rhythm perfectly. All in all, he was more than pleased that he'd summoned this unsung talent to the session; the tricky bit would be persuading Gabriel to turn the other cheek. (1)

Despite the enthusiasm of Dennis and the band, Gabriel wasn't entirely convinced and he and Victor insisted upon listening to the track multiple times, in order to discern any hint of homophobia and to propose censorship if they thought necessary. As neither was fluent in patois, Dennis acted as a reluctant translator on numerous occasions.

'What about the line, "Mi touch dung dis mawning"? asked Gabriel.

'Literally it means to touch down,' Dennis patiently explained, 'as at the end of an airplane journey. In this context Ras is saying, "I arrived this morning."'

Gabriel nodded, apparently satisfied, and went on to the next verse.

'And, "Kiss mi back side", I think I can translate that myself.'

'Pretty much,' agreed Dennis. 'Here he's declaring that, "I'm here to stay and if you don't like it you can kiss my ass."'

'Hmm,' said Gabriel. "Mi nah check wid Babylon slackness"?'

'Slackness is bad behaviour - "I don't agree with your bad behaviour." I guess you can interpret that as you wish, but essentially it's about promiscuity in general.'

'And there plenty o' dat in a Babylon,' added Ras Putin.

Bill shook his head and left them to it. As a child of the sixties and seventies he was confused and didn't know what was and wasn't acceptable anymore. Clive suggested that maybe they could employ the services of a sensitivity reader.

'A sensitivity reader,' Bill repeated; 'what the hell is a sensitivity reader?'

'Apparently they vet manuscripts for anything that people might find offensive or upsetting. I'm sure we could find one that would work on lyrics.'

'Jesus, do people actually make a living doing that? Imagine how bland and sanitised things would be if we were to let them loose on our creative processes. Over my dead body!'

Bill wandered outside to get some fresh air; except the air wasn't that fresh in this hectic metropolis. Diesel fumes filled his lungs as cars and buses vied for position, and pedestrians toyed with the traffic instead of waiting for the lights to change. It could take them all evening to translate and argue about the entire track, thought Bill with a sigh, so he purchased a coffee from a nearby café and leant on some railings. He enjoyed his occasional visits to the Smoke, but couldn't have lived or worked here. It was a great place for people-watching, though. All life was evident; from affluent to destitute, flamboyant to anonymous, pole to pole and every nation in-between. Half-an-hour later and with resignation, he thought he'd best go back inside.

Bill needn't have worried, as he returned to the fray to witness Ras Putin, Gabriel and Victor, skanking amiably to the completed masterpiece. All bonhomie and bass-heavy whine and grine; it appeared that, once again, music had the power to transcend the deepest of differences. Still, thought Bill, it was a rather bizarre sight; two gay hell's angels in their customary leathers, dancing with an exuberant, tall Rastafarian, sporting the obligatory red, green and gold tam. Dennis and the rest of the band contributed their best moves at the periphery; what else could Bill do but join in? (2)

A couple more days in the studio and the final tracks and finishing touches were applied, to complete an artefact of which they could all be proud. Bill may have been a little biased, but he thought it was bloody good and he defied anyone to match it for innovation and quality.

Gabriel was in full agreement and supplied the congratulatory champagne, as they all sat round and celebrated a magnificent achievement. Never, in his wildest dreams had Bill imagined when reforming, that the band could accomplish such a feat. But, would it sell?

'I've taken the liberty of arranging a prestigious gig to launch the album release,' proclaimed Gabriel. 'You'll be supporting Crowded Scouse at a well-known club in Liverpool next month and, if that goes well, we have the option to join them on tour.' (3)

'Wow; is the gig at the Cavern?' asked an eager Tom. (4)

'Er, not exactly, but it is a similar kind of dive. It's in a basement, anyway.'

'We'll look forward to it,' said Bill, 'I guess the only way is up from there.'

'Don't be so ungrateful,' huffed Gabriel. 'Once you have gained the approval of the general public then you may be able to command the top venues. Until then you will have to graft like any other band. Did you think it would be easy and that the whole world would be awaiting your return from the dead?'

'I don't care whether they're waiting or not,' said Bill, as he studied his glass full of fizz. 'I'll be proud to play what we've just recorded anywhere; and, if the world isn't ready, then that's their loss. Oh, and by the way, I can't stand champagne.'

1. A grammatically challenged snip from that bloody Bony M tune again!! Go on, admit it; you can't get it out of your head now.
2. Another mention for the legendary Prince Buster's rude reggae classic, *Whine and Grine*.
3. Crowded Scouse – can't claim credit for this one, as this Liverpudlian tribute to Crowded House actually exists. I would like to thank Mark Barry from the band (the brother of my work colleague Diane), for his help with some historical facts pertaining to the Liverpool episode in this book, along with permission to use their brilliant name.
4. The famous Cavern Club in Liverpool, which hosted the early Beatles' gigs and employed Cilla Black as a hat-check girl. The original Cavern closed in 1973, but a facsimile was rebuilt nearby in 1984, using many of the original bricks. Celebrating its 60th anniversary in 2017, the Cavern is still going strong.

The youth-club was buzzing tonight and Vanessa relished the chance to get involved; to do something useful. Her second night and she already felt at home; previous involvement with young people making her a natural fit to manage the boisterous but repressed teenage vibe. There hadn't been much of an induction; just general advice to assist wherever Paula and Dick thought necessary. Once she'd found her feet she was welcome to bring her own ideas to the table.

Cramped and claustrophobic, the small coffee bar would be her station for the time being. Fair enough, she conceded; I am the new girl and it will be a good opportunity to get to know the patrons.

'Do you have any vodka?' asked a young lady with large brown eyes and flowing auburn ringlets.

'Sorry, we've run out,' answered Vanessa. This girl will break

some hearts, she thought; if she hasn't already.

'I guess Coke will have to do then.'

'Diet or tooth-rot?'

'Tooth-rot, please.'

'50p please,' said Vanessa, as she handed her the can.

'Thanks. You're new here, aren't you?'

'Yes; just moved into the area and wanted to get involved. My name's Vanessa; what's yours?'

'I'm Jade. Welcome to the Big Youth Club; it's a bit of a dive, but there'd be nothing to do round here without this place.' (1)

'Thanks; it was the same where I used to live; no facilities for young people. What kind of things would you like to see happen here?'

'Live music would be good; there are some sick local bands, but they have nowhere to play.'

'Have you asked Paula?'

'Yes, but there's something about a performance license and it being in a residential area.'

'Always obstacles,' said Vanessa, 'but there's often ways around them. Give me a few weeks to settle in and I'll see if Paula and I can look into it.'

'Thanks; you're cool. See you later.'

It was a long time since Vanessa had been referred to as cool and she felt a temporary warm glow of satisfaction. She watched Jade return to her friends and initiate an animated conversation. They all looked over excitedly and Vanessa hoped she hadn't raised their expectations too high. One of the girls surreptitiously extracted a bottle of clear liquid from her bag when they thought Vanessa wasn't looking, and poured a little into Jade's can. It looked like she was going to get her vodka after all.

Paula wandered over to the hatch, placed one elbow on the counter and smiled - 'I see you've met young Jade, then; one of our more agreeable members. You seemed to be getting along well.'

'Yeah, she was telling me that they'd like to see some live music here.'

'Hmm, yes; we tried it once and all hell broke loose. One of the lads told us that his older brother was in a band, Gomorrah I think they were called, so we booked them to play one night. Turned out to be a thrash metal cacophony; a hideous and very loud racket that prompted the local residents to complain to the Council. Next day we had the noise pollution people round, wanting to know if

165

we had a licence and quoting all these rules and regulations.' (2)

Vanessa stroked her chin in thought - 'But should we let one bad experience put us off? Do you mind if I check out the guidelines and procedures; and if we can get the locals onside, hold a consultation maybe?'

'Be my guest. We're always looking for something new to keep the guys amused and, like all teenagers, they're easily bored. I'd like to get some instruments together, so they can make their own music too. We can't afford to upset the neighbours, though; there are some that would use any excuse to close us down.'

With the evening coming to a close, Vanessa collected and bagged-up the empties and hauled them out to the bins at the rear of the building. The refuse area was dark and smelly, enclosed by a dog-leg brick wall that concealed her presence to the car-park. She was about to empty the bin-bag full of cans into the one marked 'recycling', when she heard a car screech to a halt nearby. The drum and bass thud was silenced upon the cut of the engine and Vanessa listened as a door opened.

'Hey, man, pssst; over here. You have the money?'

'Yeah; how much?'

'This bag here is twenty-five. You share this with your friends and, if you good, I come back next week with more. If you bad and anyone find out, then you dead. Understand?'

'Sure, no problem; and this stuff is safe, yeah?'

'I'm not here to sell you rubbish, man. This is a business proposition; you sell for as much as you can, you make a profit and so do we - everyone happy; especially the people who take the pill.'

'Sound; see you next week, man.'

The door closed, the engine roared, the bass boomed and the car screeched away, leaving a cloud of dust in its wake. Vanessa peeked out to witness the disappearing rear-end of a lime-green Ford Fiesta, which somebody had gone to the trouble of turbo-charging; the speakers were probably worth more than the car. This guy was hardly inconspicuous and he may as well have turned up in an ice-cream van with its bells chiming 'Higher Than the Sun'. Vanessa left her bag of refuse on the floor and peeped round to see the back of a medium-built youth re-entering the club; she followed him quickly into the corridor. (3)

'Hold it right there, young man.' Vanessa was pleased to discover that her voice hadn't lost the authority gained from years

166

in the teaching profession; for the boy turned to face her with the bag of pills clumsily concealed beneath his jacket. Vanessa's heart stopped as she realised which of the boys was before her.

'In here, now,' she beckoned towards an empty room by her side. The boy checked behind him to ensure no-one was looking and did as instructed.

'OK, hand them over,' demanded Vanessa.

'But these have cost me twenty-five quid,' he protested.

'Then more fool you. Firstly, do you know what you have just purchased; are they safe to take yourself and to sell to your friends? Secondly, what happens if you get caught? You'll have a criminal record for dealing drugs; you won't be able to get a job or travel abroad. And thirdly; you could get this place closed down. Then you'd have nowhere to go and nothing to do and, more importantly, nor would the rest of the kids around here. Have you really thought this through?'

The lad stared at his shoes and handed over the bag of multi-coloured pills; the most dangerous kind because they looked like sweets. He couldn't have been more than sixteen years old and he had that awkward expression, part wounded child, part indignant adolescent. Dark hair, brown eyes and high cheekbones, perhaps he could have been in a boy-band given a passable voice and the right breaks.

'Give me one good reason why I shouldn't tell your parents about this,' said Vanessa.

'I doubt if they'd care. Mum's more interested in my sisters and I only see Dad every other weekend; and then we have nothing to talk about. We used to do all kinds of stuff together; he'd watch me play football and take me places. It all got broken when my parents split.'

Vanessa felt a pang of sympathy, but held her emotions in check - 'Look, I'm here to help and it's not for me to judge,' she said. 'You promise me that nothing like this will happen again and it can be our little secret.'

'But what about the guy who sold them to me; he's coming back with more next week.'

'You leave him to me, Nathan. I'll make sure he never sells around here again.'

'How do you know my name?'

'Oh, I make it my business to find out everyone's name. Off you go now and we'll continue this conversation next time.'

167

Vanessa thought she recognised the classic cry for help. Young Nathan wanted to get caught to regain the attention he thought he'd lost. She placed the bag of pills beneath her sweatshirt and returned to the café, where she buried them at the bottom of her bag. She'd flush them down the toilet, where they belonged, when she got home.

1. Could this youth club in the sticks be named after the distinctive Jamaican deejay Big Youth? His best known album was *Screaming Target* in 1973, on the Trojan label.
2. There exists a German thrash metal band called Sodom; therefore my logical conclusion is that they should have a support act named Gomorrah.
3. A reference to Primal Scream's ode to hallucinogenic drugs; *Higher Than the* Sun, from 1991's era-defining *Screamadelica* album.

It had to be done, but it probably wasn't the best of days to do it. A biting wind swept up the Mersey and blew quiffs, beards and hats off kilter, as the famous ferry chugged its circular route that promised views of the iconic Liverpool waterfront and skyline. The inevitable sentimental soundtrack to the experience crackled repeatedly through tinny speakers. The crew must be driven crazy by the endless recurrence, thought Bill, like the drip, drip, drip of Chinese water torture. It was one of his favourite tunes, the embodiment of an era, an attitude, a place, in just two and a half perfect minutes; but could he have listened to it every working day for years on end without going mad? (1)

A little further along the river to the north, stood the Princes Dock, like London's Canary Wharf, a prime example of gentrification. It was here that the great liners of the 50s and 60s brought the Cunard Yanks, who smuggled in blues, soul and rock'n'roll records from the U.S.A., along with the cool clothes in which to listen to them. The rebellious sounds inspired young people to form skiffle bands, their instruments cobbled together from tea-chests, washboards and pots and pans. These youthful, aspiring musicians would grow to reinterpret their American inspirations, to repackage and sell back to them in the form of the British invasion of the early sixties. What a time it must have been and, due to one band in particular, Liverpool was at its very epicentre. (2)

They disembarked at the Albert Dock; a place once bustling with honest and dishonest labour, where a working man's endeavours were generally repaid with 19th century rat-infested cut-throat poverty. Despite Tom's cynical reticence, Bill insisted that a visit to the Dock's famous museum was obligatory.

'Whether you like it or not, this is all part of our musical heritage,' he argued. (3)

'Maybe,' conceded Tom, as he took in the immaculate mop-top and suit displays, 'but I always preferred the decadent London boys with a hint of danger; these guys were too clean-cut for me.' (4)

'I loved it all,' enthused Bill, 'the romance, the innovation, the harmonies and the songs; doesn't matter where you come from, the music is universal.'

'You always were a maudlin old bugger; from the nasal twang of that song on the ferry, to your own romantic opus, there's an underlying saccharinity.'

'Nothing wrong in expressing how you feel,' said Bill, 'why else would we do it?'

'They're your lyrics,' said Tom, 'I just interpret them as best I can.'

'And we're a good team. I can't sing and you have a way with a tune; like all the best song-writing partnerships. We'll never be as prolific as these guys, though.'

That iconic white Steinway piano concluded the tour, the round NHS glasses placed poignantly on its lid. Imagine writing a song such as that, thought Bill. (5)

1. My one trip on the ferry that crosses the River Mersey in Liverpool was, indeed, accompanied by Gerry and the Pacemakers' iconic ballad *Ferry Cross the Mersey*, played repeatedly through tinny speakers. Still love that song, but imagine being employed on that boat!!
2. I will bow to the local knowledge of Mark from Crowded Scouse for the notes on this paragraph – "The first American soul/blues music came to Liverpool via GIs based at Burtonwood Air Base in the 40s and 50s, who would come to Liverpool and dance with the local girls at The Grafton and The Locarno. The base has gone completely now, but it did feature in a Teardrop Explodes video in the 80s. Another route was through the great liners of the 50s and 60s which would dock at Princes Dock/Landing stage. This is now really gentrified with new build apartments and office buildings and will be the site of the new Cruise Liner terminal in a few years. The guys who brought this music (and the clothes) from the U.S. were known as the Cunard

Yanks."
3. The Beatles' Story Museum, which promises a magical history tour, is located at the Albert Dock.
4. Tom's preference may have been for the Kinks, the Stones and the Who, the southern contemporaries of the Beatles. What a time it must have been!!
5. On my one and only visit to the museum, it concluded with the piano upon which John Lennon composed *Imagine*. His distinctive round glasses were placed on top.

It was a place to prepare, at least, but could barely be described as a dressing room; spacious enough, but sparse in its décor and furnishings. A cracked mirror above a desk, four basic wooden chairs, a grimy toilet and a sink that discharged a slow stream of murky, cold water were the only nods to its intended function. Three bare bulbs barely lit the room and did little to assuage the impression of a dungeon. The walls were covered in messages, some witty, some obscene, written by some of the previous entertainers who had graced this salubrious establishment.

A large bouquet of flowers in a vase had been thoughtfully placed in front of the mirror, an embossed card indicating that they were to celebrate the completion of the album. Tom coughed and wheezed and called them the blooms of Beelzebub, for the bunch contained lilies that stank the place out and caught the back of his throat. He implored Gabriel to remove them from his vicinity or he wouldn't be responsible for the quality of his vocals.

'How ungrateful,' huffed Gabriel, 'I thought it was a nice touch and it was just my way of saying well done and thank-you.'

'I'm sorry,' rasped Tom, 'but I can barely breathe. There are two things that I won't allow in my house; one of them is the Daily Mail and the other is lilies. Both emit an overpowering sickly stench that makes me want to vomit.'

'We do appreciate the thought, honestly,' said Bill, 'but if they jeopardise Tom's vocal chords, then I think it best we take them out.'

'Maybe you could leave them with Crowded Scouse,' Tom suggested, 'might make us sound better if their harmonies are sabotaged.'

'Very well,' conceded Gabriel, as he gathered up the blossoms and headed for the exit, 'but this is the last time I do anything nice for you ungracious lot. Have a good show.'

The door slammed behind him.

'Think you might have hurt his feelings,' observed Clive.

'I'll make it up to him later,' said Tom, apparently unconcerned, 'buy him his favourite cocktail or something.'

'I doubt if they serve cocktails in here,' said Bill. 'Now, we're on in fifteen; time we tuned up.'

Tom took a swig from a bottle of lager in an attempt to lubricate and delillyfy his larynx and Clive adjusted his strings until he was satisfied with their tenor. Ray sat back in the corner with eyes closed - his meditative pre-show ritual to relax the muscles and mind prior to his percussive onslaught. Bill plucked some sliding bass line that limbered up his fingers and ensured he was in sync with Tom.

Bill took in his surroundings and wondered what all the effort was for. Despite the optimism engendered by the completion of the album and the intermittent euphoria of recent shows, he couldn't see how they could rise above the small cult following they had originally accrued. Venues such as this, the lifeblood of the music circuit they once knew, were closing down each year, never to return.

Still, as long as people turned up, there was reason for the existence of the band; and they could carry him off the stage in a wooden box when his time was up. In the meantime they had another show to do and were ready to go, when the compere announced...

'Ladies and Gentlemen, please give it up for a band that have been around longer than me. Can we have a big Saturday night Ernie's Liverpool welcome for Skinny Ted and the Brothel Creepers.' (1)

Applause and whoops greeted Tom as he bounded onstage, closely followed by Clive and Ray, with Bill lumbering behind under the burden of his double-bass. The one-hour set played like clockwork, a proficiency developed from recent live exploits, backed up by their successful studio experience. They were playing better than ever and it was reflected in the audience reaction. They knew it too, an almost telepathic synchronicity combined with subtle nods and winks ensured a tight, professional show.

Tom howled and growled, Ray snared and crashed, while Clive wailed and wept. Bill boomed and never missed a note; not a hint of yellow in the house tonight, he played on until the final chord.

With ovation ringing in their ears, they linked arms, bowed and left the stage. Follow that thought Bill, as they made their way back to the vault.

Even the dingy surroundings couldn't dampen their jubilant mood and high-fives and clapped shoulders prevailed. No towels had been provided to mop the sweat from their brows, so already soaked stage shirts had to do. Exhausted, they crashed on the wooden chairs and congratulated one another on reaching the pinnacle of their craft. It felt good.

'That was none too shabby,' grinned Tom. 'Have we ever played that well before?'

'Not that I can remember,' said Clive. 'I've worked with some of the finest musicians in the business, but they'd be hard pressed to match what we did tonight. I know I was a bit cynical about getting back together and I don't say it very often, but it's a pleasure to be a part of this.'

'Me too,' agreed Ray. 'I'd like to thank you guys for inviting me to join the band. Even Stan, God rest his soul, in his prime, could never have experienced anything like that.'

Bill beamed and raised a hard earned bottle of beer - 'Yeah, here's to the resurrection of Skinny Ted and the Brothel Creepers. I don't know about you, but I'm too hyper to call it a night. What say we take in Crowded Scouse and then hit the town?'

'Sounds good to me,' said Tom, 'but I wouldn't mind heading back to the hotel for a shower first; we must smell like a rugby-player's armpit at the moment.'

'Speak for yourself,' said Clive. 'I'm up for a night on the tiles, though.'

'Are you OK with that, Ray?' asked Tom. 'It must be hard watching the rest of us drink when you're not allowed to.'

'I've kind of gotten used to it; and I've learnt that you don't need alcohol to have a good time.'

'That's settled then,' confirmed Bill, 'let's grab our things and get out of this pit.'

Five minutes later and they were ready for whatever Liverpool could offer.

'Hey, hang on,' exclaimed Bill, 'this door's stuck. Give me a hand, Tom.'

Bill turned the handle once more while he and Tom put their shoulders into it, to no avail. Tom felt around the rim of the door to ascertain the sticking point.

'This isn't stuck,' he concluded, 'it's locked.'

'Hey, don't fuck about,' demanded Ray, 'I suffer from claustrophobia and that's not funny.'

'It's no joke,' said Tom, 'someone's locked us in. Come and try it yourself if you don't believe me.'

Ray did as suggested and reluctantly agreed - 'But didn't they know we were in here? Surely they'd check before locking up for the night.'

Bill banged on the door and shouted, but was met with no response. Just then the thud of the headline act kicked-in and all agreed that nobody would hear their cries for help, at least until the Scouse had completed their set.

'I'll phone Gabriel,' suggested Bill, 'he'll come and let us out.'

He removed his phone from his jacket pocket and found Gabriel on his contacts but, when he tried to call, quickly discovered that there was no signal.

'Give yours a try, Tom,' he suggested.

'Nothing,' replied Tom, 'it's dead down here.'

Clive had the same result and Ray had left his back at the hotel on charge.

Bill sat down and considered their situation. 'Someone will check that everyone is off the premises at the end of the evening, won't they?'

'We'll have to hope so,' said Ray. 'I saw a notice as we came in – this place will be closed for the next month, due to refurbishment. I must say it could do with sprucing up a bit.'

'So,' said Tom, 'unless we can attract anyone's attention tonight, we could be trapped in here till Monday when, hopefully, the workmen turn up.'

'Do you think this was a deliberate act?' asked Clive.

'Surely not,' said Ray. 'Who would want to imprison us in here?'

'Didn't see our enigmatic lady in yellow tonight,' said Tom; 'did you, Bill?'

'You think it was her?' asked Bill.

'Well, I haven't seen anyone else behaving suspiciously at our gigs.'

Bill shook his head - 'I don't know, man. It's all a mystery to me.'

'OK,' said Clive, 'someone will raise the alarm. How long will it be before anyone knows we're missing?'

173

Ray looked sad - 'No-one will miss me.'

Clive thought for a moment - 'Me too; some of the family get together every Christmas, but apart from that, I have no-one.'

'Next weekend,' declared Bill, 'that's when I'm due to see the kids again. Even then, Elaine will probably think my failure to show up is down to irresponsibility.'

'Karen and I had a row before I left to come up here,' sighed Tom. 'The last thing she shouted was "don't bother coming back." Don't think she meant it, but she may think I've taken her literally. What about our meeting with Gabriel and the record company on Friday?'

'Jesus,' groaned Bill, 'it comes to something when four people can disappear off the face of the Earth and nobody's likely to notice for the best part of a week; if we're lucky.'

Eventually, the unintelligible boom from above ceased and they heard the muffled roar of the crowd morph into a slow handclap and stomp, as they demanded an encore. A couple more equally unidentifiable songs and the band that everyone had really come to see were done. In the depths of the club, four anonymous men banged on anything handy and made as much noise as possible while, above them, the routine closure of the building was taking place. Ray even used his sticks to play paradiddles on the pipes in the hope that the sound would carry through the plumbing. Finally, with fists sore from hammering the door, their desperate cries unheard, they sank back against the walls with heads in hands.

'So, what happens now?' asked Bill.

'We make ourselves as comfortable as possible,' suggested Clive. 'We're gonna be entombed for tonight, at least. In the morning we can think of a cunning plan to get us out of here.'

'Not sure I like the word entombed,' said Tom; 'can't we just say inconvenienced for now? There's one thing I did find earlier; that cupboard at the end is stacked with crates of beer and boxes of crisps and nuts. At least we don't have to go thirsty or hungry.'

Bill made his way to where Tom pointed and opened the door - 'Not exactly a balanced diet, but at least it'll stop the tummy rumbling; Salt and Vinegar, Cheese and Onion, Prawn Cocktail or Smokey Bacon? Then we have Ready Salted or Dry Roasted nuts; a bit of protein at least.'

Each expressed their preference and Bill tore open the boxes and threw a few packets over - 'Give me a hand with this crate, Tom.'

With grunts of exertion, Bill and Tom hauled the bounty to the centre of the floor. They all stared at the inviting spectacle before them, before Ray produced a key-ring with a bottle-opener attached.

'I kept this as a monument to my willpower,' he declared, as he held it in shaking hands before his eyes. 'It has cracked open many a bottle in its time, but hasn't been called into action for a while. My name is Ray Arnold and I am an alcoholic; now pass me one of those beers.'

They all stared at him uncomfortably, before Bill insisted, 'No, Ray; you've come so far and we'll all help you through this. We'll even abstain ourselves if it will help; won't we, lads?'

Tom looked sceptical - 'Yeah, if you say so; don't know if I've got that much self-restraint though.'

'I appreciate your support,' said Ray, 'but have you seen the colour of the water that comes out of that tap? I reckon it's a simple choice between botulism, beer or dehydration; unless there's any fizzy pop in that cupboard.'

'No, there's not,' said Tom, 'just lager, I'm afraid.'

'Then lager it will have to be,' asserted Ray.

Clive picked up a bottle, glanced at Bill and Tom for approval, before handing it to Ray. Tsst, the bottle was open in no time and the top rattled on the terracotta floor-tiles, before Ray handed the opener to Clive. They each followed the same ritual and held up their beer to the light.

'Cheers,' said Ray, as he swigged his back gratefully.

Bill followed suit. Somehow it didn't taste so good.

1. Never been there, but Ernie's might be based on the legendary Eric's Club, which opened in 1976 opposite the Cavern and is famous for hosting some illustrious acts, including the Clash, the Buzzcocks, the Ramones, Elvis Costello and Joy Division, to name a few.

Maybe it wasn't such a good idea, thought Vanessa, as she boarded the early train back to London. She was knackered enough from her shifts at the home, without adding clandestine trips to Liverpool to the equation. At least the first leg was a fast train that would contribute to getting her home by lunchtime. Her body-clock was yet to adjust to this new lifestyle and she doubted that she'd be able to sleep much before the alarm would wake her for earlies on Monday.

It had been a cracking gig, though; the best yet, and she wondered how much better they could get. She'd done her best to remain inconspicuous after the close-shave at Bunter's and had watched the spectacle from the back of the hall, among the wallflowers and casuals. A lonely furrow she'd chosen to plough, Vanessa had pondered where to next as she'd marvelled, once more, at the brilliant band before her. Could she leave the outcome to fate or should she act to bring things to a conclusion?

It would have to stop, this futile pursuit; it wasn't good for her health or purse, and what had she really achieved? The time was fast approaching to bring down the curtain on the whole sorry saga and she knew it wouldn't be long before it was all out in the open. Then there would be no turning back. She'd travelled the country, changed her career and home, lost contact with friends and colleagues; and all for what - revenge, reconciliation, closure?

'Can I see your ticket please, Miss?'

Thoughts interrupted, Vanessa glanced up at the ticket inspector, an amiable looking man in his late fifties with close-cropped hair and sharp sideburns. She rummaged in her bag and produced the requested item, which the inspector punched efficiently.

'Thank you, Miss, have a pleasant journey.'

She watched and listened, as he repeated the ritual all the way down the carriage. What kind of a life have you had Mr. Ticket Inspector? Do you have a family and good friends? Are you happy? Have you ever heard of Skinny Ted and the Brothel Creepers?

The countryside sped by in a blur and Vanessa plaintively whispered the words to that song - 'You left me crying in the rain, Oh, oh, stood up, again.'

'Funnily enough, this wasn't how I'd planned to spend my Sunday night either,' fumed Bill. 'You're not the only one who's a little pissed off with this situation, you know.'

Despite their best efforts, a cunning plan hadn't materialised and they'd reluctantly conceded that there was no obvious way out. Normally comfortable in each other's company, an inevitable irritability was taking over and the thought was beginning to occur that they could rot down here and no-one would know. It was bloody cold too, even with their coats and jackets on, but there was little enthusiasm for Clive's suggestion that they may have to share body heat to survive.

To Ray's disappointment, beer and nibbles were on ration, due to the fact that there was no way of knowing how long they would have to last. Bill liked a beer as well as the next man, but when the next man happened to be a recently relapsed Ray Arnold, it could only end in tears; hence, Bill had suggested that they all be limited to three bottles each per day. That way, he'd calculated, they could survive until the end of the week; by which time, hopefully, someone would have noticed that they were no longer around. Of course, they would probably have all gone crazy by then and started to eat each other.

'We must stick together to get us all through this,' pronounced Clive, 'we will emerge stronger and more united than ever.'

'You sound like that bloody psychologist that ran a help-group for addicts where I used to live,' said Ray. 'It was only a small village and there weren't enough people for exclusive Alcoholics Anonymous sessions, so this guy argued that all addictions could be treated with the same methods and lumped us all together. We had an ex-hippy who'd fried his brain with LSD, a married couple with the same problem as me, a guy who worked in the print industry who spent his breaks sniffing the chemicals they used for cleaning the cylinders and, to top it all, we had a sex addict.'

'Male or female?' asked Tom.

'Oh, very female,' said Ray. 'We became quite close, but the relationship had to be platonic, she insisted. "Every time I ask you for sex, you must decline", she'd say. I'd waited all my life to meet a beautiful nymphomaniac and I had to befriend one in remission!! I ended up drinking more than ever.'

'You've not had the best of luck, have you,' observed Bill.

'Oh, I'm not one for self-pity,' said Ray, 'most of my issues have been self-inflicted. Depression and alcoholism are just two symptoms of a deeper malaise; the fact that I have never grown up.'

'Not sure if any of us have,' Bill sympathised. 'My brother thinks it's about time I got a proper job and Karen advised Tom not to throw away his career. Isn't that right, Tom?'

'Yeah, something like that. Perhaps they were right; we should all be settled down by now and sitting in front of the fire in our carpet slippers and cardigans.'

'I thought I had settled down,' mused Bill, 'before Elaine pulled the plug; but I've never worn carpet slippers and cardigans. Thanks for the insight into your domestic life, Tom.'

'I was speaking figuratively.'

'I have slippers and a cardigan,' admitted Clive, 'very comfortable they are too; but what does it matter how I look if there's no-one to notice?'

'Loneliness can be a terrible fate,' agreed Ray, 'but you've had your moments, haven't you?'

'Not for a while,' Clive sighed. 'You can meet some lovely people through the internet, but somehow it's never quite worked out. Maybe I'm just too boring.'

'Don't put yourself down,' said Bill, 'you're a brilliant guitarist in one of the best rock'n'roll bands on the circuit, and you've played with some top stars; surely that must be a conversation starter.'

'But that's all that defines me; there's nothing else.'

'It's more than a lot of people have,' said Tom. 'Besides, you're just half of the equation; if you listen and take an interest in the other person's life too, you'll find things can develop from there.'

'There speaks the person who's been with the same woman for over thirty years,' stated Bill, 'the only one of us who can claim to be an expert.'

'Oh, those are not my words,' confessed Tom, 'they're the marriage-counsellor's.'

'You're kidding,' exclaimed Bill, 'not you as well; I had no idea. We've been drinking together for decades and you never told me.'

'Yeah, well, there are some things you keep to yourself; and, anyway, you've had enough on your plate recently.'

'And you've helped me through it; the least you could have done is give me the chance to reciprocate.'

'God, we're a sorry bunch,' said Ray, 'perhaps being buried alive is the best thing for us. Is it time for our rations yet?'

'Yeah, why not,' Bill sighed, 'nothing else to do is there.'

Could something be amiss? Vanessa speculated, as she made her way to the office to which she'd been summoned. Monday morning and there must be a reason why Wilma had made it her day's first priority to speak with her. Vanessa entered the room where, not so long ago, she'd been a bag of nerves at her interview. Wilma smiled and asked her to take a seat.

'So, Vanessa, I thought it was about time we had a chat about how things are going.'

'Why, is anything wrong?'

'Let's look upon this as a routine review. Have you settled in OK and are you enjoying the job?'

'Absolutely, yes; I like it here and everyone has been very helpful. I get on well with my colleagues and the residents. And are you happy with my work?'

Wilma hesitated - 'On the whole, yes, you have done well and you are liked by all; but it has been brought to my attention that you are spending a disproportionate amount of your shifts with one resident in particular.'

Vanessa knew exactly who she meant and felt guilty as charged - 'Oh, sorry, I hadn't realised. Who are you talking about?'

'A certain Mrs. Peggy Harris.'

'Ah, Peggy, yes; I do like her company and listening to her memories. Perhaps I lose track of time when she starts reminiscing.'

'Each of our clients deserves our attention, but we cannot be seen to favour one over the others. Duncan said he was waiting for over an hour for his bed to be turned the other day and he's not the only one to have noticed.'

'Duncan is a lecherous old sod,' complained Vanessa, 'it's no accident that he's usually in the bed when he's waiting for it to be turned.'

'That may be so; he does see himself as a bit of a ladies' man, but we're here to look after everyone, regardless of their peccadillos. Perhaps we should ensure that whoever is attending to Duncan is accompanied by another member of staff.'

'Two of us; yes, I'm sure he'd enjoy that.'

'Look, I'm sure you are mature enough to handle the clumsy advances of an eighty-five year old man and, if you have any cause for concern, then my door is always open. We are moving away from the subject here. Can you promise me that you will be more aware of your time management in future?'

'Yes, I can,' assured Vanessa. Although Wilma had every right to address the issue, Vanessa felt small and rebuked.

'Excellent,' said Wilma. 'Apart from this minor blemish, your work thus far has been well up to the standard we expect. Now, tell me about your weekend.'

'Nothing to tell; I'm still getting used to shift-work and I'm trying to make my new flat feel more like home, so no time for partying; all pretty boring, really.'

'Well, if there's anything I can do to help. Now, I'd better let you get on with your work. Thank you for understanding.'

Vanessa made her way back to the communal living area and wondered who'd grassed her up; she would have to be more circumspect in future. The next few days would be spent in redressing the balance of her attention; Peggy never left her room, so Vanessa couldn't be accused of favouritism if she temporarily passed on some of Peggy's care to Mahalia, the Filipino carer with whom she generally shared duties.

It was no lie, when she'd told Wilma that she liked it here, and Vanessa had found the role more fulfilling than expected. There would be no hardship in adherence to the guidelines for time spent with each resident. It wasn't as if they were cutting corners and each guest, as they liked to call them, had sufficient time allocated for their needs. After all, they were paying handsomely for it. Yes, she would keep her head down for a while and give no-one cause for complaint.

The day passed uneventfully, which, given the circumstances, was probably a good thing. Vanessa was exhausted and wished she hadn't promised to help at the club that evening. In a zombie-like state, she vowed to take better care of herself and not to overcommit in future. Still, she wanted to be there that night to deal with some unfinished business.

'Are you OK?' asked Paula. 'Excuse me for saying so, but you look like shit.'

Vanessa resisted the temptation to respond, 'well, you're no Mona Lisa yourself,' and merely replied - 'I'm fine, just a little tired, that's all.'

Pleasantries over, she made a beeline for Jade and her friends. Their conversation ceased as soon as Vanessa self-consciously sat among them and their eyes were all upon her, as she announced...

'Ladies, I need your help.'

To the casual observer it must have looked conspiratorial; a group of half-a-dozen young ladies nodding seriously each time Vanessa explained something. The meeting concluded with high-fives of agreement and many an excited whisper. They decided upon a signal and Vanessa returned casually to her duties. Paula and Dick were busy, clumsily constructing a new table-tennis table at the other end of the club, so she didn't think her consultation had been noticed.

With eyelids virtually stuck, Vanessa trudged through the evening on autopilot, until the hour arrived for action. Forming an O with her forefinger and thumb in a signal to Jade, she made her way outside and hid among the bins. Soon, the bass became audible from three blocks away and she readied herself for the confrontation. Upon the screech of brakes and skid of tyres she waited until this youth, who thought he was the personification of a street gangster, emerged from his Noddy-car and strode across the tarmac. Vanessa wasn't one for stereotypes, but she was amazed to find that the source of the street-talk that she'd heard last week was a short, thickset white boy with cropped blonde hair. A substantial gold chain hung out of a grey hoodie and his hands were heavy with ostentatious, chunky gold rings.

Suspicion immediately spread across his face upon sight of Vanessa and he instinctively stepped back, but too late; he was suddenly surrounded by a bevy of excitable girls. Jade stood apart from the melee and raised her phone to capture the image before her. The youth struggled to break free, but he was outnumbered and helpless.

'Hey, what's going on; I know I'm irresistible, but one at a time please ladies.' Somehow the fake ghetto-talk seemed to have temporarily deserted him.

Jade took one pace forward and smiled - 'So, you think you're something special, do you? I hear that you have something to sell. Let's see it then.'

'My business is not with you,' he said, with a look of fear. 'If my man isn't here then I'll turn around and leave.'

'Yes, I think that is the best thing you can do,' said Jade. She pointed to her phone. 'Now, I have your picture and, if you ever try to sell drugs around here again, it will be all over social media that you were chased away by a bunch of girls. The same applies if you threaten or bully anyone else from this club. Do we understand each other?'

'You think I'm scared of a gang of bitches?'

'Oh dear,' Jade sighed, 'and is that what you call your mother and sister too? Best that you go now or I won't be responsible if you upset my friends. Bitches, girls; what do you think about that?'

Vanessa stood at the periphery and wondered what she'd started, as the girls all turned and closed in on the unfortunate dealer. With panic in his eyes he wriggled free and virtually ran back to his car. A roar of the engine and he was gone as swiftly as he'd arrived. Cheers, laughter and high-fives all round, before a serious looking Paula clapped from the side-lines and all went silent.

'Well, that was some show,' she said; 'what do you do for an encore?'

She turned to Vanessa - 'I take it this was your idea.'

'Yes,' admitted Vanessa, 'I take full responsibility.'

'But not all the credit,' smiled Paula, 'that should go to Jade here and the rest of you girls. That was absolutely fantastic; well done all of you and I hope we've seen the last of him and his cronies. But we don't have to tell anyone, do we; especially parents. We could get into a lot of trouble for encouraging you to take the law into your own hands.'

'No, it's our secret,' said Jade, still shaking. 'I didn't know I could be that assertive; that was scary, but fun, though.'

As they re-entered the club, Nathan stood embarrassed at the doorway. He caught Jade's eye as she passed and whispered... 'Thanks.'

'No problem,' smiled Jade, 'you can buy me a Coke if you want.'

Back inside and Vanessa's pride turned to apprehension, as Paula demanded... 'Come and see me once all of the kids have gone home. I'd like a word, please.'

Great, thought Vanessa, two bollockings in one day. She whiled away the next hour keeping her head down, serving in the café and generally tidying up. Jade and her entourage were obviously excited by their adventure and spent the remainder of the evening talking of little else. News had swiftly got around and the club was buzzing with rumour and speculation as the story got exaggerated with each telling. By the end of the evening they'd chased away half-a-dozen drug pushers, who were all armed with knives; there was even talk that one of them had wielded a gun. Jade was a heroine and her friends were equally courageous.

As the last of them left, still chattering incessantly, Vanessa

182

nervously approached a stern looking Paula.

'OK, let's get this over with,' she sighed.

'So, are you proud of that little escapade?' asked Paula, as she brushed an errant hair from her eyes.

'No, not really; but it worked and the girls pulled it off brilliantly.'

'And you potentially put them in danger.'

'Yes, I'm sorry,' conceded Vanessa. She was probably older than Paula, but felt like a child being admonished for a grave misdemeanour.

'You know we've been trying to get rid of those bastards for years,' said Paula, 'but every time we report them, they get a slap on the wrist and are back within weeks. I never thought of getting the kids to chase them away. We've tried a drug education programme, but they're at an age where they think they already know everything.'

'Yes, it's a constant battle and I'm sure they'll return eventually; if not him, then some other scumbag.'

'Well, we can only wait and see how effective your tactics have been. I can't condone what you did, but can I just ask that, next time you want to pull a stunt like that, you run it past me first? We work as a team here.'

'And would you have agreed to it?'

'You'll never know,' smiled Paula, 'but maybe.'

There weren't any workmen. Two more days had passed without sound or hope from above and desperation prevailed. With reference to neither dawn nor dusk, they'd lost track of time, but Bill calculated that it must be at least Wednesday night. Unwashed, unshaven, unlucky and unhappy; banter and conversation exhausted, the mood was as blue as a Tory's tie and just as disagreeable. Clive and Ray were not impressed with Bill and Tom's latest masterpiece, *Down in the Dungeon*, thrashed out in twenty minutes on Tom's acoustic; and the gallows-humour was beginning to grate. They wallowed in semi-darkness, one of the bulbs already blown and no telling how long the others would last. (1)

They'd been obliged to hold a group meeting to discuss Ray's surreptitious acquisition of a few extra beers and he was full of remorse. He simply couldn't cope, he'd protested and, with head in hands and an almighty 'waaah' that echoed round the basement, he cried for forgiveness as a teardrop exploded on the floor between his feet. (2)

'Listen,' asserted Tom, 'if that stuff runs out then we're all dead. We know you have a problem, but you've already proved that you can master it. Now, more than ever, it's time to show restraint; either that or we'll tie you up and drip feed your rations.'

Ray said nothing, but nodded in agreement.

'If we ever get out of here, I'm going to become a sun-worshiper,' declared Clive, in an attempt to lighten the mood. 'I crave daylight and want to run naked through fields of daisies.'

'Well, thanks for planting that image in our minds,' cringed Bill. 'I think you'd better warn the neighbours first; they may wish to close their curtains.'

The lack of natural light caused sadness and the feeling of imprisonment provoked desperation. The walls closed-in and the blackness was all-encompassing. Could it have been a nightmare that had caused Ray to scream last night, or was it, as he insisted, that something had crawled across his face while he slept? A mouse or a rat, he couldn't tell, but he'd lain with one eye open ever since. He told a story about his eccentric Gran who'd had rats under her greenhouse; and how she used to sit on the porch in her rocking chair and pick them off with an air-rifle, whilst shouting - 'You dirty rat.'

Despite their best efforts to lighten the mood with jokes and anecdotes, any optimism left was diminishing with the culmination of each rationed beer. If continued much longer their diet of crisps and nuts would be rife with health implications; and they felt it too, the lack of energy and drive. But could a stray feline's nocturnal pursuit of a rodent offer some prospect of escape?

'Hey, where did you come from?' asked Bill, as he stroked the purring ball of ginger fur that rubbed against his leg.

'Can't stand cats,' said Tom, 'only come by when they want warmth or food; but if it can get in then maybe we can get out.'

'We've been over and over this place,' said Ray, 'if there was a way out we'd have found it by now. Besides, cats can squeeze through the tiniest of gaps.'

Bill studied the small metal disc, attached the collar - 'Well, hello Stevens,' he said; 'or should we call you Yusuf? Are you going to show us the way?' (3)

184

'It's lucky we've got no means of cooking,' said Tom, 'there's enough meat on that for a half-decent meal.'

'Don't listen to the nasty man,' Bill reassured the misdirected moggy, 'we're all friends here.'

The cat's ears stood up and it stared into a shadowy corner; nose twitching and body tensed, it sprung from Bill's arms and launched itself towards a desperate rustle. With a yowl it pounced upon its prey, a terrified mouse that had little chance of escape. Delighted with its catch, the proud pussy threw the unfortunate creature around a bit, before depositing its remains at Bill's feet.

'I think it likes you,' observed Ray, 'it wants to share its food.'

After licking the blood from its claws, the successful mouser slinked away towards the end of the room.

'Don't just sit there,' implored Clive, 'let's follow and see where it goes.'

He jumped from his chair just in time to witness a tail disappear through the tiniest hole in the wall. Barely enough light reached the depths of the basement for Clive to dive down and squeeze his hand in where the cat had escaped.

'Hey, get me one of your drumsticks, Ray.'

Ray did as instructed and they all stood behind him as he investigated, gouged and jemmied a loose brick until, fifteen minutes later, it was finally pried from its cement. Clive turned and held it up with a hopeful smile.

'I know we've all lost weight in the past few days,' said Tom, 'but there's no way we're gonna fit through there.'

'But if I can get one brick out, surely we can make the hole bigger with a bit of effort,' reasoned Clive. 'It may only lead us to the basement next door, but at least the building might be inhabited and we can get someone's attention.'

'Yeah, let's go for it.' agreed Tom. 'It's probably a supporting wall and we'll bring the whole place down around our ears; but what have we got to lose?'

A shift-pattern of half-an-hour each was agreed and Clive got to work first, arguing that, as he'd already done a bit, he only had fifteen minutes left.

'Who's counting,' said Tom, 'let's just get on with it shall we.'

After two hours they'd all had a go and agreed that walls were made to last back when this place was built; and that it may take a while to mastermind their escape. Apart from Ray intermittently, none of them were used to manual labour and, with a tired weakness due to lack of nutrition, they were making slow and painful progress. A further two bricks had been chiselled out by use of makeshift tools composed of bent bottle lids and drumsticks; there was nothing else to hand to aid their endeavours. All attempted to sleep between their parts of the relay, before being rudely awoken by a baton in the ribs.

'OK, OK,' moaned Tom. 'You bastards; that was a damn good dream you've just interrupted.'

He yawned, took a look at what had been achieved during his repose and complained - 'Jesus; is that all you've done? We'll be here till next week at this rate.'

Bill shook his head - 'It'll be a long job, but what choice do we have?'

1. A little research has revealed that there is actually a song named *Down in the Dungeon* by The Kinsey Report. Released in 1999, it's a pretty good blues tune and worth checking out. Whilst searching I also unearthed a cheerful ditty by Johnny Cash that I'd never heard before. *Dark as a Dungeon* is about the joys of mining and, aptly, his voice is at its deep finest.
2. As we're in Liverpool, a special mention in this paragraph for Pete Wylie's The Mighty Wah; Echo and the Bunnymen (again); and Julian Cope's the Teardrop Explodes. The bands are linked by their respective frontmen, who were in a band called The Crucial Three, before going their more illustrious separate ways.
3. A reference to singer-songwriter Cat Stevens, famed for compositions such as *Wild World, Father and Son*, and *The First Cut Is The Deepest*. His 1974 single *Oh Very Young* is an understated work of genius. In 1977 he converted to Islam and changed his name to Yusaf Islam, forsaking his musical career for three decades.

This is becoming a habit, thought Vanessa, as she made the short journey to the office once more. What could Wilma want this time? The shockwaves hit as she entered to see two police officers in the room. Disconcerted to note the subtle movement of the female PC that blocked her way to the door, she addressed the veteran, bespectacled sergeant before her.

'What's going on?' she quaked.

'Ms Vanessa Jones?'

'Yes.'

'I am arresting you in connection with the disappearance of

Tom Milston, Bill Harris, Clive Hunt and Ray Arnold; collectively known as Skinny Ted and the Brothel Creepers.'

'Never heard of them,' ventured Vanessa.

'Oh, I think you have Ms Jones. You do not have to say anything, but anything you do say...'

Vanessa didn't hear the rest. She was familiar with the lines from movies and TV cop shows, but still didn't know what they meant. All she did know was that she was in trouble. Well, what did she expect? There was always a chance it would come to this; that she'd be rumbled before her mission was complete.

'Disappearance; what do you mean, disappearance?'

'Have you not seen the news Ms Jones? They have not been seen since Saturday night.'

'I don't watch the news; I find it too depressing. Saturday night; they played Liverpool on Saturday night.'

'And how do you know that Ms Jones?'

'Because I was there; a great gig it was too.'

'What did you do after the show?'

'I went back to my B & B then caught the early train home the next day.'

'Can I ask what interest you have in the band?'

'I'm a big fan. Have you never listened to their music?'

'I hadn't, until some months ago, when a gentleman named Bill Harris came into the station to report that he was being stalked by a lady, and that said lady had also visited his mother on these premises. Sadly I didn't take his complaint seriously at the time. Fortunately, Ms Stephenson has kept the CCTV footage and, upon my requested re-examination, she recognised you as a recently enrolled employee here. Now, if you don't mind, we can continue this conversation at the station.'

Vanessa flinched as the PC firmly took her arm and made it clear who was in charge. Vanessa turned to Wilma.

'I'm so sorry,' said Vanessa.

'Yes, me too,' replied Wilma.

Colleagues and residents alike watched, as Vanessa was escorted from the premises and helped into the back of the police car. Well, this is a new experience, she cringed; I've never been arrested before.

187

'Reminds me of a job I used to have,' recalled Ray, as he chiselled away at the brick-face; 'they never had any decent tools either. I remember asking for a hammer once and they advised me to go and ask Wankbreak.'

'Wankbreak,' repeated Bill.

'Yeah, apparently the foreman had once objected to half the workforce stopping for a fag every couple of hours while he was still working, and enquired whether he could be allowed an official break to practice his particular vice. The poor sod never did lose that nickname.'

Bill sniggered; it was a rare moment of light relief amidst a relentless and gruelling effort to make that hole big enough to squeeze through. Clive, who was the more svelte among them, had suggested that he should engage in less toil as he required a smaller aperture through which to crawl. Apart from that, he'd argued, it was necessary to look after his hands as his playing was more intricate than his bandmates, who just thrashed around a bit. He was inevitably given short shrift, before he reluctantly took over. There was light at the end of the tunnel (figuratively speaking, as no light shone from the neighbouring property), and perhaps it wouldn't be long before they might achieve their goal.

'Another three hours, I reckon,' calculated an over-optimistic Tom; for they were slowing down and losing the will to survive in this hell-hole of damp and cold boredom.

'You know we may just be swapping one prison for another, don't you,' said Ray. 'There's no guarantee that there's anyone in there or any way out. Some say all roads lead to Rome, but I say the only place we'll all end up, sooner or later, is the graveyard.'

'Well, thanks for that you cheerful bugger,' said Tom.

'He's just being realistic,' sighed a wistful-looking Bill; 'and to think I was looking forward to this trip. I've always wanted to come to Liverpool, or do I have an over-romanticised view of the place?'

'You have an over-romanticised view of everything,' huffed Tom, as he watched Clive's feeble efforts. 'After this experience, I'll be glad to put as much distance as possible between us and this place.'

He's good cop and bad cop all rolled into one, thought Vanessa.

Sergeant Watson had tried all kinds of angles in his interrogation and she hadn't cracked yet. The inscrutable lady PC was still in attendance, ostensibly to witness fair play, but contributed nothing to the proceedings.

'So, you follow this band everywhere they play, Ms Jones?' he asked incredulously.

'That's correct. Like I said before, I am their biggest fan. You should come to a gig sometime.'

'A tempting offer, but I may be washing my hair that night. Forgive me for stereotyping but, from my limited knowledge of their music, I would have thought they would appeal more to men of a certain age, rather the likes of yourself.'

'Forgive me, but what would you know about the likes of myself?'

'Then educate me, Ms Jones. I am fascinated to learn how you can make four big ugly geezers disappear into thin air. Now, can we stop wasting each other's time and will you tell me where they are.'

'But I keep telling you; I don't know where they are, I didn't know they were missing and I am as concerned as you are. Now, do you have any evidence linking me to this supposed crime, or anything to charge me with? Because, if not, I would like to go home.'

Vanessa put on a brave front, but was secretly quaking inside. She'd refused the offer of legal representation and was beginning to regret it. Surely, any half-decent solicitor would have secured her release by now. The white-walled room was claustrophobic and deliberately intimidating; with a table, chairs, recording equipment, no windows and a firmly locked door. Nobody, apart from her boss, knew she was here and, even if anyone had known, they wouldn't be surprised. After all, her recent behaviour was hardly rational. She couldn't blame the seasoned detective before her for his suspicions.

'Yes, I would like to go home too, Ms Jones but, as we appear to have reached an impasse, we may be here for a while yet. I would like you to be our guest for the night and we'll continue this conversation in the morning, when, I would strongly recommend, that you access legal assistance.'

Vanessa found it impossible to repress a sob, as she was accompanied to the cell in which she was expected to sleep. Her shoelaces and belt had been confiscated (normal procedure, in

*case she had it in mind to do anything stupid), and she shuddered
at the metallic clunk of the door behind her. The hatch slid back to
reveal the eyes of Sergeant Watson.*

*'Sleep well, Ms Jones. Oh, and please accept my apologies;
room service has the night off.'*

Clang; the hatch closed, leaving her more alone than ever.

'So, who's going first then?' asked Clive. 'As the front man; how
about you Tom?'

At last, they reckoned, a hole of adequate proportions had been
created and they'd all shaken hands in celebration of their
monumental achievement. Tom nodded and hunched down on all-
fours, before squeezing his not inconsiderable frame through to the
other side.

'What's in there?' enquired Bill.

'How the hell should I know? It's pitch-black. Come on
through.'

Bill was next, followed by Clive and, bringing up the rear as
usual, Ray. They held hands and formed a line as Tom carefully
felt his way around the wall, hoping against hope that a door might
appear. Tom stopped suddenly, causing the others to concertina
into each other.

'Wait, there's a handle here,' he exclaimed. 'Shit, it's locked.'

'Are you sure?' asked Ray. 'Give it another try.'

'Yes, I'm positive; it won't budge. Looks like you were right
Bill; out of the frying pan and into the fire.'

There was nothing more to say, as they all groaned in defeat
and sank back against the wall.

'Shhh! What's that?' said Bill. He'd always had sensitive
hearing and could pick out the slightest sound amid cacophony or
silence.

'Can't hear a thing,' said Ray, after they'd all listened for half-
a-minute.

'Yeah, but you're a drummer,' said Bill, 'you're bound to be a
bit mutton. It's very faint, but there's something coming from over
there. Let me lead, Tom.'

Tom swore as Bill stood on his toe in the process of swapping
places, before Bill led them slowly towards the source of the
faintest of noises. He stopped every few steps and demanded

silence, then continued across the uneven floor.

'There; can you hear it now?'

'Yes,' exclaimed Tom; 'it's people talking.'

Bill walked on, his hand sweeping ahead as he went; the sound growing a tad louder and more discernible. Then Bill felt something metallic on the wall, and ran his fingers down louvre slats. He pressed his ear against it and addressed the others.

'It's an air-vent and there are human beings somewhere above us. I can hear talking and clanking noises. Did anyone notice what was next-door before the gig?'

Nobody had, but all agreed that it didn't matter; there were people there that could help. Bill shouted into the vent, causing the others to jump out of their skin. He placed his ear back against the vent and listened for any response; nothing. The conversation above continued as before, babbling and incoherent.

'There's too much noise going on up there,' he concluded. 'Maybe if we all shout at once. Ready; after 3: 1 - 2 - 3.'

'HEEELLLPPP!!!!'

He listened once more to no reply. Whatever was overhead, it was an active environment with people going about their business, oblivious to the desperate cries for assistance from beneath. Bill cursed in frustration.

'We can't have come this far, only for nobody to hear us,' he sighed.

'Perhaps if we were to sing,' suggested Ray. 'What do we have that lends itself to acapella?'

'Only one tune that I can think of,' said Tom; 'I guess it's worth a try.'

He took a deep breath, before warbling the opening lines to *Stood Up, Again*, singing as if his life depended on it; which, of course, it did. The rest of the band waited, before joining him on the chorus. Even in their current state of desperation, Bill wondered at the beautiful tones, enhanced by the resonant acoustics of their prison. As the song came to a close, Bill could just make out voices from above. The clamour had ceased and the chatter was more defined, as if they were talking directly into the ventilation system.

那是什麼聲音

('Wha' tha' noise?').

聽起來像瘦愛和妓院的人

('Soun' like Skinny Ted and Blothel Cleeper').

191

他們是誰

('Who hell they?').

搖滾樂隊

('Lock'n'loll band').

從來沒有聽說過他們

('Never heard of them').

Within minutes, the door was unlocked to reveal the outline of two shocked Oriental gentlemen. Bill could have hugged them in his relief, but exercised restraint. One of the men flicked the switch outside the door to illuminate the basement and enquired - 'Where you come from?'

'We were trapped next-door,' explained Tom, squinting in the light. 'The only way out was through there.'

The men looked to where Tom was pointing.

'You pay fix hole in wall,' demanded the one on the left.

'What, oh, absolutely,' said Tom, 'least we can do.'

'Which one Skinny Ted?' enquired the one on the right.

'You know who we are?' asked an incredulous Bill.

'You on TV; police look for you.'

'Hey, can we get out of here?' pleaded Ray. 'I need to breathe fresh air again.'

They followed their saviours gratefully up a narrow staircase and emerged in a busy kitchen, full of industrious chefs and waiters; all of whom stopped to stare as they were led through sizzling woks and boiling pans, to the restaurant. The clientele paused mid-chew to appraise the emaciated and grimy group before them. Some grabbed their phones and took pictures; they would be the first to announce the unearthing of Skinny Ted and the Brothel Creepers on social media, a band that most of them had never heard of until this week.

Bill felt disorientated and dazzled. They'd been imprisoned, with hardly any light and only each other for company; it came as something of a shock to be thrust into a packed and buzzing eatery. He looked at Tom for reassurance, but could see that he was feeling the same. The aroma of food invaded their nostrils and Clive turned to one of the men who had accommodated their escape.

'Hey, do you have a table for four?'

'Yes, sir; I sure we can fit you in.'

'What are you doing?' asked Bill. 'Shouldn't we let people

192

know we're safe?'

'Look, we haven't had a decent meal for God knows how many days. I'm starving and another hour or so won't make any difference. We can contact our loved-ones once we've ordered. What do you say?'

After unanimous agreement, they were led to a table in the far corner of the Hong Kong Garden restaurant. Bill got the impression that their hosts wanted them as far away from the other customers as possible, and who could blame them; for they were unkempt, unshaven, dirty, greasy and smelly. Bill thanked their rescuers and asked for their names. (1)

'This is Kuo and I am Laquan.'

Bill proffered his hand - 'Well, thank you Kuo and Laquan; we will repay you for setting us free. Now, may we see your menu please?'

They ordered a set meal for four then asked if they could use the phone, as each of their mobiles were out of charge. Their hosts were very obliging, as long as they were quick and didn't monopolise the restaurant's main source of income; their means of receiving takeaway calls.

Bill went first, to be met with a barrage of abuse from Elaine for putting the kids through hell. He thanked her for her concern, said he was fine and that he'd call back when she'd calmed down a bit.

Karen was virtually incoherent through her tears of relief and Tom promised he'd explain later and be home as soon as he could.

Clive called his parents to be met with sobs from his mother and a stern talking to from his father about what happens when you keep bad company.

Ray decided he had no-one to call.

A veritable feast ensued, each ravenous and eager to compensate for their recent malnutrition. Mixed hors d'ouuvre, beef in black bean sauce, sweet and sour chicken, vegetables in Szechuan sauce, crispy duck, egg fried rice… much licking of lips and expressions of satisfaction, as they tucked in appreciatively. Tom suggested red wine as an accompaniment, declaring that he never thought he'd say it, but he was utterly sick of beer. Ray was ordered back on the wagon and scowled as he sipped his Coke, with ice and lemon. It didn't take long to demolish all that was placed before them and there was a temptation to order the same again; but Bill insisted that it was time to visit the nearest police station to advise them to call off the search.

'I wonder who reported us missing,' mused Tom. 'We must be more valued than we thought.'

Ray took a deep breath and sobbed - 'I thought we were going to die down there and now we've been given another chance. It's almost like divine intervention.'

Bill and Tom exchanged nervous glances; the spectre of Stan, God rest his soul, was in both of their minds. (2)

1. *Hong Kong Garden* by Siouxsie and the Banshees, released in 1978, was one of the first post-punk hits. The classic song was named after a Chinese restaurant of the same name frequented by the band, and the lyrics concerned Siouxsie's contempt for the racist skinheads who used to pick on the restaurant's employees.

2. As previously stated, I have never been there, but a look on Google Maps reveals that there isn't a Chinese restaurant next-door to Eric's Club. However, this is a work of fiction and we'll call it artistic license.

The duty solicitor sat beside her, as Vanessa prepared herself for further cross-examination. She had barely slept, the cell cold and the rudimentary bed uncomfortable, consisting of a thin plastic mattress with no covers. Every half-an-hour the door-hatch had been slid back; police procedure to ensure that their detainee was still breathing.

Now, back in that interview room, tired and stressed, she steeled herself for the inevitable questions. The same lady PC was present for the interrogation, which somehow felt reassuring. Sergeant Watson looked Vanessa in the eye with an expression of patience, as if he was used to difficult customers like her.

'For the benefit of the tape; present are Ms Vanessa Jones, duty solicitor Michael Graves, PC Penny Jordan and, conducting the interview, myself, Sergeant Jake Watson. Any objections that we continue? Good. Ms Jones, I believe that you have recently moved into the area; can you tell me your reasons for your choice of location please?'

Vanessa glanced at Mr Graves, who advised that she didn't have to answer that question.

'No, it's fine,' said Vanessa. 'I moved here because I'd secured

a job at the Lakeside Residential Home.'

'And were there no nursing homes offering employment near to your previous address?'

'Perhaps, but I wanted to get away; start afresh.'

'Is it a coincidence that one of the residents in your chosen place of employment is the mother of a certain Bill Harris, of Skinny Ted and the Brothel Creepers' fame; a band that, it could be said, you follow to the point of obsession?'

Vanessa said nothing, but avoided eye contact, which prompted the sergeant to continue.

'I understand that you have also been offering your services to the local community, in a voluntary capacity at the Big Youth Club.'

'Yes.'

'The very same youth club frequented by Nathan Harris; the son of the aforementioned Bill Harris. Is this, too, a coincidence, Ms Jones?'

'You have been busy with the detective work,' said Vanessa, as she hung her head.

'It's my job, Ms Jones. Now, can we stop playing games and will you tell me what's going on? If there is a perfectly innocent explanation for all of this, then you will be free to leave.'

Vanessa considered her situation and concluded that she had no option but to come clean. After all, it would only be a matter of time before this experienced officer solved the mystery, with or without her co-operation. She took a deep breath and was about to speak, when an urgent knock on the door interrupted proceedings. Sergeant Watson cursed beneath his breath and spoke into the recording device.

'Interview suspended.' He opened the door and bellowed: 'What is it?'

'Sorry to interrupt Sarge,' cowered a callow young PC, 'but there's something you should know.'

Vanessa sighed and flopped back in her chair, exhausted emotionally and physically. The solicitor advised her to gather her thoughts and requested a cup of tea for them both. PC Jordan hesitated then contacted the front desk to ask for refreshments.

It took fifteen minutes for the sergeant to return, during which time, solicitor, Michael Graves, strongly recommended that Vanessa not say anything that could incriminate her. There was nothing else to do but ponder her predicament. How had she come to this? What cruel twists of fate had brought her to this point in her life; the point of no return. Despite the well-meaning advice of the solicitor, she'd already determined to tell the truth, but Sergeant Watson's re-entrance brought with it an intriguing update.

'*It seems that our missing persons have turned up, Ms Jones.*'

'*Does that mean I'm free to go?*'

'*No, it does not. Although we know they are safe, they are far from well and are being checked out at a hospital in Liverpool. They are suffering from lack of proper food and drink, not to mention serious psychological effects. It seems they have been imprisoned in the basement of the venue where they last played. By your own admission, we already have you at this location on the night in question. That, coupled with your suspicious behaviour concerning Mr Harris and his family, makes you a prime suspect.*'

There wasn't much more to say, as Bill lounged upon the sofa in his old family home. Elaine had gathered together all the kids and had been surprisingly understanding and generous in her welcome. Her new partner had made himself scarce for the occasion; a gesture for which Bill had expressed some respect. Elaine actually seemed genuinely concerned and it was she who'd reported them missing, after consultation with Karen, who'd confirmed that she couldn't contact Tom either. Elaine had wanted to speak with Bill about Nathan's somewhat disappointing school report and had become worried when he didn't answer or call back.

It was an emotional time for one and all as the Brothel Creepers were reunited with their respective kith and kin. A happy homecoming for Tom, as Karen told how much she'd missed him and, due to how worried she'd been, concluded that she must still love him.

Much to Ray's surprise, his son Keith had been in touch and they were due to meet next week. He thought he'd lost his dad and had realised that, regardless of his faults, you only get one.

Clive's elderly parents had also been worried sick and he was covered in hugs and kisses; an outpouring of affection not known since childhood. He'd also been contacted by Chloe, an ex-girlfriend, who asked if he wanted to talk about it.

Grace sat on Bill's lap, her arm around his neck as if she'd

196

never let him go again. Nathan had shaken him by the hand, a firm, manly shake that said don't be a stranger. Rosie wrested her eyes from her iPad for long enough to say welcome back and don't put us through anything like that again. Lauren had recently gained a new perspective on her old man and respect had resumed; she had burst into tears upon his return.

'Hey, Dude,' smiled Jacob, as Bill clapped him on the shoulder.

Elaine had prepared a celebration buffet and, in his hunger for proper food, Bill could have devoured the lot, but respectfully waited until everyone else had taken theirs. It was a revelation for Bill, to rediscover how lucky he was; how sometimes you have to come close to losing everything before you know how much you have. He had four wonderful kids and even his relationship with Elaine could now be put in perspective. There was no chance they would get back together, but at least they could be friends.

All members of the band were due at the local police station later that afternoon; to be formally interviewed and to be appraised of the progress of the investigation. Bill and Ray picked Tom up on the way and Clive met them there. Bill remembered Sergeant Watson from his previous visit and was pleased to note that he wasn't quite so dismissive this time.

'Ah, Mr Harris, it's a pleasure to see you again; and these gentlemen, I take it, are your fellow Brothel Creepers. Which one's Skinny Ted, then?'

Tom patiently explained the origins of the name; how Skinny Ted was supposed to be the embodiment of the Teddy-Boy icon and that Brothel Creepers were a stylish shoe of the era, favoured by said Teddy-Boys.

'The name was bequeathed to us by our ex-drummer; Stan, God rest his soul.'

'Interesting,' said Sergeant Watson. 'Now, if you gentlemen would care to join me in here; I have a few questions, before I give you an update on how our investigations are proceeding.'

The room was basic, but contained sufficient chairs for them all. The last time they'd been in a similar room, was after the gig in Margate; where they'd first met Gabriel and his gang of Angels, in very different circumstances all those years ago. Ray hadn't been there, but had experienced police interview rooms on a few occasions, due to drunkenness and vagrancy charges. A lady PC stood impassively in the corner, as they all sat down.

'This is PC Jordan,' said Sergeant Watson. 'Now, if you don't

197

mind, I will record our conversation.'

'Are we being accused of anything?' asked Ray. 'I thought we were the victims here.'

'It's just procedure, so that we have a record of everything relating to the case. Now, your perception is that you were deliberately imprisoned in the basement of Ernie's Club in Liverpool. Is that correct?'

'The door was locked when we tried to leave,' answered Bill. 'There was no signal so we couldn't call for help.'

'So, it's a logical conclusion that this was a potentially malicious act.'

'You try living in a place like that for nearly a week,' said Tom. 'I'd say it was pretty malicious to lock us in there.'

'So, if it was a deliberate, do you have any idea who would want to do such a thing?'

They all looked at Bill for the answer. He shook his head in bemusement.

'I have raised my concerns previously at this station, about a lady who attends all of our gigs. How about you start by asking her some questions?'

'We already have, sir; and our investigation is ongoing. The lady concerned denies all knowledge of the incident. Do you have any enemies that you can think of?'

Each looked at the other suspiciously, while each racked their brains for memories of anyone with whom they'd had disagreements. Nobody could come up with a single person who they'd upset so much, except Tom.

'Only person I can think of, where we parted on less than amicable terms, is Stan, God rest his soul. He's the one that split the band first time around, but it is us that should be pissed off with him, rather than the other way around.'

'So, am I to understand that we are looking for a ghost in connection with your misfortune?'

'Oh, Stan's not dead; well, not as far as we know, anyway. You see, the reason he left was because he'd found God and he couldn't reconcile the debauched lifestyle of a band on the road with his new-found faith. Last we heard he was playing tippy-tappy up in Scotland with some Christian rock outfit named the God Squad. Christian rock; now there's an oxymoron for you. It's the devil's music; always has been, always will be.' (1)

'So, why do you always refer to him as "Stan, God rest his

soul"?' asked an incredulous Ray. He was as discombobulated as the sergeant at this surprise revelation.

'It's his soul we're asking God to rest,' replied Tom, 'we always thought he lost it when he left us in the lurch. The name just kind of stuck. As far as I'm concerned, any animosity is consigned to the past. We have a much better and more versatile drummer now.'

'Well, thank you,' said Ray, 'but I think you could have told me that my predecessor was very much alive.'

'Never really thought about it,' said Tom, 'it's just a nickname as far as we're concerned.'

'And do you think this Stan, God rest his soul, would harbour any ill will towards you?' asked Sergeant Watson. 'Maybe some jealousy because you've reformed.'

'No, I can't see it,' said Bill. 'I saw him a few years back. He still has some connection with the local church. Last thing he said to me was "God bless you"; then he shook my hand, smiled and went back to his congregation. Didn't seem like a man with a grudge to bear.'

'Do you have an address for Stan?'

'No, we don't exactly exchange Christmas cards,' said Bill. 'You could try St. Mary's on Church Street; they may have contact details. But I honestly think you'll be wasting your time.'

'We have to cover every possibility, Mr Harris.'

'You say you have interviewed our mystery lady in yellow,' reiterated Bill; 'have you ruled her out as a suspect?'

'Not entirely, but call it an old copper's instinct, I give some credibility to her denials.'

'So, where do we go from here?' asked Bill.

'The lady in question is waiting in the room next door, sir. I think you should listen to what she has to say.'

'She wants to speak to us?'

'No, just to you, sir.'

Sergeant Watson dismissed Tom, Clive and Ray, who agreed to meet Bill in the pub round the corner once he'd finished his meeting. Bill was shaking; he knew who he was hoping to see when he walked through that door but, if it was her, he couldn't imagine how he'd feel; how she'd feel. Sergeant Watson knocked on the door and held it open for Bill.

'Aren't you coming in too?' enquired Bill.

'No, I think this should be a private conversation. PC Jordan will be just outside should you have any concerns.'

Bill stepped forward and saw before him the girl he'd met all those years ago. Sure she'd aged somewhat, but the eyes were the same, the smile just as radiant; but something wasn't right. He stood transfixed in the doorway, before she said: 'Aren't you going to come in, then?'

Despite his confusion, he shuffled over and sat opposite her at the desk. It was a police interrogation room and he wondered who would be interrogating who. Bill looked her in the eye and spoke first.

'Is it really you?'

'I'm really me, yes.'

'And why; after all these years?'

'You want to know why I've been following you.'

'Amongst other things, yes.'

'You could say that I'm your past come back to haunt you.'

Bill drifted back once more to that day in Brighton; a perfect day he'd never forgotten and still she kept him on tenterhooks. Now, perhaps it was time for him to reap what he'd sown. (2)

'Firstly, you must prepare yourself for a shock,' said Vanessa. 'The lady you think I am is dead. She passed away last year after a long battle with cancer.'

Bill hung his head and shook with grief; grief for a flame that had once burned so bright; for youth so cruelly trampled by life; for summer killed by the icy claws of winter; for dreams dreamt no more. He looked back at the lady before him as she continued...

'I found her diaries among her personal effects, when clearing the loft after her death. It told the story of the day you met and what happened to her afterwards. There was a Valentine's card that she never sent, a pressed rose and an old box of memorabilia relating to Skinny Ted and the Brothel Creepers, along with a complete collection of your records. A yellow mini-skirt was folded neatly at the bottom, next to a pair of vintage Dr Martens - the clothes she wore on the night you met.'

Bill was growing more sorrowful and angrier with each detail revealed.

'And what gives you the right to imitate her, to wear her clothes and to hunt me down, to harass my mother even? Who the hell are you to be so cruel?'

Vanessa hesitated and tears began to well. She was struggling to speak, but it hit Bill hard when the answer came.

'I'm your daughter,' she sobbed, 'and it was my mother's heart that was broken in two.'

Bill reeled in amazement. He could see it now; why her face looked so familiar. Not only was he looking at the features of his long-lost love, but he could see the image of his other children too. There was no doubt about the authenticity of her story. Speechless, he stared back at Vanessa; a grown-up daughter that he didn't know he had. How does anyone react to news such as this? He'd turned as white as the spectre he saw before him.

'Do you want some time out?' asked Vanessa. 'I know this is a big shock; go outside and get some air and allow it all to sink in.'

'Yes... please,' replied Bill, with mouth still agape. He almost staggered through the door and made his way to the exit, passing Sergeant Watson on his way.

'Is everything OK, Mr Harris?'

'I just need some air; I'll be back in five.'

'Understandable, sir.'

Bill almost passed out as the cold breeze hit his face. He leant on some railings and watched the blur of traffic whiz by. Did each car contain a story such as his, exposés that no-one would dream of? He took deep, deep breaths and tried to control his anxiety. Then he burst into a torrent of tears; the accumulation of stressful experiences of the last year; the roller-coaster ride of the band versus reality; culminating in the momentous disclosure he'd just heard. Eventually, he wiped away the tears, blew his nose and mastered sufficient control to return and continue the conversation.

'I was beginning to wonder if you were coming back,' said Vanessa; 'thought I'd scared you away.'

'I didn't mean to break her heart,' Bill blurted out the words that filled his head. 'I loved her and I was there the next day where we'd arranged to meet.'

'Yes, the diaries told it all. Mum was grounded so she couldn't go. She shouldn't have been at the gig and, when her father found out, he locked her in her room. She even tried to climb out of the window, but was dragged back inside the house. Imagine his reaction when, a few months later, she announced that she was pregnant. It wasn't acceptable for a good Catholic girl; she was kicked out and had to bring me up alone.'

'Oh, God, I'm so sorry.'

'Don't be; I wouldn't be here without your, what shall we call it, act of passion.'

'You know our best known song is about your mother.'

'Yes; the diaries tell that Mum suspected that the song was about her.'

'I wanted to use her name in the lyric, but Careless Eric had already written a tune called Veronica.' (3)

'Ha, and Mum always hated that name; said it sounded like some kind of fungal foot infection.'

Vanessa was almost laughing now. She'd had the last year to come to terms with her loss. Bill was still in shock from these staggering revelations.

'And did she never tell you who your father was?' he asked.

'No, she said it was best left alone; and I had a great upbringing. Mum sacrificed everything for me; she'd done well at school and could have got a decent job, or gone to uni even; she never had a proper career; she never married or had a long-term relationship; everything she did was to keep me safe and happy. The diaries tell of two occasions when she tried to find you. The first, when she was pregnant; she went to see you at some gig in London to tell you the good news. You were there with some blonde on your arm; it was just after you'd appeared on Top of the Pops, so she thought she was out of her league.'

'Never,' said Bill. 'I would have run to her like a shot.'

'The second time was when I was thirteen and had started getting curious about my father. Eventually, she gave in and said she'd search, but told me she'd been unsuccessful. It wasn't until I discovered the diaries that I learned that she had actually found you; but you were married with a young family and she didn't want to cause trouble for your wife and kids. That's the kind of lady she was; selfless and considerate to others, regardless of her own happiness.'

'And weren't you resentful, once you'd discovered all of this, that she'd kept me a secret?'

'I was at first,' confessed Vanessa, 'but I came to see that she had the best of motives, as she always did.'

'Why didn't you simply come and talk to me, as you are now; why all the subterfuge and mystery?'

'Because I didn't know how you'd react; whether you'd believe me. And I wanted to see if you remembered Mum; and I guess I wanted to make you suffer a bit, like we had to.'

'Well, you've certainly done that; but Sergeant Watson says that you weren't responsible for locking us in that basement.'

'No; please believe that it wasn't me.'

Bill smiled - 'Yes, I think I believe you. Besides, I have a lot of faith in an old copper's instincts. I never forgot your mother, you know; and I never will. Now that we've finally met, will you stick around to remind me?'

'Do you want me to; after all the trouble I've caused?'

'Of course; you're my daughter. We have a lot of lost time to make up.'

'What will you tell the rest of your family?'

'You leave that to me,' reassured Bill, 'and they're your family too. You've already met your Grandmother, of course.'

'Yes, and she's a lovely lady who told me all about you when you were a child. I have another confession to make; I've met Nathan too. I volunteer at his youth club.'

'Jesus; were you going to work your way through the whole family before you spoke to me?'

'Well, I wanted to meet my brother and sisters. Lauren seems nice too; though I'm sure she would have beaten me up at Bunter's, if you hadn't intervened.'

Bill nodded - 'Yeah, you could be right. I believe it's customary at this point to hug and cry a bit. That's how they do it on the telly anyway; on *Long Lost Family*.'

They both stood awkwardly and held each other tight; a feeling that felt as natural as a new dawn. Hugs and tears over, Bill took in their environment; not the most agreeable for a momentous occasion such as this.

'Hey, are you still under arrest?' he asked.

'No, I don't think so; but I guess we'd better ask before leaving.'

They made their way to the front desk, where Sergeant Watson stood in his now familiar pose; that of a dignified and seasoned, professional cop.

'Thank you,' said Bill, as he shook him firmly by the hand.

'It's a pleasure, sir. I can only apologise for not taking you seriously on your first visit; and to you Ms Jones for your brief incarceration here. If you had told us the truth, however, we could have reached this happy ending a lot quicker.'

Vanessa looked sheepish and apologised for wasting police time.

'And have you closed the case?' enquired Bill.

'Absolutely not. I retire in a few months' time, when they will knock this old place down to build houses; more bloody cutbacks and all that. I have been stuck behind that desk for the past five years because they deemed me too old to pound the beat. Therefore I have requested that they give me this one last case before I go. There are further lines of enquiry to follow and I will not rest until the mystery is solved. Believe me I will be in touch, sir.'

The sun had gone down whilst they were in the police station, so they emerged into a frosty evening. The usual light pollution filled the sky but, through the suburban orange glow, Bill swore he could see the prettiest star, twinkling in the heavens. Sentimental old sod that he was he liked to think that it was Veronica looking down upon them. (4)

Apprehensively, they made their way to the pub, where Bill had agreed to meet the rest of the band and entered smiling. Only Tom saw them coming, Clive and Ray with their backs to the door, deep in conversation. Bill took a deep breath – he had some explaining to do.

'Guys, I'd like you to meet Vanessa…'

1. The blues was referred to in the early 1900s as "the devil's music", by both the white establishment and the religious black community. This was reinforced by the legend of Robert Johnson, who purportedly made a deal with the devil at a crossroads in Mississippi.
2. A nod to Lou Reed's *Perfect Day* from his 1972 album *Transformer* and a double a-side single with *Walk on the Wild Side*.
3. *Veronica* is a track from the 1978 album *The Wonderful World of Wreckless Eric*. The song tells the tale of a soldier going to war and waiting for a message from his girl. Wreckless Eric was a Stiff Records contemporary of Ian Dury, Nick Lowe and Elvis Costello who, incidentally, also recorded a song named *Veronica*, co-written with Paul McCartney, on his 1989 album *Spike*.
4. *The Prettiest Star* was originally released as a single by David Bowie in 1970 as the follow up to *Space Oddity* and featured Marc Bolan on guitar. The song was re-recorded in 1972 for the *Aladdin Sane* album with Mick Ronson taking over guitar duties.

They'd dabbled with fame before, of course, albeit small-time and fleeting; but how would they cope with the demands of the modern-day media? It seemed that everyone wanted a piece of them and Gabriel had to employ an assistant to field a multitude of interview requests and offers of advertising contracts. Big venues wanted to book them, conglomerates wanted to sponsor their next tour, and social media was thrown into a frenzy of tweets and posts.

The story of their disappearance and subsequent resurrection had captured the public imagination and Bill feared that privacy was a thing of the past. No longer would people say - "never heard of them", whenever their name was mentioned. They were afforded greater exposure than ever before and their music could be heard on radios up and down the country, with the new album mooted for Number 1 and international acclaim. There was even talk that the 'lost' *Live in Holloway* tapes had been found and that they sounded amazing.

'Well, I never thought I'd miss obscurity,' said Tom, after he and Bill were stopped in the street and asked for their autograph once more. 'We can't even pop into the Red Lion for a pint anymore, without someone coming up and pestering us; it's as if we're public property.'

'Isn't this what we've always wanted, though,' asked Bill, 'to be famous, our music known to everyone? I even heard 'billy Dub played on a reggae station yesterday and you can't get better kudos than that.'

'I guess you're right,' conceded Tom. 'Gabriel says that if we manage this properly we'll never have to work again and can live of the proceeds of our music. Now, those are words that I never thought I'd hear.'

'Yeah, that would be something else; and you know what I'd really like to do? Pay John back for when he bailed us out last time around. I know he says he doesn't want the money back, but it'd make me feel good.'

'And how are things, family-wise?' enquired Tom. 'That was some bombshell you had to drop on everyone.'

'Took a while for me to come to terms with it too,' said Bill. 'Vanessa's great with everyone; although it did put Lauren's nose out of joint to learn that she wasn't the oldest anymore. I had to tell Elaine first and she wasn't even surprised; said she would have been jealous once, but now hoped we could all be happy and move on. Nathan was a bit shocked, to say the least, when he was introduced to his sibling; he looked terrified when he first came in. He says Vanessa's cool, but I'm sure they have a secret between them that they're hiding from us. Grace loves her new big sister and even Rosie has allowed her to help with the homework;

Vanessa used to be a teacher, you know.'

'Yes, she seems like a lady of many talents,' observed Tom, 'but I take it she's unemployed now.'

'No, she's not as it happens. I popped into see her boss, Wilma, at the residential home, who, incidentally, I'm taking out to lunch next week, but that's another story. I told her the whole sorry tale and she's agreed to give Vanessa her job back.'

'Wilma, ay? An unusual name.'

'Apparently her parents were big Flintstones fans; it was either Wilma or Pebbles. What about you and Karen; is everything OK?'

'Yeah, we're cool. I've promised her a second honeymoon, if we ever get out of the spotlight for long enough.'

'It's funny that it can take a calamitous event to bring people closer together,' mused Bill.

'Yeah, Karen thought it was pretty calamitous when we reformed. In retrospect she may have been right; who knows what the future has in store?'

Vanessa had never had a father before, not even one of the step variety. Whilst it felt natural to walk beside Bill, there was an inevitable awkwardness as they strolled through the municipal park. It was one of those winter days that epitomised England; damp, cold, grey and home. Their feet slid across the remnants of autumnal leaves, as they learned of each other's past, present and hopes for the future.

Bill asked most of the questions; after all, Vanessa had already done her research. She knew as much, if not more, about Skinny Ted and the Brothel Creepers than he did; their back catalogue, gigs, press reviews and interviews. She was aware of their current materiel through recent concerts and the proposed release date for the imminent album. His political and personal views could be read from his lyrics and it was obvious that they were sincerely felt. She'd now met all the family and had gleaned as much information about her dad as she could in the short space of time available. All in all there wasn't a great deal left to know about this seemingly unpretentious and honest man.

Vanessa's past however, from Bill's perspective, was cloaked in mystery and he was full of curiosity about her mother, where they'd lived, how they'd coped and how Vanessa felt about his absence. They stopped to rest on a bench by the lake and Bill took out the bag of seeds he'd brought to feed the ducks, swans and geese. Nearby, a family with three young children were excitedly going through the same ritual.

'This is what I missed when I was a child,' sighed Vanessa, 'my dad taking me to the park to feed the ducks and stuff like that.'

'Suppose you're going to want an ice-cream on the way back,' said Bill.

'Of course; you owe me lots of ice-creams.'

'You can have as many ice-creams as you want; but they won't make up for what we've both lost.'

'You're lucky, you know,' stated Vanessa, 'we can recreate the best bits like this, but you missed the time when the hormones kicked in and when my first boyfriend broke my heart; my dark period, when Mum went away for the week to visit Auntie Meg and she returned to discover that I'd painted my bedroom black. And you missed Mum's illness, where I had to watch her gradually fade away and disappear. Don't get me wrong; it hasn't all been bad, but there have been some pretty trying times.'

'We all have stressful times to varying degrees,' said Bill, 'but I wish I'd have been there to help you through them. I don't know whether you can classify what your mother and I had as love after such a brief encounter, but she sure made a big impression on me. Things could have been so different if I'd known how to find her; and the tears have never been far away since you told me she was gone.'

'Yeah, well we can't turn back the clock. We'll just have to make the most of what we have now.'

Vanessa looked down to see that they were surrounded by anticipant and noisy ducks. She threw a handful of seeds and they fought until each and every morsel had gone. She hoped that she wouldn't have to fight with her new-found siblings, the band and the fans, for the scraps of Bill's attention.

The police station was becoming a familiar haunt for the band and they had been summonsed once more, for further questioning. Bill enquired as to whether or not the police had made any further progress.

'Perhaps, sir,' said Sergeant Watson. 'I have changed the focus of my investigation, from those who might wish you ill, to those who might benefit from these unfortunate series of events. I understand that your latest record is now number 1 in the hit parade…'

'The hit parade,' interrupted Ray,' do they still call it that?'

'… and, that you have appeared on TV to tell of your ordeal and promote your forthcoming album. You have fingers in a number of potentially lucrative pies and appear to be revelling in surprising popularity. Is it unreasonable of me to suggest that you have come out of this smelling of roses?'

'We're doing OK,' said Tom.

'Indeed you are, sir. One could almost say that your recent disappearance has stoked the fires of publicity and that you have emerged triumphant.'

'Hang on,' protested Bill, 'are you suggesting that we orchestrated the whole thing?'

'Not you necessarily, but someone closely involved with your resurgent career, possibly.'

'Gabriel!!!' they all said in unison.

'My many years in the force has taught me not to reach conclusions before all the evidence is gathered, or until the criminal bastards have confessed; but I have been in discussion with a certain gentleman named Gabriel Cherubim, formerly known to the police as Bob Smith. It was he, in fact, who told us upon our original enquiry, that he'd witnessed you leaving the venue of your incarceration after the show, thereby diverting our investigation elsewhere.'

'No, surely not,' said Bill. 'He wouldn't do that to us, would he?'

'I understand that it is customary in the music business,' continued Sergeant Watson, 'for a manager to take a percentage of the performers' income. I take it you have a contract with Mr Cherubim, a.k.a. Smith.'

'Yes, of course,' said Bill, 'but he's done a lot for us; he's earned his cut so far.'

'But, is it not the case that his income will increase significantly, given your improved prospects?'

There was no denying the logic in Sergeant Watson's summation. Gabriel had the means, motive and opportunity, but none of the band could believe that someone they'd come to like and trust, would put them through such an ordeal. They sat in silent astonishment while the notion sank in, before Bill voiced their collective thoughts.

'And do you have him in custody?'

'No, we don't, sir. I had nothing to go on but my own hunch and, when challenged, he laughed in my face. I could not arrest him without further evidence.'

'So, you have nothing but a crackpot theory,' said Tom. 'It's ridiculous; I can't believe we're even considering it.'

'There is also the fact that he's nowhere to be found. When we tried to contact him for further questioning, he was unobtainable. His partner, Mr Victor Vauxhall, says he hasn't seen him for a few days. It's an old police trick; when you have no concrete evidence you confront the suspect with your theory to provoke a reaction. It seems that our Mr Cherubim was sufficiently spooked to do a runner which, one could argue, is a possible indication of guilt.'

Bill shook his head in disbelief - 'And you have no idea where he is?'

'I was hoping that you gentlemen might be able to help me there.'

'How the hell should we know,' said Ray, 'he doesn't share his itinerary with us.'

'I know of a place that he may be,' said Bill, prompting everyone to stare at him in anticipation. 'After my mother was taken into care, he came to see me to check that I was OK for the gig that weekend. He told me of a shack he has in Norfolk that he uses as a retreat when things get too much; even offered to let me stay there if I wanted to escape for a while. It's in the middle of nowhere, he said, a remote part of the Broads where no-one goes and only accessible by boat. It's a bit of a long shot, but I would imagine that Victor has the address.'

'Then I suggest that you and I speak with Victor and pay this haven of tranquillity a visit,' said Sergeant Watson.

Victor was not his usual self and Bill was shocked at his gaunt and unshaven appearance. His customary immaculate attire had obviously been left in the wardrobe and he lounged in old jeans and a grey, shapeless hoodie. The plush flat that he shared with Gabriel was in disarray, with empty beer bottles and cigarette butts in abundance. Victor invited his visitors to sit down and avoided

Sergeant Watson's gaze, as he reticently answered his questions.

'And do you know why Mr Cherubim has gone AWOL, sir?'

'He takes off sometimes when he's under stress. It's not the first time he's disappeared without warning.'

'It must be a distressing time for you, sir; and I can see that you are worried about him.'

'I will give him hell, as usual, when he returns; and he will admonish me about the state of the place. Then we will make up and things will go back to normal, whatever that is.'

'But things are not normal this time, are they, Victor? He is on the run from a police investigation and I think you know more than you are letting on. You are his business partner as well as his common-law partner; what can you tell us about recent events and Mr Cherubim's involvement in them?'

Victor looked to Bill for reassurance, but Bill sat with arms folded, a stern expression designed to convey that he wasn't happy and that Sergeant Watson and he were on the same side. Victor hesitated; he ran his fingers through his uncombed mop and fidgeted uncomfortably.

'I didn't know anything about it until afterwards, I swear,' he addressed Bill. 'I'm so sorry for what you went through and I don't know what Gabriel was thinking of. It's not like him to be so cruel, although I'm sure he'll say that the end justified the means. We had a big row about it before he left and I told him that, regardless of the happy outcome, it was unacceptable behaviour.'

'Do you think he's gone to his place in Norfolk?' asked Bill.

'How do you know about that? I thought it was our little secret place.'

'Oh, I have no idea where it is; he just offered me the use of it when I was going through a bad time.'

'Can you give us the address please, Victor,' demanded Sergeant Watson, 'I think Gabriel needs to come back and face the music.'

'OK,' sighed Victor, 'but I may have trouble giving you directions, as I've only been there once before. It was just after we met and he said it would be a romantic getaway. I hated the place; cold, damp and uncomfortable - he even brought an extra fishing rod for me, but I'm a city boy who loves his luxury. The bloody place doesn't even have a mirror, for God's sake; and have you ever tried getting into a hammock? Perhaps I should come with you, though? I may be able to talk him into coming quietly.'

'Are we expecting him to resist arrest, then? Should I bring back-up?' asked Sergeant Watson.

'You never know,' said Victor, 'he has been known to lose his rag and he was once an Angel, remember; he has an inherent distrust of authority.'

'I can vouch for that,' said Bill, 'you should have seen him in full flow, back in the day. I thought he'd mellowed though, and he won't have his gang with him this time.'

'He has mellowed and he's just a big pussycat really. He may get spooked if he sees a bunch of policemen, though. No, I think it best if it's just us.'

'Very well,' conceded Sergeant Watson, 'but I will have the local force on standby. We will leave first thing in the morning and I will pick you gentlemen up at 6 a.m. If it is as remote as you say, then it will take us some time to get there. And no prior warning to Gabriel that we are coming please, Victor.'

'There's no chance of that,' said Victor, 'he has his phone switched off and, when he's at his retreat, he is uncontactable; those are the rules. 6 a.m. though; it's a bit of an uncivilised hour, isn't it? I can't recall the last time I saw 6 a.m., unless we were still out from the night before.'

Vanessa was feeling neglected. After her astounding disclosure, she thought she'd be the centre of attention and spend more time with her new family, but the realisation hit that they all had lives of their own. Like any busy household there were routines of school runs, clubs and hobbies; barely a minute in the week to spare. Elaine had said to pop round whenever she wished, but she felt like a spare part on the odd occasion that she plucked up the courage to call in. Grace had been fascinated by her new big sister and was full of questions about why they had the same dad, but a different mum. Rosie's initial acceptance of assistance with the homework had waned, after she'd sussed that Vanessa wasn't going to do all the work for her; and Lauren was away at uni. Nathan had thanked her for bailing him out and for not grassing him up to his parents, but they'd both agreed that Vanessa should no longer volunteer at the youth club, as it would be too weird.

At least she had her old job back to keep her occupied, but her grandmother had no clue as to who Vanessa was; it broke

Vanessa's heart to know that she never would. It also felt slightly strange to learn that her dad was potentially dating her boss and, as a result, conversation between them was a little awkward. Bill had vowed to catch up with Vanessa at the weekend, but no date or time had yet been set. He was busier than ever, with the demands of fame and the ongoing police case taking up most of his days.

Elaine had asked her to join them for tea on Christmas Day, but Bill wouldn't be there. He had promised that they would spend some time together on Boxing Day, though. A possible Brothel Creepers tour had been proposed for the New Year, but it seemed that their manager was unobtainable and no details had been announced.

What did she expect? That her life would no longer be the same, that her family would drop everything to welcome her into the fold. They had all been wonderful after her sudden appearance from outer-space, but it wasn't going to happen overnight and Vanessa would have to show patience and integrate at their pace.

All in all she didn't regret the revelation of her origins and felt happier in herself that it was all out in the open. Perhaps she could have gone about things differently; employed an intermediary or wrote a letter; but that way she wouldn't have got to know her father through his music (his greatest passion and into which she hoped, she had a unique insight).

With nothing to do with her days off but vegetate, Vanessa decided to venture out to the shops and indulge in a bit of retail therapy; a sure-fire way to cheer herself up and, at the same time, regenerate her tired wardrobe. She'd always dressed simply; in her favourite hues of black and white, with jeans and t-shirts her preferred attire. Her late mother's yellow mini-skirt and Dr Martens, an indulgence for a specific purpose, she would probably never wear them again. They had however, awoken a desire for a little colour to brighten her days and to attract attention; to make some kind of a statement that she was here and wasn't going away.

In a rare mood of optimism, it was as if she was seeing colour for the first time, as she rifled through racks and racks of designer gear with designer prices. She held a lacy puce top against her body and studied her reflection: no, it wasn't right and she hung it back on the rail. The pale orange one next to it however, complimented her black hair and blue eyes to stunning effect and the attentive assistant, who hovered at her elbow, agreed. Vanessa had only once before spent so much on a top - for the wedding of an old friend - and she felt at once guilty and liberated.

To exit the shop she had to go through the men's section, where a black silk shirt boasting an extravagant, embroidered collar with pewter tips caught her eye. She immediately thought of Bill and, with no further ado, grabbed it and took it to the counter. The aloof and experienced-looking till-assistant looked at her askance, as if to say – 'Are you sure, Madam?'

'It's for my dad,' explained Vanessa, 'he's in a band.'

'Ah, yes, it is the kind of thing one might wear on stage. Anyone I might know?'

'Skinny Ted and the Brothel Creepers; my dad's the bass player and songwriter.'

'Oh, I've heard of them; they're pretty good.'

'We don't get many people hiring boats at this time of year,' said the grizzled old man at the boat-yard as he blew into his calloused hands and rubbed them together.

Sergeant Watson flashed his badge and explained - 'It's for police business. Nothing to worry about, but we need to access a certain location on the Broads. We'll have it back before close of play.'

The man tapped his nose in confirmation of confidentiality, nodded and escorted them to their mode of transport for the day; a small electric boat which, he explained had a top speed of six miles per-hour.

'The speed-limit is five, but can be four in built-up places. Keep to the right of the waterways in case you meet others coming the other way, although that's not likely on a day like this. It's the marine equivalent of the M25 in the summer, but you'd have to be a daft bugger to venture out in this weather. I would also recommend that you wear these life-vests in case you get into any trouble. '

Without further ado, the boat was untied from the jetty and they chugged out into the main channel, with Sergeant Watson at the helm. Once out of sight, Bill immediately discarded his life-vest, declaring that it was uncomfortable and unnecessary.

'I assume we can all swim,' said Sergeant Watson, as he and Victor followed suit.

'I used to be good at breast-stroke,' stated Bill, 'but I kept getting arrested.'

'Very droll, sir. Now then, Victor; we are at your behest for directions. I take it we are heading the right way.'

'Yes, but I can't guarantee that I'll remember where to turn off; it all looks the same in this mist. Last time I was here it was a beautiful summer's day.'

Bill couldn't deny that the little they could see of their surroundings evoked an eerie atmosphere (a bit like the Bayou, but without the heat, humidity and alligators), as trees and riverside houses drifted in and out of vision. The low-lying mist enveloped the boat and insidiously soaked them all in a cloak of coldness. A ghostly grey heron emerged from the gloom and glided by, barely a few feet from Bill's face. He shivered as he felt the breeze from its wings and watched it disappear as swiftly as it came.

All around was silent, the only sound the putt-putt of their modest vessel. Everywhere appeared to be deserted, most of the riverside homes used only in the summer-months, and the few other winter sailors they passed merely stared out of curiosity and nodded good morning. Victor recalled that Gabriel's hut was about forty-five minutes away and, as they approached that time, he peered into every recess in the bank for a tributary. Finally, they found a likely outlet and veered across-stream to head into the unknown. The mists had descended further and, with each bend, the river narrowed more. They could barely see the bow of the boat and the trees on the banks closed in claustrophobically.

'I don't remember it being this narrow,' declared Victor eventually, 'I think we should turn around.'

'Turn around where, exactly?' enquired Bill, who by now, had taken over driving duties. 'There's no room to turn around.'

He rammed the two-option gear-stick into reverse and attempted to retrace their trail. The engine protested at the sudden change in direction; then a judder and they were grounded. Bill revved forwards and backwards, but to no avail. Somehow, he'd managed to steer them into the bank, where tree roots snagged and held them tight. There was no other way it was agreed, than for someone to climb onto an adjacent fallen tree-stump and attempt to push them off from the shore, before jumping back on board; a dangerous manoeuvre which was likely to involve getting wet.

'You're the one that brought us down here,' Bill addressed Victor, 'it should be you who volunteers.'

'But this is an Armani coat,' protested Victor, 'I'm not going

214

out there.'

'Who the hell wears an Armani coat on a boat in the Norfolk Broads?'

'It was on the coat-stand by the door and my brain doesn't function at that time of the morning; I just grabbed what was nearest. Besides, you're the one who can't drive; it should be you who gets us out of this mess.'

'I'll do it,' sighed Sergeant Watson, 'we'll be here all day while you two argue the toss. Just make sure that one of you is ready to help me back in when I push off.'

The boat rocked as he stood and placed his leading foot on the starboard side, then it pitched violently when he used all his weight to launch his not inconsiderable frame at the fragmented bough. With a loud curse his nether-regions collided with bark, after his foot slipped and he landed, straddled, one leg either side. A philosophical Sergeant Watson took a moment to look forward to his retirement, as both boots filled up with murky water. Resigned to the discomfort he tried to stand, his balance good for one of such bulk, and in one graceful movement he pushed the boat with one foot and stepped in with the other, whilst simultaneously grabbing Bill's outstretched hand. They both crashed to the deck, while Victor attempted to control the boat. Miraculously the manoeuvre spun them around and they emerged facing the right direction and chugged back from whence they came.

'I hope our friend Gabriel is in an acquiescent humour when we catch up with him,' said Sergeant Watson, 'I'm really not in the mood for any nonsense.'

Bill concurred and sat down, as Victor continued his turn at the wheel. He steered carefully, conscious that four eyes were upon him after his criticism of Bill's and Sergeant Watson's driving. Back on the main drag, he didn't have to go far before another tributary emerged.

'This is it,' exclaimed Victor, 'I remember that sign.'

'There's a sign,' Bill huffed, 'why didn't you tell us that before?'

They remained silent whilst Victor slowly negotiated the slender offshoot, his face etched with worry, until Sergeant Watson suggested that they cut the engine.

'We don't want to warn him that we're coming,' he said, as they drifted slowly upstream, aided by an oar; 'that would spoil the surprise now, wouldn't it.'

The only sound was the water, lapping serenely around them. It was as if the world outside had disappeared and they were suspended, with no points of reference to indicate their location. Time stood still and their vessel coasted quietly. No-one spoke, for fear of revealing their presence.

CRACK!! A shotgun fired above their heads and a figure on the bank emerged from the mists. He stood defiant, with legs apart and his weapon at the ready; behind him, the outline of a modest shack, grey against the sky.

'Don't come any closer,' he shouted.

'Put that down, you stupid old fool.'

'Victor!! What are you doing here? Did you show them where to find me? How could you, of all people, betray me?'

'There's no betrayal like a lover, leaving in the dead of night, with no goodbye or clue as to when or if he's coming back. It is you who has betrayed me and, I beg of you, come back and face your responsibilities; to me, to the band and to yourself.'

'Who is there with you?' asked Gabriel.

'Only Bill and Sergeant Watson; we weren't expecting you to be armed. Where in hell did you get that thing, anyway?'

'Found it years ago, in a cupboard at the back of this place; must have belonged to the previous owner. I didn't even know if it still worked.'

'I would strongly recommend that you take Victor's advice and lay the weapon down, sir,' said Sergeant Watson. 'The further this situation escalates the worse it will be for you.'

'But it's already gone too far. They'll put me in prison for what I have done.'

'Not necessarily, sir. But I can guarantee that they will if you continue to point that thing at us. Now, Mr Smith, can we not stop all this silliness and sort things out like civilised human beings? I'm sure we'd all like to spend Christmas with our loved ones.'

'The name's Cherubim, Gabriel Cherubim; I changed it by deed poll.'

'Very well,' conceded Sergeant Watson, 'Gabriel it is. Would that we could all change our names and start anew; I always favoured Sherlock, but thought some of my colleagues might take the piss. How about we join you ashore and you can put the kettle on; I'm sure we could all do with a nice cup of tea.'

Too misty to see anything but a silhouette, no-one could see the expression on Gabriel's face, but his hesitation suggested that he was giving Sergeant Watson's entreaty some consideration. Bill kept his eye on the gun, currently pointed above their heads; he was ready to dive overboard if its trajectory changed to their direction.

'If it helps, I can promise that the band won't press charges,' offered Bill. 'I'd just like to understand why.'

'It all got out of hand,' said Gabriel, at last. 'How was I to know that it would take as long as four days for anyone to notice that you weren't around? I just thought that a little publicity wouldn't go amiss. It's my job to get you as much exposure as possible and from that perspective it couldn't have been more effective.'

'But we could have died down there,' protested Bill.

'Oh, I had you under surveillance the whole time; hidden cameras, you see. If anything had gone seriously wrong, then I would have released you immediately. The plan was to sell the footage for a reality TV show and I have interest from Channel 4. You and your cohorts are hot property, Bill; your single is number one and the album will follow, there's renewed interest in your back-catalogue and even Piers Morgan wants to interview you.'

Bill couldn't believe what he was hearing. Gabriel had set the whole thing up as a publicity stunt and, furthermore, had been watching them the whole time. He forgot about the gun in Gabriel's hand and let rip.

'You sadistic bastard; you sat there in the comfort of your own home and watched us suffer. And did you enjoy your entertainment?'

'It was a means to an end. You're more famous than ever before and that's what you wanted, isn't it?'

'Not like this, man. What on Earth made you think that we'd agree to appear on our own reality TV show? And as for Piers Morgan, I'd rather spend the rest of my life in obscurity than talk to him. We do have some standards, you know.'

'But don't you see that we needed something big to make it take off? Simply making good music isn't enough these days.'

Bill shook his head - 'I don't believe it; I can't take this in.'

'And, after hearing all that, do you still say that you won't press charges?' asked Gabriel.

'You need help, Gabriel, not prison,' said Bill in exasperation. 'Victor, how much of this sorry tale did you know?'

'Not the half of it.' He turned his attention to the apparition on the shore.

'Gabriel,' he pleaded, 'if you have any feelings for me, put the gun down and let us come ashore. It's bloody freezing out here and I need that cup of tea; or something stronger if you have it.'

Bill breathed a sigh of relief as Gabriel agreed and lowered the shotgun but, as he did so, a loud bang shattered the tranquillity.

'Shit,' screamed Gabriel, 'sorry, I didn't mean to do that. I haven't shot anyone, have I?'

Sergeant Watson and Bill both confirmed that they weren't hit then turned to see Victor, face down on the deck. Bill knelt to attend to the casualty and called Victor's name, then Sergeant Watson joined him by Victor's side.

'Oh, God; please, no,' wailed Gabriel. 'Please, tell me it isn't so.'

Bill and Sergeant Watson repeated Victor's name and shook him by the shoulder; no response. Bill searched for any sign of a wound.

Gabriel sank to his knees and sobbed. 'Victor, answer me; I'll do anything to make it up to you.'

Gently, Sergeant Watson turned Victor over to check if he was still breathing. He examined his body, but could find nothing; no bullet-hole, no blood. Victor slowly opened his eyes and winked.

'Shhh,' he whispered, 'let the bastard suffer for a while.'

'I don't think this is the time for emotional blackmail,' declared Sergeant Watson, as he felt rising water beneath his knees. 'He's shot a hole in the boat. We're sinking.'

'Please tell me he's OK,' pleaded Gabriel. 'I swear if he's gone, I will turn this gun on myself.'

'We're all alive,' replied Sergeant Watson, 'but the boat's going down. We need your help to get ashore.'

'Oh, thank God,' screamed Gabriel. 'Just step off; the water won't reach your waist.'

None of them were impressed with their welcome to Gabriel's Norfolk retreat. Bill, still in disbelief at the callous, premeditated treatment of he and his bandmates; Sergeant Watson disillusioned with the saturated indignity suffered in solving his final case; and Victor apoplectic that his beloved Armani coat was ruined.

Gabriel boiled the kettle and they all sat shivering around a basic wooden table, with hands cupped around mugs of hot tea or coffee. There were none of the trappings of the modern world; no TV, Wi-Fi or computer and there was barely room to swing a cat, should any of them have been so inclined. A single room with aforesaid table and chairs, a double-hob calor-gas oven and a hammock swung across bare wooden gables, it could only be politely described as cosy. A door at the back led to a tiny cubicle containing a chemical toilet. Victor observed that the bloody place hadn't developed any more character since his last visit, but Bill admitted that he could see the attraction; the peace and solitude, a sanctuary from the rat-race.

'So, what happens now?' asked Gabriel. 'I suppose I'm under arrest.'

'I'm afraid you are, sir,' replied Sergeant Watson, 'I have no choice but to charge you with possession of an offensive weapon, at least. Correct me if I'm wrong, but I doubt that you have a license for that thing. There are other offences to be taken into consideration and, despite the fact that Mr Harris here has declined to press charges, his colleagues may not be quite so amenable.'

One hour later and they boarded a police boat, manned by the local force. No matter how many times Gabriel declared that he was sorry for what he'd done and wouldn't resist arrest, Sergeant Watson insisted that he was handcuffed.

'Normal procedure I'm afraid; once we are back you can call your solicitor and we'll determine the next steps. The fact that you have admitted your guilt and come relatively quietly will work in your favour, but there will be consequences of your foolishness; as there should be.'

Little was said on the long journey back; Sergeant Watson remained professional and calm throughout; in the back Victor slept and Gabriel stared straight ahead, lost in thought; and in the passenger seat Bill still had the hump, to say the least, that Gabriel could be so manipulative and cruel.

Bill pondered Gabriel's words: "We needed something big to make it take off. Simply making good music isn't enough these days." He'd concocted this crazy, elaborate plan, with the sole aim that they would all become famous and prosper. At that moment Bill knew that none of it really mattered. They'd been blessed with the ability to entertain, enlighten and excite; occasionally to move strangers to dance or tap their feet, or maybe even sing, cry or think. What did it matter if they had that effect upon one person or thousands? So long as they stayed true to themselves and to those they loved, then fame and fortune could go to hell; even Stan, God rest his soul, would surely agree with that. He'd got off the ride before it got too scary and out of control; and, regardless of Bill's lack of belief, he was happy that Stan had found his way.

The New Year's Eve gig in their hometown had been booked long before their new-found infamy. It was intended to be an intimate show, for die-hard fans, family and friends; unfortunately demand for tickets now outweighed the modest venue's capacity by about one hundred to one. No matter; for the heroes' return, the leader of the Town Council had somehow pulled strings to get the show streamed live on massive screens in the Market Square. It would be some New Year's Eve party. (1)

Vanessa told Bill that she was looking forward to attending without subterfuge, alongside her new family; and this time, she promised, in her own clothes.

'Are you a medium?' she asked Bill.

'What; do you mean talking to the dead and all that?'

'No, shirt size; are you a medium?' Vanessa produced the spoils of her recent shopping trip. 'I bought you this; thought you might like it.'

Bill held it up and admired the style and sheen. He felt its elaborate embroidery and fingered the pewter tips of the collar.

'It's cool, I love it and I'm flattered, but I've got more chance of communicating with the other side than I have of fitting into this. Can I change it for a larger size; do you have the receipt?'

She looked disappointed. 'No, it was the last one in the sale. They said it couldn't be exchanged.'

Bill smiled - 'Then I guess I'd better get a corset; I wanna wear this on stage.'

As support band, the up-and-coming Jacob and the Dudes, completed their set to warm applause, Tom looked askance as Bill dressed for the performance, his face already puce with the effort.

'Are you sure about that shirt?' said Tom. 'I wouldn't want to be in the front row. As soon as you breathe out those buttons are gonna start flying.'

'It's a present from Vanessa.'

'That may be so and very nice it is too, but you'll pass out after five minutes. Look, all you have to do is wear it open, with a t-shirt underneath; simple.'

'Fashion adviser to the over-fifties; I like it, thanks.'

'No problem,' said Tom. 'Now, do you think we can get

through the evening without any drama or mishaps? It's been one hell of a year and I'd like to see another.'

Tom's phone rang, 'Hello…' He frowned as he listened intently to the response… 'I don't know; I'll have to ask the others…'

'Who is it?' asked Bill.

'It's Gabriel; says he and Victor are outside; wants to know if they can come in.'

There had been no contact between them since Gabriel's arrest. Bill had persuaded his colleagues that it wouldn't be in their interests to press charges and they had reluctantly agreed. Grudges were held however, particularly by Ray who was still deeply traumatised by the ordeal. He found it hard to forgive someone who had so carelessly jeopardised his road to recovery. With eyebrows raised, Tom looked at each of them in turn.

'OK by me, I guess,' conceded Clive.

'Yeah,' said Bill, 'I suppose it's still the season of goodwill to all men.'

'Looks like I'm outnumbered,' said Ray; 'OK, as long as I don't have to talk to the bastard.'

'You're in,' Tom told Gabriel, 'providing you behave yourself… What, are you serious?'

'What's up?' asked Clive.

'He says he'd still like to be our manager; says he has some great ideas…'

'He's got some neck,' said Ray.

'…apparently he even has some guy who wants to write our biography. …Who is it?' Tom asked Gabriel…

…'Never heard of him,' declared Tom.

'Look, can we talk about this next year,' suggested Bill, 'we have a show to do.'

'Yeah; once more unto the breach, dear friends, once more,' smiled Tom, as he cut Gabriel off.

Tom Milston, Bill Harris, Clive Hunt and Ray Arnold (collectively known as Skinny Ted and the Brothel Creepers), linked arms and stepped again into the spotlight; at the top of their game and on top of the world.

Bill beamed as he scanned the audience; they were all there – Vanessa, Lauren and Jacob, Rosie, Nathan (with Jade from the youth club smiling by his side), Grace; even Elaine with her new fella. At the front bopped Wilma, smiling back at him with all the promise of a new relationship. His brother John gave him the thumbs-up and Jessica tried to look as if she was having a good time. Tom's wife Karen with their offspring, Richard and Siobhan; Ray's lad Keith looking up at his father with pride; and Clive's ex and soon to be present, Chloe. Over to the side, Sergeant Jake Watson tapped his foot and, in the shadows at the back, a diminutive figure in black rested his soul. Gabriel and Victor had mastered the jive and cleared a large space around them on the dance-floor; they both had the audacity to look exuberant.

Jacob joined them for the encore, this time without the ladder; and Ras Putin brought the house down for the finale. Outside in the square the fireworks boomed and lit up the sky, as the clock struck twelve and the band played Auld Lang Syne. It was a cold night, but the crowd had been warmed by a red-hot performance. Skinny Ted and the Brothel Creepers were back!!

1. Musical events have been hosted in Aylesbury's Market Square intermittently for many years. It is not beyond the realms of possibility that Skinny Ted and the Brothel Creepers could conclude their adventure with such a momentous event.

Acknowledgements

As with my previous work, this couldn't have been achieved without filching the odd joke and anecdote from my longsuffering friends. Thanks once more to the following sources of inspiration and support:

Ralph Baker and Richard Packer - the best comedy double act in Southcourt.

Mark White - for the loan of his car to transport our heroes to Bunter's.

My Brother-in-Law, Bill Harrison - for almost lending me his name.

Dan Jones and Norman Van Der Lowen - for taking the time and trouble to wade through the first draft and for your suggestions and encouragement.

Town Council Leader and friend, Mike Smith, for accommodating our heroes' New Year's Eve homecoming in the Market Square.

David Walshaw and the team at New Generation Publishing.

Anna Reynolds from Cornerstones – for your advice and patience with this amateur author.

My hometown of Aylesbury and the legendary Friars Club.

And finally to my family, for putting up with this unhealthy obsession; again.